WODEN'S STORM

BOOK 2 OF THE FIRST KINGDOM SERIES

DONOVAN COOK

Boldwood

First published in Great Britain in 2025 by Boldwood Books Ltd.

Copyright © Donovan Cook, 2025

Cover Design by Head Design Ltd.

Cover Images: iStock

Map designed by CoverKitchen

A CIP catalogue record for this book is available from the British Library.

Paperback ISBN 978-1-83656-337-2

Large Print ISBN 978-1-83656-336-5

Hardback ISBN 978-1-83656-335-8

Trade Paperback ISBN 978-1-80656-033-2

Ebook ISBN 978-1-83656-338-9

Kindle ISBN 978-1-83656-339-6

Audio CD ISBN 978-1-83656-330-3

MP3 CD ISBN 978-1-83656-331-0

Digital audio download ISBN 978-1-83656-332-7

This book is printed on certified sustainable paper. Boldwood Books is dedicated to putting sustainability at the heart of our business. For more information please visit https://www.boldwoodbooks.com/about-us/sustainability/

Boldwood Books Ltd, 23 Bowerdean Street, London, SW6 3TN

www.boldwoodbooks.com

To Shaun and Emma. A thank you for their support.

BRITAIN
(449AD)

═════ Roman road

WALL OF ANTONINE

SELGOVAE

NOVANTAE

HADRIAN'S WALL

Corstopitum • ⌂ Shrine to Brigantia

PARISI

BRIGANTES

MONAPIA
(Isle of Man)

OCEANUS
GERMANICUS
(NORTH SEA)

Cair
Hebrauc

OCEANUS
HIBERNICUS
(IRISH SEA)

MONA
(Isle of
Anglesey)

Cair Ligion

Cair
Loit-Coit

ORDOVICES

CORNOVII

CORIELTAUVI

ICENI

Cair Urnahc

CATUVELLAUNI

DOBUNNI

TRINOVANTES

DEMETAE

SILURES

ATREBATES

Cair
Lundein

RUYM
ISLAND

Cair Lion

Cair
Segeint

CANTIACI

BELGAE

REGNIS

DAMNONII

DUROTRIGES

VECTIS
(Isle of Whight)

LITUS SAXONICUM

OCEANUS BRITANICUS
(ENGLISH CHANNEL)

CHARACTERS

Saxons

Octa – son of Frithowald and Berthild

Berthild – wife of Frithowald and Octa's mother

Odalric – Frithowald's friend and warrior

Reinald – leader of the Saxon foederati posted by Hadrian's wall

Jutes

Hengist – brother of Horsa and leader of the Jutes

Horsa – brother of Hengist and leader of the Jutes

Aldric – one of the brothers' warriors

Britons

King Vortigern – king of the Cornovii and high king of Britannia

Prince Vortimer – son of King Vortigern

Brigid – lover of King Vortigern and sister of Badulf

Badulf – brother of Brigid and warrior of King Vortigern

Ceretic – King Vortigern's interpreter

King Gwyrangon – king of the Cantiaci

Vettius – druid

Cadoc – friend of Prince Vortimer

Grifud – friend of Prince Vortimer

The Gods
Saxon gods
Woden – war god and chief god of the Germanic people
Friga – goddess of motherhood, marriage and wisdom, and wife of Woden
Thunor – thunder god and son of Woden and Friga

British/Celtic gods
Brigantia – chief god of the Brigantian people
Taranis – thunder god of the British and Celtic people

1

MIDSUMMER AD 450, CAIR URNAHC

Prince Vortimer pulled his cloak tighter around his shoulders as he walked through the streets of Cair Urnahc, the capital city of the Cornovii people. The morning chill seeped into his bones and made him shiver as a cockerel crowed from somewhere. Cair Urnahc was still sleeping, although the prince knew it would not be for much longer. Already he could see the first rays of the sun over the old stone walls that surrounded his father's city. A city that would one day be his, as well as the lands his father controlled. But only if he could stop the Jutes from taking that land.

A growl escaped from his throat at the thought, and the calm he usually felt on these walks fled like a hare from a fox.

'Is everything all right, Prince Vortimer?' Cadoc, one of the men following him, asked, which only soured his mood even more. There were four men with him. Two large warriors who had swords around their waists and wore the metal-plated vests the Romans had left behind. Vortimer did not need them. No one in Cair Urnahc would dare touch him. He was the son of the high king of Britannia and, as far as Vortimer was concerned, he was the second most powerful man on the island. Prince Vortimer was thirty-two years old and had proven himself in skirmishes against the Picts who raided their lands from the north. He was a skilled warrior and had been trained by his father's best men. But he had his guard follow him on these walks because it made him look important. It made him feel powerful.

Between Vortimer and the two warriors were Cadoc and Grifud, whom he had known since he was a boy. There was no one in Cair Urnahc he trusted more. They always joined Vortimer on his morning walks before the town woke up and they would talk about his plans for the kingdom of the Cornovii, the tribe that controlled much of the lands in the West Midlands of Britannia.

'I'm fine,' Vortimer said, and glanced at one house as the door opened and a woman poked her head out. The baker's wife, Vortimer recognised her before she quickly disappeared. A beauty in her youth, but age had taken that away from her. As well as her husband's beatings. Meted out to her because it was well known that she wasn't faithful to her husband. And Vortimer knew that all too well because he had spent many nights with her when he was younger. Before her beauty had left her.

Cair Urnahc had once been a Roman fort, but the prince could not remember the name the Romans had given it. Not that he cared, though, because that was in the past and his thoughts were only on the future. On a time when he would wear the crown his father wore now.

His grandfather had built another wall around the old stone fortifications, a wall made of earth and wood as they did not know how to cut stone like the Romans. But the earth mount wall, with its wooden palisade and the old Roman fort inside, made Cair Urnahc one of the strongest fortified cities in Britannia. Only the wealthy lived behind the stone walls, though. The merchants who had become rich selling furs and gemstones; the blacksmith who made weapons of exceptional quality; as well as the many cousins and half-brothers Vortimer had. Like the walls of the Roman fort, the houses and great hall were all made of stone. As well as the many other buildings the Romans had left behind. The old bathhouses where Vortimer and many of the wealthy residents would spend their days drinking wine and discussing important business. The smithy and the baker's house, as well as the merchant's part where traders sold goods from all over Britannia and even the continent.

But some of the stone walls had collapsed over time or the tiled roofs had given under the relentless pressure of the rain, and these were replaced by wood while thatched roofs covered houses that were once covered by the red tiles the Romans had made. Just like his father's great hall.

Vortimer's eyes ran over the houses laid out in squares with perfectly straight lines between them. When he became king, he would send men to the lands the Romans still held. He would bring back the knowledge the Romans had taken with them and he would make Cair Urnahc the envy of all the kings on this island. He would make the Cornovii the most powerful tribe in Britannia. A smile crept into his neatly trimmed beard as the next thought came to him. And then he would be the next high king. The king of kings.

Vortimer then remembered the Jutes, and the smile fell from his lips. They had arrived the summer before in three ships, led by two brothers, and had offered their services to Vortimer's father. And all they had asked for in return was to be provided with food and clothing. Prince Vortimer had hoped that his father would send them away, but instead he had agreed to let them stay in Britannia as long as they protected the island from the Picts who mercilessly raided the lands of the Britons from the north. The two brothers, Hengist and Horsa, had kept their word to his father. They had beaten back the Picts so many times that the savages from the north rarely raided the lands of the Cornovii, or the lands of the other tribes. Although they were based on Ruym Island, a small island in the lands of the Cantiaci people and many days' ride away, they regularly sent patrols to the lands of King Vortigern and killed any Pictish raiding party they came across. Their ships patrolled the coast and travelled up rivers as they hunted pirates from across the seas or any Picts who attempted to reach their lands by boats.

Vortimer should have been glad about that. They brought peace to the lands that would one day be his. Trade flourished in Cair Urnahc and the people felt safe again. But the Jutes were heathens, and Vortimer knew they couldn't be trusted. And it angered the prince that his father turned a blind eye to them not worshipping the one true God. Not even the priests could convince his father to encourage the Jutes to abandon their pretend gods and follow Christ.

Vortimer clenched his jaw at the thought. He knew who to blame for the fact his father was cozying up to the men from the continent. That half-breed bitch, Brigid. She was always around, listening to conversations that had nothing to do with her and whispering things in his father's ears. Not even Vortimer's mother held as much sway over his father.

The woman was a believer of the old gods, the ones who ruled these lands before the Romans came. That was how she had bewitched his father, and worse, spurned his own advances. Prince Vortimer swore that when he became king, he would burn her.

'There's a storm coming,' an old voice said, which broke Vortimer from his thoughts. He looked at the clear blue sky as the sun sat just above the walls of Cair Urnahc and saw no sign of any storm. The town had woken up while he was deep in his thoughts and Vortimer frowned as he wondered how long he had been walking around like that. He glanced behind him and saw the four men staring at him, their eyes filled with boredom. 'Aye, there's a storm coming,' the old voice said again.

Prince Vortimer turned to the old man sitting with his thin legs crossed and his lined face covered in dirt as around him women carried buckets full of shit and piss to the river to empty them out while men greeted each other. He scowled as he wondered how the beggar had got into the Roman fort. The men guarding the gates should have chased him away. 'Your eyes deceive you, old man. The sky is clear and already the sun warms my skin. There is no storm.'

The old beggar smiled, even as Vortimer signalled to one of his warriors to chase him away. But before the warrior could touch the old man, he said, 'The sky is always clear before the storm strikes. That's how she tricks you, so you lower your guard. Then she strikes while you are unprepared and everything you hold dear gets washed away.'

Vortimer raised his hand to stop the warrior as the old man's words stirred something inside him.

'The old man has lost his wits,' Cadoc said, but even as the others nodded, Vortimer sensed there was more to the old man's words, and a shiver ran down his spine before he could stop it.

He knelt down and had to breathe through his mouth not to gag at the beggar's stench. 'What storm are you talking about, old man?'

The old man smiled, revealing his blackened gums and less than a handful of rotten teeth. But even in his cloudy eyes, Vortimer sensed a hidden power that made him nervous. 'A great storm from across the seas. One like we haven't seen for many generations.'

Vortimer raised an eyebrow and wondered if the old man was talking about the weather or the Jutes. 'And can this storm be stopped?' He sensed the warriors behind him scowl, but Vortimer ignored them.

The old man's cloudy eyes drifted to the cloudless sky. 'The gods of these lands were once worshipped by all who stood below them. The sacrifices made in their names kept them strong and they protected all the lands which the blue waters surround. From the mountains in the north to the white cliffs in the south. The marshes in the west to the stony beaches in the east. But then the first storm came, and the gods were forgotten and withered away. There were no more sacrifices to keep them strong. Blood was not spilled in their honour any more and soon they were replaced by one from lands far away.' The old man's eyes went to the large golden cross Vortimer wore around his neck. Vortimer didn't know why, but he felt the urge to hide the cross behind his fine tunic. 'But there was one who was stronger than the rest. From the north, she called out to gods from another land, asking them for help.'

'What is the old bastard talking about?' Grifud asked, and Vortimer raised his hand to silence the man, even as he wondered the same. But for a reason he did not understand, he felt compelled to listen to the old man's words.

The old man carried on. 'The gods from lands covered by mighty rivers and strong mountains ignored her, but one reached out a hand and offered a weapon feared by gods from all over. But she was not strong enough to use it, and soon he washed the gods that had once stood proud on the hills of these lands away. Only a few remain now. Their names whispered in caves and dark rooms where his light cannot reach those who still worship the old gods.'

Vortimer glanced at the sun before he scowled at the old man. 'In God's name, what are you talking about?'

The old man stared at him for a few heartbeats. 'Find the spear which once belonged to a mighty god from the east and you will succeed where we had failed. Only with the spear of the one-eyed god can you stop the storm.'

Before Vortimer could respond to the old man's words, a child screamed behind them. They turned, their hands on their weapons, but all they saw were the confused faces of women carrying buckets filled with water back to their houses. Vortimer shook his head and turned back to the old man, only for his heart to skip a beat.

'Where'd he go?' One of the warriors asked the same question that was raging through Vortimer's mind. His limbs trembling, Vortimer scanned the streets on either side of him, but there was no sign of the stinking old man. The man couldn't have just vanished, and he doubted the bastard could move that fast.

Prince Vortimer turned to his two warriors. 'Find him! Now!' The warriors both nodded and, before they ran off, Vortimer said, 'And tell no one about this.'

As the two warriors ran off to find the old man, Cadoc asked, 'You don't really believe the old bastard's witless ramblings, do you?'

Vortimer ignored his friend as he marched towards the main gate of the Roman fort, eager to find out how the man had got into this part of Cair Urnahc. But as he made his way to the gate, a question kept pestering him. Where was the spear and who was this one-eyed god?

2

SOMEWHERE IN THE REALMS OF THE GODS

Friga, the mother god of the Saxon people as well as those whose lands surrounded theirs, crinkled her nose as she walked past the corpses of those slain by her son. The stench of death sent a shiver down her spine, and she wondered if that was what they would smell like when their time came. And she knew their time would come, just like it came for all those who bled and breathed. Even the mountains would one day be worn down to nothing. But new mountains would take their place and grow tall. What scared Friga was that she wasn't sure if new gods would replace them. She had stared into the flames of Woden's hearth fire, like he often did, and like her husband she saw nothing beyond the fires. He had come from lands far away and he was breaking the cycle. The way it had always been was not the way it would be any more.

A crunching noise brought her back to the present, and she saw Thunor, her son, standing over the corpse of a giant, its blood dripping from his hammer as he panted. Another dead giant to add to the many he had already killed and the many he would still kill. Men thought her son, with his thick red hair and beard and his bulging arms, protected them from the giants, but the truth was that he just loved to fight and to kill. But Tiw and Woden were already thought of as gods of war, so the people had given her son another role. A smile came to her lips at the idea that they were the powerful gods, the ones people feared, yet it was men who gave them their roles.

'Mother, what are you doing here?'

Friga smiled at her son, who towered over her and blocked what little light there was in this place. 'Thunor, have you not killed enough for one day?'

Thunor shrugged as he looked around. 'None of them breathe any more, so perhaps I have.' He looked at her again. 'What do you want, Mother?'

Friga raised an eyebrow at her son as she smiled at him again. 'Why do you think I want something?'

'You only seek me out when you need my help.' He looked at his hammer, his weapon of choice because he liked the sound it made when he broke skulls with it. It was perhaps the only weapon more dangerous than Woden's spear, Gungnir, but Friga knew that Thunor's hammer would never start a war. It only ended them.

'I need you to protect him. To keep him alive.' Friga glanced at the blood pooling near her dress and hoped it would not soak into the fabric.

'Protect who?'

'You know who. The one who found Woden's spear.'

Thunor grunted. 'I heard father's spear was found. I also heard you hid it from him.'

'I did not hide it from him. I lent it to another and we both kept it out of your father's reach.'

Thunor glared at her, but Friga knew she did not need to fear her son. 'Why did you hide Gungnir from Father?'

Friga looked at the corpses of the giants Thunor had slain and remembered the dream she had had long ago. 'Because I wanted to avoid a war that we did not need to fight. Not when we have a more important battle ahead of us.'

Thunor grunted. 'You cannot avoid war, Mother. No matter what you do.'

A small smile came to Friga. 'You sound like your father.'

'Father is wise.'

'As he is dangerous. Be careful not to follow Woden blindly, my son. He will sacrifice you if it serves his needs.'

Thunor hawked and spat as if her words meant nothing to him. 'And now a man runs around with one of the most powerful weapons in all the worlds.'

Friga nodded. 'He has a purpose. A role to play in what is to come. But there are others who seek the spear and he is not strong enough to stop them from taking it.'

'And you want me to keep him alive and the spear out of their hands?'

Friga nodded again. Thunor was not as dumb as many liked to believe. As he wanted them to believe. 'I want you to watch him and, when he needs your aid, you give it.'

'Why?'

'Because Taranis, a god of the Britons, seeks the spear and if he gets Gungnir, then he will start a war against us.'

'And you don't want to give the spear back to Father because then he'll start a war against them.' Thunor wiped the blood off his hammer. 'Father wants a war against them and he always gets what he wants.'

'Your father's lust for battle blinds him to our true enemy.'

'The one from the east? From the lands of sand and dust?'

Friga looked at the dead giants and again wondered if that was how they would go. 'We should unite with the gods from Britannia to fight him, not start a war with them.'

'The gods of the Roman people united against him and they still weren't strong enough.' Friga shook her head and Thunor sighed. 'I will protect this man, Mother. But if this Taranis tries to take the spear, then I'll rip his head from his shoulders.'

'Thank you, Thunor.'

She was about to walk away when Thunor asked, 'Why do you fear him so much? The one from the east. Even Father refuses to speak his name.'

Friga looked at the death around her. 'For as long as life has existed, there has been a cycle. Gods come, they grow old, they perish. And then new gods come, they also grow old and they also perish. We replaced those who came before us and they those before them. Like the seasons come and go, so do we gods. But he wants to break that cycle. His greed is greater than Woden's and he wants it all for himself.'

'No one lasts forever, Mother. We all know that. His time will come.'

Friga nodded. 'It will, but the real question is, what will he leave behind when he perishes?'

3

A FEW WEEKS LATER, NEAR THE ISLAND OF RUYM

Octa took a deep breath and savoured the salty air as he surveyed the surrounding lands. Rolling hills filled the landscape with patches of forests dotted between them. Thin trails of smoke from farmsteads and settlements drifted towards the clouds as birds circled the skies above him, their songs and cries washing over him and bringing a small smile to his face.

Warda, his light-coloured mare, shook her head as flies buzzed around her ears, and Octa patted her flank as he spotted a small herd of deer disappear amongst the trees of a patch of forest.

'Almost reminds you of home,' Odalric said as he also studied the British lands. Octa glanced at the Saxon warrior almost twice his age who had once fought for his father. But despite the few grey hairs in his thick beard, Odalric still looked the mighty warrior he had always been. His broad shoulders carried the weight of his chain-mail vest with ease, while the many scars on his thick arms told the tales of many battles. Unlike Octa, whose chain-mail vest sat heavy on his shoulders and he often readjusted it to make it more comfortable. Like most Saxons, Octa was tall and broad-shouldered, but at nineteen winters, he lacked the width and strength of Odalric.

'This is home now.' Octa pushed the thoughts of the Saxon lands out of his mind. Octa had been the son of a mighty warlord, but he had fled from a battle and his cousin, Uhtric, had died because of it. Uhtric's father, Witta, was his father's cousin and the mightiest warlord in the Saxon lands and he had killed Octa's father because of it. But Octa didn't know about that until his mother and Odalric had arrived in Britannia. After the battle, Octa had travelled north, to the lands of the Jutes. That was where he had met an old man he now knew was Woden, the war god of the Saxon people, who had told him of his missing spear, Gungnir. Octa tightened his grip on the spear and remembered how he had joined the army of Hengist and Horsa, the two Jutish brothers who had come to Britannia to aid the Britons against their enemies. He had found the spear in the north of Britannia, in a cave near a great wall built by the Romans, but had been warned by Friga not to return the spear to Woden. Not that Octa had planned to do that. He had wanted to give the spear to his father and redeem himself.

He had sworn that he would one day return to the Saxon lands and avenge his father, but first he needed an army. Although he knew the longer he waited, the more the chance slipped away from him. The Thuringians, a tribe to the south-east of his homelands, were being forced into Saxon lands by the Huns, a vicious people who lived on horseback and did not know the taste of defeat. Many Saxons were forced from their homes as the Thuringians took land for themselves and killed any who tried to stop them.

The Saxon people did not have a king. They had warlords who ruled over their lands and families, but when there was an outside threat, they would unite and select one warlord to lead their combined armies. That warlord had been Witta, but as spring had changed into summer, news from the continent had reached them that Witta was struggling to keep the Thuringians back. Some of the other Saxon warlords had turned against him after he had killed Octa's father, but still Octa could not avenge his father.

He glanced at Gungnir, the spear of Woden, in his hand. The spear was plain-looking, with a simple wooden shaft and an iron head, and at first glance it looked just like any other spear. If it hadn't been for the spear's name carved on the shaft in runes and the two ravens engraved onto the spearhead, one on either side and looking different from each other, then no one would have known that this was the lost spear of the war god. But even with Woden's spear in his possession, he still could not return to his homelands. And not just because he had no army. In Britannia, Octa was safe from Woden, Friga had told him that. But if he went to the Saxon lands, then Octa was certain he'd have to face Woden's wrath for keeping the spear for himself. Friga had warned him that Woden would be furious about that and that there would be a price to pay, and Octa often wondered if Woden had played a part in his father's death.

'Thunor knows it wouldn't be too bad if it didn't rain so much.' Odalric scowled at the dark clouds in the distance as he scratched his beard.

Octa chased the dark thoughts from his mind and nodded. 'Aye, it does rain a lot. But that is why the lands are fertile and food is plenty here.'

'And that is why the brothers want it for themselves.'

Octa thought of Hengist and Horsa. They were warlords from Jutland and had brought their army to Britannia to fight for the high king of the Britons against the Picts, a people from the north who raided these lands. The large island of Britannia had many small kingdoms who were too busy fighting each other instead of uniting against their enemies. That was why they were defenceless against the Picts and why they needed the Jutes to protect them. But Octa felt there was more to Hengist and Horsa's offer of friendship to the Britons. They wanted these lands for themselves, Octa was certain of it. Although now he was in the same position as them. He needed land for the Saxons who were forced from their lands by the Thuringians. Octa often wondered if his cowardice that day had contributed. Perhaps if he had stood his ground, then they might have defeated the Thuringians. But the past was not important. All that mattered was now, Octa thought as he glanced at Gungnir again, certain that the gods wanted something from him as well.

Odalric saw him look at the spear. 'Still can't believe you were foolish enough to travel to Britannia all because an old man told you an unreasonable story about Woden losing his spear.'

Octa smiled. It was not the first time they had had this conversation, and he was sure they would have it many more times. 'The old man was Woden. I'm certain of it now. He wanted me to find his spear.'

'Aye, but you did not know that then, did you?'

Octa shook his head. 'No, I didn't. But I had no other option. I had disgraced our people and my parents. I thought that finding the spear would redeem me. That it would help Father become more powerful than Witta.'

Odalric sighed, his eyes back on the dark clouds in the distance, and Octa understood why. The old warrior was there when Witta had attacked his father's village. But Octa's father had ordered Odalric to protect his wives and daughters and Octa's mother had ordered him to take her to Britannia so she could find Octa. Odalric lived with the guilt of not defending his lord and friend, just as Octa lived with the guilt of what he had done. Octa knew the older warrior also wanted to avenge his father, but there were other things that needed to be done first. 'And you still don't know why Woden wanted you to find the spear?'

Octa shook his head again. 'He wanted me to give it back to him.'

Odalric grunted, as he usually did at this point in the conversation. 'But yet, he is just letting you keep it. Gungnir, the spear of Woden.'

Octa scowled as he usually did at this point in the conversation. He had not told Odalric or his mother about his conversations with Friga and not only because he was worried that they would think he'd lost his wits, but also because he still didn't understand why Friga was protecting him. 'The gods have their plans and we rarely understand what they are.' Octa repeated the words his mother would usually say at this point.

Odalric turned back towards the small island off the coast of Britannia that Hengist and Horsa had taken for themselves. The island sat near the mouth of the large river which led to Cair Lundein and that was why the brothers had taken it for themselves.

It had been half a season since Octa's return and his fight with Eadric, the Jute who had left Octa to die in the cave in the north because he believed that he had found the spear of Woden. But the real spear had been hidden in a carving of a British god and the spear Eadric had brought south had been a decoy.

Odalric wore the dead Jute's chain-mail vest now. Octa's mother had told him that the older warrior had given his up so they could get a spot on a ship destined for Britannia and so Octa had given Eadric's armour to him. It was too large for Octa anyway and he was comfortable with the old Roman-style mail vest he was wearing.

The brothers had spent the spring and summer fortifying the island, although Octa wasn't sure if it was against threats from the north or the Cantiaci, the British tribe that controlled the lands in the south-east of Britannia, including the small island the Jutes now lived on. Both, he suspected, as Pictish raiding parties still sailed south to raid the rich lands around Cair Lundein, the capital city of the Cantiaci people, and the Cantiaci regularly attacked hunting parties sent out by the brothers. The Jutes had built a wooden wall around the town they had taken for themselves, as well as the camp where most of their army stayed. A wooden bridge spanned the tidal beach so that the island could always be reached, and was heavily guarded. The Cantiaci had not attacked the island yet and Octa doubted they would for the same reason the brothers hadn't retaliated yet, either. They were trying to convince King Vortigern, the high king of the Britons, that the others were to blame for the unrest.

'We can't stay on that island forever,' Odalric said. 'You're the son of a warlord; you need your own land.'

Octa sighed. 'I was the son of a warlord. Now I'm...' He hesitated. He still didn't understand what he was now. The fear that had been his constant companion had been replaced by something else. A calm he did not understand and he often wondered if it was the spear that was doing that to him. But even though he no longer feared battle, Octa had no desire to rush towards it. Not like other warriors his age, who were still desperate to make a name for themselves. At nineteen winters, Octa should be seeking out battles and earning his reputation, just like his father had done before him, but Octa did not want any of that. He had come to Britannia to redeem himself in the eyes of his father. But now his father was dead and even though Octa carried the spear of Woden, he was unsure of his path. Only Wyrd, the god of fate, knew that.

Even amongst Hengist and Horsa's men, Octa stood out. Hengist treated him like a friend, inviting him to their hearth fire and sharing ale with him. Horsa, on the other hand, treated Octa as if he was a threat. He scowled at Octa and barely spoke to him. And then there was the spear. Despite what Hengist had promised, Octa knew Horsa wanted Gungnir for himself. Octa glanced at the spear again and wondered why Woden had chosen him to find it and, more importantly, what Woden was planning for him. The thought sent a shiver down his spine, which Octa did his best to hide from Odalric. Warda whinnied underneath him as if she sensed his unease, and he stroked her neck to calm her.

'You are still the son of a warlord, despite what happened. And you carry Gungnir. You should be leading an army and taking land for yourself. Not running errands for the brothers.' Odalric hawked and spat.

'Octa the Coward, isn't that what you said they call me back in the homeland?' Octa turned his attention towards the dark clouds, which were slowly approaching them as if they were a bad omen from the gods. Perhaps they were. 'Who would follow a warrior who fled from battle?'

Odalric grunted and looked away from him. Octa understood why. Odalric had called him the same before. He knew it even if he had never heard it. The older man was a proud warrior who would rather die before fleeing from a battle. He didn't understand why Octa had decided otherwise. Octa himself didn't understand it either. But that was in the past, and he knew he needed to focus on the future. 'I was wrong,' Odalric said after a short while, which surprised Octa. 'You are your father's son, as well as your mother's. And the others will see that too when they see you with Gungnir in your hand and an army at your back.'

This time Octa grunted. 'First, they need to come here. And my name won't bring them.'

'No, it won't,' Odalric agreed before he too looked at the dark clouds again. 'We should get going before those clouds catch us.'

'Aye, although I think no matter how fast we ride, those bastard clouds will catch us either way.' Octa turned Warda towards the Roman road before he tapped his heels into her flank. She responded instantly, unlike Odalric's horse, who had to be threatened before she moved.

'Only the gods know how you could be lucky enough to find a good horse on this island. They're all as stubborn as the people.'

Octa smiled. 'I didn't pick her. She picked me.' Which was true and he was grateful for that strange event because she had been a good companion to him.

'So why are we being sent to...' Odalric paused as he struggled with the words.

'To Cair Urnahc? Because the brothers need King Vortigern to deliver more food. Their army has grown and with the Cantiaci attacking the hunting parties, there isn't enough food.'

Odalric raised an eyebrow at Octa as they reached the Roman road and turned north. 'And you think this King Vortigern will do it?'

Octa shrugged as he glanced at the dark clouds they were riding towards. He felt a sense of trepidation that he could not explain and tightened his grip on Gungnir.

4

LAND OF THE BRIGANTIANS, NEAR THE GREAT ROMAN WALL

Badulf ground his teeth as he sat by the fire in the clearing of a forest and tried to hide from the dampness of the north. Although it wasn't much different from Cair Urnahc. What made it worse was that every time it was wet or damp, his shoulder would ache. And that pain only fed his anger at having to sit here and do nothing. But Badulf did not know what else to do as he glanced at the men around the small clearing, their clothes ragged and faces dirty, and the tents they slept in. Some were sitting by the fire with him, while a few men skinned a deer they had caught that morning. There were others as well, sitting in groups as they spoke of things he didn't care about.

Badulf closed his eyes and remembered that day when they had left Corstopitum, the old Roman fort by the Roman wall, and made their way towards the sacred forest they had been told about, where they would find the shrine of Brigantia. The same forest he was in now. He had guided a group of the Jutes north as they searched for a weapon they claimed belonged to one of their gods, although only one of the group really seemed to believe it. Octa, the Saxon coward. They had found the fort, which was used by Saxon foederati, men who had come with the Romans and were all old now, and had been told where to find the shrine the spear was hidden in. The old healer in the fort, a Briton, had warned Badulf not to go. He had told him they would all die if they went near the forest, but Badulf's curiosity had got the better of him. Or perhaps it was that he wanted to be seen as equal to the men who came from the lands of his grandfather, a Saxon warrior who had come to Britannia to fight for the Romans.

Badulf barely remembered the man, only that he was tall, like a giant, and was strong enough to lift an ox. Or perhaps that was what his mother had told him. But as Badulf outgrew the other boys of Cair Urnahc, he believed he would be a mighty warrior like his grandfather had been. Badulf snapped the twig in his hands, which made the others around him glance his way.

'You should calm yourself, Badulf,' Bellicus said. He was older than the rest and the leader of this band of... Badulf frowned. He didn't really know what they were. They weren't outlaws, but they lived like those who had been banished from their homes: in camps hidden amongst the trees where they spent most of their time hunting or foraging for food. They called themselves the Protectors of Brigantia. Men who guarded the sacred forests and shrines of the old goddess, but all they did was sit around and tell stories of the old gods.

That day, when the Jutes and Badulf had left the fort to find the shrine, they were ambushed by these men who rained arrows down on them from the safety of the trees. Badulf had realised he did not want to die with the Jutes, and had kicked the flanks of his horse but, as he raced away from the danger, something struck his shoulder. Badulf still remembered the blinding pain that threw him off his horse. At first, he thought he had been struck by lightning, but as he landed on the ground, he felt the spear in his back. He had almost laughed at the irony of dying from a spear when they were there looking for one, but he had blacked out before he could.

When Badulf had woken, he found himself in this camp and surrounded by angry men pointing dirty daggers and arrows at him. They had believed he was a Jute and it had taken him much to convince them he wasn't. In the end, he hadn't, though. It was a druid, with his long grey beard and stern face, who had told them who he was. But Badulf never got a chance to speak to the druid.

Badulf looked at Bellicus, his face dirty and clothes ripped. Bellicus leaned forward and Badulf saw the mark of the cult of Brigantia inked on his chest. Everyone in the small band in the clearing wore the mark, and Badulf knew there were many more of them in the lands of the Brigantians. But unlike these men, many other cult members lived in the towns and on farmsteads where they still prayed to the old goddess and told stories of her past deeds.

'How can I be calm? My shoulder hurts as if it was injured yesterday and we sit here and do nothing.'

The man sighed as he poked the fire with a stick. 'And what should we be doing, Badulf?'

Badulf glanced around the fire as the others all looked at him with vacant eyes. 'We should be out there, trying to find the spear! We should warn the kings of the Jutes' plans!'

'We don't know the plans of these Jutes. And they are far to the south, so they are not our concern.'

Badulf jumped to his feet and did his best to ignore the pain in his shoulder. 'They have the spear you were supposed to protect!'

'You already sent one of us to his death by convincing him to find the spear,' another said, and many grunted their agreement. Badulf glanced away. He had convinced one man to sneak into Corstopitum when he had found out that Octa was there. He did not know if Octa had the spear or if the others had taken it south with them, but he wanted Octa to pay for what had happened. But that man had failed and soon after his attempted attack on Octa, word had reached them that he had been killed by the old Saxons who guarded the Roman wall.

'We should attack the Saxons in Corstopitum! They told the Jutes where to find the spear, all to protect one of their own. A coward who did not deserve to be protected.'

Bellicus shook his head. 'Reinald and his Saxons are not our enemies. They are our friends and they have protected us from the Picts for many winters.'

'But they told the Jutes where to find the spear!'

The leader shrugged. 'It is not their responsibility to protect the shrine. And besides, we have brothers in the fort who send word to us when others seek it so that we can stop them from finding the shrine.'

Badulf shook his head, struggling to make sense of how these men were so calm when the Jutes had the spear of one of their most powerful gods. He still didn't understand how the spear had come to be here or even if it was real, but no one here had the answers to those questions and neither did they seem to care. All they cared about was preserving the memory of the mother goddess and protecting her shrines. 'And you failed! The shrine was destroyed, and the spear was stolen!'

Bellicus lowered his head and stared at the flames. 'Aye, we failed that day and we lost many friends to the men from the continent, but you have no right to remind us of that.' He got to his feet and stared at Badulf, who almost towered over him. 'We let you stay because we were told to, but you don't wear the mark of Brigantia.'

Badulf clenched his fists as he glared at the men. He did not know why he was still in the forest with these men. He was free to leave, but every time he thought about returning south, to the lands of the Cornovii and to his sister, Brigid, something stopped him. Something Badulf did not want to admit to himself. So he had stayed, but his anger at what had happened that day refused to allow him to accept his fate. 'You are cowards! Every single one of you! How can you just sit here when your friends died to protect a spear that is now in the hands of our enemies?'

'Because I told them to sit here,' a stern old voice said, and they all gasped when they turned and saw the druid standing on the edge of their camp. The same druid Badulf had seen that day. 'And I told them to sit here and do nothing because they have failed to protect the sacred spear. Others who are more capable have been sent to find the spear.'

'Vettius!' Bellicus said, and lowered his head again as his cheeks burnt red. 'What brings you here?' Badulf saw how everyone lowered their heads as if they feared the old man with his long grey robe and walking stick. He had heard of the druids, most had, but Badulf never believed in them. Neither did he believe they possessed any magic. Not like in the stories his mother had told him. And he doubted this druid had the same gifts as Brigid had. He wondered if she would have been a druid if the Romans had not killed most of them.

Instead of answering, the druid glared at Badulf and stepped to the side. Out of the shadows walked a woman who looked older than the trees in the sacred forest, her back bent over with age and her long white hair trailing on the ground as she shuffled towards the flames without acknowledging any of them.

The men all stared at the woman, their eyes wide before they dropped to their knees.

'The wise one,' Bellicus said as he too dropped to his knees. Only Badulf and the druid were left standing as the old woman finally made it to the fire. She stood there for many heartbeats and stared at the flames as if they spoke to her and then, with a deep breath, she sat down and crossed her legs.

Badulf glanced at the druid, who was still glaring at him, before he turned his attention to the old woman, her cloudy eyes still fixed on the fire.

'There is much anger in you, Badulf, son of Brychan.' One man handed the old woman a cup of water and she nodded her thanks to him before taking a sip. 'Not like your sister. She was filled with fear when she came to me. The fear of the unknown. But you, you treat the unknown like an enemy. You want to destroy it before you try to understand it.'

Badulf's eyes widened when he realised who the old woman was and he shook his head. 'It can't be. Brigid told me you were old when she was with you. How are you still alive?'

The woman smiled a toothless smile at him. 'And yet I remember her as if she came to me yesterday. Not many like her come to me, not any more. Although I've not spoken to her for a long time. Much is happening. Much is changing.'

Badulf frowned at the woman, not understanding what she meant. 'She told me about you. About how you helped her understand her gifts.'

The wise one nodded. 'She was the last one I trained. With the new god, those like her are punished now. They are beaten until they submit to the new god instead of being taught to understand the way of nature. The way of the gods.'

Badulf glanced at the druid again, but the man was busy talking to the others. His forehead creased when he realised no one was paying attention to him or the ancient woman. He looked at the woman again, whose eyes were still fixed on the fire as if she saw something in the flames. 'The ways of the gods are done. People forget about them and turn to the Christian god.'

The woman nodded. 'Like you? You pretend you turned your back on the gods so that you can fit in with the others, despite your sister's gifts.'

Badulf gaped at the old woman, but then he closed his mouth and clenched his fists. She did not know him. 'I did what I had to to be accepted. It's not easy when everyone calls you a half-breed. When they treat you differently because of who your grandfather was. But I still heed my sister's words.'

'You are right, one should not be punished for the deeds of those who came before, but we live in a world where many are too blind to understand that.' The wise one carried on staring at the fire. 'You say you heed your sister's words, yet you rode with the one she warned you to stay away from.'

'I did what my king told me to do.'

The old woman smiled again. 'Your king told you to ride north with them?'

Badulf turned his attention to the fire and watched as it consumed the wood that gave it life. In the flames, he saw the Jutes and remembered the words they spoke to him. He remembered Octa and the fear in his eyes when they needed to fight. 'I wanted to learn more about them. I wanted to know if they can really be trusted. And I was curious.'

The wise one nodded. 'And what did you learn about the men from across the seas?'

Badulf gritted his teeth. 'They are not the friends they claim to be. They want these lands for themselves and they will destroy everything in their path. Just like this fire if we let it.'

'Many fear the fire. They fear the flames and treat it like an enemy,' the wise one said to him, and Badulf looked at her pale eyes. He frowned at the look on her face. An acceptance of things to come was the only way he could explain what he saw, but that only left him more confused. 'But the fire can be a source of good as well. The flames get rid of the old and faded so that the new and the bright can grow. That has always been the way. The old die and the flames consume them. And in their place, the young and vibrant come and life continues.' The wise one looked at Badulf and gave him a sad smile. 'Remember, Badulf. The flames take life, but in their wake, there is always rebirth.'

Badulf struggled to make sense of what the wise one was saying to him, and he wondered if Brigid had to deal with the same. But before he could find the words to respond to her, the druid cleared his throat and Badulf was surprised to see the man standing behind the wise one as if he was protecting her.

'We must go.'

The old woman nodded, and the druid helped her to her feet. 'Vettius is right. I've been here too long.'

'Wait,' Badulf said. 'What about the Saxons and the spear?'

'The spear has a purpose and so does the one who wields it,' the druid said, and the wise one nodded again.

'And what is that purpose?' Badulf's heart was racing in his chest, but he could not understand why. Perhaps it was the urgency in the druid's movement, as if they were running from someone.

'Vettius is right,' the wise one said again. 'There are those who believe I have betrayed them when I did what had to be done to protect my home from him.'

'From him? Who?' Badulf asked, but got no response as the druid and the old woman walked to the edge of the clearing. 'What is his purpose? The one with the spear?'

The wise one stopped at the edge of the clearing and, without turning back, she said, 'To bring fire to these lands.'

5

'You're leaving then?' Bellicus startled Badulf as he packed a sack with provisions, enough for half the journey south to Cair Urnahc. He would have preferred to take more with him, but these men did not have much and they had been kind to him, so he did not want to take most of their food.

'I need to. I have to warn my sister. She needs to know what's coming.' Brigid would know what to do. She spoke to the gods and they would tell her how to stop the fire. How to stop the Jutes from conquering Britannia. Badulf was sure of that as he tied the sack closed with a bit of rope before he pulled his cloak over his shoulders. It was in the middle of the brief summer night, and he had hoped to sneak away unnoticed.

Bellicus stared at Badulf, who doubted the man really understood. His family had all died from raids by the Picts. Raids the old Saxons by the Roman fort had not prevented from happening. Badulf wondered why the Brigantians still relied on them when they were too old to fight or to protect those near the Roman wall. But that was not an argument he wanted to have with these men. Not that they would care about that. They only cared about protecting Brigantia's legacy. 'Why do you need to warn her?'

'You heard what the wise one said. The one who wields the spear will bring fire to these lands. He will destroy everything we love.'

'She also said that life follows the flames. That there will be rebirth.'

Badulf's irritation grew and he turned to face the man. 'How can you just sit here and not care?'

Bellicus looked away for a few heartbeats as his eyes ran over the sleeping forms of the other men in the clearing, before he looked at Badulf again. 'For as long as I can remember, this cult has protected the secrets of Brigantia. There are many of us all over Britannia, as well as cults to the other gods. In some places, we are forced to hide in the shadows, otherwise the Christians punish us. Here in Brigantia, we can be more open about who we are, but we still have to fight the encroaching hand of the Christian god.' Bellicus sighed. 'You are right. We failed. We were supposed to protect the sacred spear as we have done for many generations. I still remember the first time I was shown the spear by the man whose place I took. I can still see the gold-rimmed spearhead in my mind and the golden rings around the shaft.' Bellicus fell silent for a moment. 'Every man here wishes we had succeeded, but the spear is gone and now we are being punished for it by Vettius. Even if we wanted to bring the spear back, we don't have the men to do it. We don't know who has the spear—'

'You were told that the young Saxon in the fort returned with a spear,' Badulf interrupted Bellicus, who nodded.

'He returned with a normal plain spear, the same type we use, and you sent a man to his death because of it.' Bellicus's face darkened for the first time in this conversation before he sighed again. 'There is much you don't understand and that I can't tell you. Vettius told us you would leave and that we shouldn't stop you.' Badulf frowned at this and, before he could respond, Bellicus signalled to another man hiding in the shadows. 'Motius has a horse ready for you and a spear. There is also enough food for you to reach the lands of the Cornovii. Be careful, Badulf. The road is dangerous. May Brigantia protect you.' He turned and walked away before Badulf could say anything.

Badulf shook his head and dropped the sack he had filled before he made his way to Motius, who, like Bellicus said, was standing at the edge of the clearing with a horse and spear.

'Just so you know,' Motius said. 'I agree with you. I think we should be out there trying to find the spear and bringing it back. Brigantia is angry with us, but Bellicus is too old and too weak to see that.'

Badulf raised an eyebrow at Motius, who was still only seventeen winters old. His father was one of the senior men in the cult and so Motius had been forced to join, even though Badulf sensed that he did not always agree with the cult. 'Then come with me. Together, we can find the spear and bring it back.'

Motius shook his head. 'I have to stay.' Badulf nodded and took the reins of the horse. 'Good luck, Badulf. I'll pray to Brigantia that you succeed.'

'Thank you,' Badulf said, before he led the horse away from the clearing and out of the forest. The moon seemed extra bright that night, as if it was trying to guide him, and in the darkness he heard an owl hooting, which made the hairs on the back of his neck stand up. Badulf glanced over his shoulder and saw a white owl sitting on a branch of an old tree, its black eyes fixed on him. He tried to ignore the shiver that ran down his spine, but couldn't.

When Badulf finally left the forest, he sighed with relief before he mounted the horse and, with one last glance at the dark trees, he turned towards the Roman road. Badulf knew he had no time to waste and as soon as he reached the Roman road he raced south, while the owl flew above his head as if it was following him. He had to warn Brigid. She had believed the Jutes could help her bring the old gods out of the shadows and back into the light. But he was certain that when the Jutes took control of Britannia, it would be their gods who ruled, not the old gods of these lands. He pushed his horse to go faster and prayed that he was not too late to stop the fire from spreading.

* * *

Brigid sat in front of the old tree in the sacred grove of the forest near Cair Urnahc, her eyes closed as she waited for Brigantia, the mother goddess, to speak to her. But all she heard were the leaves rustling in the wind and birds singing from the branches. Somewhere in the distance, a stag called out a challenge to another and Brigid could not help but wonder if that was a sign of things to come.

Brigid had been born with a mark on her chest, near her shoulder, which looked like the head of a spear and from a young age had been sent dreams by the gods of Britannia. The ones her people had worshipped before the Romans had brought the Christian god to the island. But since the Jutes had arrived the previous summer, the gods had been silent and Brigid couldn't

understand why. Were they hiding from the newcomers or had they fled the
island they had ruled over for many winters because of the gods the men
from the continent had brought with them? Brigid didn't know. All she knew
was that she had never felt so alone, so lost, before. Before the previous
summer, she had the gods, which gave her a purpose and, with that purpose,
confidence. Brigid had always been certain of her role and of what the old
gods wanted from her. And she had used that to become King Vortigern's
lover so that she could manipulate him in order to help the old gods against
the Christian god. King Vortigern claimed to be a Christian to please those
who worshipped the god from the east, but Brigid knew he also believed in
the old gods, which meant he listened to her words, but only while he
believed the gods still spoke to her.

She had also had her brother, Badulf. He was the last of her family after
their father had died in a border skirmish against the Corieltauvi, a tribe to
the east who hated the Cornovii, and their mother was killed by a drunken
Christian priest. Badulf had been one of King Vortigern's warriors and when
the men arrived from the continent, King Vortigern had sent him to deal with
them because he spoke their tongue. But now her brother was dead, and the
gods had sealed their lips to her. Brigid had never felt so helpless before, but
she was determined not to let others see it. Especially not those who wanted
her out of the way. Those like Prince Vortimer, King Vortigern's son, who once
wanted her, but now hated her because she had caught his father's eye.
Brigid's hand went to the bead necklace she wore around her neck. It had
belonged to her mother and was the only thing she had left of her.

Brigid's grandfather had been a Saxon who had come over with the
Romans and had fought for them, but when the Roman Empire took her
armies away, her grandfather, like many of his people, had stayed behind. He
had told Brigid and her brother stories of his gods, although Brigid could not
remember them well. But every time the two brothers, Hengist and Horsa,
came to King Vortigern's hall, the air was filled with a sense of chaos that left
her confused. Brigid opened her eyes and stared at the old tree as she tried to
ignore the large raven that was sitting on the branch above her where the
white owl used to sit. But in the end, Brigid could not, and so she stared at the
bird, which had its beady eye on her.

'Who do you belong to?' The raven tilted its head as if it did not understand what she was saying, but Brigid didn't fall for it. She knew ravens were

intelligent birds, just as she knew the one-eyed god of her grandfather's people used ravens to spy for him. That was one of the few things she remembered about her grandfather's gods. But so did many of the gods of Britannia. 'Are you the Morrigan, or do you spy for the Saxon gods?'

The raven hopped along the branch as if it was trying to get closer to her and Brigid couldn't help but glance around the clearing to make sure that she was still alone. Although few people knew of this clearing. And those who did were too afraid to come here, apart from those too old to fear the wrath of the gods. Even the Christians refused to come into the forest the grove was in, something Brigid encouraged by placing dead animals around the forest to scare them off. The animals she used were already dead, their bodies often covered in maggots or half rotten.

'Do you come with a message for me?' Brigid asked the raven. 'Perhaps the truth of what happened to my brother?'

The wind picked up and the raven cried out before it took to the skies, leaving Brigid staring at the branch it had been sitting on. Her hand went to her bead necklace again as she tried to calm her racing heart, before she turned her attention back to the tree. She wondered what that meant, and more importantly, why it made her think of her brother. The last she had heard was that he had travelled north with a group of the Jutes, including the young Saxon who made her nervous. Two of the other warriors that had gone with him had returned and told her that Badulf was killed in an ambush and when she had asked how they had survived, they had turned away from her. Brigid had cursed them because she was certain that they had abandoned Badulf, or perhaps had even killed him themselves. She knew there were many who were jealous of him. Badulf was taller than all the men in Cair Urnahc and was handsome. And because of their grandfather's Saxon blood, he was a talented warrior. Yet it was the other thing they had told her that had made her afraid. Something about a spear that belonged to a Saxon god. But before Brigid could ask about it, the warriors had been called away, and she had not seen them since. Brigid turned her attention back to the old tree and stared at the gnarled branches and green leaves. Her eyes went to where the white owl would often sit, although she had not seen the bird since the Jutes had arrived.

'Mother, where are you? Why do you not speak to me any more?' Brigid waited for a response, but nothing came. Just like the many days before. Since she had been told of Badulf's death, Brigid had come to the tree every day, trying to understand what was going on. And what part the young Saxon warrior played. 'What is so important about this spear?'

After a few heartbeats of nothing but rustling leaves and birdsong, Brigid sighed and placed her palm on the rough bark of the tree. Brigid looked up at the sun, which sat high in the sky, and realised she had been there for too long. King Vortigern would wonder where she was, so she tried to push the feeling of loneliness away and steeled herself so that she could return to the fort.

King Vortigern had been in a dark mood ever since he had been told of the Jutes travelling north and especially after he spoke to the men who had returned from that journey. Every day he would ask her what the gods were planning and Brigid knew it was only so long she could fool him with her non-answers. One day, he would realise that the gods didn't speak to her any more and then she would lose her control over him.

And then there was Prince Vortimer, who had been acting strange as well. She had overheard him say something about an old beggar to one of his men, and he had even gone as far as having the few warriors they had scour the town for this old beggar.

Brigid stood up and fixed her dress, and with one last glance at the old tree she left the clearing. Lost in her thoughts, Brigid made her way back to the fort. She paid no attention to the boy watching the herds outside the town walls, or the women by the river as they cleaned tunics and dresses. She ignored the warriors by the bridge, who rubbed the crosses around their necks when they saw her, and barely noticed the stench of the poorer part of Cair Urnahc, where the people went unwashed for many days and emptied their chamber pots out on the streets. Children with dirt-covered faces and ripped clothes ran around as they played games and chased each other, while tired-looking mothers tried to calm screaming babies. Somewhere, a smithy was hard at work. The beating of his hammer distracted Brigid from her thoughts and, when she looked at the Roman gates, her body tensed when she saw the last person she wanted to.

Octa the Saxon.

6

The sun was past its peak as Odalric whistled when they reached the gates of Cair Urnahc, and even though Octa had seen the fort before, it still took his breath away as they both stared at the wooden palisade on large mound walls which surrounded the city of King Vortigern, the high king of Britannia. A wide ditch encircled the fort and could only be crossed by the wooden bridge which spanned it. From behind the walls, countless thin trails of smoke drifted towards the skies and mixed in with the clouds, which were not as dark as they had been before. Something Octa was glad of. His cloak was still wet from the shower they had been caught in that morning, and he prayed that the metal plates on his armour would not rust. Even Warda looked like she'd had enough of the rain as she walked with her head lowered. Octa stroked her muscled neck and felt the dampness of her fur.

It had taken them six days on the Roman road to reach Cair Urnahc. When it wasn't raining, they had slept out in the open, under the moon and the stars. But on the few nights when it had rained, they were forced to seek shelter in farmsteads or sleep under the trees.

'I didn't think the Britons could build forts like this,' Odalric said, his eyes scanning the wooden wall and the few warriors guarding the bridge which led to an open gate. 'Reminds me of the old Roman forts they used to build on the edge of our lands when I was a boy.'

Octa nodded and thought of the old Roman forts he had seen further north and the great wall the Romans had built to stop the Picts from attacking their lands. 'They say it's one of the strongest on the island.' Octa nudged Warda over the bridge towards the gate and Odalric followed. The people of Cair Urnahc stepped aside so the two Saxons could pass and many smiled at Octa, which surprised him. The British warriors, wearing old leather vests and armed with spears, guarding the gates, on the other hand, glared at them as they rode past, and Octa felt his heart racing as Odalric smirked at them.

'They don't look like much, these warriors. Even the un-bearded boys back home could defeat them. It's no wonder their king had to look elsewhere to find men to protect his lands.'

Octa nodded, but he knew these men weren't King Vortigern's best warriors – they were inside the Roman fort which was behind the wooden walls. The warriors with the old Roman metal-plated vests, like the one Octa was wearing, and who had swords around their waists. Like Badulf. Octa's heart raced as he wondered if he would see Badulf's sister. Would she already know what had happened to her brother? He scowled as the question came to him, while Odalric grimaced at the many wooden houses and the smells inside the mound walls. An unpleasant mix of dirt and shit, blended in with the scent of animals like the goats who walked the streets as freely as the people who lived there.

As they rode past the market square, which was quieter than the last time Octa had been there, a group of boys started following them. Odalric pulled a face at them, which the boys laughed at as they danced around the horses, but Octa wasn't paying attention to them as he scanned the people of Cair Urnahc. Like those outside the fort, most smiled at them, even as they kept their distance, while the few warriors around glared at them, and as they rode past, one hawked and spat towards Warda. Octa tightened his grip on Gungnir as he frowned at the warriors.

'You'd think they'd be happy we are here,' he said to Odalric, who was scowling at the large stone walls of the old Roman fort. Even though Octa had seen it before and had seen the Roman forts and the great wall to the north, he still couldn't help but stare at the walls made of large stone blocks which were all square-shaped and stacked on top of each other.

'By Woden,' Odalric said. 'How did they build these?'

Octa had often wondered the same. 'The people here say the Romans built these walls, as well as many more around Britannia.'

'Men built them?' Odalric rubbed his head as they stopped their horses to look at the walls. 'Impossible.'

'Aye, men built them, or so they say.' Octa had told Odalric of the great wall in the north and the old warrior had refused to believe that it was real. He wondered if seeing this fort would change his mind.

'Must have been the gods who built this, or giants.' Odalric gaped at the stone wall as Octa smiled and nudged Warda towards the gates of the Roman fort.

The warriors guarding these gates were better armed than those by the outer walls. They wore metal-plated vests and simple bowl helmets. The warriors carried egg-shaped shields and long spears and all of them had swords on their hips. Like most Britons, they were shorter than Octa and Odalric, but their broad shoulders and thick limbs showed a strength that Octa was certain would challenge most Saxons.

Odalric fell silent as he scrutinised the warriors, and Octa almost smiled at the unimpressed look on the older warrior's face. 'No wonder the Romans managed to make this island part of their empire.'

Octa shook his head and was glad the warriors guarding the gate could not understand Odalric's words, but then he frowned when they barred their way. He pulled on Warda's reins and looked at the warriors.

'What do you Jutes want?' one warrior said in the British tongue, and Octa wondered if there was any point in telling the man that they were Saxons. When Hengist and Horsa first arrived, everyone called them Saxons, but over the summer and winter they were there, the people had learnt they were Jutes.

'We here see King Vortigern,' Octa responded in the British tongue. He had learnt to speak it while he was recovering from injuries in Corstopitum, the old Roman fort by the great wall, and he would often speak to the people on Ruym Island as he tried to improve it, but Octa knew he still made some mistakes.

The Britons laughed and Odalric growled as he moved his horse closer to Octa's. 'I thought this king was a friend of Hengist and Horsa,' he said to Octa, who shrugged.

'That's what they told me.'

'Why do you want to see the king?' one of the Britons asked, his tone annoying Octa because he didn't understand the aggression in it.

'We bring message from Hengist and Horsa,' Octa responded, and the British warriors glanced at each other, but they still did not move aside so that he and Odalric could enter the fort.

'Well, then tell us the message and we'll deliver it to the king. He is too busy to see your kind.'

'Our kind?' Octa asked as he struggled to contain his annoyance and had to take a deep breath to calm himself.

'Jutes. Heathens,' the Briton responded.

Octa tightened his grip on Gungnir. 'We Saxons, not Jutes.' He sensed Odalric tense beside him and knew that, even though the older warrior could not understand the words being spoken, he would have noticed the change in mood.

'Doesn't matter. You're still not coming in. Prince Vortimer has forbidden it.'

Before Octa could ask who this Prince Vortimer was, a woman's voice said from behind them, 'Prince Vortimer only has command of this fort when King Vortigern is away. And I know for certain that the king is still here, so the prince has no control over who gets to enter and who doesn't.'

His heart racing, Octa turned and saw Badulf's sister standing beside his horse, her back straight as she stared defiantly at the warriors guarding the gate. To his surprise, the warriors glanced at each other and seemed uncertain of what to do.

'You will let these men in so they can deliver their message to the king, or you can explain to him why you are treating his guests like they are our enemies.'

'But they are the enemy,' one warrior said, and looked to the others for support, but they only stepped away from him. Octa wondered what power Brigid had over these men and then remembered Badulf telling him she spoke to the old gods of this island.

'They are here to fight our enemies and the enemies of our king. Now let them enter.' Brigid glared at the warriors who, after a few heartbeats, stepped aside and let Octa and Odalric enter.

'Who's the woman and why do the men fear her like that?' Odalric asked as he glanced at Brigid, who followed them inside the Roman fort. Behind the stone walls, the fort looked much different. There were no wooden houses, only ones made of stone which were laid out neatly in straight lines, with straight paths between them. The roofs were made of red tiles, although there were a few houses which had thatch roofs and even some where half the walls were made of wood.

'I'll tell you later.'

Octa pulled Warda to a stop and dismounted so he could thank Brigid, but before he could say anything, she stepped towards him and asked in the Saxon tongue, 'What happened to my brother?'

Octa gulped as the question caught him by surprise and, out of the corner of his eye, he caught Odalric gaping at Brigid. 'She speaks our tongue?'

'My grandfather was a Saxon,' Brigid responded without taking her eyes off of Octa, who almost shrunk away from the anger in them. 'What happened to Badulf? Why did you travel north?'

'We... uhm... we were ambushed,' Octa managed to get out, and glanced at the spear in his hand. 'Badulf was killed.'

'But you somehow survived?' Brigid stepped closer to him and Octa had to resist the urge to step back, but only because he didn't want to look weak in front of Odalric.

'I...' Octa didn't know what to say. The only reason he had survived the ambush was because Eadric had led them away from the danger, after he had thrown the spear that had killed Brigid's brother when he had tried to escape. But Octa knew he couldn't tell Brigid any of that.

'Did he at least get a proper funeral?'

Octa hesitated as the people of Cair Urnahc glanced at them when they walked past. 'We never found his body.'

Brigid's eyes widened, and then she sneered at him. 'You mean you didn't look for his body?'

Octa's heart thudded in his chest, but before he could say anything, someone pushed into the back of Brigid and she fell into him. Brigid reached out to stop herself from falling and her hand landed on the shaft of Gungnir. For a heartbeat, she tensed and her face went pale as she stared at him. Octa frowned at the tear that ran down her cheek and, when she let go of the spear, she covered her mouth and shook her head.

'Brigid?' Octa asked, and glanced at Odalric, who looked as confused as he was.

'Where did you find that spear?' Brigid asked, her voice filled with fear.

Octa looked at Gungnir and struggled to understand what had just happened.

Before he could respond, Brigid said, 'That spear will bring death and destruction to these lands.' Her gaze fixed on the name of the spear carved in runes on the shaft. 'I... I must go.'

This time Octa turned pale as he remembered the white owl in Brigantia's cave saying the same words to him. But before he could say anything, Brigid turned and walked away.

'What in Woden's name was that?' Odalric asked, and Octa could only shake his head.

'I don't know.' He looked at Gungnir and saw how the ravens on the spearhead seemed to move, as if they were flying to Woden to tell him what had just happened.

7

Brigid stumbled as she rushed to get away from the young Saxon warrior. People cursed at her as she bumped into them and pushed them out of the way, but she did not care. She needed to get away from them and the spear. She struggled to breathe as she turned a corner, but she kept going, her legs unstable, until she was away from the square and on her own. Brigid leaned against the cold stone wall of a house and dropped to the ground where she closed her eyes and relived the vision she saw when she had touched the spear.

An all-consuming flame ravaging the landscape as a one-eyed god from distant lands laughed and people screamed. Countless dead littered the fields while the skies were filled with dark clouds. But not clouds, ravens. Hundreds of them, their cries piercing her ears, which Brigid covered in an attempt to drown them out, but she couldn't. Just like she couldn't stop the ravens from feasting on the dead as warriors fought a never-ending war. Fathers and sons slaughtering each other while rivers ran red with blood. And in the centre of it all stood Octa with the spear in his hands as bodies lay by his feet. The spear from a land far away with a power darker than anything she had ever felt before. But what brought tears to her eyes was that the gods were gone. The gods of Britannia whom she had devoted her life to were gone as Octa paved the way for his gods to take their place.

'Brigid?' a voice said, and Brigid opened her eyes to see Minura standing over her, her old eyes filled with concern. 'What's the matter, my dear?'

Minura had been a friend of Brigid's mother and she was one of the few who knew about Brigid's gifts. 'I...' Brigid started, and then realised she didn't know what to say. She couldn't tell Minura of the vision she had just seen, because Brigid was still trying to make sense of it. 'I miss Badulf,' she said in the end, which was also true.

Minura gave her a sad smile and nodded. 'He was a good man, your brother. I'm sure Arawn is looking after him.' Arawn was the god of death and ruler of Annwn, the afterlife, but Brigid still found it hard to believe her brother was there. Like most of the old generation, Minura still believed in the old gods, even though she went to the Christian church. To them, the Christian god was just another to add to the many gods they already knew.

Brigid shook her head as she remembered what Octa had said. They had never found Badulf's body. Ignoring the frown on Minura's face, Brigid got back to her feet and pushed the images of the vision out of her mind as she fixed her dress. She needed to find out more about the spear Octa had, and she knew of only one person who could tell her about it. The wise one. But Brigid didn't know where she was or if she still lived. The wise one had gone north soon after Brigid had finished her training and Brigid had not seen her since. Brigid took a deep breath to calm her mind. She would think of what to do, but first she had to find out why Octa had come to Cair Urnahc.

* * *

Octa and Odalric walked towards the large stone building with the thatch roof after they took their horses to large stables near the wall of the fort. Gungnir felt heavier in his hand after what had happened with Brigid and Octa couldn't stop glancing at it as he tried to make sense of what had happened. He had wanted to chase after her, but Odalric had stopped him.

'We're here to deliver the brothers' message, not run after women who lost their wits,' the older warrior had said. Octa had nodded and turned his back on Brigid, but he was determined to find her after he delivered the message. He still needed to apologise for Badulf's death and because he had not tried to find his body. The old Saxons in Corstopitum had told him they had searched for Badulf's body but that they could not find it.

Two warriors guarded the entrance to the king's hall, and like the men by the gate to the Roman fort, they wore metal-plated vests and had swords on their hips. The only difference was the helmets these warriors wore, which had cheek plates and small plumes on top. But Odalric still looked unimpressed as he towered over the Britons and glared at them. The Britons glanced at each other and then at Octa, who tried to look friendly as he approached them.

'We here see King Vortigern. Important message from Hengist and Horsa.'

Again, the warriors glanced at each other before one turned and went inside the hall, while the other glared at them. As Octa waited, he looked at the people in the Roman fort. They were better dressed than those who lived in the outer fort with many of the men wearing long tunics or cloaks, fastened by intricate brooches, over trousers and shoes made of leather. The women wore long dresses with different coloured beads around their necks, with their hair hidden under pieces of cloth, while thick gold bands adorned their wrists and their fingers were covered with golden rings. Like the women, the men also wore rings and golden bands on their wrists, and Octa rubbed his hands as he remembered how he too once wore thick golden rings on his fingers and golden chains around his neck.

When he had lived in Witta's hall, he had dressed in the finest clothes and wore more jewellery than most women. He sighed at the memory, which felt like it came from a different lifetime. Perhaps it was because the only jewellery he wore now was the spear pendant around his neck that his mother had given him before he had left the Saxon lands. Saxon women usually wore the spear pendants around their waists, but his mother believed it would keep him safe. And maybe it did, he thought as he glanced at Gungnir in his hand. He had survived where most had died and had killed a warrior better than him.

After a short while, the warrior returned and said, 'The king is busy now, so you'll have to wait. There is a tavern up the road.' The warrior pointed to a building not far from the hall. 'We'll send for you when the king is ready to see you.'

'We wait here,' Octa said, worried that if he left, then they might forget about him. Besides, he wanted to get this done with and find Brigid. He needed to know what had happened when she touched the spear.

After a long while, when the sun had started its descent and the people of

Cair Urnahc were preparing the evening meal, another warrior walked out of the hall and glanced at the two by the door before he looked at Octa and Odalric. 'The king will see you.' Octa nodded his thanks and was about to enter the hall when the warrior shook his head. 'Your weapons stay with us. You might be allies, but we still don't trust you.'

'What did he say?' Odalric said as he glared at the Briton.

'We must give them our weapons or they won't let us in.' Octa glanced at Woden's spear. He did not want to leave it with the Britons, especially not after what had happened earlier on. But he needed to deliver his message and then find Brigid. He also wanted to get back to the island. His mother was there and on her own, and Octa did not like that. Although he still didn't understand why she had suggested to Hengist that Octa deliver his message. She had claimed that it was because he spoke the British tongue, but Octa wondered if there wasn't more to it.

'Give the spear to me,' Odalric said as he held out his hand. 'And your seax. I'll wait outside.' Octa raised an eyebrow at his father's man, who only shrugged. 'The gods know there's no need for me to go inside. I won't know what you're saying and don't want to stand there and look like a fool. The only reason I'm here is because your mother wanted me to keep an eye on you.'

Octa hesitated as he thought about it, but then nodded as he handed Gungnir to Odalric. The man had fought for his father for most of Octa's life, and now he was loyal to Octa's mother. If there was anyone he could trust with the spear, then it was Odalric. He also took his seax from its scabbard, the one Reinald, the old Saxon warrior from Corstopitum, had given him before he left the fort to return south, and gave that to Odalric. 'I won't be long.'

Odalric nodded. 'I'll be here.'

Octa turned to the Briton who nodded at him. 'Follow me.'

Octa entered the hall behind the warrior, and as his eyes adjusted to the dim light inside, he raised an eyebrow at what he saw. Shields and weapons hung on the walls, much like what they had in their halls in the Saxon lands, while thick wooden columns supported the thatch roof. Holes in the stone walls let some light in, but most of the light was provided by the many torches on the walls and the wooden columns, while a large hearth fire burnt brightly in the centre of the hall. Octa almost sighed a sigh of relief at the sight of the hearth fire and hoped he'd be in the hall long enough for the fire to dry his damp cloak.

Benches lined the walls, and most of them were filled by wealthy-looking men, who all glared at Octa as he walked towards the end of the hall. Stone statues of people, half-naked men and women, also stood around by the walls and reminded Octa of the statue of Brigantia in the cave near the wall in the north, where he had found Woden's spear.

Lost in his thoughts, Octa didn't realise the warrior had stopped and almost bumped into him. The warrior glared at him, but Octa wasn't paying attention to him any more as he stared at the old man sitting on a raised chair and scowling at him.

'My king.' The warrior lowered his head. 'This Jute brings a message from Hengist and Horsa.'

'I Saxon, not Jute,' Octa said, but the warrior only shrugged as Octa turned his attention back to King Vortigern. The man looked old enough to be his grandfather, with his grey hair cut short and his grey beard trimmed. He dressed the same way that the Britons outside the hall dressed, only his clothes were of better quality and around his head he wore a simple gold band with a large gem in the centre, while a large cross, which seemed almost too heavy for the old king, hung around his neck.

A short man with a thin face which reminded Octa of a weasel stood beside the king and scowled at Octa. 'What message you have for King Vortigern?'

Octa winced at how badly the weasel-looking man spoke his language and wondered if that was what he sounded like to them when he spoke the British tongue. If it was, then he needed to practise more if he wanted to make this island his new home.

Octa took a deep breath and wished that Odalric was with him and not outside the hall, because he knew the Britons would not like what he had to say. 'Hengist and Horsa ask more provisions,' he said in the British tongue, which made the weasel man's face turn dark.

'You not speak to king. You speak to me and I speak to king!'

'My message for King Vortigern, not you,' Octa responded as he revelled in the confidence Gungnir had given him.

Before the weasel man could respond, King Vortigern raised his heavily ringed hand. 'You speak our language, although badly.' Some of the Britons in the hall laughed as Octa did his best to ignore them. He was glad now that Odalric was not in the hall. The older warrior would not like being laughed at.

'I learn it in north, by great wall.'

King Vortigern leaned forward and Octa sensed the atmosphere in the hall change. 'You went to the north? To the Roman wall? Why?'

Octa cursed himself as he realised he had said something he shouldn't have, and his mind raced as he searched for an answer. 'I heard Saxon warrior in north. Wanted to meet them,' he said, and from the look on King Vortigern's face, Octa knew the king did not believe him. Out of the corner of his eye, Octa caught a movement in the shadows cast by the torches, but before he could work out what or who it was, another man jumped up from one bench and jabbed his finger at Octa.

'He went north to talk to the Picts! The Jutes are plotting against us!'

Octa scowled at the stocky man, who looked like a younger version of King Vortigern, and shook his head. 'I fight Picts in north with Saxon brothers. Not talk to them.'

He wanted to look towards the corner of the hall where he had spotted the movement before, but then the man said, 'He lies! Father, I told you we cannot trust these heathen scum!' Many of the men in the hall raised their voices as they seemed to agree with the Briton and Octa felt his heart racing as he tried to think of what he could say.

'Enough!' King Vortigern raised his voice to be heard over the noise in the hall. Octa tensed as the hall fell silent and gave a quick glance towards the corner of the hall again, but couldn't see anyone. 'Vortimer,' the king said to the man who looked like him. 'I understand you don't like my agreement with Hengist and Horsa, but their warriors have driven the Picts back and have kept our lands safe.' King Vortigern then turned his attention to Octa and scowled at him. 'And you, Saxon. You say Hengist and Horsa ask for more provisions? Why? The other kings and I already send enough food and clothing for their warriors, and I understand that the people of Ruym also provide you with food.'

There was a muttering from the Britons in the hall as Octa took a calming breath. He had been trained on how to use spears and swords. How to defend himself with a shield, not words. And he knew he needed to choose his words carefully.

'Last carts of provisions, only half of promised. King of Cantiaci not deliver.'

Many of the men roared at Octa, who again wished Odalric stood beside him, but he took a deep breath and stood straight as he reminded himself that he was the son of a warlord and, more importantly, fought with Gungnir, the spear of Woden.

'You accuse a king of this island of not keeping his word?' the one called Vortimer said, his face red. 'See, Father, already they aim to cause dissent amongst you and your allies.'

'No cause dissent,' Octa said. 'Only tell truth. As Woden is witness.'

'Who is this Woden?' the weasel man asked, and Octa only just heard him in the noise of the many men shouting at him.

'Enough!' King Vortigern shouted again and, once more, the hall fell into a strained silence. Octa's fingers tingled as he glanced at the men around him, all of them looking like they were about to attack him. Even the warrior who had brought him into the hall stood with his hand on his sword. Octa was taller than everyone in the hall, but he had no weapons and was heavily outnumbered.

Will you fight if they attack you? A woman's voice whispered in his ears and Octa raised an eyebrow as his eyes went towards the corner where he had spotted movement before. But then something told him to look the other way. *Will you stand your ground and kill them all?* Octa gasped when he saw her walking confidently behind the men in the hall. Friga, the wife of Woden and mother of the gods. His heart raced as he wondered why she was here in the hall and why no one else noticed her. *What will you do?* She seemed to say to him before King Vortigern spoke again.

'We have heard that more ships have joined Hengist and Horsa?' Octa shook his head to clear his mind before he turned his attention back to the frowning king. 'Is this true?'

Octa glanced to where he had seen Friga before, but she was gone and it took him a few heartbeats as he wondered why she was here before he could respond to King Vortigern. 'It true, King Vortigern. More ships come. Bring people from lands of Jutes and Saxons.'

King Vortigern scowled as his son, still on his feet, said, 'They are raising an army against us!'

'Vortimer, silence!' King Vortigern glared at his son before he turned his attention to Octa. 'When do you return to Hengist and Horsa?'

Octa frowned at King Vortigern. 'Soon.'

King Vortigern nodded. 'We will go to Ruym Island. I want to speak to Hengist and Horsa myself before I agree to anything. And send word to King Gwyrangon and ask him to meet us there.' The British king then turned to the weasel man beside him. 'Find the Saxon some lodgings. It's too late in the day for him to return to Ruym Island.' Before anyone could say anything, the king stood and left the hall by a door to the back and Octa found himself facing the angry stares of those inside. The king's son walked towards him and did his best to look imposing, which was hard for him to do as he was shorter than Octa.

'My father might be blind to the threat you pose, but I am not. You better watch your back, Saxon.'

As the king's son turned and walked away, Octa heard Friga's voice in his ears again.

What would you do to defend your people?

Octa scowled as he wondered the same. What would he do to protect those he cared for?

8

'What happened in there?' Odalric asked when Octa walked out of the hall, his hands trembling. He took a deep breath to calm his racing heart as he turned to Odalric. But before Octa could respond, the weasel man walked out of the hall and glared at them. Odalric raised an eyebrow at the man as he handed Octa his spear and his seax knife. 'What's his problem?'

'The king told him to find us lodgings and I guess he isn't happy about it.'

After speaking to the two warriors outside the hall, the weasel man walked past them. 'Follow me,' he said in the British tongue.

Octa and Odalric glanced at each other and followed the man as he led them towards the tavern the warriors had pointed out to Octa earlier on.

As they walked to the tavern, the weasel man looked at Octa. 'You need to work on the way you speak our language. You sound like a child who's been dropped on his head.'

Octa gritted his teeth at the man's words, especially as he sounded worse when he spoke the Saxon tongue, but decided it was better to keep quiet.

The tavern fell silent when they entered, and Octa couldn't stop the unease he felt as everyone stared at them. Odalric didn't seem to care as he glared at everyone inside while the weasel man spoke to the tavern keeper. After handing the man some coins, the weasel man walked over to them. 'I booked you a room for the night and paid for food and drink. You are King Vortigern's guests, so behave like civilised people while you are here.' The man left without another word and, after taking a deep breath to calm himself, Octa turned to Odalric.

'Let's have a drink. I need some ale.'

Odalric smiled as Octa handed him Gungnir, before he strode to an empty bench by the wall and sat down while Octa went to the tavern keeper and ordered two cups of ale. The tavern keeper glared at him for a few heart-beats before he filled two cups with ale. Octa nodded his thanks and wondered why the Britons had to be so frustrating as he brought the ale to Odalric, who licked his lips as he took his cup from Octa. The older warrior took a large sip of the ale and swirled it around his mouth before he swallowed it.

'Not as good as the ale back home, but drinkable.'

Back home, the words echoed in Octa's mind as he drank his own ale and agreed with Odalric. The idea seemed unfamiliar to him because he knew he could never return to the lands of the Saxons. His father was dead and his village destroyed, and Octa was certain that Witta still wanted his head. Octa glanced at the spear of Woden, which leaned against the wall next to Odalric's spear. But he was different now. The fear he had felt that day and for so long after was gone. And in its place was a confidence he was still trying to make sense of. Octa almost felt like he had the day before the battle against the Thuringians. That same confidence coursed through his veins, but the arrogance was gone and in its place were the lessons he had learnt since he had fled his homeland.

Odalric drank more of his ale before he asked, 'So what happened in there? Could hear the shouting even outside the hall. The gods probably did as well.' Odalric scratched his cheek. 'Sounded like they were not happy with what you had to say.'

'I don't know, but I sense that nothing good is going to come from this.' Octa glanced at Gungnir again as he remembered Friga being inside the hall. But was she really? He was the only one who had seen her, so did he imagine her? Octa then caught sight of an old beggar standing in the tavern's door, staring at him until the tavern keeper chased the man away. He wasn't sure why, but something about the old man made him feel uncomfortable and he suddenly found that he desperately wanted to get out of Cair Urnahc. 'King Vortigern wants to go to the island. He wants to speak to the brothers, but I feel his son would rather start a war.'

Odalric raised an eyebrow as he, too, seemed to sense what Octa felt. There were many who didn't trust Hengist and Horsa and Octa knew they were right not to. The brothers might have come to Britannia with offers of friendship, but Octa knew that behind the smiles and warm words, they were planning something else. And not just them, he thought as he glanced at Woden's spear again. Woden had sent him to find the spear, but Friga then told him to keep it. That Woden was planning a war that would end all wars. Octa rubbed his forehead as he struggled to make sense of the thoughts raging in his head. He took a deep drink from his ale and signalled for the tavern keeper to bring them more ale to calm his mind. He would look for Brigid in the morning, when his mind had cleared and he knew what to say to her.

'Why would he want to start a war with the Jutes? They need the brothers and their army,' Odalric said after the tavern keeper brought them more ale.

'King Vortigern's son doesn't trust us. He believes Hengist and Horsa are plotting against the Britons.'

Odalric took another sip of his ale. 'They are. Everyone knows it. And so are we.'

Octa couldn't help but look around to make sure that no one was listening, which he knew was pointless because he doubted anyone in this tavern could speak the Saxon tongue. His mother and Odalric had tried to convince Octa he should use the spear of Woden to lead the Saxon people to a new home on this island. Somewhere they could live in peace without the dangers they had to face back in the Saxon lands. But Octa did not feel ready to lead his people. Not after what he had done.

'Things are changing back on the continent, Octa. There's barely enough land to feed those who were raised on it and now tribes from the east are pushing westwards, taking land not only from us, but from the Angles, the Jutes and even the Franks.' Odalric glanced around the tavern and seemed to study the people inside. There were a few warriors, but they were too busy drinking ale and laughing to pay any attention to the two Saxons. The rest of the people looked like traders with their fine robes and golden crosses around their necks. 'And in the wake of the eastern tribes are the Huns who drive them into our lands.'

'Have you ever fought them? The Huns?' Octa asked as he stared at the older warrior.

Odalric shook his head. 'No, and I thank the gods I don't have to.'

Octa raised his brows at the warrior, surprised the man would not want to face someone in battle.

'Even the Romans fear them. Vicious bastards who fight on horseback and kill you with their arrows before they come into range of your spears.' Odalric hawked and spat. 'That's no way to fight.' He took a sip of his ale. 'That's not the Saxon way, but it's effective. I've heard many stories of armies wiped out by them.'

The tavern filled up as more people came and went, warriors who glared at them and men who eyed the two large Saxons with wonder. But neither Octa nor Odalric paid the Britons any attention as they drank their ale and ate the stew that the tavern provided. Odalric told Octa stories of his past and the battles he had fought beside Octa's father. As Octa listened, he realised he missed his father, even though he didn't know the man well. After the sun disappeared beyond the horizon, the tavern emptied and the two warriors went to the room the weasel man had booked for them.

It was a simple room with a single straw mattress and, before Octa could even ask who would sleep on it, Odalric took his cloak off and laid it on the floor. Without a word, the older warrior lay down and went to sleep, leaving Octa alone with his thoughts as an owl hooted outside.

The following morning, Octa and Odalric were sitting on the same bench they had been the night before as they waited for their morning meal. Octa had barely slept as the conversation in the hall kept playing in his mind, especially the moment he saw Friga. Lost in his thoughts, Octa did not see Odalric nod towards the door of the tavern.

'I think we're wanted,' Odalric said, and Octa looked over his shoulder to see the warrior from the hall walking towards them.

The Briton stopped by their bench. 'The king wants to see you.'

Octa nodded and translated the words to Odalric before they finished their ale and followed the warrior outside. The morning sun hid behind clouds and Octa smelt the dampness in the air as he prayed it wouldn't rain again.

When they reached the hall, Octa was surprised that they were not asked to hand their weapons over, just like he was surprised that the hall was empty apart from King Vortigern, the weasel man and a group of warriors who all scowled at Octa and Odalric. He and Odalric glanced at each other and the older warrior only shrugged as they stopped in front of the king, who was sitting at a table and eating his morning meal. Octa's stomach rumbled as he glanced at the porridge in a large bowl, as well as bread and various fruits. Even Odalric licked his lips as he stared at the king's meal, but the king of the Britons did not tell them to sit or offer them any food as he looked up from his meal.

'The Romans brought Saxon foederati to these shores when I was a boy, and even then I marvelled at those giant men who fought like they desired to die in battle. When the Romans fought, it felt like fighting was their duty. Their movements were clean, crisp. Their warriors were disciplined and silent. But the Saxons fought as if battle coursed through their veins. There was violence and chaos. Men screamed as they used brute strength and anger to overcome their enemies.'

Octa frowned at the king as he tried to ignore the porridge in his beard. 'We Saxons, war important. Our gods want we fight well and die well.' Saying those words was difficult for Octa and he was glad that Odalric didn't understand what he was saying.

'And Woden is your god?' the king asked as he took some bread and broke it into pieces. He gave one piece to the old hound which lay under the table, the beast so quiet Octa never realised it was there, and the other he stuffed into his mouth.

Octa nodded and rubbed the shaft of Gungnir with his thumb without realising it. 'Woden one god. We have more. Woden war god, but also Tiw.'

'How many gods have you heathens got?' the weasel man asked, and King Vortigern smiled.

'Forgive Ceretic. The Christian faith does not always allow us to be open-minded about things.'

Octa frowned as he struggled to understand the king's words, so he nodded. 'Many gods,' he said.

King Vortigern leaned back in his raised chair and crossed his fingers under his chin. 'You are a Saxon, and Hengist calls himself a Jute. Are you Saxons and the Jutes allies?'

Octa shrugged. 'Saxons and Jutes, not friends, but not enemies. We trade and believe same gods.'

King Vortigern nodded and glanced at the man he called Ceretic before he said, 'The Saxon foederati fought hard to protect our lands from the Picts and others who raided our shores from the continent. Even after the Roman armies left, many of them stayed behind and continued to defend us. I hoped to use the Jutes the same way. Have them fight our enemies so that our own men don't have to die doing it. But the other kings are blind to that. They only see the fact that they are heathens and think of them as the enemy.'

Octa glanced at Odalric, who was eyeing up the food on the table, and wondered why King Vortigern was telling him this. 'Hengist and Horsa, good men. Good warlords.'

King Vortigern stroked his grey beard as he stared at Octa and Odalric before he nodded again. 'Return to Hengist and Horsa. Tell them to expect me soon.'

He waved his hand at them and Octa turned to Odalric and said to him in the Saxon tongue, 'Come, we return to Ruym.'

Odalric smiled. 'By the gods, finally.'

As they left the hall, Octa felt King Vortigern's eyes on his back and he wondered what the king of the Britons was planning. All thoughts of finding Brigid disappeared as he rubbed the shaft of Gungnir and prayed that there would be no bloodshed to come, but Octa knew there would be.

* * *

Prince Vortimer paced around his sleeping quarters, his head aching from the anger that coursed through him. 'By God, how can my father be so blind?'

Cadoc and Grifud glanced at each other, but neither answered him. Not that he wanted them to.

'These Saxons or Jutes or whatever they call themselves. They are here to steal our lands and he treats them like they are friends.' Vortimer continued to pace around his room as he thought about the young Saxon warrior who had delivered the message from Hengist and Horsa and wondered if he could get his men to capture the man. Perhaps then he could torture the bastard and find out what Hengist and Horsa really wanted. Although Vortimer already knew the answer to that. They wanted land. More importantly, they wanted the land of the Britons. Vortimer had heard of what was happening on the continent and was certain that was why the Saxons had come to Britannia. They needed land to live on because theirs was being taken from them. But Vortimer would not let them steal the land of his people. Land that belonged to God and one day to him. 'Where is that messenger?'

'In the tavern near the main hall, but he's not alone. There are two of them,' Grifud said.

Vortimer scowled at the man. 'Two of them? How did they get inside yesterday? I gave the order for none of their kind to be allowed entry.'

Grifud shrugged. 'Brigid told the men guarding the gate to let them in. She threatened to report them to your father.'

Vortimer slammed his fist into the palm of his hand. 'That bitch!' He saw the two men glance at each other and felt his irritation grow, but he swallowed it back. Vortimer had wanted Brigid for himself once. She was beautiful and tall, and she moved with a confidence that he wanted to break. But then his father caught sight of her and she decided that she'd rather bed a king instead of his son.

Vortimer knew that many believed his hatred of her and her brother was because of that, and perhaps they were right. But she was part Saxon and a witch, and the prince knew she could not be trusted. He just wished his father saw the same.

'Brigid might be useful to you still,' Cadoc said, and Vortimer turned to him.

'What do you mean? How can that bitch be useful to me?'

Cadoc took a step back to get away from his anger. 'You keep saying that she is a witch, that she worships the old gods.'

'She does!'

Cadoc nodded. 'Yes. And you still need to find out about this one-eyed god and a spear.'

'And?' Vortimer wondered what Cadoc was getting at. He had been there when the old beggar had told Vortimer of the spear that would make him king.

'Well, if she believes in the old gods, then perhaps she would know something about this one-eyed god and the spear the old beggar told you about.'

Vortimer rubbed his chin and cursed himself for not thinking of the same. His hatred of her had blinded him to that possibility. He looked at Cadoc. 'Where is she?'

'I don't know, but I'll send men to find her.'

Vortimer nodded. 'Good. Perhaps if I play this right, then I can use her against my father as well.' *And perhaps get another chance to bed her*, he thought with a smile.

The door to Vortimer's quarters opened, and he glared at the red-faced warrior who stood there panting. 'Prince Vortimer—'

'What is it?' He interrupted the man as he struggled to contain his anger at the warrior for just barging into his quarters.

The warrior straightened and glanced at the other two men there before he turned his attention back to Vortimer. 'The Saxons. They're leaving.'

'And why are you telling me this?' Vortimer raised a hand before the warrior could respond as a smile came to his lips. Perhaps there was a way to damage the relationship between his father and the heathens from the continent. 'There are only two of them?' The warrior nodded as he frowned at Vortimer. 'Take five men and hunt them down. But make sure that one of them survives, the one that speaks our language. And make sure he believes my father sent the men.'

The warrior nodded and left Vortimer's quarters as the other two men smiled at him.

'That is very clever, Prince Vortimer. Make the Saxons think your father has turned against them.'

Vortimer nodded, but his mind was still racing as he tried to make sense of the rest of the plan forming in his head. 'Send messengers to the kings opposed to my father's alliance with the Saxons. Tell them to prepare their armies. We will drive those heathens from our lands. And find Brigid!'

Cadoc and Grifud both nodded before they left his quarters, while Vortimer rubbed the cross around his neck. All he could think of was the old beggar and the spear he had told Vortimer about. He needed to find that spear and, with it, he would defeat his enemies and protect his people. Perhaps even become the new high king of Britannia.

9

Octa and Odalric left Cair Urnahc and, without a word needed to be said between them, they raced along the Roman road. Wind rushed past Octa's ears as he lowered his head, eager to get back to Ruym Island as quickly as possible, and it seemed that Warda felt the same as he barely needed to give her the command to run. He did not like that last conversation with King Vortigern and neither did he like the hostility he had felt in the king's hall before that. But all he could do was pray that Hengist would know what to do.

In the short time that Octa had known the brothers, he had seen how cunning Hengist was. The Jute had convinced the high king of the Britons to allow them to stay. And even Horsa, the younger and the more violent of the two brothers, was not a man to underestimate. Octa knew neither brother was a man you wanted as an enemy, but if the kings of Britannia united against them, then Octa doubted there was much they could do.

'Behind us!' Odalric's voice reached Octa over the wind in his ears. He glanced over his shoulder and cursed when he saw a group of warriors chasing them on horseback.

'What do we do?' he asked the older warrior, who scowled as he also looked over his shoulder.

'We keep going. I can only see five, but we don't know if there are men behind them.'

Octa nodded, glad that Odalric had decided to not fight, but then a thought came to him. 'They might have a message from the king.'

Odalric shook his head. 'The king told you what he wanted to say. My guts tell me they mean trouble.' He kicked the side of his horse and the animal jolted forward as Octa leaned closer to Warda's ear.

'Run, Warda. Run as fast as you can.' The mare picked up speed as if she understood what he had said, just as Octa knew she would. He and the horse had formed a strong bond, and she always seemed to sense what he wanted from her. It was like the gods had sent the horse to him.

They raced along the Roman road, sending the people using it jumping out of the way and almost colliding with a trader's cart who refused to move out of the way. But still the Britons chased them and, worse, they were keeping pace, even as dark clouds formed on the horizon. Warda's flanks were white with sweat and a quick glance at Odalric's horse showed they couldn't keep this up for much longer. Octa glanced at the sun poking through the clouds and knew the horses would be exhausted long before the night sky could give them cover. He saw a forest in the distance, its trees offering safety from their pursuers, but again, he doubted they would reach it. Especially as the ground towards the forest seemed uneven.

As Octa tried to work out what to do, Odalric pulled on the reins of his horse and the animal screamed as she came to a stop. Octa was forced to do the same and Warda resisted for a moment, before she too came to a stop.

His eyes fixed on the men chasing them, he asked, 'Odalric, what are you doing?'

Odalric clenched his fists as he glared at the oncoming Britons. He hawked and spat as he took his spear from his back. 'We can't outrun them. The horses won't last much longer.'

'Neither will theirs.'

Odalric raised an eyebrow at him. 'You really want to take a chance on that and find out you're wrong when you get a spear in the back?'

Octa sighed as the Britons came closer and tightened his grip on Gungnir. He did not want to fight, but Odalric was right. They could not outrun these men. 'They outnumber us.'

Odalric smiled as if he enjoyed the idea of being outnumbered. Perhaps he did. Dying with honour meant that Woden would select him to join his army, something all Saxon warriors wanted. 'We rush at them, take them by surprise.' Odalric glanced at Gungnir in Octa's hand. 'Time you showed me what that spear can do.'

Octa stroked Warda's neck and was glad that it was not fear he felt. Instead, it was the calmness of knowing that he fought with Woden's spear and that he had survived battles before. *Thunor, protect me*, he said to himself as he and Odalric kicked the flanks of their horses and charged towards the attacking Britons. Octa knew their horses would not charge straight at the enemy. They would get close and then veer to the side, because that's what horses did. These animals were not made to fight battles.

The Britons didn't slow down as Octa and Odalric charged at them. Instead, they lifted their spears and prepared to fight as Odalric called out to the gods.

'Woden, guide your spear,' Octa whispered as they were close enough to make out the anger on the faces of the British warriors and, without aiming, he threw Gungnir at them. The spear of Woden never missed. That's what they had been told when Octa was still a child. Beside him, Odalric roared as he kept hold of his spear, but pulled his arm back as he prepared to jab at the Britons.

Octa, his heart in his mouth, watched the flight of Gungnir as the spear of Woden flew as straight as a raven and pierced the chest of the British warrior leading the charge. He could not hear if the man made a sound as he was sent flying from his horse and caused those behind him to veer to the side as they tried to avoid him.

As expected, Odalric's horse pulled away from the oncoming danger and Odalric used this moment to stab his spear into the neck of one of the Britons who was distracted by his dead companion. He let go of his spear as the Briton fell from his horse and pulled his sword from its scabbard. Warda kept going straight and Octa's heart thudded in his chest, but he had no time to work out what the horse was doing as he was forced to duck under the spear of another British warrior. He reached out and grabbed Gungnir from the chest of the dead Briton, its shaft pointing to the skies as the man lay on his back, before he swung it in a wide arc. The spear caught one of the Britons on the side of his head and the man fell from his horse and, as Warda turned, Octa stabbed him in the back before he could get to his feet.

Odalric had dismounted his horse and stabbed his sword at the face of the horse and, as the animal reared to avoid the sharp blade, he shoulder barged it, knocking it over and throwing its rider to the ground. Odalric rushed at the man before he could get to his feet and buried his sword in the Briton's chest, using his bulk and his strength to drive it through the man's mail vest.

Only one Briton remained on his horse and his face paled when he realised he was now the one outnumbered. Without glancing at his dead companions, he turned his horse and fled.

'Don't let him get away!' Odalric screamed as he freed his sword from the dead Briton's chest.

Octa changed his grip on Gungnir and launched the spear. He watched as it arched through the air as if it had a mind of its own and struck the fleeing Briton in the back, throwing him from his horse.

'By Woden.' Odalric whistled and Octa could only nod as Warda took him to the man with the spear in his back.

The Briton groaned as he tried to crawl away, while reaching for the spear in his back. Octa steeled himself before he dismounted and gripped the shaft of Gungnir. And as the man screamed in pain, he remembered Badulf being killed a similar way by Eadric. He forced those memories from his mind as he leaned closer to the Briton.

'Who sent you?'

The warrior glared at him, and Octa saw the pain in his eyes. He knew the man would be dead soon as he again thought of Badulf while Odalric approached.

'Kill the bastard. He won't tell you anything.'

Octa hesitated, his hand still on the shaft of Gungnir. Fighting to defend himself was one thing, but he could not just kill a man like this.

Odalric must have sensed the same as he stepped forward and grabbed Gungnir from Octa's grip. He twisted the spear before he pulled it out of the Briton and stabbed him again. The Briton shuddered and then his body went limp as his blood spread out across the stones Romans had put down many generations before. Odalric showed no emotion as he pulled the spear free and, for a moment, he stared at the blood-covered ravens on the spearhead before he handed Gungnir to Octa.

'That was a good throw.'

Octa nodded, but he knew it had not been him. He had thrown the spear without aiming, and trusted that the stories had been true. 'Why would King Vortigern send men after us?'

Odalric shrugged as he cleaned his sword before putting it back in its scabbard. 'It doesn't matter. What does is that we live and they don't.' The older Saxon took the pouches from the dead men's belts as he collected his spear and went for his horse. 'And besides, we don't know that King Vortigern sent these men.'

Octa wiped the spearhead clean and strapped Gungnir to his back again. 'But they came from Cair Urnahc. They wear his colours.'

'Aye,' Odalric said as he mounted his horse. 'But you said there were some in the hall who are against their king's alliance with the Jutes.'

Octa walked towards Warda, who shook her head at the scent of blood. He stroked her nose and wondered what had made her run straight at the Britons. 'You think one of them sent these men? But who?'

Odalric looked at the descending sun and the dark clouds. 'Woden knows it doesn't matter, but my guess is the son. You said he was the most vocal against us.'

Octa frowned as he mounted Warda and glanced at the dead Britons, whose bodies were scattered across the Roman road. He was glad this part of the road was empty, otherwise word of what had happened would spread far across Britannia. And from what Octa had seen in Cair Urnahc, he knew that only the smallest of sparks could cause a war between the Britons and the Jutes. 'So what do we do? Do we tell Hengist and Horsa?'

Odalric turned towards him. 'What do you think we should do, Octa? You are the son of a warlord.'

Octa chewed the inside of his cheek as he considered his options. He might have been the son of a warlord, but he was not a leader. Octa had never been taught how to lead because Witta wanted him to follow his son, not lead his own armies. He tried to think of what his father would have done, but Octa barely knew the man and he was sure that Odalric wouldn't tell him if he asked. He took a deep breath to calm his mind. 'If we tell Hengist and Horsa, then they might see this as a sign of war. Especially Horsa, who is always eager for a fight.'

'Aye, and right now, they are not in a position to fight this war, and neither are we.'

'So we tell them nothing of this?'

Odalric nodded. 'Already thinking like your father. Only tell them what the king told you to tell them. They don't need to know that we were attacked. That can stay between us and the gods.'

And my mother, Octa thought as Odalric turned his horse and tapped her flank, knowing that Odalric would tell his mother of this. Odalric's mare trotted away as if she was desperate to get away from the smell of death.

With one last glance at the dead men, Octa nudged Warda, and the mare followed Odalric.

It took them five days to ride back to Ruym Island. They pushed their horses as hard as they could without injuring them or burning them out. They did not know if more men had been sent after them and were eager to stay ahead of any that might have been. Neither man spoke much on the journey. They didn't need to talk about the attack or what that meant. At night, they camped out under the cloudy skies and Octa thanked the gods that there had been no rain on the journey back.

As they rode past Cair Lundein, Octa couldn't help but glance at the stone walls and long line of people marching towards the gates of the city Hengist and Horsa had kept safe since their arrival. Yet the people of the Cantiaci still attacked their hunters or snuck on to the island at night and set fire to tents. A handful of people had been killed by these fires and most of them had not been warriors but families who had fled the flames that ravaged their homelands.

Odalric kept his gaze fixed ahead of him, but occasionally he would glance over his shoulder. Octa knew why, but doubted there was anyone chasing them. If more men had been sent, then they would have seen the bodies of the men Octa and Odalric had killed and would have known their plan had failed. Although, what that plan was, Octa was not smart enough to understand. He could only pray to the gods that it did not lead to war, because although his fear had left him, Octa did not want to fight another battle. Not if he could avoid it.

10

Berthild stood outside the house Hengist had given them, her arms crossed as she watched Hengist and Horsa talk to some of their men by the main hall. Octa had wanted to refuse the house, saying he was happy to sleep in a tent with the rest of the men, but Berthild wasn't. She had been the wife of a warlord and did not sleep in tents. Not any more. So she had accepted the house and had worked hard since to make it as much of a home as she could. Something which had not been easy, as many of the things she had been used to in Frithowald's village, she'd not been able to find. Still, it was better than sleeping in a tent.

A British woman would come to cook and clean for them and Octa insisted on paying her, but Berthild didn't trust her. Mainly because she couldn't speak to her. Only Octa could, and as much as she loved her son, he did not know what needed to be done in the house. And that he had been gone for many days only made it more frustrating. Berthild wondered if it had been a good idea to suggest to Hengist that her son should be the one to deliver the message to this high king. But Octa spoke the British tongue and Berthild knew it would bring him closer to the leaders of the Jutes. Well, one of them anyway.

She turned her attention to Horsa, the younger of the two brothers. The brothers looked almost the same. Both were tall and broad-shouldered, just like Odalric, and had light-coloured hair. They wore more jewellery than

Berthild owned at the moment, with their fingers covered in golden rings and even the clothes they wore were finer than anything Frithowald had ever given her. The only difference between Hengist and Horsa was their faces. Hengist always had a smile on his face, but there was no denying the cleverness and the ruthlessness in his eyes, while Horsa always seemed to scowl, even when he smiled. Octa had told her that Horsa didn't trust him and Berthild had seen for herself from the way he always glared at her son, especially now that he had the spear of Woden. Although, Berthild still couldn't believe that that spear was really Gungnir. What she did believe, though, was that her son was destined for greatness. She had sensed it the day he had been born, and she was determined to help him reach that greatness.

'Handsome, the brothers, aren't they?' a voice said, and Berthild's heart jumped as it startled her. She turned and saw a familiar woman standing there with a friendly smile on her face, but with eyes that spoke of a great wisdom. For a few heartbeats, Berthild only stared at the woman as she tried to remember where she had seen her before, and then it came to her.

'You're from the tavern in that village in Jutland. You're the one who told us of Britannia.' Berthild's mind raced as she wondered why the woman was here.

The woman nodded as she moved closer and stood beside Berthild. 'Aye, I worked in the tavern in Wodenberg.'

'What brings you here?' Berthild asked as she suddenly felt at ease with the woman.

The woman shrugged, her eyes on the brothers again. 'With everyone coming to Britannia, my husband saw an opportunity for us here. He believes we could thrive on this island, so we decided to come here as well.'

'Your husband is here too?'

The woman shook her head. 'He still has things he needs to take care of before he can come. So he sent me to find a suitable place for us.'

Berthild nodded. 'Your husband must trust you very much. The gods know not many men do that.'

The woman gave her a strange smile she didn't understand. 'He does, but I have my own reason for being here as well.'

'Your own reason?' Berthild frowned at the woman.

'Did you ever find your son?' the woman asked, which caught Berthild by surprise and she stuttered before she could respond.

'I never told you about my son.'

The woman nodded again. 'No, you didn't, but I heard you mention him to your man.'

Berthild shook her head faster than she should have done. 'Odalric is not my man. He is...' She hesitated, not really sure what Odalric was to her. Her protector, her warrior? He had fought for Frithowald for as long as she had been married to him and, in all that time, they had rarely spoken to each other. The only reason Odalric was here was because Frithowald had told him to keep her safe before he was slain by Witta.

'He looks to be a great warrior. A good man to guide your son.' Again, Berthild frowned at the woman's words. 'Did you find him?'

Berthild nodded as she still frowned at the woman. 'I did.'

The woman smiled a warm smile. 'Our sons are important to us, but sometimes they lose their way. Especially when they are still young.'

'You have sons?' Berthild asked, and the woman nodded.

'I do, but he is off fighting his own battles and doing what he believes he should.'

'You don't sound like you agree with him.'

The woman laughed. 'I don't always, but as a mother, it's important to know when to stand back and when to interfere.'

Berthild scowled as she thought about the woman's words. 'I had little to do with Octa while he grew to be a man. He was sent away to live with someone we once thought of as a friend. And now, he is here and I feel he hides from his destiny.'

'His destiny?' the woman asked, her eyes back on the brothers as they laughed at something one of the men they were talking to said.

'My son is destined for great things, but he was given a responsibility he was not ready for yet and I fear it made him more cautious. Too cautious, perhaps.'

'Then perhaps he needs his mother's guidance to achieve his destiny. Like the stars guide a ship to its destination.'

'Is that what you do with your son?'

The woman nodded. 'When it's needed, although he prefers to listen to his father.'

Berthild glanced at the woman. 'Your husband is a warrior as well?'

The woman smiled again. 'My husband is many things and never the same thing for too long.' Berthild frowned at the woman, who put a hand on her shoulder. 'Aye, it gets frustrating, but he likes his games.' The woman turned her attention to the brothers again. 'They are handsome, especially the older one.'

Berthild looked at Hengist and nodded as she agreed with the woman. Although he was younger than her, she had to admit there was an attraction there. The thought that had bothered her before came to her again. How far would she go to help Octa achieve his destiny? 'He is,' she said after a few heartbeats.

'He likes you. I can see it in the way he glances at you,' the woman said, and Berthild heard the smile in her voice. 'With the right words and right push, just think of what he could do for your son.'

Berthild's brows furrowed. 'But his brother doesn't trust us, especially my son.'

The woman nodded. 'I wouldn't be too concerned about the brother. The only thing you should be concerned with is how far you will go to help your son.'

Berthild's breath caught in her throat as the woman said the very words that were in her mind and, when she turned to the woman, she saw she had turned her back on her and was walking away.

'I hope I'll see you again, Lady Berthild,' the woman said over her shoulder before she disappeared around the corner of the house.

Berthild stood there, unable to make sense of what had just happened, but then she shook her head and composed herself. The woman might have been strange, but what she said was true. Hengist could help Octa reach his destiny. All she needed to do was work out how she was going to help him do that.

As the thoughts ravaged her mind, she noticed Hengist clap his brother on the shoulder before he turned and walked away. She also noticed how he glanced her way, so Berthild walked towards him.

'The gods have blessed us with a fine morning today, Lady Berthild.' Hengist greeted her with a warm smile.

Berthild glanced at the thick clouds. 'You mean it isn't raining yet?'

Hengist laughed. 'Aye, I've seen many places in my life, but never a place where it rains so much as Britannia.'

'Makes you wonder why everyone keeps fighting over the island.'

Hengist nodded. 'The lands are fertile and plenty and there are many tin mines to the west that bring in much wealth.'

Berthild raised an eyebrow at Hengist. 'You seem to know a lot about Britannia.'

Hengist gave her a mischievous smile. 'It pays to be informed. They say Woden knows all there is and yet he still seeks new knowledge.'

For a reason Berthild could not understand, the woman she had just spoken to came to her mind. 'Any news of Octa yet?'

Hengist shook his head. 'It's many days' ride to Cair Urnahc and there are many things there to distract a young man. But he has proven himself to be capable and your man looks a formidable warrior, so I wouldn't fear. They will return soon, I'm sure.'

'Odalric is not my man,' Berthild said. 'He was my husband's warrior.'

'And now he keeps you safe.'

'He is keeping my son safe. I need no protection.' Berthild squared her shoulders and gave Hengist a steely gaze, which only made him smile.

'No, I'm sure you don't, my lady. But I'll make sure that no harm comes to you while you are in my village.'

'Your village?'

Hengist nodded. 'Aye, this village and this small island belong to us now. I'm even thinking of changing its name. Something to remind us of home.'

Berthild smiled at Hengist's confidence. 'And you don't think the Britons will object?'

Hengist shrugged. 'The Britons on this island know they are better with us around. My warriors keep them safe where their so-called king left them to fend for themselves.'

'And what about this so-called king? The gods know he'll not be pleased.' For a moment, Berthild saw the ruthlessness in Hengist's eyes as he smiled at her comment.

'The gods also know there is nothing he can do about it. The man is like an insect on a hot summer's day. Annoying, but harmless.'

'And easy to kill?'

Hengist only smiled at that before he changed the subject. 'How do you find your new home?'

Berthild watched him for a few heartbeats and knew that she needed to make sure that Octa stayed on the Jute's good side. She had already seen how quick he was to punish even those who had loyally fought for him for many winters the moment they betrayed him. 'The house is fine, but the woman who helps is frustrating.'

Hengist raised an eyebrow. 'I can find you a new servant if she is not good enough.'

Berthild shook her head. 'No, she is good.' She put a finger on her chin and tilted her head slightly as she tried to find the right words. 'It's just a different way of doing things here. I guess I must adjust if I'm to live here.'

Hengist shook his head. 'We, Lady Berthild, are not the ones who must adjust to this island.'

Berthild glanced at Hengist, a playful smile on her face. 'You make it sound like you are planning on conquering the island, like the Romans did before.'

Hengist laughed before he said, 'I have things to take care of, Lady Berthild. I'll send word to you when Octa returns.' And with that, he walked away before Berthild could respond. Not that she had anything else she needed to say. Hengist had big plans for himself and his brother, and she needed to make sure that Octa was part of those plans. And not just so he could reach his destiny, but also so the Saxon people had a new place to call home. A place safe from the wars raging on the continent.

11

Brigid sat in the hall with the women in King Vortigern's life: his wife, who was older than her but still possessed the beauty of a woman half her age, and many of King Vortigern's mistresses. King Vortigern's wife knew who they were, but Brigid knew that she didn't mind. Her husband was a king and a king could do these things, and for the king's wife, it freed her from his annoying habits and allowed her to pursue her own interests.

They were sitting in the corner of the hall, weaving as they talked about the same mundane things they always talked about. The queen's grandchildren, who took up most of her time and energy, and the people from the poorer part of Cair Urnahc. The queen often complained about how the stench from the outer fort would drift over the Roman walls and how she wished they would clean themselves more often. The other women, all of them about the same age as Brigid, would all nod and agree, even though some of them came from there.

Brigid, though, was not paying attention as they chirped away about the latest fashion or the tunics they were making for King Vortigern. Her mind was on the day Octa had come to the fort. Every night since that day, she had dreamt of the vision the spear had given her and she wished she had someone to talk to about it. But there was no one that understood or that could help her make sense of it. And then there was something else. Something she could not explain.

After she had spoken to Minura, Brigid had snuck into the hall to hear what Octa had to say and she was certain that he had spotted her. More than once, he had glanced towards the corner she was hiding in and she worried he would give her away. But everyone had been too eager to argue with him to pay any attention to where he was looking. And then, near the end of the meeting, she had noticed how his posture changed. His body had stiffened and, at first, he had glanced her way before he looked the other way. And that was when Brigid had sensed it. A presence in the hall that was unfamiliar, but Brigid knew it was a god. She knew the feeling when they were around. The excitement in the air mixed with a sense of trepidation. Only those who understood knew that feeling and what it meant, and the men in the hall were too blinded by their devotion to the Christian god to sense it.

As much as Brigid had tried, she had not recognised the god in the hall that day. She knew it was not Brigantia, even though she had sensed the same motherly devotion that Brigantia gave. But there had been something else. Not a sense of danger or darkness, but something close.

'Brigid?' The queen's voice broke her from her thoughts and when Brigid's eyes came into focus, she realised everyone was staring at her. 'You've been sitting there, unmoving for a long time. Is something the matter?'

Brigid noticed how the other women smiled at each other. They did not like her because they all knew the king listened to her advice. Even the queen knew, but as long as Brigid said nothing to turn King Vortigern against her, she didn't mind. Brigid shook her head. 'I just need some air. If I may be excused?'

The queen nodded as she frowned and Brigid heard one woman whisper that she was with child. And even though Brigid knew she wasn't, she was content to let the others believe that if it got her out of the hall.

The few warriors in the hall glanced at her as she walked out before they went back to drinking the king's ale. Outside, Brigid took a deep breath and wondered where to go. She thought about going to the clearing, but then dismissed the idea. She had not been since Octa had left because she didn't want to see the raven again. After the vision, the thought of the large black bird frightened her and Brigid did not frighten easy. She then spotted Prince Vortimer, his face dark, as he walked the streets of the Roman fort while his eyes scanned every person. He had been doing that for many days and, to Brigid, it felt like he was looking for someone. Perhaps the warriors who had disappeared. Brigid had heard the rumours that some warriors had left the fort and had never returned. They had most likely been killed by bandits, or Picts, although their raids had been rare this summer because of the Jutes.

Brigid was about to turn and walk away when one of the men with Prince Vortimer saw her and pointed her way. Her hands trembled as she expected to see the same hatred in his face that she usually saw when he looked at her, but then she frowned when he gave her a warm smile.

'Brigid,' Prince Vortimer said as he approached, and even though she knew she should turn and walk away, something told her to stay and see what he was up to.

'Prince Vortimer,' Brigid greeted him as he stopped in front of her. It annoyed her how much he looked like his father, and if he hadn't been so vile, then she might have liked him. But Prince Vortimer had resented her since the day she chose his father over him and she knew he had been the one who had been spreading rumours she was a witch, a heathen lover. Which was true, but Brigid and King Vortigern worked hard to keep that hidden. 'Who are you looking for?'

Prince Vortimer smiled and shrugged. 'No one, just making sure the people of Cair Urnahc have what they need.' Brigid almost laughed at the lie. Prince Vortimer did not care about the people of the Cornovii. All he cared about was himself. 'I was hoping I'd run into you, actually.'

Brigid raised an eyebrow. 'Really? So you can threaten me again?'

There was a twitch in the prince's face as he fought hard to keep his mask on, which told Brigid he was desperate for something. Her mind raced as she wondered if she could use that. 'I have a question about the old gods of Britannia. The ones our people worshipped before we saw the light of the true God.'

'And why would I know about any of that?'

Prince Vortimer smiled again, but there was less of the forced warmth in this smile as he leaned closer. 'Come now, Brigid. We both know you still pray to the old gods. Perhaps even used their magic to bewitch my father.'

Brigid tried not to recoil from his breath. 'If you really think I bewitched your father, then that means that you still believe the old gods are real and that they have power.'

Prince Vortimer's face darkened as Cadoc crossed himself. 'The old gods are dead and whatever power they have died with them.'

Brigid's heart thudded so hard in her chest that she worried Prince Vortimer could hear it as his words struck a chord. *Is that why Brigantia is silent to me,* she wondered, before she pushed the thought from her mind. 'Then why do you want to know about them?'

The prince cleared his throat before he glanced around him, as if he wanted to make sure that no one was listening to them. 'I want to know about a one-eyed god. One who has a magic spear.'

Again, Brigid's heart thudded hard in her chest and she felt the blood drain from her face as the vision from the spear came to her. Her legs felt weak, and it took all of her strength not to collapse in front of Prince Vortimer.

'You know something.' Prince Vortimer gripped her arm, but Brigid was too numb to feel his fingers dig into her skin. He must have sensed her reaction, but Brigid still shook her head.

'I know nothing of a one-eyed god or a spear.'

'Did Brigantia not have a spear?' Grifud said, and the king's son glared at him.

'How would you know that?'

The man shrugged as Prince Vortimer still gripped Brigid's arm, so she couldn't slip away while he was distracted. 'My mother told me of her when I was a boy.'

'And why didn't you say something before?' Prince Vortimer squeezed Brigid's arm tighter, and the pain broke through the fog in her mind.

'Brigantia has a spear,' she said. 'But she has two eyes.'

Prince Vortimer turned his attention back to her, the pretence of friendliness gone. 'So which god has one eye?'

Brigid was about to respond when another question came to her. 'Why? Why are you so eager to find out about this one-eyed god and his spear?'

Prince Vortimer stammered as the question seemed to catch him by surprise and Brigid would have smiled if it had not been for the pain in her arm as he gripped her. 'I... I...'

'We heard a story and wanted to know if it was true,' Grifud said, and Prince Vortimer nodded as he let go of Brigid's arm. She resisted the urge to rub the pain away as she scrutinised the king's son. He was hiding something and again she wondered about the spear Octa had.

'None of our gods have only one eye,' she said.

She was about to walk away when Vortimer said, 'Our gods? We only have one God.'

'Then perhaps he has only one eye and a magic spear,' Brigid said as she returned Prince Vortimer's glare.

Prince Vortimer leaned in closer again. 'I'm trying hard to be nice to you, Brigid. I've never trusted the words you whisper in my father's ears, but we both know that the Jutes are a danger to our way of life. They are not here to help us fight the Picts. The Jutes are here to take our lands and to kill our people. They want to replace our God with their false idols!'

Brigid frowned as Prince Vortimer echoed the same concerns about the Jutes. At first, she had believed they could aid her by chasing the Christian god away and allowing the old gods to thrive again, but after the vision, she realised that she might have underestimated them and their gods. Her mind went to the presence she had felt in the hall the day Octa had been there. *Was that one of his gods?* The question came to her, and she took a breath to calm her heart. 'And what does this have to do with a one-eyed god and his spear?'

Prince Vortimer hesitated before he took a deep breath. 'I believe that if I can find this spear that belongs to the one-eyed god, then I can use it to drive the Jutes from our lands.'

Again, the vision came to her and Brigid pushed it from her mind. 'I know nothing about a one-eyed god or a magic spear.'

Prince Vortimer's jaw muscles clenched under his well-groomed beard. 'Are you sure about that? Remember, the Jutes don't care about the gods our people worshipped before.'

'The Jutes came as friends. Your father employs them to protect our lands and our people.' Brigid turned and walked away, her heart racing so fast that she worried she might collapse. But she needed to get away from Prince Vortimer and his questions about a one-eyed god. Because there was only one one-eyed god she knew about and all she remembered from what her grandfather had told her about him was that, wherever he went, chaos followed.

12

Brigid chewed the inside of her cheek as she walked through the market square in the outer fort of Cair Urnahc. Merchants called out to anyone who walked past their stalls, eager to sell their wares, but their loud voices drowned out the doubts and fears in Brigid's mind.

People from all over the Cornovii lands had come to Cair Urnahc because it was market day and they all wanted to buy or sell something. Farmers brought livestock, calves and chicks, recently born and hatched, to sell to others, or yarn from their goats. Merchants brought jewellery and other trinkets from across Britannia and some even claimed to have travelled all the way from Rome to sell glass cups and bowls. But even the inner fort was awash with activity as they prepared for King Vortigern's journey south. The king was old and didn't travel as well as he used to so it took longer to prepare for the long trip to Ruym Island. That was why he usually called the other kings to come to him instead of going to their halls when he needed to speak to them.

Brigid wrapped her cloak around her shoulders, even though it was a warm day. She wanted to hide the dress she wore. It wasn't the finest one she owned, but it was better quality than anything the women in the market wore and she didn't want to stand out as she glanced at the stalls of the traders and smiled at them when they tried to sell her something she didn't want or need. Brigid wasn't there to buy anything. She was there to hide from King

Vortigern because she knew he'd want her to go to Ruym Island with him, something she did not want to do. In Cair Urnahc it was easy to avoid him or to distract him so she didn't have to answer his questions about the gods' plans. That was not something she'd be able to do if she travelled with the king. But it wasn't just the king she was avoiding. It was also his son.

Prince Vortimer's words still troubled her, even though it had been two days since their conversation. She couldn't understand why the prince, a man known to be a firm believer of the Christian god, believed that a weapon which belonged to a Saxon god would help him get rid of the Jutes. And neither did she understand how he had found out about it. And then there was the spear Octa had, the spear she was certain was the one that Prince Vortimer was after. If that was the spear of Woden, a god her grandfather had once told her of, then why was it in Britannia?

Brigid considered going to the sacred tree again, but then shook her head. The gods remained silent, and she didn't want to see the raven again, not after the vision she had seen when she touched the spear. A vision that still haunted her dreams.

Lost in her thoughts, Brigid didn't notice the man following her until he grabbed her from behind, the movement so swift no one noticed it as he put a dirty hand over her mouth and dragged her away from the market.

Brigid's heart raced in her chest and she tried to reach for the knife she had under her dress, but the man had trapped her arm as if he knew about it. His scent was familiar, but she couldn't believe it was him. Not until they reached a quiet spot behind one house where no one saw them, and he turned her around.

'Badulf,' she gasped as her legs gave way under her. Her brother caught her and wrapped his arms around her, embracing her. Tears ran down her cheeks and she hugged him back, ignoring the scent of sweat and horse. They stood like that for what felt like a lifetime until Badulf stepped back and smiled at her.

'Brigid—'

Brigid slapped his face, her hand stinging from the blow. 'Where have you been? I was told you were dead! I mourned you like I mourned our parents!'

'Brigid—'

'Don't Brigid me!' She glared at her brother. His face was thinner than before and covered in dirt. His eyes, once so full of life, looked tired and there was something else, something she had never seen in Badulf. Anger and hatred. She took a step back and scrutinised her brother. Like his face, his body seemed thinner as the clothes he wore looked too large for him. He had no mail vest or helmet and neither did he have any weapons with him. 'What happened, Badulf? Octa told me you were killed.'

Anger flashed in his eyes at the mention of the young Saxon, and Brigid frowned at it.

'Octa is the reason I almost died.' Badulf gripped her shoulders. 'You were right about him. He can't be trusted.'

'What happened?' Brigid asked again, her mind reeling at the realisation that her brother was still alive. She should have guessed it, though. Octa had told her they had never found his body, and she felt a wave of guilt wash over her for not believing that Badulf could still be alive. But Brigid had been so lost since she had been told the news that she had not been able to focus on anything. Perhaps that was why she couldn't hear the gods any more.

Badulf glanced around as if he expected trouble. 'Not here. I'll tell you, but not here.' He stared at her and her heart skipped at the look in his eyes.

Brigid took a deep breath. 'Badulf—'

This time, he cut her off as he gripped her shoulders tighter. 'Brigid, they lied to us. The bloody Jutes lied to us. They are not here to be our friends or protect our lands for us. They are here to take it all for themselves.'

Brigid tried to take a step back, almost afraid of the anger she saw in her brother's eyes. 'Badulf, what happened in the north?'

The next words that came out of Badulf's mouth almost crushed her and, if it wasn't for Badulf gripping her shoulders, she would have collapsed. 'A spear. Octa came here for a spear. A weapon that he claimed belonged to one of their gods. That's why Hengist and Horsa sent men north.'

The vision flashed in her mind again. A land ablaze while people cried out in agony. A one-eyed god laughing as Octa stood on a pile of corpses with the spear in his hands. She felt the blood drain from her face and saw how Badulf frowned at her.

'Brigid? What's the matter?'

Brigid shook her head and took a deep breath to compose herself. 'Nothing...'

Before she could say anything else, Badulf said, 'You know about the spear? Did the gods tell you about it?'

Brigid shook her head. She didn't want to tell him that the gods had stopped talking to her, but then she didn't want to tell him about her vision, either.

'The gods know what is coming,' Badulf said before Brigid could work out what to say. 'She told me so.'

Brigid struggled to make sense of what her brother was saying and again she wondered what had happened to him. 'What is coming? Who told you?'

Badulf looked at her, his eyes crazed. 'The wise one. She told me this was going to happen. That he had a purpose.'

Brigid's breath caught in her throat. *The wise one.* 'She's alive?'

Badulf nodded. 'She spoke of you...'

This time Brigid grabbed hold of Badulf. 'You must take me to her, Badulf. I need to speak to her.'

Badulf shook his head. 'I don't know where she is. She came to me.'

'Badulf, it's important. Take me north. Please. I need to speak to her.'

Badulf shook his head. 'She can't help us! Brigid, we need to stop the Jutes before they destroy our way of life!'

Brigid's frustration took hold of her, and she almost screamed at her brother. 'By the gods, you sound just like him!'

'Like who?' Badulf frowned at her.

'Prince Vortimer.' She turned away from Badulf, her mind racing. If the wise one was still in the north and, more importantly, still alive, then she had to go there. She had to speak to the wise one because she would know what to do. But Brigid still had the same problem as before. The north was a large place and the wise one would be hard to find. Brigid needed the cult of Brigantia. They would know where to find her because she belonged to them. But the last person in Cair Urnahc who was part of the cult had been killed by Prince Vortimer many winters ago and the rest had fled his men.

'What did Prince Vortimer say?' Badulf asked her.

Her mind still distracted by her thoughts, Brigid told her brother about her conversation with the prince. About how he was after a spear that belonged to a one-eyed god and that he believed the spear would help him drive the Jutes away.

'The Jutes have the spear! They found it in a cave and took it south.' Badulf's words made her think of the vision again. She was about to tell him she knew, but then something made her stop herself. Her brother was acting strange, and she wasn't sure what he would do if she told him. 'That must be the one he is after. It belongs to Woden, the god Grandfather told us about.'

'Badulf, the spear is not real,' Brigid lied. 'Prince Vortimer has lost his mind. His hatred for the Jutes is making him see things that aren't there.'

'The spear is real. She told me about it. She told me it has a purpose.'

Brigid wanted to scream and was forced to take a deep breath to calm herself. 'Badulf, listen to me. You must take me to the wise one. I need to speak to her.'

Badulf took a step back. 'Why?'

Unable to control her frustration any longer, Brigid screamed, 'Because the gods don't speak to me any more!' She took a deep breath and looked around, but there was no one there other than her and Badulf. 'They haven't done since the Jutes arrived.'

Badulf's brows furrowed. 'What do you mean? They have always spoken to you. Have you been to the sacred grove?'

Brigid got annoyed at Badulf, asking her that as if she hadn't thought of it herself. 'Every day since I heard you had gone north with the Jutes. But the forest is quiet. No one speaks to me.' She decided not to tell him about the raven. Not until she knew whom the raven belonged to, but for that, she had to go back to the sacred grove. 'Badulf, you must take me to her. So much has happened and I've been so lost. Without you and the gods, I've been adrift. I need to see the wise one. She will have the answers I need. She will know what to do.'

Badulf looked at her. 'I might not be able to find her. She is running.'

'Running?' Brigid frowned. 'Running from what?'

Badulf shrugged. 'I don't know. She said she did something and others are angry at her for it.' He shook his head. 'She didn't make a lot of sense, but she told me that the spear has a purpose.'

'What purpose does the spear have?' Brigid asked.

'To bring fire to these lands.'

Brigid's heart skipped and her legs almost gave way under her as, again, she saw the vision from before and she wondered if that was what it was showing her. The fire the spear was going to bring to Britannia. Had she made a mistake by encouraging King Vortigern to accept the Jutes' offer? Had she helped bring about the end of the gods instead? Brigid struggled to breathe as the questions raged through her mind. Her heart racing, she leaned against the wall so she wouldn't collapse, but all she saw in her mind was Octa standing on the hill of corpses with the spear in his hands. Her mind reeled as she tried to make sense of everything. Octa had a weapon that would end her dreams of seeing the old gods rule again, a spear that would bring fire and death to Britannia. But also a spear that Prince Vortimer wanted because he believed it would help him drive the Jutes back to their homeland. Brigid rubbed her forehead as she struggled to find the right path to take, something she was not used to. But she couldn't. No matter how hard she tried. It was like someone or something was clouding her mind and that was why she needed the wise one.

'We need to get the spear back,' Badulf said, and she barely heard him while she was lost in her thoughts. 'Prince Vortimer can help us. He still wants you. Maybe we can use that.'

Badulf's words were like a slap to the face and Brigid had to bite back the retort before it left her mouth. She took a deep breath and shook her head. 'Prince Vortimer can't be trusted! He will kill those like us. Those who still believe in the old gods.'

'So it's better that the Jutes have the spear?'

Brigid stared at her brother, stunned by the anger in his eyes, as he asked the very question she was struggling with. With the spear in Octa's hands there would be fire and death, but if Prince Vortimer got the spear, then the old gods would never rule again. The birds would lose their song and the rivers would stop flowing because the gods would not be there to control these things. 'No,' Brigid said after a while.

'What about King Vortigern? You can use your influence on him. Get him to see how dangerous the Jutes are.'

'The Jutes have brought peace to our lands, Badulf. The raids have almost stopped and the people live without fear. King Vortigern will never go against them because he needs them too much.'

Badulf clenched his fists. 'Well, I'm not just going to sit back and do nothing. I'm going to find the spear and destroy it!'

Badulf turned and walked away before Brigid could stop him. She rushed after him, but to her frustration, she lost him in the busy market square. Rooted to the spot, Brigid grabbed the bead necklace around her neck. *Brigantia, Mother, please help me. I don't know what to do.*

13

Badulf felt a nervous energy course through him as he stared at the Roman gates and thought about his conversation with his sister. He had thought that she would understand. That she would help him because of her connection to the old gods. His fingers twitched as he struggled to make sense of her reluctance to believe him.

Badulf took a deep breath to stop his trembling hands and wished he had a weapon with him. But the spear he had been given was hidden outside the city because he knew the warriors would stop him if they saw him with a spear. It had been easy for Badulf to sneak into the outer fort of Cair Urnahc, especially on a market day. The warriors guarding the outer gate were too distracted trying to keep an eye on everyone entering to notice him. Sneaking into the old Roman part would be harder, though. As he stared at the gates while trying to come up with a plan, a hand gripped his shoulder, and Badulf's warrior instinct kicked in as he turned and was about to punch his attacker, when he saw it was Brigid.

'Brigid!' he hissed. 'I almost hit you.'

'You're right. We can't let either the Jutes or Prince Vortimer have the spear. We must get it ourselves, but then we take it north to the wise one. We don't destroy it,' she said.

Badulf stared at her for a few heartbeats and then nodded. He did not trust the cult with the spear. They had lost it before but if agreeing to that got his sister to help him, then that was what he was going to do. 'Fine, but how do we get the spear?'

Brigid's brows creased and he knew he was not going to like what she had to say. 'Go to Prince Vortimer. Tell him you know where to find the spear and that you can help him get it.'

'But I don't give it to him?'

Brigid shook her head, but he saw the doubt in her eyes.

'I still need to get to their island. I doubt I can just walk into their camp and take the spear.'

Brigid looked around her and then took a deep breath. He saw how she toyed with the bead necklace around her neck and knew she only did that when she was nervous. 'The king is travelling south to meet with the Jutes. Prince Vortimer is going with him.'

'I can use him to sneak on to the island.' Brigid nodded and Badulf smiled. It felt like it did when they were children again, plotting revenge on some kids who had attacked Brigid. But this time the consequences were more severe. If they failed, it wouldn't just be another beating, but the end of their way of life. 'First, I need to find the bastard.'

'He'll be at the baths.' Brigid turned and walked towards the Roman gate. 'Come, I'll get you inside. Just keep your head down. King Vortigern can't find out that you're still alive.'

Badulf nodded and followed his sister towards the gate. The warriors there saw her coming as he pulled his cloak over his head and lowered it so he seemed shorter. Instead of watching him, the warriors kept their eyes fixed on his sister, something that had always angered Badulf, but now he was glad for it because it allowed him to sneak into the Roman fort unnoticed.

'What will you do?' Badulf asked once they were inside the Roman fort and he saw the way she looked at the main hall.

'I'll speak to the king. Perhaps I can get him to be more cautious with the Jutes.'

Badulf nodded. 'Be careful, Brigid.'

His sister scowled at him. 'You are the one who needs to be careful. Some men went missing a few days ago and the prince has been in a foul mood about it.'

Badulf nodded again as he heeded his sister's warning and made his way to the Roman baths. He kept his head low as he walked past the townspeople, many of whom ignored him, but a few glanced his way. Badulf could only hope that no one recognised him. He didn't know how they would react if they did, especially not if they believed he was dead. When he reached the baths, he saw the two large warriors who guarded Prince Vortimer waiting outside and knew the prince was still there. Badulf made himself comfortable and waited. He knew it would be a long time for Prince Vortimer to come out of the Roman baths.

The sun was already descending before the prince walked out of the building, with Cadoc and Grifud by his side laughing at something the prince of the Cornovii had said to the two warriors.

Badulf lowered his head as they walked past him and then followed. He kept his distance as the group walked along the streets, Prince Vortimer's voice drifting towards him as he spoke with his two friends, while the two warriors kept scanning the streets ahead of them, but not once did they look over their shoulders. Badulf got the feeling that they were looking for someone and wondered if it had anything to do with the missing men Brigid had told him about, but then the group turned down a street that was quieter than where they had been and Badulf knew that was his chance. As he had followed them, he wondered how to approach them. Prince Vortimer hated him and he doubted the man would just stop and listen to him. That left him with only one choice. He had to make the prince listen to him.

He clenched his fists and sped up, closing the distance between himself and the two warriors. 'Oi, you ugly bastards!'

As the warriors turned around with snarls on their faces, Badulf punched the one on the left and, as his head snapped back, Badulf turned and kneed the other one in the groin. The man slumped to the ground while clutching his crotch.

Badulf turned to the one he had punched and grabbed the man by his mail vest. He threw him into the wall and heard the thud as the man's head struck the stone and he collapsed in a heap. Badulf ignored the man as he turned and faced Prince Vortimer and his two companions, all of them pale in the face.

The prince freed his sword from its scabbard, and rushed at Badulf. 'You dare attack me?'

Badulf twisted out of the way of the attack and grabbed Prince Vortimer's sword arm. He was tempted to punch the bastard in the face, but knew he couldn't. Instead, he moved behind Prince Vortimer and put his arm around the prince's neck.

Cadoc and Grifud hesitated, but Badulf knew they wouldn't attack. The men were smart, especially Cadoc, but they weren't warriors.

Badulf leaned closer to Prince Vortimer's ear. 'I hear you are looking for a spear.'

He heard Prince Vortimer gasp and noticed how the man's sword trembled. 'Who told you that? Who are you?'

'I know where to find this spear, the one you are looking for.'

Prince Vortimer tried to turn his head to see who he was, but Badulf moved his head away. He was not ready to reveal himself. But as he moved his head, his cloak hood fell off and Grifud recognised him.

'Badulf?' His face paled even more and Badulf worried the man was going to faint.

'You're supposed to be dead,' Cadoc said as Badulf pushed Prince Vortimer away from him.

Prince Vortimer turned and sneered at him as he raised his sword. 'He is now.'

Badulf glared at Prince Vortimer and, before the king's son could attack him, he said, 'Kill me and you'll never know where to find the spear of Woden.'

Prince Vortimer stopped and frowned at him. 'Woden? The god of the Jutes?'

Badulf nodded as the warrior he had kneed in the groin got to his feet and pulled his sword from its scabbard. Prince Vortimer raised his hand, and the warrior frowned at him.

'You are looking for his spear, aren't you?'

'Who told you that?' Prince Vortimer glanced at his friends, who only shrugged.

'Brigid told me. Said you believed the spear will help you defeat the Jutes.'

Prince Vortimer's face turned dark. 'That bitch! I'm going to kill her.'

Badulf's heart raced, but he took a breath to calm himself. 'You harm me or my sister and you will never know where to find the spear.'

'So it's real?' Cadoc asked, his voice filled with shock. Prince Vortimer glared at him. 'What? It's a hard story to believe.'

'Where is this spear?' Prince Vortimer asked, and Badulf shook his head.

'Swear that my sister will not be harmed. Not this day, or any other day.'

Prince Vortimer curled his lip and then nodded. 'I swear. Now tell me where to find this spear.'

Again, Badulf shook his head. 'If I tell you now, then you'll have your men kill me.'

'Why are you doing this?'

Badulf's heart raced in his chest and he prayed their plan would work, although he wasn't sure to which god he was praying. 'Because, for once, we agree on the same thing. The Jutes are not our friends. They want to take Britannia for themselves.'

'And why do you care about that, half-breed?' Cadoc asked. 'Thought you'd want to live with your kind.'

Badulf clenched his fist. 'They are not my kind. My grandfather was a Saxon, but I am a Briton, like all of you. And I don't want to see my home burnt.'

'So what do you suggest?' Prince Vortimer asked.

'We work together. I help you find the spear and together we drive the Jutes from our home. I know the Jutes. I know how they think and how they fight.'

'And what do you get from this?'

Badulf hesitated for a heartbeat. 'I get to right a wrong.'

Prince Vortimer glanced at the other two and Badulf saw how Cadoc nodded. But he knew he still needed to be careful. 'So where is this spear?'

'The Jutes have it.'

Prince Vortimer's eyes widened at this. 'The old bastard didn't tell us that!'

Badulf frowned and wondered who this old bastard was, but then pushed the thought from his mind. 'That was why they sent men north. They were looking for the spear.'

'So how in God's name do we get the spear from them?' Grifud asked.

'How do we even know which spear it is? There must be hundreds of spears in their camp,' Cadoc added.

'Because I know what it looks like,' Badulf lied. 'And who might have it.' Which was half true. Eadric had led the group and, if Octa didn't have the spear, then that meant the older Jute must have taken it. And if he did, then he would have given it to Hengist and Horsa.

'I don't trust him,' Grifud said, and Cadoc nodded as Prince Vortimer glared at him.

'I don't trust you either, but we all want the same thing.'

'If the Jutes have the spear, as you say, then how do we get it?' Prince Vortimer asked.

Badulf smiled at them. 'Get me on to their island and then I can find the spear. I know their tongue, which means I can blend in.'

Cadoc shook his head. 'How do we know you won't keep the spear for yourself?'

'I don't want the spear. And besides, even with the spear, we will still need an army to drive the Jutes off our island. And I don't have an army.' Badulf could only hope that they believed him, but he knew he'd need to watch his back.

'Leave that to me.' Prince Vortimer smiled. 'You find the spear and bring it to me, and then we rid Britannia of those heathens.'

Grifud scratched his head. 'How will he get on to the island? It's well guarded.'

'My friends, it looks like the Almighty has given us the answer to that already.' Prince Vortimer smiled as the other two crossed themselves. 'Tomorrow, my father leaves to talk with the heathens. We can sneak Badulf on to the island then.'

'But how?' Cadoc asked. 'The other warriors will recognise him, which is something we don't want.'

Prince Vortimer scowled as he thought about that. 'We'll think of something.' He turned to Badulf and came closer until they were face to face. 'But if you betray or fail me, then by God I swear your sister will suffer a fate far worse than death.'

The others smiled as Badulf's heart raced in his chest. Again, he prayed that his and Brigid's plan would work. And not just for the sake of his people, but also for the sake of his sister.

* * *

Vortimer smiled as he walked back to his quarters, with Cadoc and Grifud alongside him. This day had sprung a surprise on him that could only have been a gift from God. For a moment, he wondered if the old man had been the Almighty himself. The more he thought about it, the more sense it made. The heathens from the continent threatened his people, and the priests always liked to say that God was a shepherd who protected his flock.

'Do you really think we can trust Badulf?' Cadoc asked, which chased Vortimer's smile away. He scowled at his friend and wondered why the man always had to question everything. 'He comes back from the dead and tells us he knows how to find this magical spear.'

'Aye, doesn't sound right to me,' Grifud said, and Vortimer sighed.

He glanced around to make sure they weren't being followed or that anyone was listening. That was something else Badulf's appearance had done. It had made him more nervous. Vortimer had always felt untouchable in Cair Urnahc and yet Badulf had taken out his two guards and could have killed him if he wanted to. The thought of that made him chill to the bone. From now on, he would have more warriors around him. 'We don't have to trust him,' Vortimer said as he tried to push the thoughts from his mind. 'We use him to find the spear, unless one of you wants to sneak around Ruym Island and look for it?' Both men paled as they shook their heads.

'But if you don't trust him, then why have we agreed with him?' Cadoc asked.

'Because Badulf will do anything to protect his sister,' Vortimer said as he looked at Cadoc. 'Besides, he claims he knows where to find the spear and what it looks like. If he is right, then we get the spear and use it to kill the Jutes.'

'And if he's lying to us?' Grifud asked.

Vortimer shrugged. 'Then he dies. Most think he is already dead, so no one would know if we kill him.'

'And what if he brings us the spear?' Cadoc asked, and Vortimer smiled.

'Then he still dies. Along with his sister.'

14

Brigid walked into the hall, her hands trembling as she prayed she had done the right thing. But as she had stood in the market, she thought of what Badulf had said. The spear would bring fire to these lands. It would burn away everything they knew, and the more she had thought about it, the more that idea frightened her. The vision had shown her that, and she knew Badulf was right. Octa could not have the spear.

The gods had warned her about Octa, and she had been blind to that. Perhaps that was why they didn't speak to her any more. If she got the spear from Octa and took it to the wise one, then maybe the gods would speak to her again. But they could not get the spear on their own. Neither she nor Badulf could just walk on to the island the Jutes had taken for themselves and take the spear. And she doubted that Octa would give it to them. As much as she hated it, they needed Prince Vortimer. His hatred of the Jutes would blind him to their plan and make it easy to use him. But Prince Vortimer had a cruel streak when it came to non-Christians, and that was why he could not get his hands on the spear either. Brigid knew that if he got the spear, then he would be as dangerous to the gods as Octa was.

Brigid looked at where King Vortigern was sitting on his raised seat and resisted the urge to rub the bead necklace around her neck as she prayed for Badulf's safety. The high king of the Britons looked like the old man he was, and she wondered when he had aged so much. Brigid had once believed that

King Vortigern would help her chase the Christians out of Britannia so the old gods could flourish again, but she saw now that she had been wrong. All he cared about was his crown, and he had been using her as much as she had been using him. Just like he believed he was using the Jutes. Brigid still didn't know if she had made the right choice by encouraging King Vortigern to employ the Jutes. She had believed that they hated the Christians as much as she did and that she could use that, but so far she had not been able to get close to the Jutes.

All that mattered now, though, was that Brigid needed to go north, especially now that she knew the wise one still lived, but she needed the king's permission. Being his mistress protected her from others, but it also imprisoned her to his whims.

King Vortigern looked up from his conversation with a trader and turned to Ceretic, who nodded and made his way to her. But Brigid ignored the man and went to the king's sleeping quarters. She knew that was what he had sent Ceretic to tell her, and if she hadn't been so nervous for her brother, she would have smiled at Ceretic's red face as she just walked past him.

'You've been avoiding me,' the king said when he entered his sleeping quarters not long after. 'I am your king, and you do not avoid me.'

Brigid stiffened at the change in his tone towards her. She might have been his mistress, and she knew there were no real feelings between them, but King Vortigern always treated her well because he believed the gods would honour him if he did. Just like he treated the Christian priests well, so that the Christian god would look kindly on him. The king knew his position as high king was perilous, and so he made sure to keep as many gods as happy as possible. 'Forgive me, my king, but much has happened, and I needed time to understand what it means.'

King Vortigern stood by his bed, but did not tell her to come to him. Instead, he waved her words away with his old hand. 'That doesn't matter. Soon I'm leaving to go south and I want you to come with me.'

Brigid took a deep breath. She had known this was coming, but still, she wasn't prepared for it. The vision came to her again, and she doubted she could face Octa or the spear. 'Forgive me, King Vortigern, but I cannot go to Ruym Island with you.'

King Vortigern's mouth twitched in his grey beard before he asked, 'And why is that?' She knew he was angry at his son for the way he had behaved when Octa was there, and even she had heard the rumours that many of the kings of Britannia agreed with Prince Vortimer. 'You told me to accept the Jutes' offer. That it was what the gods wanted, and now I have to travel south to deal with their new demands and calm the other kings. And I want you to come with me.'

Again, Brigid resisted the urge to grip her bead necklace. She straightened her back and tried to be as confident as she was before. 'Forgive me, my king, but the gods demand that I go north.'

King Vortigern raised an eyebrow. 'And why do they want you to go north?'

Brigid knew she had to choose her next words with care. The king was still unhappy about the news that Hengist and Horsa had sent men north the previous summer, and she doubted he believed what Octa had told him. Just as she knew that if she told him about the spear, then he'd only get more agitated. 'I don't know yet, my king. That is why I must go. To find out what the gods want from me.'

The king's face turned red. 'I am your king, and if I say you're coming with me, then you will come with me!'

'But, my king, the gods—'

'I don't care about the blasted gods! What have they done for me?'

King Vortigern's words angered Brigid, and before she could stop herself, she said, 'The gods made you the high king of Britannia!'

'Gold and iron made me the high king! Not the gods!' The king's face was so red that Brigid would have worried for his health if his words had not been so disrespectful to the gods.

Brigid clenched her fists as her blood pumped in her ears. 'The gods made the gold you used to pay off some of the kings, and they made the iron you used to threaten others. And it was me who used my body to convince those who weren't convinced by the promise of riches or threats of war!'

For many heartbeats, Brigid and King Vortigern glared at each other, and even though she knew where his anger was coming from, she still would not allow him to dismiss the gods like that. Brigid knew that King Vortigern was angry at his son for disrespecting him in front of Octa and the other kings. It made him look weak, which threatened the crown he liked to wear so much. That was why he was going south. He wanted to look strong in front of the other kings and remind the Jutes that they worked for him. Brigid knew the king better than he knew himself, and she knew the reason he wanted her there was because she knew the words that gave him strength. But the gods were more important to her than the king's ego, and that was why she refused to obey him.

After a while, the king let out a strained breath and said, 'I don't need you or the gods any more. I will go south without you, but you are forbidden from leaving my city.' The king turned, and before he left his sleeping quarters, he looked at her. 'I will deal with you when I return.'

Brigid gritted her teeth as the king left his quarters, and when he was gone, she gripped her bead necklace and prayed that Badulf returned soon with the spear. Then they would go north and give the spear to the wise one.

15

Octa breathed a sigh of relief when he and Odalric rode over the bridge that led to Ruym Island.

'Never thought I'd be glad to see this island,' Odalric said, his words showing that he felt the same as Octa, who nodded his greeting at the Jutes guarding the bridge.

The warriors smiled at them and nodded back, without bothering to stop them. Everyone knew who Octa was, and many knew about the spear. Whether or not they believed it was Gungnir was not his concern, but he had heard many say that he had lost his wits in the north. That he had come back with an ordinary spear left behind by an old Saxon in the past. But Octa did not care about that and, if he was honest, he preferred people believed that, because it meant that there was less chance of someone trying to steal the spear from him. Octa still carried it everywhere with him, though.

They rode past the spot where Hengist and Horsa's ships had originally landed and Octa tried not to think of that night when they were attacked by the natives of this small island. Much had changed since that day, though. Many of the tents the warriors had slept in that night had been replaced by small wooden houses. Not the type that Octa saw around Britannia, but like the ones they lived in in Jutland and the Saxon lands. As well as the lands of the Angles and Franks. The sounds of wood being cut and timbers being split filled the air while men laughed and swore as more houses were being built for those who had arrived since.

There was not enough wood on the small island, so parties had to be sent to the mainland to chop trees. Recently, though, warriors had to be sent to protect those men as the native Britons had started attacking them. It was a stark contrast to the Britons on Ruym. They treated the Jutes as friends, and many were trying to learn the language of the men from the continent. Some of the Jutes had even married the women on the island, and even Octa's loins stirred when he thought of Lucilia, the Briton who was helping his mother in the house Hengist had given them, but who also warmed Octa's bed at night.

Octa glanced at the wooden palisade Horsa had ordered to be built around the town they had taken over. It was not as impressive as the walls of Cair Urnahc or even Cair Lundein, but it would protect the town if anyone attacked the island. His hand went to the spear pendant around his neck and he prayed that never happened because he knew the brothers' revenge would be bloody and brutal.

As they approached the gate to the town, the warriors guarding it lowered their spears and moved to stop them. Octa and Odalric slowed their horses down and one of the Jutes smiled when he recognised them.

'It's the Saxons. Let them through.'

Once inside the walls, Octa and Odalric dismounted their horses and Octa gave Warda to the older warrior. Octa was tired and longed for a good night's rest under his furs, but he needed to speak to Hengist and Horsa. He needed to tell them what had happened in Cair Urnahc, even though he knew Horsa would not be pleased that King Vortigern had not agreed to what they had asked for. As he glanced at the seabirds flying over the houses and soaring on the strong wind from the sea, he wondered how they would feel about the high king of the Britons coming to the island instead.

'Remember, tell them nothing of the attack on us. We don't need to give them reason to start a war,' Odalric said, and was about to walk away when Octa's mother approached.

'My son and Odalric.' She smiled at them before she embraced Octa and then pulled away with a grimace. 'You stink.'

'It's lovely to see you as well, Mother.' Octa was still adjusting to living with his mother, something he had not done since he was a young boy and, he had to admit, her demanding nature was hard to deal with. Yet he was glad she was there, especially after what had happened to his father and his village. At least Octa knew she was safe.

'Lady Berthild,' Odalric said, and Octa almost laughed at how the gruff warrior tried to soften his voice.

'Odalric, I trust you kept my son out of trouble.'

Odalric nodded. 'He's back with all his parts where they should be.'

Octa's mother smiled. 'Good. Now come, Hengist is waiting for you.' Odalric turned and led the horses to the stables where he would clean and feed them as Berthild led Octa towards the brothers' hall. He wondered why she had only mentioned Hengist when she asked, 'How did it go with the British king?'

Octa sighed and knew he should have expected this from his mother. She had always been around power and was used to being treated that way. And Octa knew it annoyed her that Horsa did not allow her to have a say in anything. Something she was not used to. 'Not well.' Octa told his mother what had happened as they approached the hall, but he left out that they were attacked, even though he was sure that Odalric would tell her. He still treated her as a woman above his station, although Octa was sure he detected some affection towards his mother from Odalric.

His mother scowled as she considered what he had told her and when they stopped in front of the hall, she said, 'Choose your words carefully in there, Octa. Hengist likes you, but Horsa will see this as a failure and use it against you. And we need them on our side to achieve our plans.'

Your plans, Octa thought before he nodded. 'I know, Mother. But I am not good at this.'

His mother smiled at him. 'You are the son of a warlord. And the grandson of one of the greatest Saxon warlords. This is in your blood. Just stand strong and don't back down.'

Octa nodded again. No matter how many times his mother had said that to him, it never encouraged him like she thought it did. It only made the armour he wore feel heavier and made his mouth feel dry. He took a deep breath and handed Gungnir to his mother because they would not allow him to enter the hall with the spear and Octa did not trust the warriors guarding the doors. They were men more loyal to Horsa, and Octa knew he still wanted the spear.

His heart raced as he walked into the hall, especially when it fell silent and everyone inside stared at him. Warriors sat on the benches drinking ale while servants, Britons mostly, kept the hearth fire going and carried jugs of ale to the men inside. In the corner, a group of women sat spinning yarn, their heads lowered as they whispered things to each other.

'Octa,' Oisc, Hengist's son, cried out, and ran to him, which made Octa smile. He had saved the boy's life from an enraged horse in Jutland and had earned Hengist's trust. Oisc had stayed behind in Jutland, with a family Hengist trusted, when Hengist and Horsa left for Britannia. The boy had told Octa that he spent more time with that family than his father because Hengist and Horsa would be away raiding, and Octa knew how Oisc felt. Hengist had sent for his son as soon as he had felt it was safe enough, but with the news Octa had to bring, he wondered how safe they all were.

Octa knelt down, still surprised at how much the boy had grown. 'Hello, Oisc. It's good to see you.'

'Did you kill any Britons?'

Octa's eyes widened as for a heartbeat he wondered how Oisc knew about that, but then realised that he couldn't have done, as Hengist laughed.

'Don't mind him, Octa. Horsa has been telling him stories of our battles against the Picts.'

Octa nodded and straightened up. He ruffled Oisc's hair before he walked towards the end of the hall where the brothers were sitting with some of their senior men.

'What news do you bring?' Horsa said, his customary scowl on his face, which made him look older than Hengist even though he was the younger brother. 'Did Vortigern agree to our new terms?' Horsa refused to use his title, although Octa never understood why. He guessed it made Horsa feel important, but he didn't really care about that.

'Forgive Horsa,' Hengist said with a warm smile. 'He has the patience of a bull during rutting season.' The men around laughed as Horsa glared at Hengist, who raised a hand to show he meant no offence. 'Sit, Octa. Have a drink.'

Octa glanced at Horsa and took a breath to calm himself as he sat down at their bench and took a cup of ale from one man. He emptied the cup without taking a breath and sighed with relief as the ale quenched his dry throat and helped calm his nerves.

'So, tell us, Octa,' Hengist said as his son sat down beside him. 'What did King Vortigern say?'

'I don't know what you expected him to say,' Octa said. That was something else he had thought about as they rode back to Ruym Island. The brothers must have known he would not agree to their new terms. 'But he is coming here. He says he wants to speak to you.'

'By Woden, I knew we shouldn't have sent you!' Horsa slammed his fist on the table, but Hengist only nodded as he seemed to consider what Octa had said.

'And when can we expect him?' Hengist asked.

Octa shrugged. 'I don't know, but soon I'd say.'

Hengist nodded again and turned to one of the men at the table. 'Make sure everyone is aware of King Vortigern's arrival.' The warrior nodded and finished his ale before he stood up and left the hall.

'And what about the king of the Cantiaci?' Horsa asked. 'Is he going to do anything about that bastard?'

'He sent word for King Gwyrangon to meet him here, but there is something else,' Octa said, and his palms felt sweaty as both brothers frowned at him. 'Prince Vortimer, King Vortigern's son, does not agree with his father's alliance. And he is less than pleased about your increasing numbers.'

Hengist waved a hand at him. 'The little bastard has never liked us, but he is of no concern.'

Octa's brows creased as he shook his head. 'That's not the feeling I got. He openly challenged his father and there were some in King Vortigern's hall who agreed with him.'

The two brothers glanced at each other before Horsa said, 'Vortigern's position might be weakening.'

Hengist nodded. 'Aye, the gods know there have been many sons who overthrew their fathers.'

'And if he does, then our position will be less than secure.' Horsa scratched his beard.

Hengist stared at the table, his arms crossed as he seemed to think about the news Octa had brought them, while his son tried to copy his demeanour. 'Life is never without its challenges and the gods reward those who overcome them. And that is exactly what we will do.' He smiled at Octa. 'Thank you, Octa. You did well.'

Octa nodded, but before he could respond, a warrior ran into the hall. 'Ships!'

Horsa looked at the warrior. 'How many?' The warriors in the hall all stopped drinking and stared at the man as they waited for his answer.

'Two. They look like Frisians.' The Frisians were a people from lands to the west of the Saxon lands, but Octa had never met a Frisian before. Like the Saxons and the Jutes, they worshipped Woden and the other Aesir gods and were formidable warriors. Some of the Saxon warlords often went raiding with them and even his father had joined Frisian warlords on raids in the past.

'Are they coming to the island?' Hengist asked, putting a hand on his son's shoulder.

The warrior shook his head. 'They're headed for the river.'

'Could be traders?' one warrior at the table said, but the man who brought the news shook his head.

'They're warships.'

'Could just leave them. Let the Cantiaci deal with them, especially as the bastards refuse to pay us.' Horsa scratched his cheek and Hengist smiled. For a moment, Octa thought that was what they were going to do, but then the older brother shook his head.

'At tempting as that sounds, the gods know we can't do anything to turn the Britons against us. King Vortigern is still high king and we will honour our side of the deal.' He turned to the warrior. 'Get the men ready. Two ships.' The warrior nodded and rushed out of the hall. After a few heartbeats, a horn blew outside the hall to tell the men to prepare for battle as Hengist eyed Octa, who was still wearing his dust-covered armour. 'Octa, join me while I go welcome our visitors.'

Octa wanted to object. He was tired and needed a wash, but he knew he couldn't, so he nodded. 'I'll just need to get my spear.'

Octa ignored the glare on Horsa's face as Oisc said, 'Woden's spear? Can I see it?'

'Later,' Hengist said to his son before he turned to Octa. 'Meet me by the ships.'

Octa nodded as he stood up, and as he was about to leave the hall he glimpsed a face he did not expect to see there, but when he turned to make sure, she was gone. He scowled as he left the hall and wondered why Friga was watching him so closely. His hand went to the spear pendant around his neck and he was about to pray that the gods had nothing bad planned for him, but then he didn't know which god to pray to.

16

Octa left the hall and glanced at the blue skies, the first he had seen in many days. The town was awash with activity as warriors rushed to get armour on and collect their weapons. Hengist had ordered only two ships to be made ready, and Octa wondered how these men knew who would go and who would stay behind. He guessed it came with experience. Most of the Jutes had sailed with the brothers for a long time and he guessed they knew what to do, even as he was still trying to make sense of things.

'What is happening?' Odalric asked as he came rushing from the stables. Like Octa, he was still in his armour, and also like Octa, his was also covered in dust from the ride back, but Octa knew that the older warrior would want to take part in the fight before he even needed to say anything. The man had been itching to show the Jutes how a Saxon warrior fought.

'Frisians,' Octa said as he watched the warriors get ready. Some of them ran to the walls of the town while others ran towards the wharves where the ships were. 'They sailed up the river and Hengist is taking two ships to see what they want.'

Odalric grinned at the news as he loosened his shoulder. 'Good. The gods know it's time I have a proper fight,' he said, and Octa wondered why the older thought there'd be a fight. He was about to tell Odalric to stay and look after his mother, but the look in Odalric's eyes told him that the warrior needed this. Octa knew that Odalric still felt guilty for not fighting by his father's side, even though Frithowald had ordered him to protect his wives and daughters. That guilt was eating away at Odalric, so perhaps he needed this fight to dispel it. For a moment, Octa wondered about the other wives of his father, and their daughters, his half-sisters. His mother had told him that they had travelled to the lands of the Franks after his father's village was destroyed, but she didn't know if they ever made it because she and Odalric had come to Britannia. Octa pushed them out of his mind as the horn blew again, but prayed they were safe even if he didn't really know any of his half-sisters.

'I just need to get Gungnir and then we meet Hengist by the ships.'

Odalric nodded. 'Then let's go.'

They both rushed back to the house, where his mother, still holding the spear in her hands, and Lucilia were waiting for them.

'What is happening? The men are talking about ships up the river,' his mother said, and Octa explained. 'Hengist asked you to join him?' she asked when he had finished.

Octa nodded. 'He did, but I need the spear.'

His mother smiled as she handed him Gungnir and Octa barely had a moment to look at Lucilia when Berthild said, 'Remember, Octa. You are the son of a warlord and you fight with Woden's spear. Show Hengist your worth.' Before Octa could respond, she turned to Odalric. 'And you keep my son alive.'

Odalric nodded, his face grim. 'I will, Lady Berthild.' He turned to Octa. 'Come, let's go.'

Octa glanced at Lucilia and smiled at her before he turned and heard his mother say, 'Fight well, my son. The gods watch you.'

Her words sent a shiver down his spine as he thought about how he had glimpsed Friga in Hengist's hall, but then he pushed the thought out of his mind as he gripped Gungnir tight in his hand.

When they got to the wharves, they saw both Hengist and Horsa were already there. Both brothers were dressed in their war gear, with spears in their hands and swords on their waists. Their chain-mail vests shone in the sunlight and their eyes were fierce under their helmets. The brothers frowned when Octa showed up with Odalric.

'Does your dog follow you everywhere, Saxon?' Horsa asked with a sneer on his face.

'Call me a dog when you're not surrounded by your protectors and you'll see what happens.' Odalric stepped towards Horsa, who grinned at him as his Jutes came closer.

'Enough,' Hengist said, and pushed his brother back. 'Lady Berthild told me that Odalric is a great warrior, so if he wants to join us, then I welcome him.' Odalric nodded his thanks to Hengist, who turned to his brother. 'Keep the men on the wall and ready until I return. Those ships might be a decoy.'

Horsa nodded to his brother. 'Woden knows that if anyone is foolish enough to attack us, then they'll be sorry.'

Hengist gripped his brother's shoulder and laughed. 'Aye, that they will be.' He turned and signalled for Octa and Odalric to join them.

'You really want to get on Horsa's bad side, don't you?' Octa asked as they boarded the ship with Hengist.

Odalric grunted. 'I will not be called a dog by any man, unless he defeats me in battle and, even then, only if I'm dead because I'll rip his tongue out of his mouth.'

Octa couldn't help but smile at the older Saxon and was glad that Odalric was by his side. The man was more than a great warrior. His name was spoken across the Saxon lands and he had been one of Frithowald's most feared warriors. Octa guessed that was why his father had told Odalric to protect his family.

Hengist stood by the prow of his ship and ran his eyes over his men, all battle-hardened Jutes, and then looked at the other ship. The man by the prow, one of the brothers' senior warriors, nodded to show they were ready. Hengist smiled.

'Let's go introduce ourselves to these Frisians.' The warriors all cheered as the order was given to row. Octa and Odalric stood by the prow with Hengist, who waved to his son on the wharf beside Horsa.

'Why risk your men to defend the lands of a king who doesn't want you here?' Odalric asked as the ships rowed towards the river which led to Cair Lundein.

Hengist smiled. 'Because I swore an oath to King Vortigern that I will protect this river and the lands around it and, like you Saxons, Tiw compels us to be honourable. And besides, the men are bored and, like you, Odalric, they need a good fight.'

Odalric raised an eyebrow at Hengist, and Octa struggled to understand how the Jute could sense that. Perhaps experienced warriors just understood each other. They fell silent as they scanned the river for any signs of the Frisians and after a long while, when the sun started making its descent, a shout came from the other ship where a warrior was pointing towards a thick, dark cloud of smoke not far from them.

'Well, now we know they are not here to trade.'

'Or at least not to trade with the Britons,' Odalric said, and Hengist nodded. Octa guessed Odalric meant the Frisians would trade the British captives somewhere on the continent as Hengist gave the order for the ships to turn towards the smoke.

When they got close, they saw two warships beached on the riverbank. A small group of warriors guarded the ships and, as soon as they spotted Hengist's ships, they blew a horn and one man ran inland.

'He's going to warn the others,' one of the Jutes said, and Hengist grunted.

'Good. That means we don't have to go running after them.'

Octa resisted the urge to rub the spear pendant around his neck. 'How do you know they'll come to us?'

Hengist smiled. 'I forget you Saxons do most of your fighting on land. Ships are more important to some warlords than their wives. But more importantly for these Frisians, without those ships they can't go home.'

'They'll have to attack or they can't go home. All that plunder will mean nothing to them then,' Odalric said, and Hengist nodded.

Octa took a deep breath as a calm washed over him and he glanced at the spear, wondering if Gungnir had caused it. He still wasn't sure what effect the spear had over him, but he was glad the fear that had controlled him was gone.

'Get ready, men!' Hengist ordered as he readied his shield and spear. Odalric handed Octa a shield, who tested its weight and rolled his shoulder as he rubbed the shaft of Gungnir. As soon as the ships hit the riverbank, Hengist and Odalric jumped off and rushed at the few Frisians guarding the ships. Octa hesitated for a moment and scanned the landscape, although he wasn't sure what made him do that, before he joined the other Jutes as they followed Hengist.

The few Frisians, no more than a handful of men, seemed unsure of what to do, but then they attacked. Hengist stabbed one through the chest with his spear before the man could raise his own and Odalric ducked under the spear of his attacker before he punched the man in the throat with the rim of his shield. Octa saw the man drop and clutch his throat before Odalric stomped on his head. The remaining three Frisians turned and ran, and Octa could not blame them. He still remembered the crippling fear that made him flee instead of protecting his cousin. The memory still shamed him, but he had learnt to use it to stand his ground and fight. The past was not important, he had been told once, but to Octa, it was all that mattered. It gave him the strength to overcome his fear.

Hengist grinned at Odalric as Octa reached them. 'And I thought my brother was a vicious bastard.'

Odalric grunted and then turned to Octa, but he did not see disappointment in the older warrior's eyes. Odalric had seen Octa fight and knew he was no coward.

'Now what?' Octa asked, and Hengist glanced at the sun.

'We wait.' He turned to his men. 'You know what to do. Form a shield wall and be ready. The Frisians could return at any moment.'

'And if they don't?' Octa asked before he could stop himself.

Hengist scratched his bearded chin. 'Then we take their ships and leave them stranded here. Let the Britons deal with them.' Hengist walked away, and Odalric turned to Octa.

'I'd have thought you'd want to be first off the ship to show Hengist what you can do.'

Octa shrugged and glanced at the spear in his hand. 'Running head first into an unknown battle without knowing the enemy didn't seem like a smart thing to do.'

Odalric grunted as he raised an eyebrow at Octa. 'Witta never taught you that. Running head first into battles is what the bastard does best. Your father as well.'

Octa shrugged again. 'I'm not like them.'

Odalric smiled at him. 'No. Like your mother says, you'll be better than them.'

Octa turned his attention to Hengist and watched as the Jute prepared his men for the battle against the Frisians. They did not know how many men the Frisians had, and from the size of their ships, they probably had as many men as Hengist had brought with him, if not more. Some of the Jutes would not return to the camp and Hengist must have known that, yet he had to get them to fight for a cause many of them were unaware of. Octa wondered if he could ever do that. 'What if she's wrong?'

Odalric grunted again. 'I'll be honest with you, Octa. I also doubt your mother, even though I have never known her to be wrong. Even your father sought her advice more than that of his other wives. You ran from a battle and brought shame to your family, but you did not let that break you. Like a true Saxon, you fought through that and now I see a young warrior fighting with a spear that he believes belongs to Woden. A young warrior who defeated a man who had fought many battles in single combat.' Odalric glanced at the skies. 'We don't know what Wyrd has in store for us. All we can do is fight and die glorious deaths so that Woden comes for us.' He looked at Octa again. 'So you use that spear and you fight as if you are Woden yourself. Let Wyrd worry about the rest.'

For a few heartbeats, Octa's voice was stuck in his throat as he listened to Odalric's words. He glanced at the spear, not knowing how to respond, so instead he said, 'You don't believe this is Gungnir?'

Odalric smiled. 'I'll believe it when Woden tells me it is.' He clapped Octa on the back. 'Now come, we must prepare to fight the Frisians.'

Octa smiled back as he realised Odalric was right. His wyrd was not something he could control. All he could do was face what was in front of him. Octa gripped the shaft of Gungnir. He had faced his fear and had conquered it, just like he would conquer anything the gods put in front of him.

17

The Frisians returned to their ships as the sun sat low on the horizon and Octa surprised himself by sighing with relief as they arrived, their faces set in angry snarls and brandishing their weapons. The tension of waiting had tired him and his stomach rumbled to remind him he had not eaten since before he and Odalric had returned to Ruym. He glanced at the others around him, but as before, Hengist and Odalric showed nothing on their faces other than the desire for violence.

'Who are you and what do you want?' A Frisian stepped forward. The man seemed shorter than Octa, but his shoulders were broad and he had an ugly scar on his face. 'The gods know there are plenty of other places to raid, so why attack my men?'

Hengist scrutinised the Frisians and their leader, and Octa took a moment to do the same. Even in the late-evening sun, Octa saw these men were all hardened warriors. Some of them wore chain-mail vests, but most had leather jerkins on. The Frisians all had spears, swords and axes and from the blood on the blades it looked like they'd had a good day pillaging nearby settlements. King Gwyrangon would blame the Jutes for this, Octa was certain of that.

'I am Hengist and it is my duty to protect these lands from men like you.'

The Frisian leader hawked and spat. 'And why is a Jute protecting lands that don't belong to him?'

Hengist smiled at the Frisian. 'The high king of the Britons pays me and my brother to do so.'

There was a tense silence, and Hengist and the Frisian leader stared at each other. The Frisian's sword twitched in his hand, but Hengist seemed unconcerned as he smiled at the man.

'Bastard,' Odalric whispered, and Octa glanced at him. 'That's Reiner and his men.'

Octa followed his gaze and saw Reiner, a minor Saxon warlord. The last time Octa had seen him was at the feast before the fight against the Thuringians. Octa knew that some Saxon warlords went raiding with the Frisians, but he couldn't understand why Reiner was there when the Saxon lands were being overrun by the Thuringians.

'So are you are planning to attack us?' the Frisian said as Reiner noticed Octa and Odalric. His eyes widened for a moment before he sneered at them.

Hengist shook his head. 'There's no need to fight. Your men equal mine in number, but I have the better warriors. So, I will give you a choice.'

The Frisian leader tilted his head as he gave a crooked smile. 'A choice?'

'Aye. Your men all look capable, and I am always in need of capable warriors. So return what you have taken from the people. Join me and my brother. Help us defend this island and you can reap the rewards when they come.'

The Frisian, his face twitching, glanced over his shoulder at his men, who laughed. 'You hear that, lads? The Jute wants us to fight for him.' More of his men laughed as he turned back to Hengist. His arm muscles tensed as his sword twitched again. 'And if I say no?'

Hengist shrugged. 'I have your ships, so if you say no, you die. Say yes and you live.'

The Frisian bared his teeth at Hengist and Octa felt his limbs tremble at the prospect of a pitched battle against experienced warriors. He gripped Woden's spear as he prayed. *Woden, guide your spear.* A calm settled over him, but still he felt the nervousness in the pit of his stomach and he took a deep breath to chase it away. Odalric stepped closer to him and raised his shield. As did many of the Jutes. They all knew what was about to happen as the breeze picked up.

'Keep your shield up and spear ready,' Odalric whispered. 'Show these Jutes what we Saxons can do.' Octa nodded, but said nothing. He wondered how many more times those words would be spoken to him as the leader of the Frisians raised his sword.

'We'd rather die than join you bastard Jutes.'

Hengist didn't respond to the Frisian. Instead, he lifted his shield and readied his spear. 'Men! Shield wall!'

'Attack! Kill them all!' the Frisian leader shouted, as the Jutes formed a shield wall in front of the Frisians' ships. The Frisians roared and charged and, for a moment, Octa felt the urge to turn and run as Odalric stood beside him.

'Finally, a proper fight,' the older Saxon said as he locked his shield with Octa's. Octa glanced at him and remembered Reinald, the old Saxon foederati, and the words he had spoken to him when they had fought the Picts by the wall. *Use your fear. Feed on it and use it against your enemy. You fight with Woden's spear.*

Octa used the words to plant his feet to the ground and raised his shield as the Frisians reached them. He barely noticed the missing teeth of his attacker as he blocked the Frisian's spear with his shield and stabbed Gungnir over its rim. Octa felt it hit its mark, but paid no attention to the blood on the spearhead as he pulled it back and was forced to duck behind his shield as another Frisian hacked at him with an axe. Odalric stabbed the man in the throat with his spear, but then the Frisian grabbed hold of it and, as he collapsed, he ripped it from Odalric's grip.

Odalric did not seem to panic, though. Instead, he punched out with his shield and gave himself some room to pull his sword from its scabbard.

'Fight me, you bastards!' he roared as he hacked at the shield of a Frisian, driving the man back. Octa saw the small gap open between the Frisian shields and stabbed Gungnir through it. A warrior cried out and Octa felt a brief tug on the spear before he twisted it and pulled it back.

A spear came towards him and Octa lifted his shield to block it when he felt something strike his mail vest. He resisted the urge to look down as he remembered something else Reinald had said to him. *Never take your eyes off your enemy.* Instead, he punched out with his shield, hoping to give himself some more space, but he did not possess Odalric's strength and was pushed back instead. Octa ducked behind his shield as another spear came for him again and felt himself being pushed back again.

'Hold your ground, Octa!' Odalric shouted, but Octa barely heard him over the sounds of the men fighting and his heart beating hard in his chest. He felt the fear creeping up his spine again, a fear he thought he had defeated when he fought Eadric. But fighting in a shield wall was more terrifying than facing a single man. Octa struggled to understand where the attacks were coming from and every time he tried to use the spear, he was forced behind his shield. He closed his eyes and took a deep breath to force the fear back, but unlike Odalric, who was roaring to the gods as he hacked and stabbed at the Frisian with his sword, Octa struggled to stand his ground.

Blood sprayed over him as the Jute beside him was killed and, before the gap in the wall could be closed, a large man stepped into it and killed another Jute before he turned around and sneered at Octa.

'Time to die, Octa the Coward!' The warrior pulled his sword arm back to stab him and, to Octa, it felt like the fighting stopped. He sensed that the battle was not going Hengist's way as in that moment of unexpected calm he saw holes in Hengist's shield wall before he focused on the man about to kill him. Octa recognised Reiner. A man his father had considered a friend and had shared mead with.

Will you stand and fight? The words were whispered in his head and Octa glanced at the spear as the large Saxon stabbed his sword at him. *Will you fight to protect your people?* Octa twisted out of the way of the sword, like he had been taught to do so many winters ago, and felt it grate along his mail vest before punching the Saxon on the shoulder with his shield.

Reiner cried out as his arm went limp and he dropped his sword before Octa struck him in the face with his shield again. Octa snarled as the Saxon warlord's eyes rolled in his skull, before he collapsed, and raised Gungnir to kill Reiner, when Odalric shouted, 'Octa, behind you!'

He glanced over his shoulder and saw another Saxon rush at him. His heart stopped because he knew he could not turn in time to avoid the man's spear, but then one of Hengist's Jutes shoulder barged the Saxon and knocked him to the ground. The Jute buried his sword in the Saxon's throat before he could get back to his feet, but that left his back exposed. Octa turned and stabbed a Frisian under the armpit as he tried to kill the Jute as Odalric blocked another attack with his shield and killed the man he was facing.

For a moment, no one came at them and Octa used the time to see what was happening. It was hard to see who had the upper hand, as he saw Hengist laughing while he cut another Frisian down. Octa frowned when he saw

Hengist wasn't fighting the leader of the Frisians, and he ran his eyes over the battleground trying to find him.

'Octa! Fight!' Odalric shouted as he and the Jutes closed the shield wall, but they were being pushed back by the Frisians.

What will you do? The voice came to him again and Octa wondered if it was Friga as he spotted the leader of the Frisians hacking away at the Jutes. Without thinking, he changed the grip on Gungnir and raised it over his head.

'Octa!' Odalric shouted again, but Octa ignored him as he took a deep breath and threw Gungnir at the leader of the Frisians, trusting that the spear of Woden would find its mark.

Again, time seemed to stop for Octa as he watched the spear fly over the heads of the Jutes and strike the leader of the Frisians in the face. The gods seemed to laugh in his ears as the spearhead broke through the back of the Frisian's skull and his head snapped backwards before he disappeared from sight.

The Frisians cried out as their leader died and Hengist wasted no time. 'Kill them all!'

Octa felt his battle lust take over him, and he pulled his seax knife from its scabbard and charged at the Frisians. He killed the first man while he still gaped at his dead leader, while Odalric sliced another's throat open with his sword. Octa pushed a Frisian to the ground before one of the Jutes killed the man. He turned towards another Frisian, but then the man dropped the sword and shield, before lifting his arms in the air. Many of the other Frisians did the same and even the Saxons that fought with Reiner stepped back, but they kept their shields raised and their weapons ready.

The fight was over and Octa's legs trembled as Hengist walked over to the dead Frisian leader. He looked at the spear in the man's face and then glanced at Octa.

'That was a good throw,' Odalric said, and Octa nodded. 'Like Woden guided the spear.'

Octa glanced at Odalric before he walked towards Hengist, still standing over the dead body of the Frisian.

Hengist stepped back and let Octa pull the spear from the Frisian's face. For a moment, Octa and Hengist stared at each, before the Jutish warlord smiled. 'If I didn't believe you before, then I do now, Octa. That was some throw.'

Octa shrugged, not knowing what to say. He might have thrown the spear, but he never aimed it. Gungnir never missed.

'Wasn't needed though,' one of the Jutes said, an older warrior with a missing eye that made Octa think of the old man who had told him of the spear. Woden. 'We were beating them.'

Hengist gripped Octa's shoulder. 'Octa did what he felt was needed, but these Frisians put up more of a fight than I thought they would.'

'Because there were Saxons fighting with them,' Odalric said as he approached, his sword still in his hand. He nodded towards the small group of Saxon warriors who still had their shields raised and then at Reiner, who seemed to come to.

Hengist looked at the Saxons and then asked, 'Do you know the man?'

Odalric nodded, even though Octa felt that the question was aimed at him. 'His name is Reiner. He is a minor warlord in the Saxon lands. His lands were to the east and were the first to be overrun by the Thuringians as they pushed westward.'

Reiner sat up and rubbed his head with his left hand as his right arm hung limp by his side. A handful of the Jutes surrounded him, which made the other Saxons angry. They shouted insults at the Jutes who had surrounded them, while Reiner glared at Octa.

'Talk to him, Octa. See if he will join us.'

'Me?' Octa's eyes widened.

'You are the son of a warlord.' Hengist looked at him and Octa took a deep breath as he glanced at Odalric, who nodded at him.

Octa, Gungnir in his hand and Odalric beside him, walked towards Reiner, who hawked and spat.

'Never thought I'd see you fight beside him,' Reiner said to Odalric, who scratched his beard with blood-covered fingers.

'Aye, thought the same once, but I was wrong about the lad. And so are many others.'

Octa's heart raced at Odalric's words, but before he could say anything, Reiner said, 'He is a coward. The gods have cursed him and they curse you for fighting with him.' He glared at Octa. 'Just like they cursed your father, who is dead because of you. Him and his family. All killed by Witta because you are a coward.'

Octa's heart thudded in his chest as Reiner's words punched through his mail vest like an arrow. He tightened his grip on Gungnir as Odalric said, 'Frithowald's family still live, as do many from the village.'

Reiner's eyes widened at that, but before he could say anything, Octa knelt down in front of him.

'You are right. My father was cursed. But not by the gods. He was cursed by me and by what I did.' Octa stared at Reiner, who only glared at him. 'I am not the same as I was last summer, though. My fear no longer controls me. And I swear by Woden that one day I will return to the Saxon lands and avenge my father.'

Reiner curled his lip as he continued to glare at Octa. 'The gods still see you as a coward.'

Octa glanced at Gungnir and shook his head. 'The gods see me as the warrior who defeated you, but we do not have to be enemies. The past is not important. The future is and, here on this island, we can have that future. We can build a new home for our people. For all those who had to flee theirs because of the Thuringians and the Huns.'

'Neither me nor my men will ever fight for a coward like you.' He looked at Hengist over Octa's shoulder. 'Octa the Coward! That is what they call him. Octa the Coward! The boy who ran from a battle with his tail between his legs.'

'You should kill him,' Odalric said as many of the Jutes glanced at each other and Octa's cheeks burnt with shame. He had done his best to hide what he had done from Hengist and his men. But still, he shook his head as he got to his feet.

'His wyrd is not in my hands.' Octa turned and walked away. He would not kill a man in cold blood. Reiner was defeated and injured. But as he walked away, he heard a cry behind him and turned in time to see Reiner charging at him, his sword in his left hand.

Octa lifted his shield to block Reiner's sword, but the Saxon warlord never made it that far as Odalric hacked his sword into the back of Reiner's neck. Octa could only stare as Reiner's life left his eyes, and he dropped to the ground.

'Kill them!' Hengist ordered his men who were guarding the Saxons, and there was nothing Octa could do as they slaughtered the remaining Saxons and Frisians. He turned to face Hengist, his anger making him blind to his position, when Odalric grabbed his shoulder and glared at him.

'Never turn your back on the enemy, even if he is injured!'

Octa stared at Odalric, stunned as he remembered those words being said to him before. 'I...' He turned as the last of the Saxon warriors were killed, their blood soaking into the ground. Men who had wives and children back in the Saxon lands.

Odalric shook his head. 'You fought well, Octa. But you still have much to learn. Reiner might never have joined us, but some of those warriors could have been convinced if you had killed the bastard.'

This time Octa shook his head. 'They think I'm a coward. They wouldn't have joined me.'

'Doesn't matter. They saw you defeat their warlord and, if you had killed him, then they would have seen what your mother sees in you.'

'Odalric is right,' Hengist said from behind them. 'Men follow those who show strength. Words mean nothing to most, but actions matter.'

Octa looked at the Jute, not sure what to say.

'It doesn't matter what that man said about you. Me and my men know you are brave. I saw it when you saved my son and these men saw how you fought today. But if you want the Saxons to follow you, then you need to be more ruthless.'

'Take this.' Odalric handed Reiner's sword to him and Octa shook his head.

'I don't need a sword. I fight with Gungnir.'

Odalric pressed the sword into his chest. 'That doesn't matter. Take this sword and wear it every day. Use it to remind yourself of the lessons you learnt today.'

Hengist nodded. 'Show compassion when it is needed, but be ruthless when it's necessary.'

Octa took the sword from Odalric and stared at the blood-covered blade. The sword wasn't as beautiful as his father's. Its guard, which was the same width as the pommel, was simple and not adorned with gems or gold. Instead it was made of plain iron, while the grip was wrapped in leather which was worn down and needed to be replaced. But Octa's heart still raced as he looked at the sword. His sword. 'And how will I know?'

Hengist smiled at him. 'Sometimes you don't and all you can do is trust the gods.'

18

The sun was setting as the Jutes boarded the ships after they looted the dead and filled their pouches with valuables. The plunder the Frisians had taken from the Britons was left behind for the Britons to collect themselves. The warriors were exhausted and Octa struggled to keep his eyes open, but Hengist did not want to stay on the riverbank so he did not send men to take the plunder back to the people. He didn't want the locals to mistake them for the men who had raided them and attack them during the night.

Hengist took the two ships of the Frisians and had split his men amongst the four ships, after he had the heads of the pirates put on stakes along the riverbank. A warning to other raiders, but also a message to the Cantiaci. That the Jutes protected them while their king did nothing.

'Your mother is some woman,' Hengist said out of the blue as the ships travelled around a bend in the river.

Octa fought back a yawn as he looked at the warlord while Odalric tensed beside him. 'My mother?'

Hengist smiled. 'Aye. Lady Berthild. She's not afraid to speak her mind. A strong woman. I can see why your father married her.'

Octa shrugged. 'I don't really know. I was raised by another warlord.'

'Lady Berthild is as fierce as any warrior,' Odalric said as he stared at Hengist. 'So watch your words and actions around her.'

Hengist raised an eyebrow at the older Saxon warrior and smiled at the man. 'I mean no offence. But it is hard not to notice her. Perhaps that is how Woden feels about Friga.'

Octa's heart raced as Hengist mentioned the mother goddess. He had felt her presence again during the battle and struggled to understand why she was watching him so closely or why she kept asking him those questions. The same questions she had asked him in Cair Urnahc. Was it because of the spear? When they had spoken in Corstopitum, she had told him she would make sure that Woden couldn't find him or the spear. Was that what she was doing?

'Octa?' Odalric's voice startled him.

Octa shook his head and frowned at the warrior as Hengist laughed.

'The gods know I've never known a young warrior to be so serious.'

'Aye, never used to be like that,' Odalric said. 'Used to think with his prick and not his head.'

Octa's cheeks burnt as Hengist laughed again. 'Didn't we all when we were his age?'

They fell silent after that and Octa was glad when the warriors started singing a war song, although it surprised him that they sang a song he had heard in Witta's hall. As the ships reached the island, Hengist waved to Horsa and Oisc, who were both standing on the wharves. Oisc was beaming at them and had to be held back by his uncle, who looked as serious as always as the ships docked and were tied up. The dead and injured were taken off first and, as Octa waited by the prow, he saw his mother waiting, her brows creased as she looked like she was deep in thought.

'Your mother is up to something,' Odalric said, and Octa frowned at him. 'That's the face she pulls when she is planning something. Your father knew it well and so do most of us.'

When the dead and injured were off the ship, Hengist disembarked and embraced his son as Horsa scowled. 'You lost some men.'

'Aye, the Frisians fought well. It's a pity they didn't want to join us. But we have more ships now.'

Horsa looked at the new ships on the wharves. 'We don't have enough men for those ships.'

Hengist smiled as he gripped his son's shoulder. 'Then we sell them. More gold for us.'

Horsa glanced at Octa as he got off the ship. 'King Vortigern is on his way.'

'How far away?' Hengist asked.

Horsa scratched his bearded chin. 'Should be here tomorrow, but the king of the Cantiaci has already made camp near the island.'

Hengist nodded. 'Make sure the men keep an eye on them. And no one leave the island until the kings of the Britons leave. We don't want to give King Gwyrangon a reason to start a war against us.'

'You really think he would?' Octa asked, and regretted it as Horsa glared at him.

'The Britons can't be trusted. They'll never accept us.'

Octa's brows furrowed as he remembered Corstopitum. There the old Saxons and the Britons lived together as one people. The Saxons had families there and many of the Britons had started following the Saxon gods. If that was possible there, then why could they not do the same in the south? But even as the question came to him, Octa remembered King Vortigern's son. *Because of people like him*, a voice said to him, and Octa wondered if Horsa wasn't right.

'The Britons on this small island accepted us,' Hengist said. 'They treat us well and don't cause us any problems.'

Horsa grunted. 'Only because they fear what will happen if they turn against us.'

Hengist nodded as he looked at his son, who was staring at the surrounding warriors. 'The gods know that one day we'll have to teach the British kings the same.'

* * *

Berthild watched as the high king of Britannia entered the town on another day where the clouds threatened rain. The gates had been opened and Hengist had his best warriors standing there, all of them in their war gear. Berthild knew the message the brothers were sending. It was a welcome befitting an honoured guest, but it was also a warning. A show of power.

Octa stood by the main hall with Hengist and Horsa, and Berthild felt it was a good sign. Hengist trusted her son, even if Horsa didn't. Odalric had told her how well Octa had fought against the Frisians and that he had been the one who killed their leader. He had also told her that Reiner had joined the Frisians. The man had always been weak, but Berthild had been surprised to find out that he had been raiding with Frisians. It made her wonder about what was happening in the lands of her people. And then there was something else, something she felt Odalric was not telling her. She did not like it when men hid things from her, but she did not want to push. Not yet.

Berthild watched as the king of the Britons' carriage came to a stop by the main hall. Short warriors on horseback surrounded it, most of them wearing the same mail vest that Octa liked to wear and with scowls on their faces, but even from where she stood, Berthild could sense their fear. They were surrounded by men larger and more vicious than them. Men who would kill them without a second thought, but Berthild admired the way the Britons squared their shoulders and faced the Jutes.

Behind the high king's carriage rode another who looked like a king. Like King Vortigern, he was surrounded by warriors, and Berthild frowned at the hatred in the man's eyes. He must have been the king of the tribe that kept attacking the Jutes.

'You'd think the high king would look mightier than that,' a woman's voice said, and Berthild turned to see the tavern woman standing next to her. She raised an eyebrow in surprise and glanced at Odalric, who was standing beside her, but was not paying any attention to the woman. Instead, his eyes were fixed on the Britons as his finger on his right hand twitched.

Berthild looked at the high king of the Britons as he climbed off his carriage and realised the woman was right. The man looked old enough to be her father and his shoulders were slightly stooped with age, even as he tried to stand straight. But it was the younger man beside the high king that really caught her attention. He looked much like the king, but Berthild could sense the hatred from him. A shiver ran down her spine as he reminded her of Witta and her hand went to the spear pendant she wore around her waist. The one she had got to replace the pendant she had given Octa.

'A snake,' the tavern woman said. 'That's what he reminds me of.'

Berthild nodded as she watched the tense way the Britons greeted the Jutes. 'My son thinks he will cause problems for us.'

The woman was silent for a heartbeat and then said, 'Your son is smart. He thinks with his head and not his sword.'

A small smile came to Berthild. 'Yes, he has changed much over the past two seasons. I almost don't recognise him.' Berthild turned to the woman. 'I have not seen you around since our last talk.'

The woman smiled, but her wise eyes were still fixed on Octa. 'I've had business to attend to, but I'm always around. All you need to do is call my name.'

Berthild frowned as she realised she didn't know the woman's name. But before she could ask, there was a commotion as one horse reared and kicked out at one of the men. The warrior dodged the horse, before Octa rushed forward and grabbed the animal by its reins and calmed it down. Berthild smiled at that. Octa had always been good with horses. She turned to ask the woman her name and then frowned when the woman was gone. 'Where did she go?'

'Where did who go?' Odalric asked, and Berthild looked at him.

'The woman I was just talking to. The one from the tavern in Jutland.'

Odalric raised an eyebrow at her and shook his head. 'I didn't see a woman.'

* * *

Octa waited for the Britons to enter the hall before he followed them in, his heart still racing from the incident with the horse. It reminded him of that day in the town in Jutland when he had saved Hengist's son and he couldn't help but wonder if that was a sign. He glanced towards his mother and Odalric and frowned at the look on his mother's face, but then the son of the high king stopped in front of Octa and glared at him.

Octa glared back and wished he had Gungnir with him, but the spear was back in the house. And so was Reiner's sword. All Octa had was the armour he wore, which had been cleaned and the metal plates polished so it glowed, and his seax knife. That was all the other senior warriors had as well. Only Hengist and Horsa carried their swords. A show of power, especially as the Britons had to leave their weapons outside of the hall. Even the kings who had accompanied King Vortigern. Only the high king of the Britons was allowed to carry his sword. Octa's mother had told him it was to show the other kings who their alliance was with. That they saw King Vortigern as a friend they trusted, but not them.

'You are good with horses,' Prince Vortimer said to him, and Octa nodded as he looked down at the prince, who was shorter than him. 'Perhaps because, like them, you are an animal.' The man laughed at his own joke and all Octa could do was shake his head as he followed them inside.

The tables in the hall had been filled with food. Fish from the seas and river, along with birds caught in traps and venison they managed to hunt without being attacked. The Britons had worked hard all night and day to prepare the feast for their king and high king, but Octa sensed it was more to impress the brothers. Despite the threats the brothers had made the day before, they treated the Britons well, but unlike the old Saxons in the north, they did not treat the Britons as equals. Jugs with ale and mead had been laid out, and Octa's stomach rumbled at the smell of the food as he looked for a place to sit.

Hengist and Horsa sat at the main table with King Vortigern and King Gwyrangon. The others had to find seats where they could, and Octa ended up sitting with Aldric, one of the senior warriors who had fought against the Frisians.

'I'm surprised they let you in the hall,' the man said with a warm smile. 'Although, I'm glad. Otherwise, that horse might have started a war.' Some of the other warriors laughed, which caused Horsa to glare at them.

Octa smiled at Aldric and licked his lips at the food in front of him. He had not eaten that morning because he was busy cleaning his armour, even though his mother had told him to make the Britons do it. But before Octa could take a bite, Hengist signalled for him to join them. That was the real reason he had been allowed in the hall for this meal. Hengist needed him to translate.

Silence fell over those in the hall as Hengist stood and cleared his throat. Even the Britons stopped their conversations as they stared at the warlord, who stood head and shoulders above them all, while Octa made his way to Hengist.

'My friends, we welcome you to our home,' Hengist greeted the Britons, and Octa translated as best he could. 'The people of Ruym have worked hard to prepare and the ale is from your lands. Today, let us enjoy this feast as equals and as friends.'

Again, Octa translated, but had to pause now and again to find the right words. He saw how some Britons scowled at him, especially the king of the Cantiaci and Prince Vortimer, but they remained silent and allowed him to finish.

What would you do to protect your people? The voice came to him again. *Would you wage a war and burn their lands?*

Octa stammered and scanned the hall, but saw no sign of Friga. Again, he wondered what she was planning, when Horsa cleared his throat and Octa realised everyone was staring at him. His cheeks burning, he stepped back to show that he was done, before he rushed to his seat, eager to get away from the attention.

'What happened to you there?' Aldric asked, and Octa frowned at him. 'You froze and turned pale.'

Octa shook his head. 'I thought I saw something.' He took his cup, filled it with ale and emptied it in one gulp.

'Must have been something terrifying,' Aldric said, and others laughed, but Octa ignored them as they dug into the food. But the hunger he had felt before had left him, and all Octa could do was scan the shadows of the hall.

What do you want from me, he asked in his head. Something drew his attention to Prince Vortimer and Octa wondered what the son of the high king was looking at until he realised it was the spear Eadric had brought back from the cave. The one they had first thought was Gungnir. Hengist had liked the spear, with its gold-rimmed spearhead and the golden rings on the shaft, which had been fixed with a thick golden band after Eadric broke it during his fight with Octa, and had decided to keep it. So now the spear leaned against a stand, decorated in runes, while two human skulls and many animal skulls sat beneath it. And amongst the skulls was a small wooden statue of Woden, its one eye always fixed on Octa when he was in the hall. Only those who were there when Octa and Eadric had their duel knew it wasn't the real Gungnir, but those who had arrived after that day believed it was and the others liked to make fun of them for it.

Octa wondered why Prince Vortimer was so interested in the spear as the king's son whispered something to one of the men he was sitting with. The man stood up and left the hall as if he was in a rush and the warrior sitting beside Octa laughed.

'Bastard can't hold his drink.'

Octa smiled and nodded, but he sensed it was more than that, especially as the voice came to him again. *Will you fight to protect us?*

The meal carried on for much of the day, but apart from picking at his food, Octa did not eat or drink much. Something about the way Prince

Vortimer kept glancing at the spear made him nervous, and the last question the voice asked made his hands tremble. *Who is us,* he wondered when King Vortigern cleared his throat.

The hall stayed as noisy as it was, forcing the high king to do it again, and it was only after Hengist slammed his fist on the table that the hall fell silent. King Vortigern, red in the face now, nodded and stood, and so did Ceretic, who stumbled as he rushed to get to his king's side.

'We thank you for this fine meal and the warm welcome you have given us on the island of Ruym,' King Vortigern said, and Ceretic translated. Octa noticed how many of the Jutes scowled at his bad pronunciation and almost felt sorry for the man. Again, he hoped that was not what he sounded like to the Britons when he spoke their tongue. Both Hengist and Horsa smiled at the high king before he continued. 'But now that the meal is finished and our bellies are full, it is time to discuss some serious matters.' Ceretic translated the words and Horsa glanced at Octa, who nodded to show that the words were correct. The younger of the two brothers did not trust the Britons and had asked Octa to make sure that no one was trying to cheat them.

Hengist raised his cup and smiled at the high king. 'My King Vortigern. The gods know that my brother and I are curious about your visit. But already the moon sits high in the sky and you and your men must be tired after your journey from Cair Urnahc. I ask that we enjoy this meal and say what must be said tomorrow with rested minds and bodies.'

Ceretic translated the words and King Vortigern scowled, as did the other Britons. But after a long while, King Vortigern nodded, and the Jutes cheered.

As the night wore on and men ate and drank, Octa saw his chance to slip out of the hall. The Britons and the Jutes did not mix, so there was no need for him, and on the few occasions that the brothers spoke with King Vortigern, Ceretic was there to translate. So Octa finished his ale and left the hall.

For a moment, he stared at the sky, trying to see the moon behind the thick clouds, but then shivered as he sensed someone watching him. He clenched his fists and wondered why Friga didn't just come to him, like she had done that day in Corstopitum.

Taking a deep breath, he walked to the house he shared with his mother and Odalric. The older warrior was sleeping by the hearth fire, where he usually did, and from the pause in his breathing, Octa knew he wasn't really sleeping. He was doing what he had been told to. Protecting Octa's mother. But Octa forgot about all of that when he went to his sleeping quarters and saw Lucilia waiting for him.

She smiled as she removed the furs and Octa felt a stirring in his groin when he saw she wasn't wearing anything. With a smile of his own, Octa removed his clothes and embraced her as she came to him. He breathed in her scent and, for the first time in many days, forgot about all the questions that ate away at his mind.

19

Octa woke the next morning when his mother walked into his sleeping quarters. Lucilia stirred beside him as he rubbed the sleep from his eyes and he felt her hide under the furs to avoid his mother's glare.

'By the gods, you couldn't wait until the Britons left before you did that.'

Octa sat up and looked for his trousers. 'Nothing happened last night, Mother.'

His mother raised an eyebrow at him and Lucilia under the furs. 'That's not what it looks like from where I'm standing.'

'I meant at the feast. All everyone did was eat and drink while pretending to be friends.'

His mother scowled at him. 'And I still want to know about that. Get up and get dressed. Hengist is looking for you.'

'Yes, Mother.' Octa nodded and, after his mother left, he turned to Lucilia, who poked her head out from under the furs.

'Your mother doesn't like me. I see the way she always looks at me. Like a wolf at a rabbit.'

Octa smiled at Lucilia. 'My mother not like many. And she look at everyone like wolf. Very angry wolf.' Octa stood up and stretched before he put his trousers on and pulled his tunic over his head.

'Will there be war? Between your people and mine?' Lucilia's question caught him by surprise and he thought of the questions Friga kept asking him as he looked at the spear in the corner of his room.

'I not know.' Not knowing what else to say, Octa left his sleeping quarters. He did not want there to be a war, but he sensed one was coming. One that would change not only his life, but the lives of many in Britannia.

'Someone had a good night,' Odalric said as Octa walked past him. 'Just like your father, you are.'

Before Octa could respond to that, his mother walked into the main room. 'I hope that Briton is just a bit of fun. A way to get rid of your urges.'

'Mother—' Octa started, not wanting to hear that from his mother, but she carried on.

'You need a Saxon wife. The daughter of a strong warlord.'

Octa rinsed his face in a bowl of water before he combed his long hair. 'There are no Saxon warlords on Britannia, Mother.'

Berthild crossed her arms and scowled at him. 'There is one. You.'

'I need an army to become a warlord,' Octa responded, and frowned at his mother's smile.

'One day, my son. You will have a mighty army behind you and your enemies will cower before you. But until then, you need to be smart. Now, go. Hengist is waiting for you.'

Odalric finished his morning ale and got to his feet before he gripped Octa by his shoulder and the two of them left the house before Octa could respond to his mother.

'I'm sometimes glad my mother is not a man,' Octa said as he took a deep breath of the fresh morning air. There was still a slight chill in the air which cooled his face and the salty air from the sea helped him focus his mind. Octa had never seen the sea before he left his homeland, but he had found that he enjoyed it. The smell of the sea and cries of the birds calmed him.

'Aye. Even the gods would tremble before her wrath,' Odalric said as they walked towards the main hall.

Already some of the Britons were making their way there, many of them looking worse for wear, and Octa saw Prince Vortimer and his two friends talking to a fourth man who was hidden from him. He would have wondered about that, but Horsa walked out of the hall and grabbed Octa by his tunic.

'You snuck off last night.'

Octa stared at the younger of the brothers. There was a time when the taller man frightened him, but not any more. Still, Octa knew he had to be careful around Horsa. The man was the more ruthless of the two brothers and wanted Gungnir, which Octa had left in the house. 'I saw no reason for me to stay. Everyone was either drunk or asleep.'

Horsa glared at him as Odalric stood nearby, his eyes fixed on them. 'Aye, not much happened last night. It was a dull feast. Not a single bloody fight.' He glanced at Odalric and his mouth twitched. For a heartbeat, Octa wondered who would win in a fight between the two warriors. 'The gods know I hate to say this, Saxon, but I need you in that hall.' Octa's eyes widened, but he kept quiet. 'King Vortigern insists on using his man to translate, but my brother and I want you there to listen. Make sure the bastard doesn't try anything funny.'

'You really think Ceretic won't translate his king's words properly?'

Horsa shrugged. 'I don't trust these Britons. They're like rats who try to eat your grain when you aren't looking. And you will be our cat to make sure that doesn't happen.' Horsa let go of him and went back inside the hall, leaving Octa and Odalric to stare at each other.

'I would have liked him if he wasn't such a prick,' Odalric said, and Octa couldn't help but smile.

They went inside the hall and Odalric went to a bench near the door, while Octa walked to where Hengist and Horsa were sitting. The benches were slowly filling up with the same people that had been there the night before, although Octa was certain that some of them had never left the hall as he saw one Jute lift his head from the table, his eyes still half closed, before it dropped again. Many of the others looked like they had been drinking deep into the night, even some of the British warriors.

As Octa took a seat near the brothers, the British kings arrived, their dark faces betraying a tense conversation that must have happened before. Prince Vortimer and his friends followed, and the king's son glared at the Jutes as he walked to the front to sit near his father. Octa wondered about the fourth man they were talking to as Ceretic stood up.

'King of Britannia thank you for feast night before. Food good, drink good.'

Hengist smiled and nodded, while Horsa only glared at the Britons. The atmosphere in the hall was very different from the night before, and Octa was glad that no one had weapons with them. Not that that would stop any fights, though.

'Tell your king we are glad he enjoyed the feast laid out for him and his companions. Hospitality is important to us and the gods demand that we treat our guests with honour,' Hengist said, and Ceretic translated, although Octa noticed how he left out the part about the gods. 'My brother and I would like to know why you didn't treat Octa with the same respect?'

Ceretic's face paled, and he glanced at Octa, knowing that he spoke the British tongue, before he translated the question. There was a growl from some of the Britons, but King Vortigern raised his hand to silence them. He got to his feet and Octa noticed how he was dressed differently than the day before. He wore a thick gold band around his head and golden rings on his thin fingers. A large gold buckle adorned his waist and even the knife he wore on his belt was gold and had a large gem on the hilt. It was as if he wanted to display his power and his position as the high king of Britannia.

'Your man was treated as well as we could, even though the message he delivered caused some upset,' King Vortigern said, and Ceretic translated. Horsa glanced at Octa, who nodded to show the words were correct. 'You came to me offering your services and your men to help defend our lands against our enemies from the north. And in return for this, you asked for only food and clothing for your men.'

'As well as land in my kingdom,' King Gwyrangon said, his face an angry scowl, but King Vortigern raised a hand to silence him. Ceretic hesitated and King Vortigern nodded, so he translated the king of the Cantiaci's words. Horsa's face twitched, but Hengist only nodded, his face unreadable.

'Our agreement was for your men on the three ships you arrived with,' King Vortigern continued. 'And yet, when we arrived yesterday, we saw many more than that. And now you ask for us to increase the amount of provisions we give you.'

'Your army is growing and you expect us to feed them!' Prince Vortimer jumped to his feet and shouted. 'For how long? Until you decide to turn your swords and spears against us?'

King Vortigern glared at his son, even as King Gwyrangon grunted his agreement with what the prince had said. Ceretic kept quiet, maybe too afraid to translate Prince Vortimer's words. But then Horsa looked at Octa, who knew he had no choice, so he told them what was said.

The flames of the torches seemed to flutter as the air got more tense. Some of the Jutes in the hall glared at Prince Vortimer, who was still on his feet as he returned their glares. Octa had to admit he was impressed with the man's braveness. Even Hengist seemed to enjoy it as he laughed.

'Your son has the heart of a bear, King Vortigern,' he said.

'In the body of a pup,' Horsa muttered under his breath. Octa looked at Prince Vortimer like he had seen him for the first time and disagreed with Horsa. Vortimer might have been smaller than them, but he was still larger than many of the Britons. His broad shoulders and thick arms showed a man who trained often, and the hatred in his eyes made Octa realise the man was dangerous.

Hengist put a hand on his brother's shoulder and Octa was glad that Ceretic did not translate his words. 'You are correct. Our agreement was for the men in our three ships, and your eyes do not deceive you. There are more than three ships here. Some have arrived from our homeland, bringing with them people who had to flee their homes, like Octa's own mother.' Vortigern pointed at Octa, whose cheeks turned red. He glanced at Odalric and saw the anger on the man's face. 'She had to flee her lands because of tribes from the east who push west day by day, taking lands that don't belong to them. And even those people are being chased by an enemy so vicious, even the mighty Romans fear them.'

'The Romans fear no one,' the king of the Cantiaci said, and Hengist smiled at him.

'If that is so, then why did they not return the warriors they took from these lands? Why did they not bring their armies to you when you begged for help?' The Britons bristled at the word begged, but Hengist continued as Ceretic translated. 'Because they are too busy defending their own lands from the Hun. They abandoned you to protect themselves. But as war rages on the continent, many are forced from their homelands and come here looking for a new start. Those people need food we cannot provide because our hunters are attacked. Our fishing boats sunk. So we were forced into asking for more food from you, King Vortigern.'

'And how many of those who came on those ships are warriors?' Prince Vortimer asked, ignoring his father's glare.

Hengist nodded. 'Many are warriors, yes. Men who follow their wives and children. But not all those ships are from those who joined us. Two of them belonged to a Frisian warlord who attacked your lands a few days ago.' Hengist looked at King Gwyrangon, whose face turned red as Ceretic translated the words. 'They attacked your people and burnt their homes and yet, it was my men who died fighting them.'

King Vortigern looked at the king of the Cantiaci. 'Is this true?'

King Gwyrangon glared at Hengist for a heartbeat and then nodded. 'There was an attack a few days ago on some settlements.' Octa translated the conversation because Ceretic kept quiet, and the Briton scowled at him.

King Vortigern turned back to the brothers. 'And where are these Frisians now?'

Hengist shrugged. 'Theirs heads are on their spears along the river. A warning to others and a message to those who live along the river.'

'And what is this message?' Prince Vortimer asked.

After Ceretic translated, Horsa said, 'That it is us Jutes who defend them while you drink your wine and feast.'

Prince Vortimer's hand went to where his sword would usually be and when he remembered it wasn't there, he glanced at the fake Gungnir. Octa wondered about that while King Vortigern tried to calm everyone as some of the Britons shouted their displeasure at Horsa's words.

'I want those heads removed!' King Gwyrangon ordered. 'God does not condone this barbarianism!'

'Then remove them yourself.' Horsa got to his feet and leaned forward, his scarred knuckles resting on the table. Ceretic looked like he wanted to be elsewhere as he translated the words and Octa almost felt sorry for the man.

There was a tense silence in the hall as the king of the Cantiaci and Horsa glared at each other. The flames on the torches fluttered again and Octa felt that the slightest insult now could cause a brawl that many would not walk away from. He resisted the urge to rub the spear pendant around his neck, but sensed that this was a sign of things to come.

Hengist must have sensed the same and placed a hand on his brother's shoulder. 'You must forgive Horsa. He knew the men that died well and he is still affected by their loss.'

'If you are too afraid to fight, then you shouldn't have come here,' Prince Vortimer said, and the smile fell from Hengist's face. Even Ceretic's eyes were filled with panic as he translated the words.

Hengist walked around the table and towards Prince Vortimer, who stood his ground as the Jute towered over him. Many of the Britons in the hall glanced nervously at each other while the Jutes, all of them men who had fought for the brothers for many winters, got to their feet as if they were preparing for a fight. But Hengist raised his hand, and they all sat down again.

'We are here risking our men because you are too afraid to go out and fight yourself. When we arrived, you were all hiding in your halls behind walls of stone built for you by the Romans. Your *warriors* grow old and fat, their weapons as dull as their wits, while your people suffer and die at the hand of your enemies. Even the people of Ruym have resorted to fighting for themselves because they have learnt that their king never sends out his warriors to protect them.' His nostrils flared. 'Our gods compel us to fight, to stand tall and to face our enemies while yours tell you to drop to your knees and to pray. Do not question the bravery of us Jutes while we fight your enemies for you.'

Ceretic paled and looked like he was about to faint. In the silence of the hall, while everyone waited for him to translate Hengist's words, Octa felt her presence again and knew she was watching him. At that moment, he realised Friga was testing him and, as much as he did not want to because he feared it might start a war with the Britons, Octa knew he had to do it. So he got to his feet, took a deep breath and translated what Hengist had said.

20

Men jumped to their feet and kings hid behind their warriors as cups were grabbed to be used as weapons. Benches were pushed out of the way and the flames of the torches fluttered as Octa finished and braced himself for the fight he knew was coming. This could not have been what the brothers or King Vortigern had planned, but there were those who seemed determined to start a war between the Jutes and the Britons.

'Enough!' a woman's voice thundered over their heads, and Octa groaned as he recognised his mother. He turned toward the entrance of the hall and saw his mother, her face as hard as the iron of his new sword, standing straight and with her shoulders squared. Her eyes were filled with enough venom that no man dared argue with her and, to everyone in the hall, even the Britons, his mother looked like what she was: a woman of power and influence. The Britons all gaped at her as she glared at every man in the hall.

Octa glanced at Odalric standing behind his mother and knew he must have gone to fetch her when things had started getting tense. Odalric shrugged at him and Octa was still trying to understand if the man had done a good thing or not.

Berthild fixed her eyes on Hengist, who had a small smile in his beard, and Prince Vortimer, whose face was too red to be healthy as he glared at Octa's mother.

'How dare a woman enter this hall and interrupt us!' His hands clenched into fists as Octa's mother walked towards them. Octa's heart raced in his chest at the look of contempt on his mother's face as Ceretic finally found his voice again. Many of the Britons agreed with Prince Vortimer, and even Horsa looked annoyed.

'I am not just a woman,' his mother said as she stopped in front of the prince and stood taller than him. Octa cleared his throat and translated his mother's words. 'I am the daughter of a mighty Saxon warlord and the wife of another. I gave birth to a son who has faced the fires of war and others who were taken too soon. I watched my husband die and my village burn to the ground. I have ventured far from my home and killed men with my own hands.' She leaned closer to Prince Vortimer as Octa translated her words. 'What have you done?'

Prince Vortimer looked like he was about to choke on his tongue as Octa translated, and he worried the man might attack his mother. But before the son of the British king could respond, Octa's mother continued.

'You come to our home as friends, but even outside the hall we can hear you squabble like children over a stick.'

'This is my land!' King Gwyrangon shouted after Octa translated the words, and his mother smiled at the man.

'And we thank you for your gift, gracious king of the Cantiaci.'

King Gwyrangon stammered at Berthild's response and Hengist took the opportunity to take back control.

'Lady Berthild is right. We are here as friends and not enemies.' He turned his attention to Prince Vortimer, whose face was still too red. 'Even if some are determined to cause conflict between us.'

'I am only saying what everyone thinks.' Prince Vortimer took a step closer to Hengist.

'That may be so, but you are not the high king of the Britons or even a king.' Hengist looked at King Vortigern, whose face was pale as he gaped at them all. 'King Vortigern, wise king of the Britons, may I suggest we continue this conversation without those who mean to disrupt it?' Ceretic hesitated and, encouraged by his mother's look, Octa translated the words, which made the Briton glare at him.

King Vortigern hesitated for a moment and then straightened his back and nodded. 'Hengist is right. We are here to solve a misunderstanding and we do not need some of you to antagonise those who risk their lives to protect our lands.'

'But, Father—'

'No, Vortimer.' King Vortigern stopped his son and then looked at King Gwyrangon as well. 'We are here as friends and allies. Leave the hall, Vortimer. Go walk around the beach and clear your head. King Gwyrangon, I understand your feelings as well, but these men are protecting your people as much as mine. Stay if you want, but I ask in God's name, do not seek to cause conflict.'

Octa whispered King Vortigern's words to Hengist and noticed the small smile in his beard. For a moment, he wondered if that was what the warlord wanted. To get the high king of the Britons on his own as the other kings left the hall. Octa's mother stood where she was, her face stern, and many of the Britons looked away from her as they left the hall.

King Gwyrangon got to his feet and glared at the Jutes. 'I have important business to deal with. Things that go against the teachings of Christ.' He turned and walked away, with his warriors behind him, and Octa noticed how King Vortigern shrank with exhaustion.

'And what of woman?' Ceretic asked.

Hengist smiled. 'Lady Berthild is a woman of high standing amongst the Saxons, who, like us, regard women as equals. If she prefers to stay, then I will not stop her.'

Horsa grunted, but he kept quiet as Octa's mother said, 'I will leave. I do not want our honoured guests to feel uncomfortable.' She gave Octa a stern glance and left the hall as Hengist leaned closer to him.

'What a woman.'

'Aye,' was all Octa could say as he watched Odalric leave with his mother.

'Mead!' Horsa ordered, and some of the men rushed to fill the cups with mead served only to important guests. Hengist took two cups from a warrior and handed one to King Vortigern, who nodded his thanks.

'Your son's blood runs hot, much like Thunor, our god of thunder. Always eager for battle.'

King Vortigern raised an eyebrow as Ceretic translated. 'That is my concern. He is filled with anger and rarely agrees with me on things these days. But that is my cross to bear as his father.'

Hengist nodded. 'In our lands, if a son becomes too troublesome, we send them raiding. That way, they're out of the way and find their own path.'

'And if your son returns with a mighty army to challenge you?'

'Then we kill them,' Horsa said, and both King Vortigern and Ceretic paled at his words. Hengist laughed and shook his head.

'My brother jests. Our father did the same to us and we have not set foot on his lands since. Even though we are both stronger than him. He can keep his small lands while we make names for ourselves.'

The king of the Britons nodded, and Octa noticed the sadness in his eyes. 'I fear that if I send Vortimer away, then he might cause more problems for me. I keep him close so that I can keep an eye on him. But some of what they say is true, Hengist. Your numbers have grown and many are concerned about that.'

Hengist nodded and then his face turned serious as he led King Vortigern back to his seat. 'My King Vortigern, we came as allies, as friends. We fight for you to protect your lands. That others have come here after fleeing the wars back in their homelands is not in our control. Does your god not say that we should be compassionate to others?'

King Vortigern nodded. 'He does, but I didn't think you'd listen to the words of our God.'

Hengist smiled. 'We listen to the words of any god when it helps us.'

King Vortigern nodded again as Ceretic translated the words. 'But with your increased numbers, it will be harder to provide the provisions to feed and clothe them. Many of our own people are still recovering from raids by the Picts and pirates from across the seas. That is why King Gwyrangon doesn't send provisions. He claims he needs them for his own people.'

'Gwyrangon lies,' Horsa said, and Octa noticed the glance Hengist gave his brother, who ignored it. 'His men attack those we send out to hunt for food or to cut wood. He filled the forts on the coast with men who watch us. He means to start a war with us.'

'King Gwyrangon won't do anything I tell him not to. I am the high king of Britannia.'

Octa wondered if that was true, as he remembered the hatred and anger in the man's eyes.

'I pray to our gods that you are right, King Vortigern.' Hengist drank his mead as Ceretic translated the words. 'If we have become a burden, then we will board our ships and leave.' Octa was stunned by Hengist's words, but then he glanced at Horsa, who seemed unconcerned. 'But if we leave, who protects your lands from the Picts to the north? From those like the Frisians who raided here only a few days ago?' He leaned closer to King Vortigern and Octa had to strain his ears to hear the words he spoke next. 'Who will protect you from the other kings when they unite against you?'

King Vortigern's eyes widened, and even Ceretic struggled to say the words. 'No one will turn against me. I am the high king of Britannia.'

Hengist nodded. 'You are, but your son openly speaks out against you. King Gwyrangon does not seem pleased with your decisions either. Already he doesn't send us the provisions you told him to. And Octa tells me there are other tribes to the north that don't support you. Even Woden, the mightiest of our gods, makes sure he keeps a close eye on the other gods so they don't betray him.'

A shiver ran down Octa's spine as he thought of the spear. He had betrayed Woden by keeping it for himself, and even Friga, Woden's own wife, was helping him do it. But even though Woden had already killed Octa's father because of that, Octa knew he still needed to be wary of Woden's wrath.

King Vortigern's face turned dark as Ceretic translated Hengist's words and Octa thought he saw a glimpse of the man the high king had been once. The man who had made himself the high king of the Britons. 'They would never turn against me.'

Hengist leaned back and looked at his brother. 'That was what we thought of our father once. Until he became jealous of our wealth and sent his men to kill us.' Hengist drank more of his mead as Octa glanced at Horsa. 'Even Eadric, a warrior we thought of as a brother and had given much to, lied to us for his own gain.'

'And what did you do?' King Vortigern asked.

'We killed our father's men and burnt his hall to the ground with him still in it. And Eadric' – Hengist nodded towards Octa – 'Octa killed him with our blessing. The most important lesson we have learnt, King Vortigern, is that you can't always trust those around you. Even Woden knows this. Your son is hungry for power, and King Gwyrangon wants us gone. Do you have enough capable warriors to defend your crown if they unite against you? And if not them, what about the other tribes? The Brigantians, the Corieltauvi, the

Iceni?' Octa frowned as Hengist named the other tribes of Britannia. He had not realised the warlord had taken the time to learn about them. 'Do you have enough warriors to fight them?'

King Vortigern stared at Ceretic as he stumbled over the words and, when the man was done, all the king could do was shake his head.

Hengist smiled, and Octa thought it was the smile of a hunter about to ensnare his prey. 'My brother and I have many more men in Jutland. Let us send for them and we will fight for you and only you. We will defend you not just from the Picts and those who seek to raid your shores from across the seas, but also from the other kings who seek to take your crown from you.'

Octa heard Woden laughing in the silence that filled the hall as King Vortigern stared at Hengist. Even Ceretic looked like he might collapse after he had translated the words.

The king of the Britons glanced around him, as if he was seeking someone and, after what felt like a lifetime, he said, 'Perhaps you are right, Hengist. Perhaps I have been blind to what the others are doing. Send word to your homeland, bring your men here.'

'As you wish, wise king,' Hengist said, and smiled. And from his wolf smile and that of Horsa, Octa knew that King Vortigern had fallen into the brothers' trap.

21

Anger coursed through his veins as Prince Vortimer rode over the bridge that connected Ruym Island to the mainland, with Cadoc and Grifud by his sides, as well as ten of the best warriors in Cair Urnahc. As soon as his father had told him to leave the hall, Vortimer had left the island. He'd had enough of the stinking heathens and their smug smiles as they looked down on him.

He kicked the flanks of his horse, urging the beast to go even faster in his desperation to get away from the Jutes and his father. The wind rushed past his face, making his eyes water, but Vortimer ignored all of that, even the dark clouds that promised more rain. All he wanted to do was scream. He could not understand why his father was too blind to see the danger the Jutes posed, but Vortimer knew who to blame for that. Brigid, that half-breed bitch who had whispered things in his father's ears. She had convinced him to join the Jutes. He was certain of it. The only thing he didn't understand was why. What did she hope to gain from that?

'Do we return to Cair Urnahc?' Cadoc asked, his words hard to hear, and Vortimer pulled his horse to a stop along the Roman road so that Cadoc could repeat the question. His horse protested at the sudden stop, but Vortimer ignored it.

Vortimer scowled as he looked back along the Roman road and saw the island in the distance, and he wished he could wipe out the Jutes who now called Ruym Island their home. But he couldn't. Not until he got his hands on the spear. And Vortimer was certain the gold-rimmed spear he had seen in the Jutes' main hall was the spear he was after. Badulf might have tried to be clever by not telling him what the spear looked like, but that spear looked like it belonged to a god. A powerful god. And the shrine underneath the spear only convinced him more that that was the spear he was after. Vortimer shuddered, though, when he remembered the shrine, with the skulls and the small wooden statue. Only heathens would do something as vile as that.

Badulf was still on the island, left behind to retrieve the spear, and what frustrated Vortimer the most was that all he could do now was pray the bastard didn't fail or betray him. That was one reason he didn't want to return to Cair Urnahc. It was too far away, and he wanted to be nearby for when Badulf got the spear. The other reason was that he didn't want to face his father, not with the rage still coursing through him. 'We go to Cair Lundein.'

'Cair Lundein?' Cadoc repeated. 'You want to be nearby when Badulf gets the spear?'

Vortimer nodded, not surprised that Cadoc understood. 'And I want to talk to King Gwyrangon.'

'King Gwyrangon?' Cadoc asked, and rubbed his horse's neck.

Vortimer took a breath to calm himself down. 'It's time we rid ourselves of these Jutes before they get too strong.'

'Do you really think King Gwyrangon will help with that? It means going against your father,' Grifud said as the warriors with them hung back so they couldn't overhear the conversation.

Vortimer gritted his teeth and felt his temples throb. 'By God! I can't believe my father is foolish enough to trust the heathens over his own son. Can he not see how dangerous they are?' Vortimer had done his best to disrupt the meeting with the Jutes. He had tried to provoke them so that they attacked him, hoping that would encourage the kings of Britannia to unite and drive them from Britannia. Instead, it had the opposite effect. Vortimer knew, though, why his father sided with the Jutes. He wanted to protect himself because he must have known that many of the other kings were against his deal with the warlords. He was becoming weak, blind, and the other kings saw that. Vortimer saw that as well, and he knew his father was trying to protect his crown and power. But power, like the seasons, never lasted.

'Do you really think King Gwyrangon will attack them?' Cadoc asked the same question as Grifud.

Vortimer glanced at his friends and then back at the island. 'We need to make sure he does.'

'What about the spear?' Grifud asked.

Vortimer frowned. He needed the spear, but he worried that if they took too long, then the Jutish army might grow too large for them to fight. 'Grifud, take four of the men and keep an eye on the island. Wait for Badulf to return. Let's hope he is as good as he believes he is.'

'How long do we wait for?' Grifud asked, and Vortimer shrugged.

'A few days. If he hasn't returned with the spear, then he's probably dead.'

'And if he retrieves the spear?'

Vortimer looked at his friend. 'Then you kill him and bring the spear to me.' With that, Vortimer turned his horse towards Cair Lundein as Cadoc and the remaining six warriors followed.

They reached Cair Lundein just as the rain started and Vortimer cursed the old gods of Britannia, certain that they were the ones who always made it rain. Vortimer rode through the gates and into the city of Cair Lundein, barely acknowledging the warriors who guarded the gates or the people they knocked over.

He did not like Cair Lundein and rarely came here. The old Roman part, which stood empty, made him feel uncomfortable. It was like he could feel the eyes of those who had died in the city on him. And the part of the city where the people lived was too crowded and stank. The rain did not help either and by the time he reached King Gwyrangon's hall, he was soaked to his skin.

The doors to the hall were closed because King Gwyrangon was not in the city, which made Vortimer curse again, especially when the warriors guarding it refused to open them for him.

'Do you know who this is?' Cadoc asked the old warrior, who only shrugged. 'This is Prince Vortimer, son of the high king of Britannia.'

The old warrior glanced at his companion before he turned his attention back to Vortimer. 'Aye, his father might be the high king, but my king has ordered me not to open the hall until he returns.'

'My father rules over your king!' Vortimer said, unable to control his anger.

'Only God rules over my king.' The old warrior stared back at him and Vortimer swore to have the man flogged. 'But I will send word to Cunittus. He is in charge while King Gwyrangon is out.'

'You do that,' Cadoc said before he tried to calm Vortimer down.

'I am not a child!' Vortimer berated his friend before he cursed the rain again that lashed down on him.

Cunittus took his time reaching the hall and, when he did, his bloodshot eyes widened and he turned to the warriors guarding the doors. 'Open the doors, you fools!'

The warriors glanced at each other and then shrugged.

'It's on your head, Cunittus,' the old warrior said as they pushed the doors open.

'I want this man flogged,' Vortimer said as he walked into the hall and shivered because of the cold from his wet clothes. He was glad to see that the hearth fire was going.

Cunittus lowered his head. 'My prince, he only did what he was told by our king.'

Vortimer glared at the man. 'I don't care. He insulted my honour. I want him flogged. And bring me wine!' he ordered Cunittus as he left the hall while Vortimer stood by the hearth fire to dry his clothes. 'Bloody rain!' He looked at his leather boots. 'New boots as well. Ruined! It's no wonder the Romans left. They were probably fed up with the rain!' Cadoc smiled as he joined Vortimer by the fire, even though he had said that many times before.

It didn't take long for a servant to bring cups of wine, and Vortimer savoured the taste of it before he finished his cup and ordered the servant to bring him more. He might not have liked Cair Lundein, but King Gwyrangon had the best wine in all of Britannia. Vortimer knew he bought all the best stuff from the merchants who came from the continent.

'Welcome to my hall, Prince Vortimer,' King Gwyrangon said as he walked in not long after, his scowling face showing his displeasure. 'Please, by God's grace, make yourself at home and have my men flogged.'

'He was disrespectful,' Vortimer said without looking at the king of the Cantiaci.

'That is why he guards the hall when I leave, so that I don't have to deal with him. But he is still my man, and this is my city. I don't care who your father is, you have no authority in my city or over the Cantiaci.'

Vortimer looked at King Gwyrangon as the king took a cup of wine from the servant girl and sat down on his raised seat, not bothered by his wet clothes. He clenched his fists, but then took a deep breath to calm his anger. He needed the man to help him fight the Jutes. King Gwyrangon had at one point been his father's strongest ally, but the man was angry that his father had allowed the Jutes to take land from his people and did not allow him to do anything about it. Trade in Cair Lundein might have been flourishing, but a king's pride is everything, and King Gwyrangon's pride had been hurt. 'Your attacks on the Jutes have not had the desired effect.'

King Gwyrangon drank his wine before he responded. 'I told you it wouldn't drive them off. They are a hardy people used to war. Attacking their hunting and foraging parties only makes them more determined to stay.'

Vortimer, his clothes dryer now, walked to a bench near King Gwyrangon and sat down. He wondered if the king had sent men to deal with the heads left behind on the riverbank by the Jutes, but doubted it. 'We need to do more to get rid of them.'

King Gwyrangon raised an eyebrow at him. 'We? It's my men who attack their hunters. My men who risk their lives sneaking onto Ruym Island to burn their tents and supplies. And some of those men never returned. And for what? They've not attacked or left like you said they would.'

Vortimer nodded as he tried to calm himself. He did not like being spoken to like that, but only because nobody ever did. But King Gwyrangon was a king, and he was only a prince, and for now he would ignore the man's tone because he needed him. 'I admit, they are more stubborn than I thought they were.' They sat in silence for a few heartbeats, staring at each other as servant girls kept the hearth fire going and refilled the cups of Gwyrangon's warriors. Cadoc was sitting with the Cornovii warriors at the far end of the hall, while outside the city bustled. Vortimer heard the voices of the people drift into the hall and was annoyed by how happy they sounded. 'My father trusts the Jutes more than us. He believes they are more capable than our own warriors. I believe it's time we show him and the heathens how wrong they are.'

King Gwyrangon leaned forward, his face darkening because Vortimer was certain he knew what that meant. 'What are you saying?'

Vortimer shrugged. He did not want to give too much away, or even say the words that needed to be said. Not until he had the spear. 'How long before you think more ships arrive, with more men to fight for Hengist and Horsa? More warriors who will one day turn their weapons against us.'

The king of the Cantiaci drummed his fingers on his knee as he glared at Vortimer. 'And where will these men stay? The ones you seem to believe are coming.'

'On Ruym Island, I'd say, with the rest of the Jutes.' Vortimer took a sip of his wine. 'But whether the island will be large enough for them all is hard to say.'

'What are you saying?'

Vortimer stared at the flames of the hearth fire, for a moment transfixed by the way they moved and the destruction they promised. 'I'm saying, King Gwyrangon, that we need to get rid of those heathens before they can bring more men from their homeland.'

'Get rid of them?' Gwyrangon scowled at him. 'Fight them, you mean, even though your father, the high king, has employed them to defend us?'

Vortimer waved a hand at King Gwyrangon. 'My father was a fool for doing that. Those brothers are wolves. You can see the hunger in their eyes. Hunger for our lands and our women. You, more than any of us, must see that. They took some of your land for themselves. They marry your women and get them pregnant. And which god do you think those children will follow? Christ? Already symbols of their gods are all over the small island.' King Gwyrangon stared at Vortimer as he spoke. 'And when their numbers grow too large for the small island, where are they going to go? Whose lands are they going to take first? It won't be the lands of the Cornovii, the Trinovantes or the Iceni. It will be the lands of the Cantiaci. Lands your father and his father fought hard for.'

King Gwyrangon jumped to his feet, his face red. 'Don't you think I know that? By God, every day I hear stories from across my kingdom of how the Jutes take more for themselves! How the names of their gods get whispered by young Cantiaci warriors who want to be as strong as those heathens! I trusted your father! And how did he repay me? By giving my land to those heathens from the continent!'

'And that is why we must act now, before they bring more warriors in.' Vortimer got to his feet and took a step towards King Gwyrangon. 'There are many others who don't like that my father employed the Jutes. Many of the Cornovii as well are unhappy. King Gwyrangon, muster your men, arm them and prepare them. I will bring what men I can from my lands, as well as those from other kingdoms. Together, we will have enough men to drive those heathen Jutes from Britannia.'

King Gwyrangon stared at him, his cheeks puffed as he huffed. 'And what of your father? He will not be pleased by this.'

Vortimer thought of the spear he had seen in the hall of the Jutes. The gold-rimmed spearhead and the golden ring in the shaft. A spear that belonged to a one-eyed god. That was what the beggar had told him and that was what he was certain that spear was. Badulf had told him that was the reason the brothers had sent men north to the wall. To find that spear. The spear that would help him punish his enemies and become the mightiest king in Britannia. 'My father is old, and it is not just his eyes that are losing sight. He should have seen the brothers for what they were.' *He should have seen Brigid for what she is*, he thought. 'It's time for a new king of the Cornovii.'

22

Badulf's hands trembled as he hid behind a house and stared at the main hall. King Vortigern had left that morning and all those who came with him had followed, so the town was quiet and the Jutes relaxed. Which was why Badulf had decided that tonight he would steal the spear. He didn't want to do it while the king was still there. The Jutes had been more alert and Badulf didn't want to think of the consequences if they had found out the spear was missing while the high king of Britannia was still there.

Badulf did not know the name of the town on Ruym Island, not that it mattered because he was sure the Jutes had given it a new name in their tongue. Already he had seen how the Jutes had changed it. And not just the wall they had built around the town, but in the carvings of their gods and letters on some houses.

Badulf had left Cair Urnahc the day before King Vortigern and when he reached the island he joined the Cantiaci nobles, who barely noticed him because of the fine tunic Prince Vortimer had given him, as they camped near the island and waited for King Vortigern to arrive. To them, he was just another noble trying to find favour with the kings of Britannia so no one paid any attention to him.

When King Vortigern arrived, Badulf kept his head low and followed the entourage as they crossed the bridge on to Ruym Island. Once on the island, all he had to do was find a place to hide, something he was good at because, as a young boy, before he outgrew everyone, he was often picked on because of his sister. Even then, people had known she was different and when she was sent away, many of the boys in Cair Urnahc had picked on him. So he had spent a lot of time hiding from them. That had all changed, though, as he became a man. Where the others had stopped growing, he didn't and soon, like a mighty oak tree, he outgrew all of them and suddenly everyone wanted to be his friend.

Badulf smiled at the memory, but that smile disappeared when he saw a large Jute walking with one of the British women. The look on her face showed her attraction to the man, even though they seemed to struggle to communicate. But Badulf doubted that mattered to the Jute. All he wanted was to conquer the woman like they had conquered the island. And it grated on him that it was not the first time he had seen that in the two days he had been on Ruym Island. Many of the women seemed to carry the children of the Jutes, but what irritated him more was that the British men, instead of fighting the invaders, spent their days running errands and doing all the work around the town while the Jutes walked around and laughed or sat and drank ale. Some would guard the walls, and others had spent the day training, but the Jutes had become the masters and the Britons the servants. It was another reason Badulf had to do what he could to stop the Jutes. He refused to be a servant to another man other than his king. And that his king was treating the Jutes as brothers angered him.

Somewhere nearby, Badulf heard men laugh, and he pressed himself into the shadows as two warriors walked past, too busy talking to notice him. Again, Badulf was surprised by how relaxed the Jutes were. It was like they didn't fear an attack from the Britons. He watched as the warriors replaced the ones who were guarding the main hall. Cadoc had told him about the spear in the hall that looked like it belonged to a god and, when he described the spear to Badulf, his heart had raced as it matched the description Bellicus had given him. All he needed to do now was find a way into the hall without being noticed and steal the spear. Then he would go to Cair Urnahc and he and Brigid could travel north. Badulf still would have preferred to destroy the spear, but his sister wanted to give it to the wise one, if they ever found her. Badulf would use that time to convince her that the spear needed to be destroyed.

Badulf glanced at the house he had seen Octa go into and gritted his teeth as he thought about sneaking into the building and killing Octa. But then Badulf remembered the older warrior who had followed Octa into the house. The warrior watched his surroundings like a threatened wolf and always stayed close to Octa, so Badulf decided it was best to avoid them. Octa he knew he could kill, but he wasn't sure about the warrior. And besides, he was here for the spear, not Octa.

Badulf turned his attention back to the hall, not once wondering why Octa didn't have the spear if the gods of Britannia were afraid of him. Perhaps it was because the Octa he had seen the previous summer had been a coward. Badulf was surprised to see Octa on the island, though. He thought Octa had stayed in the north with the old Saxons. That he would have been too afraid to return to Ruym Island, but then Badulf frowned as another thought came to him. He had not seen Eadric, the Jute who had led the party north, once since he arrived, and he knew the man had been close to Hengist and Horsa. Just like he knew Eadric had been the man who had brought the spear south. He felt like he was missing something, but then reminded himself why he was there as he turned his attention back to the main hall.

Badulf knew he would never be able to just walk in, so he needed to think. Luckily, the gods were with him, or perhaps the Christian god. He wasn't really sure any more, because with all the Britons in the town, he had walked around unnoticed and studied the hall. Again, no one paid any attention to him other than a few curious glances, and because Octa was in the hall, he didn't have to worry about being recognised. That was when he had seen a spot on the roof where the thatch had come loose and knew he could use that to sneak into the hall.

Badulf looked at the sky and thanked god and the gods that it was cloudy and the moon was hidden. That made it easier for him to sneak around the houses until he reached the back of the hall. Once there, he waited a short while just to make sure that there weren't any warriors on patrol and for the clouds, which had parted, to cover the moon again. The town was quiet as most of the villagers were sleeping, apart from the warriors on guard, who seemed too relaxed to be effective, but Badulf still didn't want to take any chances of being spotted.

He didn't have long to wait for the clouds to cover the moon again and took a deep breath before he walked towards the hall. With one quick glance around, Badulf used his strong fingers to climb onto the thatch roof of the hall.

Badulf used his knife to pull the thatch loose and make a hole large enough for him to sneak through. He took great care to move slowly and to make sure that none of the thatch fell onto the ground. The last thing he wanted was to be caught because he was careless. Badulf had heard stories of how cruel the Jutes could be and did not want to die by having his stomach cut open and being hanged by his insides. He wasn't sure if they really did that or if those were just stories to scare them, but he didn't want to find out.

Once he was finished with the hole, Badulf prayed to whichever god was listening and snuck through. He bit the inside of his cheek as the thatch grazed and cut his skin, but soon he was through and standing on the beam which supported the roof. Badulf pulled a piece of straw out of his arm as he studied the hall. There was barely any light as the hearth fire was nothing but embers and it took many heartbeats for his eyes to adjust to the darkness inside.

Three people were sleeping by the hearth fire, and Badulf guessed they were women or children from their smaller frames. Perhaps servants who would need to get the fire going again in the morning. Warriors slept on the benches by the walls, their snores making Badulf feel confident that he had woken none of them. He wondered where the brothers were as an idea came to him, but then he shook it from his mind. He might kill one of them in their sleep, but he wasn't sure if he could kill both of them. And besides, that wouldn't matter once he got the spear, because without it, they couldn't bring fire to the lands and kill the Britons.

Deciding he'd waited long enough, Badulf shimmied down the wall and hid in the corner of the hall as he tried to work out where the spear would be. The corner of his eyes glimpsed light, and when he turned to the side, he gaped at the spear, which was like a beacon in the darkness. The gold around the spearhead shone as bright as the stars on a clear night and Badulf, almost too scared to be so near the spear, took a step back and bumped into a table. He covered his mouth to stop himself from crying out and waited for a few heartbeats to make sure that he had not woken any of the warriors or the servants. But no one stirred and Badulf released the breath he had been holding.

He reached out for the spear with a trembling hand when the door of the hall opened. Badulf dropped to the floor as one of the warriors from outside stood in the door and scanned the inside of the hall.

'Nothing,' Badulf heard him say to the other man outside. 'You're just hearing things.' The man closed the door and Badulf sighed with relief as he got to his feet. He shook his hands to calm his nerves and reached out for the spear one more time. As his fingers wrapped around the shaft of the spear, Badulf held his breath and closed his eyes. He felt his hand grip the cold, thick gold band around the shaft, which sent a shiver down his spine and brought a smile to his lips as he opened his eyes.

'The spear of the gods,' he whispered to himself as he gripped it. *The Jutes' days are numbered*, he thought. Soon, they would be driven from Britannia, and the gods would reward him. The fire that would end life on the island would not come and life would continue as it always did.

Badulf looked around and cursed as he realised he could not sneak out the way he had come in. The only way out of the hall was through the door. He looked around and, for a moment, he thought of using the spear to kill the sleeping Jutes inside the hall, but then dismissed the idea as soon as it came to him. If one of them woke up and screamed, then he'd be dead and Britannia would belong to the Jutes and their gods.

Gripping the spear tightly, he crept towards the door, pausing often to make sure he hadn't disturbed anyone. When he reached the door, he took his knife in his left hand and held the spear in his right. There had only been two men guarding the door earlier on and he prayed that was still the same, because Badulf knew he only had one chance to escape this place.

With one last prayer and a deep breath, he pushed the door open. The two Jutes were slow to turn, perhaps thinking it was one of their own who had come out for a piss, and Badulf used that to his advantage as he drove the spear into the back of one of the Jutes. As the man arched backwards, Badulf turned and stabbed the other in the neck with his knife. Badulf pulled the spear free as the blood of the second Jute sprayed over him and he ran from the hall as fast as he could, smiling as he believed he would escape without being spotted.

23

Badulf kept his head low as he ran, his heart racing in his chest. He was halfway to the gate when a horn blew and he knew the men he had killed had been found. But he didn't care. With the spear in his hand, the spear that belonged to their war god, he felt like he could kill them all. And it took all of his self-control not to turn around and to challenge the Jutes to a fight.

As he ran, he felt the urge to glance over his shoulder and, when he did, his heart skipped when he saw Octa standing outside the house, his arm pulled back as he aimed his spear at Badulf. But then he frowned and shook his head, and before Badulf understood what was happening, Octa lowered his spear.

Badulf turned by one house, knowing he would not be able to get out of the gate. Especially not now. He had not really thought about how he was going to get out of the town. Perhaps he had hoped he could just walk out of the gates, but that would mean hiding until daybreak and then hoping that they wouldn't notice that the spear was missing. That was not an option any more, and he would have cursed himself for killing the men outside the hall, but that had been his only way out. Hiding in the hall with all the sleeping warriors did not seem like a great idea.

He hid behind a house near the wall the Jutes had built, panting as he tried to catch his breath. The bloodlust had worn off now and his legs felt weak, but Badulf knew the night would be long. He strained his ears as he tried to listen out for pursuers, but all he heard were shouts of confusion. And over those shouts, he heard the waves as they lapped on the beach. A smile came to his lips. The gods were with him after all because, unknowingly, he had run towards the only part of the wall he could get through. The path that led to the wharves near the town. It seemed the Jutes never closed that gate and, while the men from the continent were still trying to understand what had happened, he ran towards the sea.

Another sign that the gods wanted this was that the tide was in and Badulf thanked them because he was a good swimmer. But before he got to the water, he heard Octa's voice behind him.

'Badulf, stop!'

At first, Badulf thought of ignoring the coward, but then he wanted to see the shock on his face when Octa saw he had the spear of his god. The spear Octa had believed would redeem him. He turned around and held the spear with the golden-rimmed spearhead in front of him. Close up and in the darkness, Octa seemed different from the last time Badulf had seen him. The fear that had been in his eyes was gone, replaced by a look of uncertainty, but what annoyed Badulf was that the shock he had hoped to see wasn't there. Just a look of regret.

'You can't stop me, Octa,' Badulf said as he tightened his grip on the spear. He saw Octa glance at the blood on the spearhead and shake his head. 'I can't let you.'

'I thought you were dead,' Octa said. 'If I knew you were still alive, I would have searched for you.'

Badulf wanted to laugh at Octa's fake sympathy. 'You never cared about me. All you wanted was the spear of your god! And now I have it!'

Octa looked at the spear again as he lowered his own spear and Badulf struggled to understand why, especially by the way Octa looked at the spear in his hands. 'You didn't believe in the spear.'

'I didn't believe in a lot of things, but my eyes have been opened. Now I know you and your people are not here to help us, but to conquer us!'

Octa shook his head. 'I am not here to conquer. I only came for the spear.'

'And yet, you don't have it. Why?' Badulf tilted his head. 'I heard the old Saxons found you injured in the forest. That they healed you and yet here you are. Fighting for the brothers who have the spear you wanted so desperately.' Badulf tightened his grip on the spear, his eyes darting towards the town. Perhaps the gods were giving him the chance to kill the man they feared. But why they were afraid of Octa, Badulf could not understand.

'I am not your enemy, Badulf.' Octa took a step towards him, but Badulf noticed how the spear trembled in his hand. 'In the north, I saw how our people can live together. Saxons and Britons sharing the land in peace.'

Badulf shook his head. 'You are my enemy and the enemy of my people.'

Octa stared at him, but Badulf struggled to see the look on his face as a cloud briefly covered the moon. 'You want to kill me?'

Badulf felt his own limbs tremble with rage. 'I want to protect my sister and my home.'

Octa sighed and seemed to look at the sea behind him. 'And I want to find a new home for my people who are being driven from theirs.'

'Then we are enemies.' Badulf prepared himself to attack, but then Octa tilted his head as if someone spoke to him.

With a deep sigh, Octa said, 'That spear will not give you what you want, Badulf.'

Badulf glanced at the spear in his hands as he tightened his grip around its shaft. 'This spear will stop the fire that will destroy our way of life.'

Octa took a step closer. 'Our people can live together as one. I saw that in the north. You must have seen it too.'

'Stop talking!' Badulf shouted, tired of Octa's words and angry that he didn't see the fear he expected to see. 'I will not let you stop me!'

Octa frowned and for a heartbeat it looked like he was trying to work something out, before he said, 'Then go.'

Badulf's eyes widened. 'You're not going to try to stop me, then?'

To his surprise, Octa shook his head. 'That was not why I came here.' And with that, he turned and walked back to the village.

Badulf was too confused to even think of rushing at Octa and sticking the spear in his back. But then he heard the horns from the village again and before he ran towards the sea and plunged into the water, he shouted, 'You're a coward, Octa!'

* * *

Octa watched as Badulf jumped into the water and swam away, his hands trembling as he wondered if he had done the right thing. But Octa could not kill Badulf. He didn't understand it, but as he faced Badulf on the beach, he got a feeling that the gods did not want him to kill the Briton.

'Why did you let him go?' Odalric asked, and Octa shrugged, not wanting to tell Odalric the truth. 'The brothers won't be pleased about that. He killed two of their men.'

'I know,' Octa said. Like everyone else, he had been woken up by the horn from a dreamless sleep. He had jumped out of his bed and pulled his trousers on while Lucilia hid under the furs, before he grabbed Gungnir and ran out of the house. That was when Octa had seen Badulf.

At first, he just saw a figure running away from the hall with the golden spear in his hands. Octa pulled his arm back, trusting that the spear would find its mark. That was when a voice whispered in his ear.

Don't. Unlike before, it wasn't Friga's voice, but a man's, and he wondered if that had not been Woden. But as he had tried to make sense of the voice, the man looked at him and Octa recognised him. His heart had skipped a beat, and he thought of the last time he had seen Badulf. Racing away from the ambush by the wall in the north. Before Eadric had thrown the spear at him.

Octa didn't know what had made him go to the wharves when all the others ran around the houses to search for Badulf. But as he had stood there, facing Badulf, he knew he could not kill him.

'He thinks he has Gungnir,' Octa said.

Octa felt Odalric stare at him. 'And why does he want Gungnir?'

Octa rubbed the shaft of the real Gungnir. 'He said something about stopping a fire.'

'Stopping a fire?' Odalric raised an eyebrow at him and Octa nodded, even if he didn't understand it either.

Octa looked back at the water, but couldn't see Badulf any more as he wondered what had happened to the man in the north.

'We should go back,' Odalric said, and again Octa nodded as he turned and followed the older Saxon back to the hall.

'Did you find him?' Berthild asked as they got to the square in front of the hall. Octa shook his head, not wanting to tell his mother that he had let Badulf go. She would be disappointed in him and he had already disappointed her enough. Besides, she wouldn't understand why he had done that, because Octa didn't understand either.

Hengist and Horsa were in front of the hall, their faces as dark as the night sky, while Oisc's head poked out from inside. Hengist stood as still as a stone carving, his arms crossed across his chest as he stared at the bodies of his men killed by Badulf while Horsa paced up and down, shouting orders and calling for war.

But what worried Octa was the three servant girls who were on their knees, their faces bloodied as they cried. And behind them stood three warriors with their swords in their hands.

'These Britons helped that bastard sneak into our hall to kill us!' Horsa was shouting, and some men jeered as the Britons of the island stood in stunned silence.

'Sister!' Lucilia screamed from behind, and Octa turned in time to see her running out of the house. Odalric grabbed her and lifted her up as Octa turned his attention to the three women and realised that one of them was her sister. His heart raced as he knew he needed to stop what was happening, but the anger on Horsa's face made him hesitate.

'We treat you well,' Horsa said as he glared at the Britons. 'We make sure you have plenty of food and homes to sleep in. We protect you from pirates and the Picts and this is how you thank us!' Horsa turned his attention back to the three women on their knees, their heads lowered as they cried. 'These women will pay the price for their betrayal and the rest of you consider this a warning. Betray us again and we will kill you all.' He raised his hand, and the three warriors behind the women raised their swords. Behind Octa, Lucilia screamed, begging him to stop this, as Odalric struggled to hold her.

Octa glanced at Hengist, who stayed silent as he stared at the men who had been killed. And at that moment, Octa felt the familiar presence of Friga, but what confused him was how his mother tensed beside him, as if she also sensed the presence of the mother goddess. Before Octa could make sense of it, his mother stepped forward.

'Stop!' Even though she was dressed in her sleeping gown and her hair was loose, she still had a sense of authority which made even Horsa hesitate as Hengist looked up from the bodies of his men.

'You dare tell me what to do?' Horsa rushed towards Berthild. Before Octa could react, Odalric dropped Lucilia and stepped in front of his mother. His fists clenched, he glared at the Jutish warlord who looked like he was ready to kill Odalric.

Octa's mother put a hand on Odalric's shoulder and he stepped aside so she could face Horsa. 'I only ask that you think.' Berthild looked past Horsa at Hengist. 'You say the man wanted to kill you? Then why didn't he? Why did he sneak into the hall only to kill the two men outside?'

Hengist frowned at Octa's mother as Horsa responded, 'Because there were warriors inside the hall. They scared him off.'

Berthild raised an eyebrow at Horsa. 'And not a single one of those warriors spotted the man or raised the alarm? And yet you want to punish those women when it was your warriors who failed you?' The warriors who had slept in the hall glared at Octa's mother and he prayed they would not hold a grudge against her for her words, even if she was right.

Horsa clenched his jaw and Octa sensed Odalric tense beside her, when he heard Friga's voice again.

What will you do to protect your family? Will you kill him?

Octa looked at the three women, their faces bloodied and bruised, and then at Horsa, who looked like he was about to attack his mother. Would he kill him to protect his mother? Octa wondered to himself and knew the answer was yes, as Hengist said, 'Lady Berthild is right. If we punish these women, then we have to punish the men who were supposed to protect us.'

'But they did protect us!' Horsa said, his face turning red. Octa sensed this had nothing to do with punishment. Horsa was angry and wanted to take that anger out on someone. He glanced at Lucilia, who was on her knees, her eyes red with tears as she stared at her sister, and then at his mother, who stared defiantly at Horsa.

What will you do? The words came again.

With a deep breath, Octa stepped between Horsa and his mother. 'The Briton that killed your men did not come for you.'

Horsa glared at him, and Octa saw the vein throbbing on his forehead. 'Then why did he come?'

'He came for Gungnir.'

Horsa glanced at the spear in Octa's hand and leaned forward. 'How do you know that?'

Octa steeled his nerves. 'Because I saw him flee with the spear in his hand and let him escape.'

Thunder struck in Octa's skull as Horsa punched him. He knew the punch was coming as soon as he said the words, but he did nothing to stop it. Not that there was much he could do. Horsa reacted faster than Octa had expected and, as he hit the ground, he raised a hand to stop Odalric from doing anything because he knew his father's warrior was just looking for a reason to fight Horsa. Odalric didn't like the Jute, but Octa knew that if he struck the warlord, then his life would be over. He had seen how ruthless the brothers could be.

Octa wiped the blood from his busted lip and glanced at Hengist as he got to his feet again.

'Stay down,' Horsa hissed at him as the spear vibrated in his hand. 'Before I kill you.' Odalric tensed beside Octa and he could almost feel the anger coming off the older warrior, but again, he raised his hand to stop Odalric.

What will you do? The voice came to him again, and Octa took a breath as he stared into the angry face of Horsa. All he had to do was use the spear, which was still in his hand. Kill Horsa and then throw the spear at Hengist. With both brothers dead, he could lead the Jutes and avoid a war. Octa wasn't sure where these dark thoughts came from and glanced at the spear as he pushed them from his mind. He did not want to kill anyone, and he knew the Jutes would never accept him if he killed the brothers. Instead, he gave the spear to Odalric, who gaped at him.

'Octa, what are you doing?'

Octa ignored the warrior as he stared at Horsa. 'There is more happening here than what we understand.'

Horsa punched him again, and as Octa hit the ground, he kicked him in the stomach. Octa's mother held Odalric back, perhaps sensing the same thing that Octa had, or perhaps she wanted to see what her son was made of. 'I will kill all of you treacherous Saxons!' Horsa screamed as he kept kicking Octa in the stomach, although Octa barely heard the words over the blood pumping in his ears as he curled into a ball to protect himself. Fear coursed through him, and all he could do was pray that Horsa didn't kill him.

24

A mother knows when to stand back and when to interfere. The words came to Berthild as if the woman from the tavern was standing behind her. And perhaps she was, because Berthild was certain she could feel her presence as she watched Horsa kicking her son. Octa lay there, his eyes screwed shut as he curled into a ball. It reminded her of the night he had come to Frithowald's hall. He looked broken, lost, and it had torn at her heart to see him like that. Yet she did not feel the same now. Her hand went to her chest when she realised she was oddly proud of her son. He had stood his ground and had faced Horsa even after admitting he had let the Briton go. She might not have understood why, but she had to trust that Octa had his reasons.

Beside Berthild, Odalric bristled, and she knew that if she didn't act then the warrior would kill Horsa, who was still raging that he couldn't trust the Saxons.

'Enough!' Berthild stepped forward and glared at Horsa, who towered over her as he stopped kicking Octa. Octa coughed as he tried to catch his breath, but she kept her eyes fixed on Horsa. Her heart was racing in her chest, but she was the daughter and wife of Saxon warlords and she had never feared them, so she refused to be afraid of Horsa. 'How will you live with the Britons if you can't even live with us few Saxons?' Berthild looked at Hengist and then the three women, on their knees and crying. The blood on their faces angered her and the wailing of Lucilia broke her heart. 'We are only a handful of Saxons, so we can't harm you, but if you treat the Britons like this, how long before you unite them against you?'

'The Britons hate each other more than they hate us. They will never unite,' Horsa said.

Berthild stared at him for a while, surprised the man could not see what was already happening. Only a couple of days ago, the son of King Vortigern had been trying to sow dissent between the Britons and the Jutes. 'We Saxons don't have a king like you Jutes. Warlords rule over their families and lands.' She looked at Hengist again. 'For most of the time, the warlords will battle each other as they try to grow their power, and many Saxon men have died for the power lust of their warlords. But when we are threatened by an outsider, we unite as one people. We vote for a chief warlord who leads us in battle against our enemy. My father was once such a man and he sent our enemies fleeing with their tails between their legs.'

Horsa stepped over her son so that he stood right in front of her. 'And yet, your lands are now being overrun by the Thuringians and your people do nothing.'

Berthild's nose wrinkled at the smell of sweat and ale coming from the man, as well as the stench of anger, but she refused to cower in front of him. She needed to be strong. For herself and her son, and the three women whose lives depended on her words. 'Our lands are overrun because we chose the wrong man to lead us.' Berthild was still angry at her dead husband for the role he played in that and for what had happened to Octa afterwards. 'But the gods know you should not underestimate our strength and you should know not to underestimate the strength of the Britons because then they will crush you.'

Horsa raised his hand to strike her and Berthild could only pray that Odalric did not skewer the man with Octa's spear.

'No, Horsa, enough,' Hengist said, and Horsa hesitated. Berthild wanted to smile at that because again it showed that the older brother was the real leader here. 'You got to take your anger out on someone. Now it's time for calm.'

Horsa turned to face his brother. 'Octa let the Briton escape! He betrayed us like I said he would!'

Hengist looked at Berthild's son, who was still on the ground, his face stern. 'Aye, and I'm sure Octa has a reason for that. But there has been enough violence for one night.'

'You are blinded by the fact that he saved your son!' Horsa said as he glared at his brother. 'Will you wait until he sticks a knife in your back before you see him for what he really is?'

'And what is he?' Berthild asked as her own anger took hold of her. She was tired of men deciding who Octa was. 'Tell me what my son is.'

Horsa stared at her. His nostrils flared as Octa wiped the blood from his mouth and struggled to his feet. 'Your son is weak. A coward and a traitor.'

'My son did what no one else could. He found the spear of Woden and used it to kill one of your best men.' Berthild turned her attention to Hengist. 'If you really are as wise as you want others to think, then you will understand that my son was not the only one who let the Briton escape.' Horsa raised an eyebrow at her and Berthild looked at the men who had slept in the hall. She saw how they glared at her, but she was not afraid of the men who were willing to let women die to protect themselves. Because to her, they were the real cowards. 'You have all these warriors and not a single one of them found or stopped this Briton.' She looked at Hengist. 'Not a single one of them saw him sneak into your hall and now you want to punish my son for their mistakes?' She pointed at the women on their knees. 'You will kill them when your men failed you?'

Berthild thought she saw a small smile in Hengist's beard as he walked towards them. All around, the Jutes and the Britons, the Angles and Saxons, even the gods, held their breath as Hengist walked past the three British women and stopped beside his brother. Hengist looked at Octa, and Berthild was glad her son stood his ground, even as he seemed to struggle to stand up straight.

'Could you have stopped the Briton?' Hengist asked Octa.

Octa stayed silent for a few heartbeats, and Berthild thought she could see his mind working, as if he was trying to work something out. 'I don't know,' he said after a while. 'I came out of the house and saw him run away from the hall with the golden spear in his hands, but everything happened too fast for me to react.'

Hengist nodded as Horsa shook his head. 'He lies! He has the spear of Woden. All he needed to do was throw it!' Many of the men looked at each other and Hengist put a hand on his brother's shoulder.

'Calm yourself, Horsa,' he said in a quiet voice that only they could hear. 'You sound like a witless fool.'

'He's right,' Octa said, and Berthild almost shook her head as she wondered what her son was doing. 'I could have done, but when I saw who it was and what he had, I froze.'

Everyone, including Berthild, frowned at Octa, not sure what he meant.

'You recognised him?' Hengist asked, and Octa nodded.

'It was Badulf.'

'Who?' Hengist frowned.

'The Briton who spoke our tongue. The one with the Saxon grandfather.'

Berthild glanced at Odalric, who still had Octa's spear, as he shrugged at her. It seemed he didn't know who this man was either, but from the confused looks on the faces of the brothers, they did.

Horsa now frowned at Octa. 'Eadric told us he was dead.'

'Who is this Briton?' Berthild asked.

'He was one of King Vortigern's men,' Octa said as the brothers looked at each other. 'He spoke our language, so the king used him to speak to us. He also guided us north when we looked for the spear.' Octa fell silent for a moment and Berthild guessed he was reliving that day which she knew still haunted him. 'When we were ambushed, Badulf fled and Eadric threw his spear at him. We all thought he was dead.'

'It seems that no one stays dead on Britannia,' Hengist said with a sigh, and then looked around him. 'But this is not a conversation we should hold out here. We go to the hall. Lady Berthild, please join us.'

'Why must she join us?' Horsa asked, and Berthild almost smiled at his anger, but she was glad that Hengist wanted her in the hall as well. It meant he valued her opinion. All Octa had to do now was not say anything dumb.

'Because out of everyone here, she speaks the most sense.'

'And what of the women?' Berthild asked. 'I ask that they be spared.'

Hengist looked at the women, who were all staring at him with pleading eyes. Even Lucilia had stopped crying, as if she understood what was going on.

'Someone needs to be punished for allowing Badulf into our hall,' Horsa said, his face turning red.

'Then punish the men who were supposed to guard your hall,' Berthild said. 'Not three young women whose only crime is that they are British.'

'How did he get into the hall?' Odalric asked, the first words he had spoken since all this began. Everyone looked at him as they seemed to wonder the same. 'There's only one way into your hall.'

Hengist nodded. 'There is. Then it seems the ones responsible have already been punished,' he said as he looked at the dead warriors by the hall. Berthild followed his gaze, but her eyes were not on the bodies. Instead, they were on the young boy in the hall who looked frightened as he stood there and, again, she thought of Octa that night. 'But the men need to see someone punished. So it's them or Octa.'

Berthild's heart raced as she was given the choice. Would she kill three innocent women to save her son? Her brow furrowed as she thought about it. Octa always came first, but as she looked at the three women, she thought of Frithowald's daughters with his other wives. The last time she had seen them, their eyes were filled with tears and fear and Berthild had often wondered if they had made it to the lands of the Franks and if they were safe. She took a deep breath and looked at Hengist. 'Then I ask that you don't kill them, but banish them. That way, you are seen as punishing those you deem responsible and they don't have to die for something they had no part in.'

'How do you know they had no part in this?' Horsa asked.

'How do you know they did?' Berthild retorted, and glared at him.

Hengist put a hand on Horsa's shoulder. 'Lady Berthild is right. We don't know that they let Badulf in. Just as she is right about the Britons. We kill those women and we risk turning the people of Ruym against us.'

'Then we kill them all.' Horsa's face contorted in anger.

'And turn the rest of Britannia against us.' Hengist leaned closer to Horsa, and Berthild only just caught his words. 'We need to be smart, brother. We need the people to support us. To see us as being better than their kings and nobles.'

Horsa stared at his brother before he huffed and walked away without another word, and Berthild sensed she needed to watch him, certain that he was her enemy now.

Hengist turned to his men and said, 'These women and their families will be banished from Ruym Island. At sunrise, they will be escorted off this island and will be left to fend for themselves.'

'Why don't we just kill them?' one warrior asked, and Hengist glared at the man.

'Because I said so and the gods know what will happen to any man who disobeys me.' The warrior nodded and looked away like a scolded child. 'Now, free the women and watch them until they leave.' Hengist then turned to Berthild. 'Don't worry about my brother. He gets his temper from our mother. As dangerous as a lightning storm.'

Berthild nodded. 'The weather always calms after a storm.'

Hengist smiled at her. 'And so will he. Now let's go to the hall so we can make sense of this.'

Berthild glanced at the moon and realised the sun would be up soon, but even though she was tired, she knew she could not think of sleep yet. First, she had to talk to Octa because she was certain there was something he was hiding. Him and Odalric. And then she needed to make sure that her son did not become the scapegoat for this. 'Allow Octa to clean himself and then we will join you in the hall.'

Hengist glanced at her son, his face covered in blood and dirt from the beating Horsa had given him, and nodded. 'So be it.' He turned around and walked back to the hall as Berthild turned to her son.

'Tell your woman that her sister is spared, then go inside and clean yourself up. And then we talk.'

'Mother—'

Berthild raised her hand. 'Don't, Octa.'

Octa looked at her and then at Odalric, who only shrugged as he gave the spear back to her son. 'Yes, Mother,' Octa said, turning to Lucilia and speaking to her in the British tongue. Lucilia jumped to her feet and hugged Berthild, who after a moment's hesitation hugged her back as she wondered if the girl would stay on the island. As Lucilia went to her sister, Berthild saw the woman from the tavern near their house. The woman smiled as she nodded at Berthild, who had the sudden urge to grip the spear pendant she wore around her waist.

25

Octa returned to his sleeping quarters, desperate to collapse on his bed and sleep. His stomach and ribs ached from Horsa's beating and his lip stung from the cut. He looked at his midriff and saw the red marks from where Horsa kicked him and wondered why he had spoken out. It would have been easier just to keep quiet or say that he had not seen anything. But Octa knew he couldn't do that, because if he had kept quiet, then Lucilia's sister, as well as two other innocent women, would have been killed. Although Octa knew he had his mother to thank too for saving them.

Lucilia had gone to her sister and Octa was certain he would never see her again. Octa wasn't sure how he felt about that. He enjoyed their time together, but he didn't feel like she was important to him, and he was certain she felt the same about him. He pushed the thoughts from his mind as he leaned Gungnir against the wall and went to the bowl of water on the table in his sleeping quarters. There wasn't much water in there, but he didn't want to get more, so he scooped what little was left and wiped his face clean. Octa winced as his lips stung and looked at the red water that dripped back into the bowl. His hands trembled as he remembered the fear that had coursed through his veins when Horsa attacked him. There was a moment when he felt like the Jute might kill him and Octa was not ready to die yet. There were still too many things he needed to do.

Still lost in his thoughts, he turned towards his bed and his heart skipped when he saw her sitting there with a smile on her face. She wore a dress that looked like something his mother would wear, but hers shone as if it was made of gold, while gold jewellery covered her neck and hands. Her long hair framed her ageless face while wise eyes scrutinised him.

'Friga.' He gaped at her.

'Octa, son of Frithowald.' She ran her eyes over his torso. 'You did well tonight. You acted like a true leader.'

Octa raised an eyebrow at the mother of the gods, his heart racing as he tried to understand why she was there. 'I am no leader.'

Friga picked at something on her dress. 'No, not yet.'

Octa stood where he was, too afraid to get any closer. 'I let Badulf go when I could have stopped him. Because of me, there will be war.'

Friga stood up and walked towards him, her eyes fixed on Gungnir. 'War is coming regardless of what you do. Even if you killed the Briton, the son of their king would still raise his army.'

Octa stared at Friga. 'I thought you wanted to stop this war? That is why you wanted me to keep the spear.'

Friga smiled. 'Woden believes that war is coming, regardless of what I want or do.'

Octa thought back to when he had spotted Badulf fleeing from the hall, when the voice told him not to throw the spear. 'That was Woden, wasn't it? He told me not to throw the spear?'

Friga shook her head. 'Woden is preoccupied with other things at the moment. He gets like that.' Octa frowned while his heart raced as Friga walked around him. 'I still remember the day Woden got Gungnir. Terrible visions came to me, to him as well. But where they frightened me, they made him smile.'

'Visions of what?' Octa couldn't help but ask as his skin grew cold.

'Chaos, son of Frithowald. Visions of chaos and fire.'

Octa felt the shiver run down his spine as he remembered what Badulf had said to him on the beach and he glanced at the spear leaning against the wall. 'If it wasn't Woden who stopped me from throwing the spear, then who did?'

Friga walked past him towards his bed. Octa couldn't help but look at the way she moved. Graceful, but commanding at the same time, similar to the way his mother moved. 'We are not the only gods around. There are those who once controlled these lands and they are not pleased with our presence.'

'Brigantia?'

Friga shook her head. 'Not her. She sees the truth, but there are others who are blinded by their own greed. They long for the power they once wielded.'

'And they want the spear?'

Friga nodded. 'That was why Brigantia allowed you to take it. She could no longer protect it from them or Woden.'

Octa looked at the scars on his arm as he remembered that day in the cave when the white owl warned him about the spear, before it gave him those scars. He had always thought the owl was Brigantia and often wondered why she never stopped him. 'Why do they want the spear?'

Friga turned, and the seriousness in her eyes sent another shiver down his spine. 'Because they want war and Gungnir will give them the power to kill us.'

Octa wanted to look at the spear as he wondered if that was why Badulf wanted to steal Gungnir, but couldn't take his eyes away from Friga. He had never thought about the spear's true capabilities. 'But they don't have the real spear. The spear Badulf took is fake.'

Friga smiled at him, like a mother at a child who struggled to see what was in front of them. 'Their gods might not, but the people believe they have, and that will give them strength. It will give them the courage to unite against you, which will give their gods the strength to fight us.'

Octa frowned as his heart raced in his chest. 'And yet you tell me I did well?'

Friga smiled. 'You did, Octa, son of Frithowald. You did very well.'

'How?' Octa asked, and then turned when he heard a noise behind him. When he turned to face Friga again, he cursed when he saw she was no longer there. Octa looked at Gungnir and his head ached as he tried to make sense of what the gods were up to. For a moment, he wished he had never found the spear, but then he remembered Reinald's words again. The past was not important. Octa had found the spear and now he needed to understand what role he played in the games of the gods.

'What are you not telling me?' His mother walked in, with Odalric behind her, as Octa stared at the spot where he had last seen the goddess.

Octa turned to his mother and saw the frustration in her eyes. He considered lying to her, but then saw how Odalric shook his head and, with a deep sigh, he said, 'I spoke to him.'

His mother scowled at him. 'Spoke to who?'

'Badulf, the Briton.' Octa rubbed his forehead as he tried to chase the headache away. 'I went to the wharves while the others searched the town. That's when I saw him.'

'And why didn't you kill him?' Berthild's face turned red with anger and Octa almost took a step back. He had never seen his mother like this before and understood why his father had respected her so much. She was as fierce as any warrior he had ever met. For a moment, he wondered if his mother was not the one who should wield Gungnir. But then he thought of her question. The answer was simple, but he doubted she would understand. He didn't even really understand.

'Because I couldn't.'

His mother raised an eyebrow at him. 'You couldn't?'

Octa shook his head.

'Why is this Briton so important? I've worked hard since I arrived to make sure Hengist favours you and sees your value to him and you risk it all for a man you barely know.'

Octa sighed again. He just wanted to be left in peace and rest. He felt like a man who had seen too many winters to count, and his ribs still ached from Horsa's beating. 'It doesn't matter, Mother. He doesn't have the real spear.'

'He came for Woden's spear?' his mother asked, and Octa nodded.

'Badulf told me that he took the spear to stop the fire from ending their way of life.'

The scowl on his mother's face turned to a frown, and then she looked at him. 'What does that mean? What fire?'

Visions of chaos and fire, Friga's words came to him. Octa opened his mouth to respond, but then realised he couldn't tell them that Friga had told him. They would think he had lost his wits. For a moment, he wondered if that was what Brigid had seen when she had touched the spear.

'It doesn't matter, does it?' Odalric said. 'The Briton lost his wits and, as Octa said, he doesn't have the real spear.'

'He believes he does,' Octa said.

'And we don't know what he plans to do with it.' Berthild looked at the older warrior and Octa. After a few heartbeats, Octa's mother shook her head and rubbed her temples. 'That doesn't matter for now. We are in a perilous position. And not just with the Britons and the Jutes.' She looked at Octa, who now saw the tiredness in her eyes. 'Octa, I know you don't want this, but the gods have given you a chance to be the man you are destined to be. To be better than your father and your grandfather. Our people need a home. Countless of them are homeless. They are lost, and they have lost everything, just like we have.'

Octa nodded. He knew that, but he also knew he was not the right person to lead them, even if he had Gungnir. But Octa did not have the strength to argue with his mother. 'So what do we do?'

His mother took a deep breath. 'We go to the hall and see what Hengist has to say, and whatever you do, Octa, do not tell them you spoke to the Briton. We'll keep that between us and the gods. And try not to anger Horsa again. I doubt I'll be able to stop him next time.'

Octa nodded again as Odalric gave him a clean tunic and he winced as he pulled it over his head. He looked at his mother, who seemed to possess far more strength than he had. Even that night after he had fled the battle, she had been strong even as he wept. She had told him to go north and to make a name for himself. It was because of her that he met Woden and found the spear. So he took a deep breath and tried to straighten up, but the pain in his ribs made that difficult. 'I'm ready.'

As they left the house, Octa was surprised to see the orange colour light up the sky as the sun rose. The clouds that had been there before were gone and the early morning calls of the birds were greeted by tired faces and angry warriors. The men who had been killed had been removed and, near the gate, Octa saw Lucilia's family loading carts as they prepared to leave the island. Lucilia stood with them, her cloak wrapped tightly around her as she held her sister.

'It doesn't have to be this way,' Octa said as he stopped and looked at Lucilia.

'The brothers think it does,' his mother said, but Octa heard the sadness in her voice. He knew she had cared for the people of his father's village – of her village – and it must have been hard for her to have left them behind. Perhaps that was why she was so determined to find a new land for the Saxons.

'We can live with the Britons, in peace. As one people.'

His mother looked at Lucilia, who stared back at them, before she turned her attention to him. 'That's not just up to us, my son.'

Octa nodded as Lucilia waved at him. He wanted to go to her, to say farewell, but didn't think that was a good idea. So instead, he waved back and followed his mother and Odalric to the hall.

Inside the hall, the mood was grim. The hall was empty, apart from the brothers and the few warriors they trusted. Men who had fought with them since the beginning. Oisc sat in the corner of the hall, his face breaking into a smile when he saw Octa, and Octa smiled back before he turned his attention to Hengist and Horsa, who were deep in conversation with each other. He wondered what they were talking about when one of the Jutes cleared his throat and the brothers looked up from their conversation.

'Why does he want Gungnir?' Horsa asked before Octa or his mother could say anything. Octa glanced at the older brother, who had his head tilted. 'You said that he came for Gungnir. Why?'

He looked at the corner where the golden spear had been and then at his mother as he tried to work out what to say, when Hengist said, 'Don't be rude, Horsa. I'm sure they are as tired as we are. Sit, have some ale and some bread. That's all we have for now until we get the hearth fire started again.'

Odalric didn't wait for Hengist to finish talking before he grabbed a loaf of bread and broke it in two. He gave one piece to Octa's mother, who nodded her thanks, and started chewing on the other piece.

'Some ale, Lady Berthild.' Oisc appeared with a cup in his hand and Octa's mother smiled at him as she took the cup.

'Thank you, Oisc.'

The boy beamed as he ran back to his seat while Octa took a cup and emptied it. He sighed as the ale calmed his nerves and then looked at the brothers again.

'Why does the Briton want the spear?' Horsa asked again.

'Have you found him yet?' Odalric asked before Octa could respond.

Horsa glared at him as Hengist said, 'Not yet. The men are searching the island.'

Odalric nodded. 'I saw someone run towards the wharves, it might have been him.'

Hengist glanced at some of his warriors, who shrugged, before he looked at Odalric again. 'You think he went towards the water?' This time Odalric shrugged and Hengist looked at his men again. 'Take one of the ships. See if you can find him.'

As one of the warriors left the hall, Horsa asked again, 'Why does Badulf want the spear?'

Octa thought of his conversation with Badulf, but knew he couldn't tell them about that. 'I don't know.'

'Perhaps the son of the high king was behind this,' Octa's mother said, and Octa wondered why she blamed the prince for this, but decided to trust that his mother knew what she was doing. 'He made his feelings towards you clear. He could have told this Briton to steal the spear.'

'That bastard!' Horsa slammed his fist on the table, which knocked some of the cup over.

'We still don't know that he came for the spear,' Hengist said, before he broke a chunk of bread from the loaf and put it in his mouth. 'He might have been sent to kill us and, when he saw it was impossible, he decided to take the spear instead.'

Octa was about to object to this when his mother gripped his hand. 'That is true,' she said.

'But what if they came for the spear?' Horsa asked. 'How would Prince Vortimer know about it?'

'Badulf guided us north,' Octa said. 'And he knew why we were looking for the shrine.'

Hengist chewed on some more bread as he thought about it. After he washed it down with some ale, he said, 'If Prince Vortimer is behind this, why does he want the spear of Woden? He is a Christian and does not believe in our gods.'

'There is much we don't understand,' Octa's mother said as she glanced at him. 'And many of those things we never will, but if I were you, Hengist and Horsa, I'd be preparing for war.'

26

Badulf sucked in a lungful of air when he reached the beach. The swim had been harder than he had anticipated and even though he wasn't wearing any armour, there were moments where he thought the current would take him. He thanked the gods that he had survived and, more importantly, that he had the spear as he lay on the beach. Catching his breath, Badulf listened out for any sign of pursuit, but all he heard was the waves lapping on the beach.

Badulf sat up and ran his hand through his hair while staring at the island. He wondered if Octa had alerted the brothers, but then he frowned as he wondered why Octa had let him go. Octa had come to Britannia to find the spear of his god, and yet he let Badulf leave with it. Badulf's head started hurting as he tried to make sense of it, but he could not ignore the feeling that he was missing something.

Badulf lost track of time as he sat there, trying to understand what had happened. He kept thinking of his conversation with Octa and, by the time the sun rose, he decided Octa was just too afraid to fight him. That was the only thing that made sense.

None of that mattered, though. Badulf had the spear of their war god, and Octa was too frightened to fight him for it. Just like he would be too frightened to let the Jutes know he had let Badulf go. A smile came to Badulf's lips, and he thanked the gods again, because he was certain they had helped him steal the spear. And with it, he would prove the wise one wrong. There would be no fire and the people of Britannia would be able to protect their island from the invaders. All he had to do now was return to Cair Urnahc and then he and Brigid would go north. Neither the Jutes nor Prince Vortimer would have the spear.

Badulf got to his feet and looked at the spear, which was more breath-taking in the sunlight than it had been in the hall. For a moment, he saw himself wielding it in a battle against the Jutes and couldn't resist smiling at the idea. But he had no army so he knew that would never happen.

Badulf heard a noise behind him and turned around to see Grifud and a group of warriors standing behind him. His heart raced at the smiles on their faces, especially when he recognised the two warriors he had attacked to get to Prince Vortimer in Cair Urnahc amongst the group. He gripped the spear in his hand and cursed himself for wasting time on the beach. Badulf should have guessed that Prince Vortimer would have men waiting for him.

'Badulf, back from the dead,' one of them said. 'I'd say I was sorry when I heard you were dead, but that would be a lie.' The others laughed as Badulf gripped the spear.

'What do you want?'

Grifud shrugged. 'Prince Vortimer told us to wait for you here. It seems he doesn't trust you to deliver that spear to him.'

Badulf glared at Grifud. 'Where is Prince Vortimer?'

'He is waiting for the spear in Cair Lundein.'

Badulf frowned. 'He didn't return to Cair Urnahc?'

Grifud shook his head. 'There's no need for him to return there, but don't you worry. He has men watching your sister.'

Badulf's heart raced and, as he glanced at the warriors with Grifud, he got the sense that he would not make it to Cair Urnahc. He took a breath to calm himself, but the anger that he felt at Octa for not fighting him still coursed through him. 'Let's go to Cair Lundein then, so I can give Prince Vortimer the spear.' He hoped that would get them to drop their guard so he could kill them, but the smiles on their faces made him realise they weren't going to fall for that.

Grifud nodded. 'Yes, let's go. Prince Vortimer is eager to get his hands on the weapon.' He stepped aside so that Badulf could walk past, but Badulf stood his ground as he noticed the other warriors moving closer to him.

'I had a deal with Prince Vortimer. I get him the spear of their one-eyed god and he lets me and my sister live.'

Grifud smiled at him for a few heartbeats and then shrugged. 'Yet, the prince didn't quite believe you would honour your part of the deal.' He gave a signal to the warriors, who smiled as they charged at Badulf.

Badulf gritted his teeth and gripped the spear. He was taller than the men Grifud had brought with him and stronger, and he had the spear of Woden, but as he turned the spear at the oncoming men, someone struck him from behind.

Blinding pain shot through him, and Badulf cried out as he dropped to his knees. He looked over his shoulder and saw another warrior who must have snuck around, smiling at him.

'I never liked you, Badulf,' the man said. 'You always thought you were better than us.'

'I am better than you,' Badulf said. 'Your wife told me so.'

The warrior struck Badulf in the face as the others surrounded him, their spears pointed at his chest. 'You'll regret that,' the man said as Grifud came closer, his eyes on the spear.

Badulf glared at Grifud as he reached down to take the spear from him. 'I'm sure Prince Vortimer will have lots of fun with Brigid before he passes her on to his men. Perhaps after that he will kill her.'

Grifud's words added fuel to the anger he already felt at Octa for not fighting him, as well as at himself for not leaving for Cair Urnahc as soon as he reached the beach. He roared as he dropped the spear and launched himself at Grifud. The others froze in shock as Badulf pulled Grifud's knife from its scabbard and stabbed him in the chest. His sister's face came to him as he twisted the knife while Grifud's body tensed underneath him.

'Kill the bastard!' one warrior shouted, and Badulf rolled off Grifud in time for the warrior's spear to miss him. The warrior gaped as he speared Grifud instead and Badulf wasted no time in stabbing him in the throat with Grifud's knife before he could react.

Badulf pulled the warrior's spear free and barely glanced at Grifud's body as he faced the remaining three warriors.

'You're going to pay for that, half-breed,' one of the men said, and as soon as he finished the words, Badulf rushed at him. He stabbed the man in the throat with the spear, but was forced to twist out of the way as the other stabbed at him. Badulf didn't turn fast enough and felt the spear slice his arm open, but he had to forget about that as another spear came towards him.

Badulf deflected this spear with his own and used the butt of his spear to knock his attacker's teeth out. As the man fell to the ground, his mouth missing some teeth and filled with blood, Badulf turned to the last man standing.

He tightened his grip on his spear as the warrior glared at him. 'I'm going to enjoy killing you, you bastard.' He rushed at Badulf, who stepped to the side and tripped the man up. As the warrior fell to the ground, Badulf buried his spear in the man's back.

'You're not good enough to kill me,' Badulf said, and then turned his attention to the man whose teeth he had knocked out. But to his dismay, he saw the warrior running towards Grifud's horse with the golden spear in his hand. Badulf screamed and threw his spear at the man, but the throw was rushed and all he could do was watch as it missed the warrior who mounted the horse and raced off. He stood there as the man disappeared before he dropped to the ground, his arm stinging and his strength gone. There was no point in trying to catch the man. Even if he could catch the bastard, then what? As soon as Prince Vortimer found out that Badulf had killed Grifud, he would send men to Cair Urnahc.

He sat like that for a while, panting as he tried to regain his strength, but his body was exhausted. He had spent the entire night stealing the spear and swimming to the mainland, and that fight had taken the last of his strength. But Badulf knew he couldn't lie down and rest, as much as he wanted to. He had to get up, and he had to get to Cair Urnahc. Prince Vortimer would have the spear soon, and with that spear, he would make himself king. Badulf didn't know if Vortimer really wanted to use the spear to drive the Jutes out of Britannia. All he knew now was that Brigid was in danger and it was all because of him. But he couldn't waste more time than he already had. Badulf had to get to Cair Urnahc. He might not have the spear any more, but he would still take his sister north. Even if it was just to get her out of Prince Vortimer's reach.

Badulf struggled back to his feet and stumbled towards the horses of the warriors. Most of them backed off, frightened by the stench of blood, apart from one horse which only stared at him. Badulf thanked the gods as he mounted the horse and, with one last glance at the men he had just killed, he kicked the horse's flanks and raced towards Cair Urnahc, praying to Brigantia and the other gods that he was not too late to save Brigid.

* * *

Vortimer paced up and down the hall of King Gwyrangon while Cadoc sat and drank ale. How the man could be so relaxed infuriated him, but the stakes weren't the same for Cadoc as they were for Vortimer. His entire life he had looked up to his father, the cunning king who had made himself the high king of Britannia. Vortimer had always known his father wasn't much of a warrior, but he had been smart. That was until Brigid had come into his life. His father had changed and Vortimer still believed that the witch had placed a spell on him.

Vortimer had prayed every day, asking the Lord to break whatever spell Brigid had put on his father, but nothing worked. Still, Vortimer had never thought that he would usurp his father. He had always believed that he would be the next king of the Cornovii. He was the oldest of Vortigern's four sons and had the support of the nobles, but he had always thought it would happen after his father's passing. Not like this.

'Lord, forgive me for what I am about to do,' he prayed as he gripped the cross around his neck. 'I swear that when this is done, I will destroy the heathen weapon.'

'You need to get it first,' Cadoc said, but Vortimer noticed how he crossed himself first.

'Grifud won't fail me.'

Cadoc nodded as he stood up and brought Vortimer a cup of ale. Vortimer took the cup and wished it was Gwyrangon's wine instead. 'Grifud might not mean to fail you, but that half-breed can be a slippery bastard.'

Vortimer nodded as the same concerns darkened his already sour mood. It had been two days since they had left Ruym Island and he had come to Cair Lundein and the waiting was eating away at him. King Gwyrangon had left Cair Lundein the day after to summon his army, which left Vortimer and Cadoc on their own. The nobles had done their best to entertain him, but Vortimer was not in the mood to be courted.

'Do you think God will forgive you if you use the heathen god's weapon?' Cadoc asked, and the question made Vortimer's heart skip a beat, but before he could respond or even think about the question, a warrior with dried blood around his mouth walked into the hall.

'Printh Vortimer, I hath it! I hath the sthpear.'

Vortimer stared at the warrior as he struggled to understand what the man was saying, but then he dropped the cup of ale in his hands as his eyes fell on the spear in the man's hands.

'The spear,' Cadoc said, his eyes wide.

'Where's Grifud?' Vortimer asked as he rushed towards the warrior and ripped the spear from his hands.

The warrior dropped to his knees. 'Baduth killed him, my printh. I esthcaped with the sthpear.'

'Badulf killed Grifud?' Vortimer felt like he had been kicked in the chest and he looked at the spear in his hands as he struggled to make sense of the death of one of his closest friends.

The warrior nodded. 'He goth too clothe and Baduth attacked him.'

The words washed over Vortimer as he stared at the spear, which looked even more beautiful than it had done in the hall. His heart raced, and he forgot about everything else as he took in the gold-rimmed spearhead and the two golden rings on the shaft. But it was the thick gold band around the centre that drew his eyes. The gold there shone as brightly as if it had only been placed there recently and, as Vortimer wrapped his fingers around the golden band, he imagined the one-eyed god of the heathens holding the spear in the same place. The last time he had felt this way was the first time he had seen Brigid, but unlike her, the spear belonged to him.

'Prince Vortimer,' Cadoc said, his voice heavy. 'What do we do about Badulf?'

Vortimer smiled as he lifted the spear and felt a surge of confidence course through him. He now had the spear that belonged to the one-eyed god of the Saxons, and with it, he would drive them out of Britannia. Grifud's death would not be wasted and Vortimer promised God that Badulf would pay. Vortimer looked at the warrior, who was still on his knees. 'Take men with you and bring me Grifud's body. He will get a proper funeral.' He turned to another warrior in the hall. 'Get the fastest horses you can and race to Cair Urnahc. Tell the men watching the bitch to grab her, but keep her alive until we get there. And if they see Badulf, they can beat him, but I also want him alive. I knew I couldn't trust that bastard.' The two warriors rushed out of the hall to do as he asked before Vortimer looked at the spear again. The more he looked at it, the more he believed that the old beggar had been sent by God to tell him of the spear. 'God wants us to use this weapon to protect His flock. We are His shepherds and with this spear, we will kill the wolves who threaten His people.'

27

Brigid stood at the edge of the forest, her heart racing as she stared at the trees and the green leaves as they lifted in the wind. Her eyes fell on the rotten corpse of a rabbit, more bones than meat now, and she tried to remember if she had been the one who had put it there.

Her hand went to the bead necklace around her neck as she tried to summon the courage to enter the forest, something she had never had to do before. But she had to go to the clearing. She had to confront the raven, if it was still there, and try one more time to talk to the gods. Badulf had gone south and Brigid could only pray they had made the right decision to steal the spear. Badulf was a capable warrior, but he had gone into the wolves' den and he had no one to help him. What also worried Brigid were the two warriors who always followed her around. Everywhere she went, she saw them. Always the same two men. And she knew they were following her because they did not try to hide from her. They wanted her to know they were there, and that made her fear for her brother even more.

Brigid glanced over her shoulder and was relieved when she saw the warriors weren't there. She had lost them, which hadn't been too hard, and she was sure they'd be running around the streets of Cair Urnahc trying to find her. They would never think of coming here for her because they didn't know about this place.

Brigid turned back to the trees again and took a deep breath. 'The forest won't hurt me. The trees are my friends and she watches over me,' she said to herself, and let go of the bead necklace as she walked into the forest. Her hands trembled as she followed the familiar path towards the clearing, but it did not feel the same as before. The air felt heavier, even as the birds sang their songs while darting from branch to branch, and Brigid sensed a change in the trees. Hungry eyes seemed to follow her and Brigid resisted the urge to turn and run as she walked towards the centre of the forest, where the clearing was. 'The forest won't hurt me,' she repeated, but noticed the quiver in her voice.

By the time Brigid made it to the clearing, her fear had taken hold of her and it took all of her strength not to turn and run away. She took a deep breath, summoning what remained of her courage as she prepared to go into the clearing. But as she stepped into the clearing, her heart stopped when she saw the carcass of the fox by the sacred tree, its eyes missing and its stomach torn open. Her body felt weak as she glanced at the raven sitting on the branch above the body of the fox, knowing that was a sign from the gods. But which gods and what it meant, she did not know.

The raven cried out to her, as if it was challenging her, and Brigid swallowed back her fear and took a step towards the tree.

'I am not afraid of you,' she said to the raven, but even she heard the doubt in her words as the raven seemed to laugh at her. The large bird hopped to another branch and flapped its wings as if it was about to fly off, but all it did was scream at her again. Brigid forced herself to put one foot in front of another, her eyes on the raven so she didn't have to look at the fox. She had to get to the tree, although what she would do when she reached it, she didn't know.

As Brigid got close enough to the tree to almost touch its rough bark, something grabbed her from behind. Fingertips dug into her shoulder and Brigid screamed as her heart felt like it was going to rip out of her chest. The raven cried out as her hand went to the knife under her dress, when she was turned around. Brigid closed her eyes, not ready to face the monster that had come to take her, and her legs gave way under her. Strong arms caught her and picked her up, and then a familiar voice said, 'Brigid, it's me. It's Badulf.'

Brigid opened her eyes and stared at the tired and strained face of her brother. 'Badulf!' But all the anger she felt at him for scaring her fled as she saw the pain in his eyes. She looked at his arm and saw his tunic was ripped and covered in blood and, as she looked at his hand, she saw the dried blood there as well. 'Badulf, what happened? Where's the spear?'

Badulf closed his eyes and shook his head. 'I lost it, Brigid. I had the spear and then I lost it.'

Brigid's eyes went to the dead fox and the raven, which had now gone quiet and was staring at them, its head tilted as if it was listening to them. 'Badulf, what do you mean you lost it?' she asked, although Brigid already knew the answer to that. They had underestimated Prince Vortimer.

'Prince Vortimer. He had men waiting...' Badulf's words trailed off as he opened his eyes and saw the tree. 'What in the gods?'

Brigid guessed he had just seen the fox as he let go of her. 'Badulf? What happened?'

'Did you do that?' He pointed to the fox and Brigid shook her head. Badulf knew she would lay dead animals around the forest to scare people away. He was one of the few who knew of the clearing, although he didn't know where it was. That thought made her frown.

'How did you find me here?'

'I... I followed you,' he said as he stared at the fox. 'I saw you standing outside the forest and then followed as you came in. If you didn't do that, then who did?'

Brigid glanced at the raven, wondering if it had killed the fox. 'I don't know.' She turned her attention back to her brother, whose face was pale as he stared at the fox. 'Badulf, there is much happening and I understand very little of it.'

Badulf looked at her. 'It doesn't matter. Prince Vortimer has the spear of the one-eyed god of the Jutes.'

Her heart skipped in her chest, and she couldn't help but look at the raven again. 'Prince Vortimer has Octa's spear?'

Badulf frowned at her. 'Octa's spear? No, the spear of their god.'

Brigid shook her head as she tried to make sense of her brother's words. 'Badulf. What spear did you steal?'

'The one Eadric had taken back to the Jutes. The one in their hall with the gold-rimmed spearhead.'

Brigid's mind raced as the vision from before came to her. The raven went wild as if it saw the vision as well, and Badulf's eyes widened as he stared at the raven. 'You didn't take the spear from Octa?'

Badulf blinked rapidly. 'Why would I want his spear?'

Brigid stared at the raven as it flapped its wings and cried out to the skies. 'Octa has the spear of their one-eyed god.'

Badulf's brows creased as he stared at her. 'Brigid, what are you talking about? The gods know Octa can't have the spear. The one he has is just a plain spear.'

Brigid shook her head again, this time to dismiss his words, and told him about the vision she had seen when she had touched the spear Octa had with him. She had not known it before, but now she was certain. Octa had the spear of his god and that was why the gods of Britannia were nervous of him. They had known that he would find it. But what Brigid couldn't understand was why the gods didn't stop him. Surely they had the power to do that, yet they just watched as he found the spear. A spear Badulf had told her had been in a cave with a shrine to Brigantia. Her eyes went back to the fox. Was it there to tell her that Brigantia was gone, or was it a warning of her death? 'Octa has the spear the wise one told you about.'

Badulf collapsed, his face too pale to be good for him. 'Octa has the spear?' His forehead creased as if he was trying to make sense of something. 'It can't be. He is a coward, weak. He didn't even...' Badulf paused and he looked like he had been struck by something. 'The bastard. He let me go because he knew I didn't have the right spear. The Saxon bastard.'

Brigid dropped to her knees in front of Badulf and grabbed his face so that he would focus on her. 'Badulf, you have to take me north now. I must find the wise one. I must talk to her.'

Badulf stared at her, but she could tell his mind was somewhere else. 'If Prince Vortimer finds out...'

Brigid shook her brother. 'Badulf! Prince Vortimer is not important. Octa still has the spear. We need to go north!'

Badulf's eyes focused on her, and she almost smiled when she saw his old self. 'Prince Vortimer has men watching you. Grifud said—'

'Yes, there are warriors following me, but I lost them,' Brigid said, sensing what Badulf was talking about. 'But none of that matters. The only thing that matters is that I speak to the wise one. Badulf, you have to take me north.'

'All I wanted to do was to stop the fire.'

Brigid wanted to scream, but she took a deep breath. 'Then take me north! Take me to where you saw the wise one and together we can stop the fire.'

Badulf nodded, even though Brigid wasn't sure if they could do anything. If the gods wanted this, then it was going to happen regardless of what they did, but she still had to try. And she still believed the wise one would have the answers. 'I will take you north, but we need horses and supplies.'

Brigid smiled, glad to see her old brother back. But then the raven cried out and took to the skies before it flew away. It was the first time Brigid had seen it leave the clearing, and a shiver ran down her spine as she wondered what that meant.

* * *

Badulf was exhausted as they left the clearing. His mind was still reeling from the fact that he had stolen the wrong spear and that Prince Vortimer had outsmarted him. But how could he have known that Octa had the real spear? His brows creased as he tried to remember the spear Octa was holding on the beach of Ruym Island that night, but he couldn't. In the light of the moon, it had looked like an ordinary spear. He cursed himself for being so foolish. He had even mocked Octa for being a coward for not trying to take the spear from him. But then that led to so many other questions, the most important one being: what was the spear that he had stolen?

Bellicus had told him that was the spear the cult was protecting, that was why he believed he had stolen the right spear from the Jutes. Did Bellicus lie to him, or did the old man really believe that was the spear of the gods? Or perhaps it was just not the spear of the one-eyed Saxon god. His mind was numb from all the thoughts and that he had not slept in many days was not helping.

After Badulf had left the beach and the bodies of Grifud and Prince Vortimer's men behind, he had raced north as if he was being chased by a pack of wolves. He didn't know if the order to kill Brigid had already been sent, but he knew he had to get to Cair Urnahc before any messenger from Prince Vortimer. So Badulf had pushed his horse hard and on more than one occasion the animal had refused to go any further and Badulf was forced to wait for it to recover. He glanced at the animal grazing near the forest and wondered if it had enough left in it to take him north, but then shook his head. The horse had done enough. It deserved its rest. Unlike the men Prince Vortimer had ordered to follow his sister.

Brigid had told him what they looked like, and he was glad that he knew them. Badulf pushed his exhaustion away and turned to his sister, her eyes focusing on something in the distance that wasn't there, as if she was trying to make sense of something. He guessed they both were. Badulf couldn't explain it, but it felt like they were caught in the middle of something more important than a battle over Britannia. And that frightened him more than any fight he had ever been in.

'You wait here,' he said to his sister. 'I'll find us some horses and supplies and then we'll go north.' He didn't want to tell her he was going to kill the two warriors as well, because he knew she might try to stop him.

It was harder for Badulf to sneak into Cair Urnahc this time. There was no market today, which meant the warriors guarding the gate paid more attention to people coming and going. And Badulf knew he would be easy to spot because he was taller than everyone else, even if the men were half asleep.

He watched the gate for a while, waiting for the right opportunity to come his way. And then he smiled when he saw it. A farmer bringing a cart filled with jugs of milk to sell to the bakers. Badulf pulled his cloak over his head, ignoring the sting from the cut to his arm, and crouched behind the cart so that he was hidden from the warriors guarding the gate.

The warriors didn't stop the farmer because they knew him well, as did Badulf, because he often came to Cair Urnahc, and they barely looked at the cart as it trudged past them. Once inside, Badulf took a deep breath and, keeping his face hidden, he walked to the market square. He wasn't sure if he'd find Prince Vortimer's men, and he knew he couldn't spend too much time searching for them. They had to leave the lands of the Cornovii as soon as they could. Prince Vortimer would have already sent men after him. He was sure of it, just as he was sure that the prince would have sent the order for the men to kill Brigid.

As he walked through the streets of Cair Urnahc, hoping that he would run into the two warriors, he thought of everything that had happened to him. Badulf still didn't understand how Octa had the real spear, but he knew that if Brigid believed it was the spear of their god, then it was. But to him, that made even less sense because the cult believed the one they were protecting was the spear with the gold-rimmed spearhead.

Lost in his thoughts, he did not notice the two warriors rushing at him until one of them grabbed him from behind. Badulf's heart skipped a beat, but his warrior instinct kicked in and as he turned and caught a glimpse of metal, he twisted out of the way and felt the warrior's knife slice his cheek open. The second warrior pulled his arm back to stab at him, but then the man arched backwards and cried out.

Both Badulf and the other warrior were stunned as Brigid pulled her knife out of the man's back, the ugly sneer on her face enough to frighten the most experienced of warriors. Badulf recovered first and punched the warrior in the throat with his elbow, and the man's eyes bulged as he struggled to breathe before Brigid lunged at him. She buried her knife under his armpit and twisted it as she snarled at the warrior.

'The gods will gladly accept your blood. Brigantia will feed off your soul while the earth devours your corpse.' The warrior paled and Brigid stopped his hand from going to the cross he wore around his neck. 'Your god can't save your soul. It belongs to the old gods now.'

Badulf felt the shiver run down his spine and thanked the gods he was not Brigid's enemy. He had never realised how terrifying his sister could be. 'Why are you here? I told you to wait by the forest,' he said once he got a hold of himself again.

Brigid looked at him as she cleaned her knife on the dead man's trousers. 'I followed you because I knew you would be looking for them.'

Badulf shook his head and then looked at the dead warriors, before he glanced around them, glad that there was no one around. 'I could have dealt with them.'

Brigid straightened herself and fixed her dress. She looked at the blood-stain on it and grimaced. 'I know, Badulf. But we don't have time to waste. We need to leave now. Every moment you spend hunting these men is a moment the answers slip away from us.'

Badulf nodded and looked at the dead men, not sure how they found him first, but that was not what bothered him. What bothered him was that for the first time in his life, he was afraid of his sister.

28

Prince Vortimer walked into the hall of Cair Urnahc, the golden spear in his right hand and his warriors behind him. Anger and determination coursed through his veins as his eyes were fixed on his father, who looked up from his conversation with Ceretic. It was midday, and the hall wasn't busy. Apart from the king and his advisor, Vortimer saw two of his three brothers, Pascent and Catigern, sitting near their father while a handful of warriors relaxed on the benches as they pretended to protect their king. His youngest brother, Faustus, was most likely off hunting and making the most of the sunny day outside, while these two were trying to get closer to their father. Although Vortimer knew there was no point in doing that. King Vortigern's days were over.

'What is the meaning of this?' King Vortigern asked as his eyes widened at the sight of the spear while Ceretic paled. The man had always been a coward, and Vortimer never understood why his father kept him around. Vortimer's brothers jumped to their feet when they saw him, but Vortimer didn't pay any attention to them. It was his father he was after.

Vortimer's men spread out as the warriors in the hall looked at their king, but King Vortigern raised his hand to stop them from doing anything, just like Vortimer knew he would. Just like he knew his father wouldn't summon the warriors outside. Not that it would matter. Vortimer had his own men guarding the doors so no one else could enter the hall.

'Brother, what are you doing?' Pascent asked.

Vortimer stopped a few paces away from his father and glared at the old man. He wasn't sure how he had never seen it before, but as his father sat on his raised chair, his thin golden crown around his head, he looked old, feeble and, worst of all, tired. The strength Vortimer had always admired in his father was gone. The broad shoulders and thick limbs were replaced by deep lines and a crooked back. 'What should have been done a long time ago. What God commands me to do.'

'And what does God command you to do?' King Vortigern said as he stood up from his seat. He straightened his back and squared his shoulders. But Vortimer was not intimidated, not like he used to be.

Vortimer tightened his grip on the spear and felt the gold band warm to his fingers. He took a deep breath and felt strengthened by having the spear of the Saxon god. 'What you should have done, Father. But you are too blind to see the real danger the Jutes pose. Blinded by the half-breed bitch and by your lust for power.'

His father took a step towards him and, despite his age, still stood the same height as Vortimer. 'And what is that, Vortimer? What should I have done? Leave our people to fend for themselves? Cower in my hall while our enemies ravage our lands and kill our people? Warm my bed with young women while the Picts take many others with them over the wall to breed with?'

Vortimer glared at his father, who for the first time in a long time showed the strength that made him the high king. But it was too late for that now. 'You should never have let the Jutes stay! You should have sent them back to their ships! Instead, you gave them land and now they grow stronger. But no longer, Father. You let the wolves into our homes and God commands I chase them out!'

'Vortimer, what are you talking about?' Catigern asked, but Vortimer saw how he stared at the spear.

Vortimer smiled as he looked at his brothers. 'Did Father tell you why he agreed to let the Jutes stay? Why he accepted their offer? Did you ever wonder why they never asked to be paid in gold and silver, but in food and clothing?' His brothers shook their heads as he knew they would.

'They protect us from our enemies!' King Vortigern said, his face turning red.

'What enemies, Father?' Vortimer asked. 'You tell us that the Picts don't raid our lands as much because of the Jutes. So why do we still need them?'

King Vortigern leaned closer, his nostrils flared. 'The Picts are not our only enemies, Vortimer. The other kings are forming alliances against me. King Gwyrangon is gathering his army and there is talk of the other kings doing the same.'

Vortimer wanted to laugh at how blind his father had become. Or perhaps he had just overestimated how smart his father was. 'I know, Father. I told King Gwyrangon to raise his army. Just like I told the other kings to do the same.'

Vortimer's father stepped back as if he'd been slapped, and Ceretic almost collapsed.

'You raise an army against our father?' Catigern asked, his face pale.

Pascent, though, showed only anger as he glared at Vortimer. 'You were always so desperate to be king, weren't you? Couldn't wait for Father to die so now you plan to take the crown from him. That's why you are raising an army, isn't it?'

Vortimer turned on his brother. 'I raise an army to protect our people! To protect our lands!' He looked at his father, who was sitting on his seat again, exhaustion and defeat all over his face. 'The heathens want to take our lands for themselves! They want to destroy our churches and build their monuments to their gods! And instead of resisting them, our father, the wise high king of Britannia, opens his arms and lets the wolves in!'

'Have you already forgotten how the Picts raided our lands?' his father asked, his voice weak. 'Have you forgotten how our people lived in fear, how their farms were burnt and livestock was stolen? And not a lifetime ago, but two summers ago. We needed the Jutes to defend our lands because the Romans had left us to fend for ourselves.'

'Our warriors could have dealt with the Picts!' Vortimer said.

'Then why didn't they?' Pascent asked. 'Why didn't our warriors stop the Picts?' The warriors in the hall bristled at that, but Pascent ignored them as Vortimer stared at his brother. 'We don't have enough warriors to fight the Picts. Not a single king has enough warriors to defend their kingdoms from the Picts to the north and the pirates from across the seas.'

Vortimer smiled. 'Not a single king, no. But God knows that if the kings united, then we could have driven the Picts out of Britannia and taken the entire island for ourselves.'

'Ha!' King Vortigern barked. 'Don't you think I've tried? Me, Gwyrangon. How many messengers have we sent to the Brigantians, the Corieltauvi? They never wanted peace! They never wanted to unite! As long as the Picts raided our lands, they left theirs alone.'

Vortimer smiled at his father. 'Perhaps you were not the king to unite them.'

'And you are?' Pascent asked.

Vortimer looked at his brother, his smile still on his face. 'Yes. I am. God has given me the weapon to unite the kings of Britannia and to fight the Saxons. To get rid of the heathens that plague our lands.'

'That spear?' Catigern asked, his voice filled with awe.

Vortimer looked at the spear, which still shone brightly, even in the dim light of the hall. He wasn't going to say anything about the spear, but then changed his mind. 'Yes, Catigern. This spear belonged to the one-eyed god of the Saxons, and God told me to find it. God told me that, with this spear, I will stop the storm.'

Many of those in the hall crossed themselves, which only made Vortimer smile.

'You're a fool if you think that pretty spear really belonged to a god!' his father spat. 'And a bigger fool if you think I'm going to let you send our men to their deaths all because you want the crown on my head!'

Vortimer shook his head. 'No, Father. You're the fool who listened to a whore because she opened her legs for you. You're the fool who let the wolves into our homes and now I must send our men to their deaths to chase them out.'

'And where will you stand while our warriors die? While they die?' Pascent pointed to the men in the hall. The warriors that would fight against the Saxons.

'Where God wants me to be.' Vortimer turned his attention back to his father, who glared at him from his seat. 'You are my father and our king, and for that I love you, but God knows I can no longer do nothing as you allow the Jutes to take over our lands.'

'So you are going to kill me?' King Vortigern sat straight in his seat and did his best to look like a king as Vortimer shook his head.

'No, Father. If I kill you, then the men will never follow me. You will keep your head and that crown of yours, but I will rule in your name.'

'The people will not agree with that,' Pascent said.

'The people will do what I tell them to do because that is what God commands!' Vortimer turned to Cadoc. 'Take my father to his quarters. Make sure he is comfortable and has everything he needs. And make sure that only my men guard his door.'

Cadoc nodded and selected a group of warriors as everyone just stared silently at them.

'Vortimer, don't do this,' Pascent said. 'What would Mother say?'

Vortimer glared at his brother. 'Why don't you run to her and find out?' He turned his attention back to his father and Ceretic as his warriors surrounded the king. For a moment, it looked like King Vortigern would refuse, but then the old man let out a long breath and struggled to his feet. Vortimer was almost shocked at how much he had seemed to age in a matter of heartbeats, but as Cadoc led his father to his quarters, he smiled and turned to his father's men in the hall. 'From this day forward, you will obey me and only me. God commands that you do. So put down your cups and sharpen your weapons for soon we will march south and, with the men of the Cantiaci, we will drive the heathen scum from our lands.' Vortimer did not get the cheers he had hoped for as the warriors all glanced at each other. But as one, they put their cups down and left the hall, leaving behind a deathly silence that annoyed him more than it should have done. He didn't care, he told himself. They did not need to love him as long as they obeyed him.

Pascent glared at him and then spat at his feet. 'You will regret this, Vortimer. Catigern, let's go.'

'No,' Catigern said, which made Vortimer smile. 'I agree with Vortimer.'

'Catigern?' Pascent's eyes widened and even Vortimer was surprised. Pascent and Catigern had always been close, but to Vortimer it showed again that God was with him.

'You heard him, Pascent.'

Pascent glared at them before he left the hall.

'Should we stop him?' one of Vortimer's warriors asked.

Vortimer shook his head. 'No, Pascent is harmless.' He turned around and looked at his father's seat. The seat of the king of the Cornovii. A seat his grandfather had sat in, but Vortimer was not king and he did not want to anger his ancestors by sitting in their seat without the crown on his head. So instead, he sat on the bench where he always sat and filled a cup with wine.

'Is that really the spear of the Jutes' god?' Catigern asked as he stared at the spear in Vortimer's hand.

'It is, and with it, we will free our lands from the heathens.'

'Where did you get it?' Catigern asked, and Vortimer thought of Grifud and clenched his fist.

'A good man died so that I could get this weapon and that is why I had to act now. If I waited any longer, then it would be too late.'

Catigern frowned at him. 'You really believe the Jutes will destroy our way of life?'

Vortimer stared at his younger brother. 'They will not only destroy our way of life, but they will make sure that God's light gets swallowed by their darkness.'

Catigern raised an eyebrow. 'But why?'

Vortimer shrugged. 'Because they fear God and His almighty power. That's why our churches will be destroyed and our children will be sacrificed to their gods.'

'How do we stop them?' Catigern asked. 'Father said they are skilled warriors.'

Vortimer nodded as he thought of the large men he had seen on Ruym Island. Even the shortest Jutes seemed taller than the Britons. 'We attack them now, before they can bring more warriors to Britannia. If the kings unite, then we will have more warriors than they do.'

Before Catigern could say anything else, Cadoc returned. 'Your father is in his quarters. He will be given wine and some food soon.' Cadoc glanced at Catigern and then lowered his voice. 'He asked for Brigid. Demanded that I bring her to him.'

Vortimer felt a spark of anger at that and then swallowed it down as he reminded himself that she would be dead soon. That she would no longer be able to cloud his father's mind. 'And Ceretic?'

'Fled. But I sent some men after him.'

Vortimer nodded as he drank more of his wine. He thought of Grifud again, a man he had known since he was a boy, and the thought of him being buried in the lands of the Cantiaci and not those of his ancestors angered him. 'Find Brigid and her bastard brother, and bring them to me.'

29

Vortimer screamed as he threw his cup against the wall of his father's hall. The clay cup shattered into small fragments, just like his quest to avenge his friend and kill the bitch who had shunned him long ago.

'What do you mean, they are gone?'

The warrior stepped back from his anger. 'My prince, we searched her quarters and all of Cair Urnahc for the last few days, but there was no sign of her. No one had seen her for many days.'

Vortimer gritted his teeth at the news. His mother had told him the same, and Vortimer cursed his bad luck. 'Where are the men who were supposed to watch her?'

'Their bodies were found in the outer fort, near the stables,' said the warrior: the man Vortimer had sent from Cair Lundein while he was still there to tell those men to grab Brigid and Badulf if they found them.

Vortimer grabbed the spear which was lying on the table in front of him and pointed its golden point at the warrior's neck. The warrior stood his ground as the point of the spear pressed against his neck, but his eyes showed his fear. 'This is your fault! You took too long to get here!'

'My prince, I travelled as fast as I could. Almost killed my horse to get here, but when I arrived, I couldn't find them. I searched everywhere.'

'Badulf had a head start. He would have reached Cair Urnahc long before this man and killed the two who were watching Brigid,' Cadoc said, and

Vortimer cursed because his friend spoke the truth. And because he knew that no matter how much he wanted to kill the warrior for failing him, he couldn't. That would turn the other warriors of Cair Urnahc against him. For now, they obeyed him because he had told them that his father had fallen ill, but he knew it was only a matter of time before they learnt the truth. Even though those in the hall had been sworn to silence about what had really happened, Vortimer knew warriors liked to talk. It had been two days already since he had returned to Cair Urnahc, and Vortimer knew he needed to gather his men and march south.

He took a deep breath and pulled the spear back, but not before wondering what it would feel like to kill someone with the weapon of a god. 'Badulf and Brigid might be out of my reach for now, but I swear on the Almighty, I will find them one day and they will pay for what they did!'

Cadoc leaned towards him and whispered in his ear, 'Perhaps there is a way we can get everyone to look for them so we can focus on the Jutes.'

Vortimer raised an eyebrow at his friend. 'How?'

Cadoc looked around to make sure that no one was listening, but the few warriors in the hall made sure they were busy with something else. Only Catigern looked their way, but Vortimer's younger brother was too far away to hear what Cadoc said. 'Spread the rumour that Brigid is responsible for the king's *illness*. Say that she cursed the king or poisoned him.'

Vortimer smiled, and for a moment was glad that it was not Cadoc who had been killed because he was the more cunning of the two. 'Make sure it's done. Tell the people that my father had found out she was a witch and so she poisoned him.'

Cadoc nodded and left the hall as Vortimer looked at his younger brother, still surprised that Catigern had sided with him. Pascent had left Cair Urnahc and had gone to his lands in the north of their father's kingdom. Vortimer knew he couldn't stop Pascent from returning to Cair Urnahc after he had left, and neither could he send men to kill his brother. Not after some of the warriors saw them argue. All he could do was hope that by the time Pascent freed his father, it would be too late to stop him.

'Catigern, tell the men to get ready. We march south at sunrise.'

'Are we going to fight the Jutes?' His brother's eyes widened in anticipation, and Vortimer smiled as he looked at the spear.

'Yes, brother. We go to fight the Jutes.'

Catigern rushed out of the hall to carry out his orders and almost bumped into one warrior in his eagerness. Vortimer shook his head and then looked at the spear again, sensing that his time for greatness was at hand.

'Everyone out,' Vortimer said as he wanted to be alone with the spear. The warriors in the hall glanced at each other before they got up from their benches and left the hall. 'And make sure no one disturbs me. I need to think.' The last warrior nodded as he closed the door of the hall, leaving Vortimer on his own. The only noises he could hear were his own breathing and the flames of the hearth fire. And when he was certain he was alone, he turned and stared at his father's raised seat. In the two days since Vortimer had locked his father away, it had got more tempting to sit in the seat of the king of the Cornovii. Vortimer's heart raced at the thought and he took half a step towards the seat.

'A storm is coming,' an old voice said. Vortimer turned, the spear in his hand, and pointed at the old man standing by the closed door of the hall. The same old man who had told him about the spear. 'A storm is coming. A storm that will wash away the old and bring in the new.'

The spear trembled in Vortimer's hand as he wondered how the old man had got into the hall, but if the old man was who Vortimer believed he was, then that would explain it. 'And I will stop the storm.' Vortimer lowered the spear and straightened his back, determined to look like a warrior prince to the one he believed was his God. 'I will stop the storm in your name. I will drive the heathens from our lands.'

The old man walked around the hall but stayed in the shadows cast by the torches and the hearth fire, but Vortimer felt his eyes on him. He frowned, though, when instead of the warm glow he expected to feel, all he felt was a bitter anger, a desire for vengeance similar to his own. *Is God testing me*, he wondered. *Is he looking at my sins?*

'Only the spear of the one-eyed god can stop the storm.' The spear felt heavier in Vortimer's hands as the old man's voice echoed off the stone walls. 'Only the spear of their god can stop the fire they will bring to our lands. To my lands. Only his spear can punish her for her betrayal.'

Vortimer frowned at the old man's words. Was the old man talking about Brigid? Was he saying that Vortimer had to use the spear to kill her? He looked at the spear and a smile came to him. He liked the idea of that. Killing the half-breed bitch with the spear of her grandfather's god. 'I have the spear,'

Vortimer said, even though he couldn't see the old man who was now behind him. 'I have the spear of their one-eyed god and I will kill her with it. Just like I will drive the heathens from your lands. This I swear to you, my Lord Almighty.'

Vortimer sensed the old man, his God, standing behind him as he stared at the front of the hall, too afraid to turn and face Him, when the door to the hall opened and Catigern walked in.

'Brother, it is done. The men are ready.'

Vortimer's anger flashed at his brother and he turned around to see if the old man was still there, but there was no sign of Him. He looked at the spear in his hand and his anger at his brother vanished. It did not matter that Catigern had entered the hall when he had told everyone to leave, because God had come to him again and had told him what he needed to do. A smile parted his trimmed beard as he looked at his frowning brother.

'Tell the servants to prepare a meal worthy of kings. Bring out Father's best wines and mead. Tonight, brother, we feast for tomorrow, we march south to do God's bidding.' Catigern crossed himself as Vortimer laughed. He was God's warrior, his hound sent to kill the wolves that threatened God's flock. And with the spear of the one-eyed god, he would kill every single one of the Jutes. And when he was done with them, he would find Brigid and make her pay for all the embarrassment she had caused him.

* * *

Vortimer's heart raced as he left Cair Urnahc, his friend and his brother on either side of him. And behind, the army of Cair Urnahc. Seventy of the best warriors of the Cornovii, all of them dressed for war and riding south to fight the Jutes alongside the armies of the Cantiaci and the Trinovantes. The sun shone brightly and there wasn't a cloud to be seen, another sign that God was with him. Vortimer resisted the urge to look over his shoulder at the army of the Cornovii. At his army. But he pictured the men in his mind, all of them on horseback, their spearheads pointing to the sky and glinting in the morning sunlight. Mail vests and helmets shining brightly while grim faces stared ahead as they marched towards their enemy.

Vortimer had to leave twenty warriors behind to protect Cair Urnahc and keep his father locked up, but he was certain that, combined with the armies of the other two tribes, they would have enough to drive the Jutes out of Britannia. Vortimer knew, though, they had to do more than just defeat them. The heathens had to be crushed, otherwise they would just return with more men. With the spear of the one-eyed god of the Saxons, Vortimer was certain that would happen. God had come to him again and had told him that.

A handful of priests travelled with them, their songs of God and Christ lifting his spirits, and would have brought a smile to his face if it had not been for the people of Cair Urnahc. Instead of the cheers and joy he had expected as he rode off to fight their enemies and the enemies of their God, the people looked sullen. Some even asked where the king was, which only annoyed Vortimer even more as he left his father's city. But he knew that when he returned triumphant, then they would forget about his father and declare him as their king and victor.

'How long before we get there?' Catigern asked, who, like the warriors, wore a mail vest and had a shield strapped to his back. He carried his spear awkwardly, which also annoyed Vortimer, even though Catigern had never fought a battle before.

'Seven or eight days to reach the lands of the Cantiaci with the army behind us,' Cadoc said. 'And then another few days to reach Ruym Island.'

'It's that far away?' Catigern asked with his eyes wide, and Vortimer shook his head.

'It's not that far away. Without the army, we can reach Ruym Island in about six days, but an army moves slower, even on horseback. But have patience, brother. We will get there soon and, before the summer is out, we will have rid ourselves of the heathens who plague our lands.' Vortimer puffed his chest out to look like the leader he wanted to be, and smiled as his younger brother gaped at him.

It took them longer than anticipated to reach Ruym Island and by the time they reached the lands of the Cantiaci, Vortimer could barely contain his anger. Every day they had to stop earlier than he wanted so the men could set up camp and, in the morning, it took them longer than he liked to pack up and continue on their journey. And then there were the regular stops along the way for the horses to rest.

'You can't rush a march to war,' one priest had said. 'Jesus was not rushed as he was marched to his crucifixion.' The priest was one of the oldest in Cair Urnahc and had been a warrior a long time ago, but even though he spoke with knowledge and experience of these things, his words had still angered Vortimer.

But that anger vanished when he saw the army of the Cantiaci camped outside Cair Lundein. It was hard for Vortimer to tell, but it looked as if King Gwyrangon had more men and he knew the men of the Trinovantes still had to arrive because he could not see their banner.

'We'll have more than enough to drive the Jutes from Ruym Island,' Cadoc said with a smile, and Vortimer nodded. It was not just the size of the two combined armies that filled him with confidence. It was the spear and God's words to him.

Vortimer tightened his grip on the spear as a smile spread across his face. 'We won't just drive them from our lands. We will crush them. We will drown them in the sea and then we will destroy everything they touched on our lands. We will make it seem as if the Saxons and Jutes never came to Britannia and, for generations to come, they will be too afraid to ever come to our shores again.'

30

Brigid tried to forget about the men she had killed as they rode north. She had never killed another person, only animals that she had sacrificed to the gods, and she could still smell their blood on her hands, no matter how many times she washed them. She glanced at Badulf, who scowled as he sat comfortably on his horse, and wondered how he dealt with that. All she saw every time she closed her eyes were their frightened faces as she buried her knife in them. Did Badulf see the same? she asked herself as she thought of all the minor battles he had fought for King Vortigern. All the men he must have killed.

They had hidden the bodies of the two warriors after Badulf emptied their pouches and took weapons from them. He had also taken the armour of the bigger of the two warriors and even though the man was shorter than her brother, he had had wide shoulders, which meant his mail vest fit Badulf. After that, she had cleaned the cut to his cheek and dealt with the wound to his arm, which took some time as she had to clean the dried blood away before she could bind the deep cut. Brigid would have preferred to stitch the cut, which was already many days old, but there was no time for that so all she could do was pray to Airmed, the goddess of healing, that the wound would not get infected. Then she had gone to the market and bought enough food for the journey while Badulf found them fresh horses.

That had been three days ago, and now they were on the edge of the Cornovii lands. Brigid pulled on the reins of her horse and stared back along the Roman road. Badulf did the same and said, 'I doubt anyone is following us. Even if they found the bodies and work out it was us, they wouldn't know where to look for us.'

Brigid nodded. 'That's not it.' Her hands trembled as she looked at the lands of her ancestors. Her grandfather might have been a Saxon, but her grandmother had been born on these lands. Brigid didn't know why, but she wondered if she would ever see the hills and valleys of the Cornovii again. The rivers that cut through the land like giant serpents travelling towards the seas. Dark forests grew in large patches as thin trails of smoke showed how man had taken over the lands the gods had created. Brigid watched birds glide on the wind as if unseen hands held them in the air and, for a moment, she wondered what that felt like. 'I've never left our lands before.'

For a moment, she thought of King Vortigern and the influence she used to have over him. But after their last conversation, Brigid knew that the king would no longer listen to her words. Not that it mattered any more. Brigid had believed the king would allow her to go north to find the answers, but the king was not what she thought he would be and his desire to protect his crown was stronger than his desire to please the gods. The king would have to make his own decisions while she tried to work out why the gods seemed to be hiding and what this fire was that Badulf had told her about.

Badulf nodded. 'It can be frightening at first.' He turned and looked north. 'And even though Britannia is a large island, you'll find it's much the same everywhere.'

Brigid looked at her brother and felt comforted by the smile on his face. For a reason she could not understand, she thought of Octa and wondered what he had felt like when he left the lands of his people to come to Britannia. 'Let's go,' she said as she pushed the young Saxon from her mind.

They rode north for many more days, often stopping at roadside inns to sleep, but some nights they were forced to make camp under the stars. Badulf never slept on those nights as he kept watch, but neither did Brigid. She would stare at the moon – if thick clouds didn't block it – and try to make sense of everything. Too many uncertainties still clouded her mind and the vision the spear had given her still gave a sense of trepidation that she could not shake. The further north they went, the more nervous she became as well. The thought of seeing the wise one made her heart race, but it also filled her with dread. What if the wise one didn't have the answers she needed? What would she do then? Brigid shook her head to rid herself of those questions as they stopped on top of a hill. Badulf had taken them away from the Roman road when they entered the lands of Brigantians, the people who thought of Brigantia as their chief god. When she was a child, Brigid had often wondered why Brigantia had chosen her and not one of her people, and all the wise one had ever said when she had asked was that you should never try to understand the gods. Brigid's hand went to the bead necklace around her neck at the memory, because that was what she was trying to do now.

In the distance, Brigid saw a large city surrounded by thick walls like Cair Urnahc. Too many trails of smoke to count drifted towards the skies while many farmsteads filled the landscape around the city. Badulf had been right about one thing, though. The lands in the north looked similar to the lands of the Cornovii and even the people they had come across spoke the same language, only with different dialects.

'Cair Hebrauc,' Badulf said. 'The capital of the Brigantians.'

'Why are we not going there?' Brigid asked as she stared at the city.

'We have no need to go there. The wise one won't be in Cair Hebrauc.'

Brigid looked at her brother and wondered about the thoughts in his mind as his face darkened. 'You said before you don't know if you can find the wise one. Perhaps someone in Cair Hebrauc might know where she is.'

Badulf shook his head. 'To find her, we must go to the sacred forest, but even then, we might not. I told you, she seems to be running from something.'

Brigid frowned as the excitement of seeing the wise one was replaced by doubt, which she pushed away. 'What about the cult? You stayed with them, didn't you?'

Badulf shrugged. 'I can try to find their camp, but I don't know if they will still be there.'

'Then let's go,' Brigid said, and nudged her horse forwards. Badulf followed, and they rode around the capital of the Brigantians.

As they rode, Brigid tried to feel Brigantia's presence in the blue skies and in the song of the birds. Children smiled and waved at them as they rode past farmsteads, while men glared at them and women frowned. But just like the sacred grove in the forest by Cair Urnahc, Brigid felt nothing. She still wondered why the mother goddess had fallen silent to her. And not just Brigantia, but the other gods as well. Badulf had said that the wise one was hiding from something, and Brigid wondered if that was what the gods were doing as well.

The following day, they reached the Roman road again, and Badulf took them north. Brigid wanted to ask him where they were going, but in the distance she saw something that took her breath away. A wall, larger than any she had ever seen before, that cut through the lands like a giant blade separating a limb from a body.

'The great Roman wall,' Badulf said when he saw what she was looking at. 'The stories of it never prepare you for seeing it.'

Brigid nodded, her voice lost in amazement. It didn't matter which way she looked; she saw no end to the wall. She remembered Octa asking about the wall and how she had been so confident when she had told him of it, as if she knew it well, but never had she thought she would ever see it. 'The shrine is near here?'

Badulf's face darkened, and she regretted asking as he pointed to the east. 'Somewhere in that forest over there.'

Brigid looked at where he pointed and saw the dark trees on the landscape. 'Is that the sacred forest?'

Badulf nodded.

'Then why aren't we going there?' Brigid wondered if she would get to see this shrine to Brigantia. Perhaps there she could feel Brigantia's presence.

Badulf sighed, and she looked at him. 'Because I don't know where it is. Only that it's in there.'

'And the cult?'

Badulf shrugged. 'The same. Only that they are somewhere in the forest.'

'So how are we going to find them?' Brigid asked, as she tried to hide her disappointment. She had hoped it would be a simple task to find the cult and that they would lead her to the wise one.

'Someone in there will know and I think I know who.' Badulf pointed to the Roman fort at the end of the Roman road and Brigid felt her heart race as she stared at it.

A short while later, they stopped by the gates of the fort and Brigid was surprised to see two young Britons guarding it. 'I thought Saxon foederati guarded this fort?'

Badulf nodded. 'They do, but they're old men. The locals here seem to respect them, though, and many join their ranks. Even the cult considers the Saxons as friends.'

Brigid raised an eyebrow at this as Badulf approached the guards. The gates were open and, inside the fort, Brigid saw the same buildings that she was used to seeing in Cair Urnahc. Warriors, old and young, walked around, some wearing armour and carrying weapons, while some didn't. Children ran around the fort as well, often with wooden swords, while women shouted at them or laughed.

The two young warriors frowned as Badulf stopped in front of them and glanced at each other while Brigid looked at the top of the fort, where she saw more warriors staring at them.

'I seek Reinald, the Saxon foederati.'

The two young warriors only stared at Badulf, and Brigid wondered if they spoke the British tongue, when a voice shouted from the top of the fort.

'And what do you want from him?' The words were British, but the accent sounded strange, yet familiar, and Brigid couldn't help but smile as it reminded her of her grandfather. Brigid looked at the source of the voice and was surprised to see an old face with a long grey beard staring down at them.

Badulf looked up at the old man speaking to them. 'I seek his advice, that's all.'

'Advice about what?' the old warrior called down. 'On how to please your woman?'

Brigid saw how Badulf bristled at that and prayed her brother kept calm.

'She is my sister, not my woman.'

The old man shrugged. 'I don't think Reinald can give advice about that.'

The two young warriors by the gate smiled and Badulf glared at them when a new voice said, 'By the gods. I thought you were dead.'

Brigid looked at the gate and saw an old warrior, a man old enough to be her grandfather, standing there and staring at Badulf with a raised eyebrow. The old warrior wore his mail vest with ease and, as she looked at his face, she couldn't tell which were scars or age lines. But his thin frame and sinewy muscle showed a strength not to be underestimated. As Brigid stared at the warrior, she wondered if he had known her grandfather.

'So did I,' Badulf responded as he glared at the old warrior, and Brigid wondered about that.

The old Saxon shrugged. 'Well, the gods know that explains why we never found your body.' He looked at Brigid, who shivered under his gaze. 'And this is your sister?' Badulf nodded and for a short while he and the old warrior stared at each other, until the Saxon said, 'Well, there's no point standing here and doing nothing. Those clouds will bring rain soon and you two look like you need a bath and some warm food.' The man turned and walked back into the fort and Brigid moved her horse closer to Badulf.

'You don't like him.'

Badulf gritted his teeth. 'He told the Jutes how to find the shrine, all to save Octa. It's because of him that Octa has the spear.'

Brigid frowned. 'Why did he need to save Octa?'

Badulf glanced at Brigid, and she realised she had never asked him about the journey north, only of what had happened after. 'It's a long story.'

They nudged their horses forwards and entered the fort. A young boy, no older than seven winters, led them to the stables and took the horses' reins when they got there.

'I'll take good care of them, don't you worry,' the boy said, and Brigid smiled at him as Badulf scowled.

'Thank you,' Brigid said, and followed Badulf as he made his way to the main hall. Again, Brigid was struck by the mix of old Saxon warriors and the Britons, although she noticed how some of the Britons had Saxon features and, for once, Brigid wasn't taller than most. 'They live together as one people,' she said to Badulf, who only grunted. 'How long have the Saxons been here? Do you think they knew Grandfather?'

'There were many Saxon warriors fighting in Britannia for the Romans, but it's possible. I didn't think of asking the last time I was here.' She saw how he looked at one building as they walked past it, but then she forgot about it as she saw an old Saxon showing a young boy how to hold a spear correctly. The old man laughed the way a proud grandfather would as the boy lunged forward with the spear and Brigid wondered if her grandfather had ever laughed at her or Badulf that way. They walked past what looked to be a Christian church and near it stood a stone column with a carving of a one-eyed man on it. Brigid froze as she stared at the carving. She didn't recognise the symbols carved on the stone, but she recognised the spear in his hand as the vision came to her again.

Brigid looked at the church again, surprised that it was near the monument to the Saxon god. In Cair Urnahc, the Christians tried hard to wipe out any mention or image of other gods, whether they were Roman or British, but here it looked like they thrived side by side. Just as the people did.

31

Brigid walked around the streets of Corstopitum, her arms crossed and lost in thoughts. It was a short while after they had arrived at the fort and she had cleaned her face from the sweat and dust of the ride north and her stomach was filled with freshly baked bread and fresh fish caught in the river nearby. Badulf was still in the hall, talking to Reinald, but Brigid wanted to explore more of the fort.

The fort was strange to her. In some ways, it reminded her of Cair Urnahc, but it was also different. Men taller than her walked past her, something that was still strange to her because she stood as tall as most of the men in Cair Urnahc. The people spoke a mix of languages, which took her some time to get used to. Most in the British tongue, even the old Saxons, but some spoke the Saxon language, which almost made her feel like she was in her grandfather's homelands.

Brigid stopped and looked around her as she tried to picture her grandfather in a fort like this, but she couldn't. She couldn't remember what he looked like. Perhaps a bit like her brother as she saw him walk towards her, his face as dark as his mood. Brigid knew why he was angry. He had thought he had helped stop the fire the wise one had told him about, only to learn that he had stolen the wrong spear from the Jutes. Perhaps part of the blame belonged to her as well. Brigid had never thought of telling Badulf that Octa had the spear because she had assumed he already knew. But Brigid had not known about the other spear.

'Vellocatus's gone,' Badulf said when he reached her. 'The bastard is gone. Killed by the Picts when he went to a nearby farm to treat the family who got ill a few days ago.'

Brigid frowned and tried not to let the news bring her down. Badulf had told her he believed the man who treated the ill and the injured in the fort was part of the cult and that he could help them find the others. But if that man was dead, then where did they go? 'There is no one else we can ask? I have to find her, Badulf. What about the leader of the foederati? You said he knew where the shrine was. Perhaps he knows where to find the cult.'

Badulf looked at her and then sighed. 'Reinald? No, I don't trust him. He's a Saxon.'

Her brother's words angered her. 'Why does that make him our enemy? Our grandfather was a Saxon, Badulf. Saxon blood runs through your veins! Open your eyes and look around you. Saxons and Britons living together, as one people!'

Badulf scowled at the people of the fort and said, 'The wise one told me that Octa would bring fire to these lands. And I'm sure she was talking about a war. A war between us and the Jutes. And who do you think these Saxons will fight for? Us or those from their homelands?'

'We will fight for our families,' the old Saxon leader said from behind them, which startled both Brigid and Badulf. 'We will fight for the wives and children we buried in this ground. We will fight for the children who will one day bury us in this ground.' Even at his age, the old warrior was still intimidating as he stood taller than Badulf. 'If there is a war with the Jutes, then it will be in the south, not here by the wall. And we don't concern ourselves with what happens in the south. Not when we have our own war to fight.'

Badulf glared at Reinald before he turned and stormed away, leaving Brigid behind with the old Saxon.

'Forgive my brother. He feels like he is responsible for what is to come.'

Reinald, his eyes still on the back of Badulf, shrugged. 'We cannot control what is to come, just like we could not control what has been. Wyrd decides what was and what will be.'

'Wyrd?' Brigid frowned at Reinald, who smiled at her.

'Aye. Wyrd is the god who decides our fate, or our wyrd, as we say. He decides how and when we die. Whether we achieve greatness or die nameless.'

Brigid shivered at the thought of that, but then she knew her ancestors also had gods they believed did the same. 'So if you can't control what happened yesterday or what will happen tomorrow, what do you do?'

Reinald looked around him, smiling at those he knew, and then he looked at the sky as thick clouds covered the sun. 'We live in the now and we live it to our best abilities. We enjoy the songs of the birds and cherish the moments we get to share with the ones we love.'

Brigid couldn't help but smile at that, but her smile faltered as soon as it arrived. She had never been allowed to enjoy the moment. Her entire life had been dedicated to serving the gods. To serving Brigantia. Her mind had always been occupied with ideas of how to manipulate King Vortigern in order to keep the Christians from getting too strong. Of finding ways to spread the names of the gods who once ruled Britannia. 'If only life was as simple as you make it seem.'

Reinald nodded. 'Aye, if only.' He looked around him again. 'If you need anything, just ask.'

Before Reinald walked away, she asked, 'Did you know my grandfather? He was a Saxon foederati, like you. His name was Badulf.'

'Your brother was named after him?' Brigid nodded, suddenly nervous even though she didn't understand why, as Reinald scratched his bearded chin. 'It's a good name. A strong name. I knew many Badulfs, some older than me, some younger, but the gods know I can't say if any of them was your grandfather.'

Brigid's heart sank. She had hoped to hear some stories of her grandfather, something to add to the few faint memories she had of him. 'Thank you.'

Reinald stood there for a few moments and, after a deep sigh, said, 'I know why you are here. Your brother either seeks the shrine again or the cult that protects it.'

'It's not him who seeks them. It's me.'

Reinald's old eyes stared at her for a few heartbeats and, in them, Brigid saw the countless battles the man had fought and the many friends he had buried. Those who loved him and those who betrayed him. 'Why do you seek them? The last time your brother was here, it ended with him getting a spear in his back and us thinking he was dead.'

Brigid nodded. She still remembered the crushing pain when she had been told that Badulf was dead. 'I have my reasons and they are mine alone.'

Again, the old warrior stared at her for a while, before he glanced at the sky. 'The last time I told them how to get there, most of them died. I don't care about Jutes. The gods know they deserved their wyrd, but what happened to your brother weighed heavily on me for a long time.'

'But you told them. And Badulf said it was to protect Octa, the young Saxon.'

Reinald sighed. 'Aye, and still to this day, I wonder if I did the right thing.'

Brigid thought of the vision she had when she had touched the spear and wondered the same thing. But that was why she was there. To find out. 'Why did you? Octa meant nothing to you.'

'He reminded me of my son, who died beyond the wall. I couldn't keep him alive and believed that if I could help Octa, then I could forgive myself for failing my son. I didn't see it at first, only after when we found him by the shrine and believed he was dead as well.'

'And did you forgive yourself?'

Reinald frowned for a short while. 'I don't know. Octa lives and he found what he came for.'

'The spear.'

Reinald nodded. 'I often wonder if he got the redemption he was after.'

Brigid frowned as she wondered what redemption Octa was after, but then she pushed those thoughts from her mind. 'The spear Octa found... it...'

'It is just a spear,' Reinald said. 'A weapon made of wood and iron, like all the others around the fort.'

Brigid stared at the old warrior and wondered if that was what he really believed, or was he just saying that to her? 'No, the spear is more than that. And that is why I need to find the cult. I need to find the wise one.'

'The wise one.' Reinald raised an eyebrow at her and Brigid wondered if she had said too much. 'She has not been seen for many winters. Not since I was a young man, and yet, over the past season, many have seen the old crooked-back woman wandering the lands.'

Brigid shook her head. 'Badulf saw her when he was with the cult. She came to him.'

The old warrior stared at her, the lines on his face deeper in his seriousness. 'Why do you seek her and what does this have to do with the spear?'

Brigid hesitated for a few heartbeats, not sure what she should tell the old warrior. 'She told Badulf that the spear will bring fire to these lands. He thinks it means there will be a war.'

'And you want to stop this war?'

Brigid took a deep breath. 'Badulf wants to. I want to understand what this means for the gods.'

Again, Reinald stared at her as the people of the fort continued with their lives, unaware and uninterested in their conversation. 'The gods of these lands are fading away and they have been for a long time.'

'And what of your gods?' Brigid asked. 'Are they still as strong as they were before your beard grew grey? I see monuments of your gods all around the fort. Symbols carved into the stone walls and small statues of your gods, and alongside them, the symbols and words of the Christian god.'

Reinald looked around him and nodded. 'We keep our gods alive with us. We honour them with sacrifices and we call out their names while we kill our enemies. But the Christians are free to follow their god. We found a way to live in peace, something I know doesn't happen everywhere.'

'And what of my gods? The gods of Britannia? Brigantia, Morrigan and Taranis? I see no inscriptions of them in the fort.'

'Your gods still live, but like I said, they are fading away. There are many who still speak their names and worship them, but more and more people turn to the Christian god.'

'And that is why I must find the wise one. I believe something is coming and that Octa and the spear will play key roles in that something. I need to understand what that is.'

'And you believe the wise one will tell you? Why?'

Brigid wanted to scream with frustration from all the questions, but she sensed Reinald would not help if she didn't tell him the truth. For a moment, she wondered if Octa had to go through the same. With a deep breath, she pulled her dress down to show Reinald the mark. 'I was born with this symbol. The wise one taught me what it meant and how to communicate with the gods. If I can find her, then I know she'll help me.'

Reinald looked at the mark of the spear on her shoulder and then nodded. 'Tell your brother we leave in the morning.'

'We?'

Reinald nodded. 'This time, I'm going with.'

32

Octa stroked Warda's side, his mind lost in the events of recent days. Lucilia and her family had left the island, but their house had not stayed empty for long as one of the Jutes took it for himself and his new family. The brothers had spent most of their time arguing. Hengist felt it was prudent to take Berthild's advice and prepare for battle, but Horsa refused to listen. He claimed women knew nothing about these things, but Octa felt it was more than that. Part of it, he thought, was because of Horsa's dislike of him, which meant he didn't like his mother either. Another part, Octa thought as he looked up and saw his mother walking around the town like she used to in his father's village, but this time with Oisc by her side, was because of the growing bond between Hengist and Octa's mother.

'Every day, the boy walks with her,' Odalric said as he poked his head out from behind his horse, and Octa nodded.

'Aye. Oisc likes her and his mother died a few winters ago. Perhaps that's why he spends so much time with my mother.' He turned his attention back to Warda and stroked her muzzle. The horse shook her head and turned away from him and he smiled at that. 'I'm sorry, Warda. I know I've been neglecting you, but much has happened these last few days.'

'Only you can get a horse to be mad at you,' Odalric said, and then frowned at something behind them.

Octa looked over his shoulder and saw that Hengist had joined his mother and Oisc. He raised an eyebrow at the way his mother laughed at something Hengist had said and then sighed. 'Mother is up to something.'

'Aye,' Odalric said as he put a saddle on his horse. 'And only Wyrd knows whether that's going to be good for you or not.'

'Aye.' Octa looked beyond his mother and the warlord, and his heart raced. Warriors were walking around in full armour and many were doing drills as they prepared for the war his mother felt was coming. Horsa might not have agreed with her, but Hengist had convinced his brother that the men should be ready for battle at all times, at least until they knew for sure. Even Octa and Odalric had their armour on and their weapons with them. Those not practising were working on the walls of the town, making them taller and stronger, while more barriers had been placed between the bridge and the town. Octa turned back to Warda and picked up her saddle. 'Come, Warda. Let's go for a ride.'

'Are you sure this is a good idea?' Odalric asked, and Octa shrugged.

'I need to get away from all this. And besides, you don't have to come with.'

Odalric grunted. 'I do because your mother told me to protect you.'

Octa shook his head. He had fought battles and had the spear of Woden, yet his mother still treated him as if he were a child. 'I thought you were supposed to protect her.'

Odalric checked the saddle was tight enough and said, 'She's safe enough here. I might not like the Jutes, but I'm sure Hengist will protect her. He likes your mother.'

Octa looked at his mother again, who was now walking with Hengist by her side. Oisc was walking ahead of them with a stick in his hand, which he swung around as if it was a sword and he was fighting a battle. His hand went to the sword around his waist and he prayed the boy would never have to fight a battle. 'But does she like him too, or is she using him?'

Odalric shrugged. 'I'm only a warrior, and that question is for someone a lot smarter than me. Now, let's go before they see us and stop us.'

Octa glanced at Odalric, already on his horse, and sensed the man was also eager to get away from the town for a short while. He finished putting the saddle on Warda and, with Gungnir in his hand, mounted her before he stroked her neck. The mare pawed the ground, and he guessed she wanted to get out of the stables. Since they had returned from Cair Urnahc, Octa had been too busy to take Warda out for rides. He still tried to visit her every day so she wouldn't feel abandoned, but he knew she needed to run. Horses needed space. They needed to stretch their legs and run free, not be locked up in stables all the time.

'Aye, let's go.' He nudged Warda, and they rode towards the gates of the town, when he heard his mother's voice.

'And where in Friga's name are you going?'

Octa sighed and looked at his mother. 'Warda needs to stretch her legs.'

'And I guess this can't be done on the island?'

'Perhaps Octa and Odalric can scout the lands for us. The last group of scouts we sent out yesterday have not returned.' Hengist's brow furrowed, and Octa understood why. Every day they sent scouts out to see what the Cantiaci were doing and today was the first time the scouts had not returned.

'Perhaps they rode out further,' Odalric said, and Hengist nodded. Unlike his brother, Hengist seemed to like the older Saxon. 'We'll keep an eye out for them.'

Again, Hengist nodded. 'Thank you.'

'Can I go with?' Oisc asked, his eyes wide.

'I'm not sure that is a good idea,' Octa's mother said, but then Hengist smiled.

'No, it might be good for my son to see more of Britannia other than Ruym Island.' He looked at Octa and his eyes fell on Gungnir in Octa's hand. 'I'm sure Octa and Odalric will take good care of Oisc. And if Octa and Odalric don't mind waiting, I can have some of my men join them.'

A look of annoyance flashed across his mother's face. She did not like to be disobeyed, but Octa saw no reason to disagree. Besides, he also felt like Oisc might enjoy getting off the island. The boy had been stuck in the village since he arrived, and there wasn't much for him to do. The other children his age avoided him because of who his father was and because they couldn't speak to him, and his father had been too busy to spend much time with him.

'We can wait,' Octa said, and noticed how Odalric raised an eyebrow at him.

They didn't have to wait long for Hengist to gather six men to join them and, because the warriors were already in their armour, it only took them a short while to get ready. Horsa watched them from the hall. Octa had thought the man would complain about this, but he just stood there and watched them.

Octa recognised one of the men as the man he sat next to when King Vortigern had been here. Octa remembered his name: Aldric. The Jute was a similar age to Odalric and somehow looked like he had fought more battles, but Octa liked him. A horse was prepared for Oisc, who looked uncomfortable as he was helped onto it.

'Stay calm,' Octa said. 'If she senses you are nervous, then she'll get nervous. Just relax and trust her. She'll look after you.' Oisc looked at Octa and nodded before he took a calming breath.

'Listen to Octa,' his mother said. 'He's always been good with horses.' Oisc smiled at her as the Jutes all mounted their horses.

'So you want us to keep the Saxons safe?' one of the Jutes asked, and the others laughed, especially Oisc, who seemed eager to be one of the men.

'First, you'll need to make sure you don't fall off your horses,' Odalric said as he turned his towards the gate. 'Come, before the sun decides it's had enough time waiting for us.'

'Listen to the men, son,' Hengist said. 'And stay close to them.'

'And if you see any Britons, throw some stones at them,' Horsa said as he approached. Oisc nodded with a wide grin, and the warriors laughed as Octa nudged Warda towards the gate and the Jutes followed before they rode to the bridge. People waved at the boy as they rode past, and Octa frowned as he looked at the many houses being built on the island. Most of the tents had been replaced by wooden houses, but that still didn't stop the Britons from the mainland from sneaking on to the island and burning the houses. Octa glanced at the blackened remains of a house that had been burnt soon after the king of the Britons had left, one of a handful that night. The gods had been with them that night as those houses were empty, but to Octa, it felt like the attacks were happening more often.

'Why do they do that?' Oisc asked as they rode past the burnt-down houses.

'Because the Britons are weak and, instead of fighting us, they sneak around in the middle of the night and try to kill us while we sleep,' Aldric said, and Octa glanced at the warrior.

'Or perhaps they are angry because this land belonged to them before your father and uncle arrived,' Odalric said. 'But they can't fight back because their king tells them not to, so they try to hurt us in other ways.'

'You speaking from experience there, Odalric?' Aldric asked, and Odalric only grunted as they rode over the bridge and on to the mainland.

Octa scanned the skies, not sure what he was looking for, when one of the Jutes asked, 'Where do we go?'

'That hill looks like a good place to see the land,' Aldric said, and Octa nodded. He glanced at Oisc, who seemed more comfortable on his horse, and smiled at the boy.

'Let's see who can get there the fastest.' Before anyone could respond, he nudged Warda, who took off as if she knew what he wanted.

'You bastard!' one of the Jutes shouted, but soon they were all racing towards the hill, with Warda in the lead. Octa closed his eyes, trusting the mare to run straight, and smiled as the wind rushed past his ears and through his long hair. Behind him, he could hear the others cheering and pushing their horses to go faster, but over that, he heard Oisc's shrill laughter. Octa opened his eyes and glanced over his shoulder, and saw the others were gaining, but he didn't care. He just wanted Warda to run. He smiled as he saw Aldric holding on to the reins of Oisc's horse and the joy on the boy's face reminded him of how he and his friends used to race around Witta's village when he was Oisc's age.

Octa reached the hill first, and Warda stopped without him needing to do anything. She pawed the ground as she snorted, and Octa smiled as he patted her neck. 'There you go, girl.'

The others reached the hill soon after, and Octa smiled as Oisc laughed.

'You bastard,' Aldric said with a smile on his face.

'Should have known you were going to do something like that.' Odalric patted his horse, who looked like she had also enjoyed the run.

'The horses have been in the stables too long,' Octa said, and looked at Oisc, who beamed at him. 'They need a good run now and again.'

Aldric nodded. 'Just like warriors need a good fight now and again.' He scanned the lands behind the hills and scratched his ear. 'Looks quiet.'

'How big is Britannia?' Oisc asked as he copied the older warrior.

'Big,' Octa said. 'It takes many days to reach the town of the high king and then many more days to reach the lands of the Picts in the north.'

'You've been there?' Oisc asked him, and Octa nodded, but he didn't want to think about that. He wondered, though, how Reinald was. 'Is that where you got the spear?'

Again, Octa nodded. 'That is where I got the spear.' The Jutes all glanced at him and Octa sensed Odalric tense near him. He turned his attention back to the land and frowned when he saw what looked like many fires behind the forest in front of them. 'What's that?'

Everyone turned serious as they looked at the smoke.

'Which way did the missing scouts go?' Odalric asked, and the Jutes glanced at each other.

'That way,' Aldric said. 'We went south, and they went west, but that smoke wasn't there the day before.'

Octa's hands trembled as he wondered if that meant his mother was right. He looked at Oisc, who stared at the smoke like everyone else.

'We should return to the island,' he said, and Aldric shook his head.

'Not until we see what is causing that. If we return without that knowledge, then we all get flogged, even you, Octa.'

'He's right,' Odalric said as he glanced at him.

Octa rubbed the shaft of Gungnir as he stared at the smoke and then the forest they'd have to go through to get to the source of the smoke. He wasn't sure why, but he didn't feel like it was a good idea to go through those trees, but it would take too long to go around the forest. He glanced at the sky. The sun was just past its peak, so there was still plenty of daylight left and the clouds didn't look like they would bring rain. 'Then we should at least send Oisc back.'

'No, I'm coming with,' Oisc said, and Aldric laughed.

'The boy's spoken. Let's go, unless you Saxons are too afraid.'

Odalric grunted, but then looked at Octa. 'What are you thinking, Octa?'

Octa glanced at the older Saxon and wondered if this was one of those you're-the-son-of-a-warlord moments, but he didn't see the same look on Odalric's face when he usually asked that question. Only concern. He took a deep breath and tightened his grip on Gungnir. *What will you do,* he asked himself before he responded. 'I think we should stay close and keep our eyes open.'

One of the Jutes laughed. 'Look at Octa. Fights some Picts in the north and now thinks he's the god of war himself.'

'He fights with Woden's spear,' Aldric said, glancing at Gungnir. 'Let's do as he says. Those trees could well hide an army.'

They fell silent as Aldric moved his horse closer to Oisc's and they rode downhill towards the forest. Octa's heart raced in his chest as he remembered what Friga had told him. They might not have the real spear, but that they believed they did would give them the strength. Again, he wondered if he had done the right thing by letting Badulf go. He could have avoided a war if he had killed the Briton, but that was not who Octa was.

They slowed down as they approached the trees. The older warriors all scowled at the trees, their spears ready, while Octa looked at Warda. Her senses were better than theirs and Octa did not like the way she lowered her ears. Something or someone was amongst the trees.

'We shouldn't go in there,' he said, but Aldric shook his head.

'It'll take too long to go around the forest. We stay close, like you said.' He looked at the other Jutes. 'Keep Oisc between us.' Oisc looked afraid as he stared at the trees and Octa remembered when his own fear had crippled him. 'Don't be afraid, Oisc. We Jutes don't feel fear, remember that. Be strong, like your father.'

Oisc nodded, but Octa saw the words only made him more nervous. He glanced at Odalric when he sensed his eyes on him and he wondered what the older Saxon was thinking.

Octa took a deep breath. 'Come, Warda, let's see what that smoke is.' The horse seemed to hesitate, as if she didn't want to enter the forest, and Octa stroked her neck. 'I know, I feel it too.'

'Feel what?' Oisc asked, and Octa looked at the young boy.

'Fear.'

33

Badulf glared at the old Saxon as they left the fort. His fists were clenched around the reins of his horse and his shoulders were tense, as if he expected Reinald to attack him at any time. And as much as Brigid tried to ignore it, she couldn't. She still didn't understand Badulf's hatred for the old Saxon, but felt that he had become infected with the same disease that Prince Vortimer had. A hatred for everything not from Britannia.

When Brigid had told Badulf that Reinald would take them, he had refused at first and said that they would go by themselves instead, that he would find the shrine and the cult. But Brigid did not believe that he could, otherwise he would have taken her there instead of the fort. The only reason Badulf was with them now was because she had told him she was going with or without him.

'It's a fine day today, barely a cloud in the sky,' Reinald said as he rode his horse with the ease of a man who had done so more times than could be counted. 'The gods are smiling on us today.'

'Your gods have cursed this island. They want to burn everything we have and replace it with their monuments,' Badulf said as he glared at Reinald, who only smiled at him.

'Young man, I am too old to be affected by your misplaced anger. I am not the one who threw the spear that injured you, neither am I the one who took the spear from the shrine.'

'He is right, Badulf. Your anger at the Saxon is blinding you to the fact Saxon blood runs in our veins, something we were proud of once.'

Badulf hawked and spat. 'That was before I knew how treacherous they are. You can't trust the Saxons.'

Reinald stopped his horse and stared at the surrounding landscape. His old eyes creased as if he was searching for something. 'You see that hill over there?' He pointed to a hill in the distance. 'My cousin died there defending the village behind the hill from men who rebelled against the Dux.' He glanced at Badulf. The Brigantians weren't ruled by a king like the other tribes. Instead they gave their leader the title of Dux, which was what the Romans called their generals. 'Britons attacking other Britons because they believed their leader should be the Dux. Over there' – he pointed to a valley not far from the hill – 'twenty of my friends, Saxons and Angles, died fighting a large raiding party of Picts. They outnumbered us, and the British warriors who were supposed to support us decided they didn't want to die, so they fled.' He turned his attention back to Badulf, but Brigid saw no anger in his eyes. 'Do not think that we are the same as the Jutes in the south. Just like I don't think you are the same as the many Britons who have betrayed me and my men over the long time we have been here. We have shed our blood on the very ground we ride over defending these people and not because we want to take their land. Because it is our duty and Tiw demands we honour that duty.'

Badulf looked away, his cheeks red, but then he said, 'But you still told the Jutes where to find the spear.'

'No, I told them how to find the forest the shrine was in. And I expected the cult to kill them, which was another reason I tried to convince Octa to stay behind. Like you and the cult, I underestimated them.'

'Enough of this, Badulf. I know you blame yourself for the part you played, but you didn't know what the Jutes were planning,' Brigid said as she tried to calm her brother and carry on. She was eager to get to the shrine and was getting frustrated with this distraction.

'But you warned me to stay away. You said the gods were afraid of Octa.'

Reinald raised an eye at Badulf's words and Brigid wished Badulf hadn't said that.

'But I still don't understand why. The man is a coward.'

'A coward?' Reinald asked, and then shook his head. 'Octa is no coward.

He should have been dead when we found him, yet he survived. He spent the winter with us while he recovered from his wounds and I got to know him well.' Reinald looked at Brigid. 'Your gods have no reason to fear Octa, unless they threaten what he loves.'

'How can you be so certain?' Brigid asked, her heart racing.

'When you fight beside a man in the shield wall, you get to know him very well.'

'Octa fought in a shield wall?' Badulf asked, his voice filled with disbelief.

Reinald nodded. 'Aye, we fought a large force of Picts not far from here. Octa stood his ground and fought like a Saxon warrior.'

'That's not the Octa I saw,' Badulf said, and Reinald smiled.

'No, the Octa that left us to return south was not the same Octa that came with you and the Jutes.' Reinald nudged his horse and they carried on as Brigid and Badulf frowned at each other. Brigid wasn't sure if the old Saxon's words had any impact on her brother, but they added even more questions in her mind. Was the vision she got when she touched the spear a sign of things to come, or did it show her the fears of her gods? Of what they were afraid might happen?

They rode in silence after that as Brigid, her fingers toying with the beads around her neck, struggled with the thoughts in her mind. She did not notice the scowl on Badulf's face or hear the song the old Saxon sang to himself as they turned off the road which ran along the wall.

'This was where it happened,' Badulf said, breaking her from her thoughts.

'Where what happened?' Brigid asked.

'The ambush,' Badulf said, and Brigid looked around her. They were near the forest, which surprised her as she had not realised how far they had travelled since their last conversation.

'They would have had archers hiding in the trees,' Reinald said. 'We found two dead Jutes with arrow holes in them, but the arrows had been removed. They usually try to drive those seeking the shrine away from the forest and must not have expected the Jutes to go towards it instead.' Brigid tensed as if she expected arrows to come flying out of the trees and Reinald gave her a comforting smile. 'There's no need for that. They no longer need to protect the shrine, so they left.'

'The cult left?' Brigid's heart sank at that news, and she wondered why the gods were making it so hard for her to reach them. *Am I being punished*, she wondered.

'Most have. The ones who lived in the forest, anyway. We found many bodies hanging from the trees and I suspect they were punishing those who failed to protect the spear.' Reinald scratched his neck. 'Although why now when a season has passed, only the gods would know.'

'But I was with them the entire winter,' Badulf said. 'I only left when summer arrived. There was no talk of punishment.'

Reinald raised an eyebrow at her brother. 'Then something must have changed.' They paused as they approached the forest and, for the first time since she had met the old Saxon, he seemed nervous. 'They say an old magic guards these trees and the secrets they hide. I never knew if that was true or not, but whenever I enter this forest, I always feel as if something dangerous is watching me. Stay close and keep your eyes open.'

'I spent the winter amongst these trees, old man. I don't need your concern,' Badulf said, but Brigid noticed how he gripped his spear.

'You spent the winter amongst those who knew its secrets and they kept you in one place, away from the shrine and the magic that protects it.'

'How are you so sure of that?' Badulf asked, and Reinald smiled.

'There is little that happens along this part of the wall that we don't know. We might not know the exact locations of the cult, but we usually know what they are up to.'

'How?' Brigid asked as she stared at the dark trees which reminded her of the sacred forest by Cair Urnahc. Without meaning to, she glanced around the ground, trying to see dead animals that had been laid there to scare off those who were not welcome.

'There are those who tell us and we pay them.'

Anger flashed in Badulf's eyes. 'You are spying on the cult?'

Brigid looked at her brother, wondering why he was suddenly so protective of the cult of Brigantia. He had never cared about them in the past, even when Brigid had asked him to help protect the few members of the cult she had known in Cair Urnahc.

'Not spying on them, no. Making sure they don't cause any problems. Other than that, we leave them alone.' Reinald turned and led his horse into the trees and Brigid shook her head at her brother before she took a deep breath and followed the old Saxon.

This forest seemed darker than the one by Cair Urnahc, although Brigid couldn't understand why as the hairs on the back of her neck stood on end. She closed her eyes, trusting her horse to follow Reinald's, and tried to feel the presence of Brigantia amongst the trees. But just like the forest by Cair Urnahc, she felt nothing. And all she heard were the birds singing from the trees, a raven's crow and a cuckoo calling out. As well as leaves rustling in the breeze and Badulf's angry breathing.

'We're here,' Reinald said as he stopped and Brigid opened her eyes. She stroked her horse, thanking the beast for guiding her as she searched for the gods amongst the trees.

'I don't know this part of the forest,' Badulf said, and Reinald nodded.

'They wouldn't have brought you were. Only the cult members know the location of the shrine.'

'So how did you find it?' Brigid asked.

Reinald shrugged. 'We were hunting outlaws who had killed some farmers a long time ago when we stumbled on the clearing.'

'Why didn't you take the spear?' Badulf asked, and Reinald looked at him.

'I had no interest in the spear or the stories told about it. I had my wife and my children. Them and my duty was enough for me. And besides, I always sensed the gods, yours and mine, didn't want me to take it.'

Brigid took a deep breath and moved her horse past Reinald's before she entered the clearing. Her horse's muscles quivered, which made her think that the animal had sensed something she couldn't, so she dismounted her, not wanting to stress the horse more than necessary.

'Brigid,' Badulf said, but she ignored him as she stared at the cave in the clearing. She had expected to see the same as the clearing in Cair Urnahc, but there was no sacred tree or carved stones. All she saw was the cave in the small hill in the clearing, but even that seemed unremarkable. Nothing she saw or felt would have made her believe that this was a shrine to the mother goddess of the Brigantians.

Behind her, Badulf and Reinald dismounted their horses, but they stood back as she wondered how Octa had learnt of this place. With a deep breath, she walked towards the cave. Her heart raced in her chest and her palms felt sweaty.

Brigantia, Mother, are you here? Please talk to me.

Brigid stopped at the entrance of the cave, suddenly too afraid to enter.

But then the vision from the spear came to her again, and she knew she had to. She had to find the goddess. Brigid clenched her fists to stop her hands from shaking and walked into the cave. The stench inside the cave caught in her throat and almost made her gag and, as her eyes adjusted to the darkness inside, her hand went to her mouth to stop herself from screaming.

The corpse of a dead man, the skin dried and pulled tight against the bones, lay in the middle of the cave, its empty eye sockets and white teeth giving her a welcoming smile. The chain-mail vest and the weapons told her the man had been a Jute, perhaps one of the men who had travelled with her brother. She scanned the rest of the cave and, at the back wall, she saw the feet and what must have been a statue. Around the feet lay broken stone and, in the dim light that came in from outside, she could make out the face of the statue. Without needing to be told who it was, Brigid knelt down by the stone and said, 'Brigantia.'

34

Brigid sat in the cave, her eyes closed as she tried to feel the presence of the gods. Her breathing was slow and calm, her heartbeat relaxed. Focusing on her breathing, she blocked out the sounds from outside: the birds singing from the branches; leaves rustling in the wind; insects buzzing over flowers; even Badulf as he coughed. She lost track of how long she sat there as she did what the wise one had taught her to do.

If you ever need to speak to the gods, then all you need to do is listen. Her voice came to Brigid. *The gods are everywhere. In the sun that shines from the sky, in the wind that cools your skin. The water that flows in the river and even the smallest insect crawling on a flower. The gods are there. All you need to do is listen.*

But it didn't matter how hard Brigid tried to listen. She could not hear Brigantia or any of the other gods. Exasperated, she opened her eyes and stared at the stone head of Brigantia. 'Mother, why won't you speak to me? Why are you ignoring my calls?'

'Because she is not here, not any more,' an unfamiliar voice said behind her from the shadows in the cave, and Brigid screamed.

Reinald and Badulf came rushing into the cave, both men with their weapons ready, as Brigid jumped to her feet and pulled the knife from its scabbard.

'What happened?' Badulf asked as he scanned the cave. His eyes fell on the corpse of the Jute and he stared at it as Brigid searched the shadows for the source of the voice. For a heartbeat, she wondered if she had imagined it, but then an old man stepped into the dim light of the cave and scowled at her. He wore an old robe with tattered edges, his grey beard all the way down to his waist while his hair hung over his shoulders. A rope was tied around his hips and from the rope hung many small pouches and a knife. 'Vettius!' Badulf's eyes widened, but what surprised her more was the smile she saw on Reinald's face when he saw the druid.

'Vettius, I thought you were dead.'

Badulf turned to the old Saxon. 'You know him?'

Reinald lowered his spear. 'Aye, me and this old bastard have known each other for more winters than I can remember.'

'How?' Badulf asked.

'That is not important, Badulf, son of Brychan,' Vettius said. He turned his attention to Brigid, who was still frozen to the spot. 'What is, is that you have arrived. Just like she knew you would.'

'She?' Brigid asked, and the druid smiled at her. It was not a friendly smile, or a comforting one, but Brigid sensed no danger in it, or from the man.

'The wise one?' Badulf asked, and Brigid looked at her brother as the druid nodded.

'You know the wise one?' Brigid asked, her heart racing in her chest.

The druid nodded. 'I am her protector, her guardian. I watch over her and ensure that she has everything she needs.'

'Can you take me to her? I need to see her. I have so many questions, but no answers. And... and the gods, they are silent. They don't speak to me any more.'

'The answers you'll get when you are ready to hear them. As for the gods.' The druid glanced around the cave and then he looked at the corpse of the Jute. 'Reinald, you really could have removed the body.'

Brigid's mind reeled, and she frowned at the sudden change in the druid's words as Reinald responded, 'It serves a purpose, and you know that neither me nor my men ever enter the cave.'

'The bastard Jutes defiled the shrine of the goddess,' Badulf said, his face contorted in anger again. He jabbed an angry finger at the remains of the statue. 'They stole the spear and destroyed the statue of Brigantia!'

'The men from the continent did not destroy the statue,' Vettius said as he stared at the broken stone.

'Then who did?' Badulf asked.

'I did,' the druid said.

Badulf's eyes widened, and even Brigid was surprised by this. 'Why?' she asked.

'It had served its purpose and, like the body, it sends a message.' Vettius looked outside the cave. 'Come, it is time to go. We have stayed here too long.'

'What message does it send?' Badulf asked, but the druid did not respond as he walked out of the cave.

'Don't bother trying to make sense of what the old druid is saying. He'll only ever tell you what he wants you to know. Never more and never less,' Reinald said, before he followed the druid outside.

Brigid looked at Badulf. 'I still couldn't sense her. She's not here.'

Badulf put a hand on his sister's shoulder after he took a deep breath. 'The druid is with the wise one. He'll take you to her and then you can get your answers.'

Brigid nodded as she took strength from her brother's words, but she still couldn't help but think of the vision, certain that that was the reason Brigantia was hiding from her.

They left the cave and saw Reinald and Vettius deep in conversation and Brigid frowned at that, especially when they stopped as soon as Brigid and her brother came near.

Vettius looked at the old Saxon. 'You can go, Reinald. There is no more need for you at the moment.'

Reinald shook his head. 'I'm staying. Much has been happening and many of the cult members have been found dead.'

Vettius nodded and then glared at Badulf. 'There were some who were encouraged by Badulf's rage and they rebelled. They believed it was wrong to sit back and do nothing, but they have been dealt with.'

Brigid looked at her brother and saw his cheeks turn red as he turned away from the druid.

'I'm a warrior. I can't just sit back and do nothing,' he said.

'Yet that is all you were doing before they arrived. Sitting around and doing nothing while the Picts raid your lands,' Vettius said with an edge in his voice. 'I warned you not to meddle. There is much you don't understand.'

'I understand that the spear the cult believed they were protecting was not the real spear.' Badulf glared at the druid as his own anger took hold and Brigid stepped between her brother and Vettius. 'But the Saxon found the real spear and yet you still do nothing.'

The druid glared at her brother for many heartbeats, before he said, 'You still know nothing.' He turned around and walked to the edge of the clearing where he stopped. 'Follow me. And Reinald, you don't need to follow. They will be safe with me. And take the horses with you. They're not needed.'

Reinald nodded and said to Brigid, 'Listen to him and tell your brother to calm himself. The druid is not a man to anger. Many have been disembowelled alive for making that mistake.'

Brigid glanced at her brother as she nodded. 'How do you know him?'

'He was my wife's brother before she called to him.' Reinald's eyes misted over as if he remembered the past.

'She?'

'The wise one.'

Brigid looked at the druid. 'He is the reason you know so much about the cult?'

Reinald smiled. 'One of the reasons. Now go, he is not a patient man.' Reinald turned to Badulf. 'I know you believe your anger is justified, but be careful who you aim it at. Like a sharp blade, it can hurt those who never meant you harm and those who only want to help.'

Badulf grunted and then walked towards the druid as Brigid shook her head and sighed.

'Thank you, Reinald. May your gods watch over you.'

Reinald smiled at her. 'And I pray you find yours once more.'

Brigid watched as the old Saxon took the three horses and led them out of the clearing, before she followed the druid as he walked through the trees, his pace almost too fast for her and Badulf to match.

'Why couldn't we take the horses?' Badulf asked, but the druid did not respond, and Brigid noticed how her brother clenched his fists.

'Badulf, calm yourself.' She put a hand on her brother's arm as they walked and he took a deep breath, but she still sensed the anger in him. Brigid struggled to understand what had caused it. Badulf had always had a smile on his face and was well liked by many of the warriors. Just as he had always been proud of the Saxon part of them. When they were children, they would often talk of travelling to the lands of the Saxons to see where their grandfather was from. But then life got in the way. He had become a warrior for King Vortigern and she had found her calling.

'I don't trust the druid.' Badulf glared at the back of the druid. 'How did he know you would be there? He could have killed you if he wanted to.'

'But he didn't.' Brigid shook her head. 'He's going to take me to the wise one.'

'Why isn't she with him? The last time I saw him, the wise one was there as well.' He turned to the druid, his face creased with anger. 'Where is the wise one?'

'Badulf!' Brigid grabbed her brother and spun him around so that he faced her. 'Where is this anger coming from? And don't tell me it's because Octa has the spear!'

'Badulf doesn't care about the spear,' Vettius said as he stopped and looked at them. 'As for his anger. It's not me or the cult he is angry at. Neither is he angry at the Jutes or the Saxons.'

'Then who is he angry at?' Brigid asked as she glanced at her brother's contorted face and clenched fists.

Vettius stared at her brother for many moments as if he was waiting for something and then said, 'He is angry at himself and instead of dealing with the source of his anger, he deflects it on to others. The wise one had hoped he could be useful to us in what is to come, but she saw he was too blinded by his anger to see the truth.'

Badulf glared at the druid, but before he could say anything, Brigid asked, 'Why is he angry at himself?'

Vettius stared at her brother again for a few heartbeats. 'Because he is a warrior, but when the arrows flew from the trees, he ran. He didn't face death like your grandfather had, or the Jutes he hates so much. Or even the one he calls a coward. He ran while they rushed into the storm. That is why he is angry and that is why he is doing everything he can to make sure there will be a war. So that he can fight and show to himself that he is worthy of his grandfather's blood that runs in his veins.'

Badulf clenched his fists. 'You know nothing of me, druid.'

Vettius smiled. 'I might not, but she does. Those are her words I spoke, not mine.' Without another word, the druid turned around and carried on walking.

Brigid looked at her brother and saw the tears in his eyes. Tears of regret and anger and her heart broke as she looked at him. 'Badulf—'

'He doesn't know what he is talking about,' Badulf said, and then carried on walking before she could say anything else.

Brigid sighed and looked at the surrounding trees, which reminded her of the forest near Cair Urnahc as she closed her eyes. *Mother, please talk to me. Help me make sense of this.*

As before, she heard nothing that told her the goddess was there, so she lowered her head and followed the druid and her brother.

They walked in silence after that, Brigid lost in her search for the gods. From the look on her brother's face, he was lost in his anger, whether at himself or the druid's words, she didn't know. Brigid looked at the druid, his walk confident and with the gait of a man half his age. He was the protector of the wise one, but when she had known the wise one, she hadn't needed a protector.

'What do you protect the wise one from?' Brigid asked.

Vettius tilted his head, but he kept on walking. 'Much has changed since you last saw her in the south. There are those who want to wash her memory away. They say she only brings evil and should be banished.'

Brigid glanced at Badulf and remembered that he had told her it seemed like the wise one was running from something. Brigid wondered who would want to harm the wise one, but then remembered how some of the Christians in Cair Urnahc destroyed anything they found that mentioned the old gods, even those the Romans had brought with them.

Brigid glanced at the sky above the trees and saw it had darkened. She wondered how long they had been walking for and did not realise the forest was so large. 'How long before we see the wise one?'

'I'm not taking you to the wise one.'

Vettius's words stunned Brigid, and she stumbled as she gaped at him.

'See, I knew you couldn't trust him. He said he'd take us to her and then decided not to,' Badulf said.

Vettius stopped and looked at them. 'I never said I'd take you to her. I only told you to follow me.'

Brigid struggled to hide her frustration and had to take deep breaths to calm down. *Why does everything have to be so hard now,* she wondered to herself, but after a long moment she felt calm enough to speak to the druid.

'Why aren't you taking me to her? I need to speak to her. I have so many questions I need to ask her.'

Vettius looked at Brigid, his face unreadable, as Badulf glared at the druid. 'Because I don't know where she is.'

'What do you mean?' Badulf asked. 'You are her protector! You said so!'

'I am, but there are times when she must go places I cannot, and then, just like you, all I can do is wait for her to return.'

'Where did she go?' Brigid asked. 'Tell me so I can find her. I travelled all the way to the wall for her and I will travel further if I have to.'

Vettius smiled at her, which only confused her. 'I can't tell you, because I don't know. She has gone to confront another who wants to start a war that none of them will survive.'

'What does that mean?' Badulf asked, and even Brigid struggled to understand.

'It means what it means and now our time together is over and I must leave you.'

'What?' Brigid looked around and saw they were at the edge of the forest, and even more surprising was Reinald waiting for them with the horses.

'We walked in circles!' Badulf said, and tensed as if he was about to attack the druid, but then Brigid stopped him.

'Why?'

'You are both important to her, but neither of you is ready for what is needed from you. And yes, Badulf is correct. We walked in circles and that walk told me that what she believes is true. You need more time, both of you.'

'But I don't understand what is happening. The vision, what does it mean?' Brigid's limbs trembled as she struggled with her frustration.

'That you need to ask shows you are not ready yet. You are both blinded by your own desires, and until you learn to see past them, she will not come to you. None of them will.'

Brigid felt like collapsing as the druid's words struck her like a stone. Even Badulf looked confused. 'What do we do? Where do we go?'

Vettius smiled, the first kind smile since she had met him earlier in the day. 'You are exactly where she wants you to be. Go with Reinald. He will keep you safe. Listen and learn and, when you are ready, she will come.' With that, the druid turned and walked back into the forest, leaving both of them staring at the trees.

'I don't understand,' Badulf said.

'I think I do,' Brigid said, and turned to Reinald, who was waiting for them. 'She is testing us, Badulf. We have a part to play in the fire you had hoped to stop.'

'And what part is that?'

Brigid took a deep breath and looked at the sky. 'I don't know. Not yet, but I have a feeling Reinald does.'

'So what do we do?'

Brigid looked back over her shoulder but saw no sign of the druid. 'We do as Vettius said. We go back to the fort with Reinald and we wait. And while we wait, we listen and learn.'

35

They rode through the forest in silence while following a track they had found. Odalric was in the lead, his spear ready as he scanned the trees and the shadows between them. Octa was second, his hands trembling as he gripped Gungnir, but his attention was more on Warda than the trees around him. If there was any sign of danger, then his mare would spot it long before them. Behind them rode the Jutes with Oisc between them. Like the two Saxons, they had their spears ready and their eyes focused on their surroundings as they too searched for any threats.

It would have been a relaxing ride if it hadn't been for the silence of the trees and the animals that lived amongst them. The sun was shining and there were no rain clouds on the horizon. But that there was no birdsong or animals calling out to each other made everyone, including the horses, nervous.

Octa glanced over his shoulder at Oisc and saw the fear in the boy's eyes, but he tried to hide it as he puffed out his chest and copied the postures of the Jutes around him. He smiled at Oisc when the boy looked at him and Oisc smiled back. Octa prayed they had not made a mistake by bringing the boy with them as his hand went to the spear pendant around his neck.

Friga, if you hear me, please protect the boy.

He wasn't sure why he prayed to Friga when Thunor was the god of protection. Perhaps it was because he knew she was nearby, even though he couldn't feel her presence amongst the trees.

They rode for a short while longer, when Odalric raised his hand.

'Well, now we know why the scouts never returned.'

Octa rode past Odalric so he could see what the warrior meant and grimaced at the sight in front of him.

'What is it?' Aldric asked.

'Keep the boy back and come see for yourself,' Odalric said, and Octa felt that was a good idea, because Oisc should not see this.

'By the gods,' Aldric said as he saw the bodies of the three scouts who had been tied to the trees. 'And they call us dogs.'

Octa rubbed the shaft of Gungnir as he felt an unfamiliar feeling burning in his chest. Anger. Anger that the Britons had done this to these men. Men Octa knew, and he gritted his teeth as he looked at one of the men who had just become a father.

The three bodies had been stripped naked, their feet and hands cut off and placed underneath their bodies. Their eyes had been stabbed out and their ears cut off and, from the blood stained around their mouths, Octa guessed their tongues had been cut out. He felt the bile rise in his stomach and looked behind him to make sure that Oisc could not see this.

'What is it? Let me see,' Oisc said, and tried to nudge his horse towards them, but one of the Jutes gripped its reins and held the horse back.

Aldric turned and looked at the son of Hengist. 'No, this is not a sight for young boys.'

'Why would they do that?' Octa asked, struggling to make sense of the needless brutality of what had been done to the men and to stop himself from vomiting.

'A warning,' Aldric said as he covered his nose at the stench.

'Aye,' Odalric agreed. 'And to make sure their spirits can't warn us, either. That's why they cut their feet off, so they can't run to us.'

'And the rest so they can't tell us what they saw or heard?' Octa asked, and Odalric nodded.

'We used to do the same to enemy scouts in the homeland.' The older Saxon turned and scrutinised the surrounding trees. 'We should be near the edge of the forest by now, which means—'

Octa glanced around the trees as Odalric spoke when he heard: *Run!*

Eyes wide, he looked amongst the trees and saw movement. Too many to be animals. 'Run!' Octa turned Warda in time to see a spear pierce the chest of the Jute closest to Oisc. The man gaped at him and let go of the reins of Oisc's horse before he fell to the ground.

Oisc screamed, his face pale as he stared at the dead Jute, which startled his mare and the animal shot off into the trees.

'Protect Oisc!' Aldric roared before a spear flew past his head. None of the men had any shields, only their spears and swords, and all they could do was lower themselves as more spears flew from the trees. One more Jute was killed and another's horse was struck. But Octa paid attention to none of that as he kicked Warda's flanks and chased after Oisc's horse.

'Octa!' He heard Odalric scream at him, but he knew he couldn't stop. If the Britons got their hands on the boy, then... he didn't want to think about it, not after seeing what they had done to the scouts.

Branches slapped him in his face and his cheek stung from where one cut him, but he kept his head low and eyes fixed on Oisc ahead of him. He heard the boy's screaming and urged Warda to go faster.

'Come on, girl. You can catch them. We need to save Oisc.' He felt the mare push herself harder as he gripped her reins. 'That's it, girl.'

Octa didn't know what had happened to the others and prayed that they had found a way to escape the ambush as he gained on Oisc. He pushed the thoughts of the others out of his mind. All that mattered now was getting Hengist's son.

Octa reached out as he was gaining on Oisc, but the boy was just out of reach.

'Help me!' Oisc screamed as he clung on to his horse. He looked over his shoulder and Octa saw the terror in the boy's eyes. 'Octa! Help me!'

'Hold on!' Octa urged Warda to go faster, even though he sensed the mare was already going as fast as they could. But they were gaining on Oisc's horse and Octa reached out one more time. His fingertips just grazed Oisc's tunic, and he cried out in frustration. 'Come on, Warda!'

'Octa!' Oisc shrieked as Warda found more speed in her legs.

'That's it, Warda! Keep going!' Octa screamed as his mare drew level with Oisc's horse. He reached out to grab the reins, but just before his hand gripped them, something struck him and Octa's heart stopped as he was thrown from Warda. He flew into Oisc, knocking the boy from his horse as well, and they both tumbled to the ground. Octa hit the ground hard and bumped his head on something as he rolled until he eventually stopped. His head ached as the forest spun around him and it took Octa many heartbeats before he could get to his knees. 'Oisc.' He struggled to get the boy's name out and had to take deep breaths so the spinning would stop. 'Oisc!' he called again, but there was no response.

His heart raced as he got to his feet, and was glad when nothing seemed broken, although there wasn't a part of his body that didn't hurt. Octa felt something wet on his forehead and, when he reached up, he saw the blood on his fingertips, but he ignored that. He lived, the pain told him that, but now he had to find Oisc.

Octa searched the forest floor and then saw him, lying on his stomach and not moving. His heart skipped as he tried to rush to the boy, but his legs struggled to obey him. He was almost by Oisc when something struck him from behind and, again, Octa was sent flying. As he landed, Octa opened his eyes and saw the feet of an old man standing by his head. He groaned as he looked up and saw an old face glaring at him. Confusion clouded his mind as he struggled to make sense of what was happening and then he realised he no longer had Gungnir in his hands. He looked around, trying to see the spear, but he couldn't, and panic tore through him as the old man leaned closer. Cloudy eyes filled with anger stared at Octa and the old man's lips parted to reveal rotten teeth and blackened gums.

'I sent another to do this, one whose hatred of you I thought would be useful. But you men are too dumb to understand what must be done.'

Octa looked at the man. 'Who are you?'

'I am the lord of thunder and lightning! I control the skies and the storms.'

'Thunor?' Octa struggled to get up as he wondered why the thunder god had attacked him. Had Woden sent him? 'I must get to Oisc. I must help him.'

The old man put his foot on Octa's back and pressed him to the ground. Octa cried out and the old man laughed. 'I am not your god of thunder, you fool!' He pressed his foot down harder and Octa feared that the old man might break his back. 'I ruled these skies for more of your generations than you can count. I have watched others come and go and I have survived. But because of her weakness, I have to fight for my survival.'

Octa frowned as he tried to work out what the old man was talking about, and who he was. 'What do you want?'

The old man pressed harder on Octa's back, making him scream out again. 'I want the spear!'

'I... I...' Octa tried to lift his head to look at the old man, but with his foot on his back, he couldn't. He found it hard to believe the old man was a god, but the man's strength was unnatural and Octa's mind raced as he tried to work out what to do.

'Save your words,' the old man said. 'I—'

Before he could finish, a white owl swooped down from the trees and sunk its talons into the old man's shoulder.

'You bitch!' The old man screamed and lifted his foot, and Octa wasted no time as he ignored the pain in his body and rolled away. He jumped to his feet, his head swimming and body swaying, and pulled his sword from its scabbard, but all he could do was watch as the old man waved his arms at the white owl as it kept attacking him. Octa couldn't understand what was going on, but then he heard Oisc groan. His heart skipped as he realised the boy was still alive and he ignored the old man and the owl as he rushed towards Hengist's son.

'Oisc,' he said as he reached the boy and dropped to his knees. He rolled Oisc over and saw the gash on his head as well, when he sensed movement behind him. Octa rolled out of the way as the old man stomped his foot down on where he had been and narrowly missed Oisc's head.

Octa looked for the owl, but couldn't see the white bird anywhere. He turned his attention back to the old man, who was sneering at him, before he looked at Oisc.

'The boy is important to you?'

Octa's hands trembled and he almost dropped the sword at the malevolence in the old man's eyes. 'He... he's just a boy. Let... let him live.'

The old man laughed. 'Exactly. He's just a boy, like the ones they sacrificed to me once. But not any more! You men really don't understand how insignificant you are to us. Let me show you.' He raised his foot and hovered it over Oisc's head as he smiled at Octa.

What will you do? The voice came to him again. *Will you run or will you fight?*

Octa roared as he charged at the old man. At a god of Britannia. He stabbed his sword at the old man's face, but the old man barely moved as he avoided the blade and punched Octa in the stomach. As Octa bent over, he grabbed Octa by his hair.

'You are dumber than the one I sent to find the spear.' The old man barked a laugh. 'The fool believes I am the Christian god and even now thinks he has the spear I want, and that he can use it against you. But at least his idiocy brought the real spear to me.' The old man pulled Octa upright, and he screamed at the pain in his scalp. 'And to think the one-eyed bastard sent you to find the spear. You are weak, pathetic. Just like the gods you follow. And after I kill you, I'll take his spear and stick it in his other eye.'

Octa screamed and stabbed his sword into the old man's leg, not caring whether or not the old man was a god. He refused to die here in this forest, and more than that, he refused to let Oisc die. The old man cried out as Octa's sword pierced his skin and he threw Octa through the air.

Octa bounced off a tree and a fresh wave of pain tore through him as he landed on the ground. The sword fell from his hand and Octa just had enough time to see the red on the sword's tip, before the old man screamed at him.

'You fool! You dare attack me? A god!'

'You bleed,' Octa said, struggling to make sense of it. He had never thought of it, but had always believed that gods didn't bleed.

The old man looked at his leg and then glared at Octa. 'And the price you pay for learning that is your life and the life of this boy.' The old man turned and faced Oisc.

Octa struggled to his feet, determined to stop the old man from killing Oisc, when her voice came to him again. *Gungnir.* Octa looked around, but he did not know where the spear was. He had lost it when he fell from Warda, but he didn't know where. That was when he heard the owl and, when Octa looked for it, he saw the white bird on the ground. And below its feet was Gungnir.

He glanced at the old man, who raised his foot again, before he pushed the pain from his mind and ran for the spear. The owl hooted, which made the old man turn around, and as Octa reached Gungnir, he picked up the spear of Woden and launched it at the old man.

36

Thunder sounded over the trees as the spear left Octa's hand and flew straight at the god of the Britons, his foot hovering over Oisc's head. The old man gaped as he stared at the spear, but before it struck him, a hand reached out and grabbed it.

Octa watched, stunned, as a warrior larger than him, his shoulders as broad as the mountains and his limbs thicker than any tree he had ever seen, swung the spear around and struck the old man with the shaft. The old man cried out, his eyes wide, as he flew back and landed on his back, while the large warrior turned and glared at Octa, whose heart felt like it had stopped.

The thick red beard of the warrior parted as he sneered at Octa. 'Men do not kill gods!' The warrior turned and gripped Gungnir in his hand as he stomped towards the old man, who was struggling to get to his feet. 'Only gods kill gods.' He stood over the old man and raised the spear above his head. 'I am Thunor, son of Woden, and with your death I will take your place as the thunder god of these lands.'

Octa could not move, even though he knew he needed to get to Oisc, as Thunor stabbed down with the spear. But the old man rolled out of the way before he jumped to his feet and punched Thunor in the face. To Octa's surprise, Thunor's head snapped to the side, and he staggered a few steps, but the thunder god recovered quickly enough to dodge the old man's next attack. He tried to stab the spear at the old man, but the god of the Britons grabbed hold of Thunor's hand and the two gods strained, their faces red as they fought for control over Gungnir.

'These are my lands!' the old man shouted, his rotten teeth bared.

Thunor smiled as he leaned forward. 'Not any more.' He let go of the spear and punched the old man in the stomach and, as the old man bent over, kneed him in the face. The old man's head snapped up and Thunor grabbed the spear from his hands before he punched the old man in the face. The old man collapsed, the fight over for him, and Octa struggled to make sense of what he was seeing as, for a second time, Thunor raised Gungnir above his head.

'Thunor, no,' Friga's voice said as she walked out of the trees. 'His death will not benefit us.'

Octa was numb with shock as Thunor glared at his mother before he took a step back and lowered the spear.

'You fool. You are as dumb as those who worship you,' the old man screamed as he jumped to his feet and attacked Thunor. But then the white owl appeared and sliced his cheek open with its claws, before the bird disappeared amongst the trees.

'Enough, Taranis,' an old woman said as she walked out of the trees, as Friga had done before. Octa wondered how old the woman was as she leaned on a stick, her back almost bent double and her long white hair touching the ground. 'You have gone too far.'

The old man looked at the old woman, his face contorted in rage. 'I've gone too far! You gave them the weapon that will kill us all!'

'The weapon belongs to them. It was never ours to use,' the old woman said as she stopped beside Friga.

'We do not need to fight each other. We have a common enemy,' Friga said. 'One that threatens us all.'

'Your husband doesn't feel the same way as you do. That's why he keeps sending men to look for the spear.' The old man glared at Octa, who wanted to run, but he couldn't. And not because his fear was stopping him, but because of Oisc. 'For many of their generations, you hid the spear from them. Protected it from their grasps, and now you let this weakling take it.'

'She hid the spear because I asked her to,' Friga said as the old woman stepped forward.

'Like you, my life is fading. With each passing season, he takes more.

More land, more followers. Those who speak our names grow old and pass, while the young ones are scared into following him by his priests. Hiding the spear took more than I could give.' The old woman looked at Octa and he shivered as her pale eyes fell on him. 'He was chosen by Woden and Friga told me to give him the spear.' Octa was struck by the sadness on her heavily wrinkled face. 'Only time will tell if he is strong enough to carry the burden.'

A growl escaped from Taranis's throat as he glared at Octa and then the other three gods. 'You betrayed us. Your own kin for them.' He wiped the blood from his cheek.

'Our days are done, Taranis.'

Taranis shook his head. 'Not while I still breathe.' He glared at Octa again. 'You made me bleed. For that, you will pay. While you walk these lands, you will not be safe.' The old man looked at Thunor and a smile appeared on his face. 'We will finish this one day.' With that, he turned around and disappeared amongst the trees.

Octa froze as the three remaining gods all looked at him. His heart raced in his chest, but then he remembered Oisc and rushed to the son of Hengist.

'He'll live,' Friga said. 'The boy is strong, but you must get him back to his father. Before it's too late.'

As if she had been called, Warda came out from the trees and Octa smiled as he saw his horse. 'You were supposed to protect us,' he said as the mare nudged him with her nose.

'She is a brave horse, but even she is smart enough to know you can't fight the gods,' the old woman said, and Octa looked at her.

'You sent her to me?'

The old woman nodded. 'I knew you'd need a friend you could trust.'

'Are you...?' Octa couldn't finish the sentence as he stared at the old woman.

'Yes, she is Brigantia, the mother goddess of the people who live in the north of these lands,' Friga said.

'But there are those here who also speak my name.'

Octa shook his head and frowned as he struggled to make sense of the way the goddess looked. Friga looked old enough to be his mother and Thunor could have been the same age as Hengist and Horsa, but Brigantia and the one called Taranis looked ancient.

As if reading his mind, Brigantia said, 'Our strength and beauty come from those who worship us. Sacrifices made in our names keep us young and strong. They give us the power to control the weather, the trees and the seas. But if those sacrifices stop, if those who say our names dwindle, then so does our strength and we age like you men. Many of my kind have already perished and have been replaced by the gods the Romans brought with them. But then those gods perished when he arrived.'

'He?' Octa asked, his eyes still fixed on the gods.

Friga nodded. 'The one from the lands of sand to the east. The one whose son was elevated to a god though he was a man just like you.'

'The Christian god?' Octa's eyes widened when he realised who Friga was talking about. The mother goddess nodded and Octa saw the anger on Thunor's face. 'And you are trying to stop him?'

Friga shook her head. 'We cannot stop him, though we will still try. Woden will fight—'

'And so will I,' Thunor said. 'I will crush him like an egg and wipe his name from the tongues of men.' His arms bulged as he tensed.

'But he does not fight you,' Brigantia said.

'No, he does not.' Thunor scowled. 'No matter where I look, I can't find him or his son.'

'Because the son is not real, I told you that.' Friga shook her head.

'Then why do they say his name? Why do they worship him like he is a god?'

Friga looked at Octa. 'This is not a conversation to have now.' She turned her attention back to Thunor. 'Give him Gungnir. He will need it for what is to come.'

Octa frowned. 'What is coming?'

But Friga did not respond as Thunor towered over him and Octa felt the fear in the pit of his stomach as the thunder god glared at him.

'This spear should be returned to my father, but Mother knows more than me, so if she says you need it, then I give it back to you.'

With trembling hands, Octa took Gungnir from Thunor. He looked at the spear in his hands as Brigantia walked towards him. She put a hand on his shoulder and in his mind, he heard, *I warned you about the spear. I told you it would bring only death. Woden cannot be trusted, but sometimes we must make allies with our enemies to fight a greater threat. Be strong, son of Frithowald. Stand tall when the flames come. That is the only way you will survive.*

Octa frowned at the old woman and, when he looked at Friga, he saw that both she and Thunor were gone.

'I don't understand.' He looked around and saw no sign of Brigantia. Only Oisc and Warda were amongst the trees with him. 'What must I do?'

The leaves of the trees rustled in the sudden breeze and, somewhere, Octa heard an owl scream.

Run.

* * *

Vortimer got to his feet as he watched the men on horseback break out from the forest and race towards them. His hands trembled as he wondered what that meant and he glanced at King Gwyrangon, who looked just as concerned as him.

They had moved their combined army, over two hundred men, closer to Ruym Island and the king of the Cantiaci had suggested the camp behind this forest. It was as close to the island as they could get without being seen by the Jutes, so Vortimer had agreed.

The men from the continent might have had fewer warriors, but they were bigger and stronger than many of the Britons and Vortimer knew that the only way to defeat them was by taking them by surprise. To storm the island before the Jutes had enough time to prepare themselves. He knew the town they had taken had been fortified, but he also knew that if he could trap them inside those walls, then it was only a matter of time. While he was there with his father, Vortimer had tasked Cadoc with studying the town's defences. So Vortimer knew their defences better than themselves. All he needed to do was make sure that the Jutes did not get to their ships. If they escaped, then they would return with more men.

But it seemed that the Jutes suspected something as they sent scouts out every day. One of those groups had bumped into some of King Gwyrangon's men and Vortimer had got a bit carried away when he told the men what to do with the Jutes.

'Perhaps they found your message,' Cadoc said, as if he had read Vortimer's mind, while they watched the horsemen approach.

'They're mine,' the king of the Cantiaci said, which only made Vortimer more nervous. He glanced at the spear in his hand and wondered what had happened amongst the trees.

'They found the bodies!' one of the men said as he jumped off his horse and ran towards them. He dropped to his knees in front of his king and looked up. 'A group of Jutes. They found the bodies.'

'And did you kill them?' Prince Vortimer asked before King Gwyrangon could say anything, but Vortimer ignored the glance the king gave him.

The man shook his head. 'We killed most of them, but some got away. They got separated, though.'

King Gwyrangon frowned. 'Separated?'

The man nodded. 'There was a boy. His horse got spooked and ran off. One warrior chased after him. Three others tried to follow, but our spears kept them away.' He wiped the sweat from his brow. 'They returned to the island.'

Vortimer looked at the man. 'A boy?'

'There was a boy in the hall when we arrived,' Cadoc said. 'I think he is Hengist's son. Could be a valuable hostage.'

'But why would Hengist allow his son to leave the island?' King Gwyrangon asked as he glanced at Vortimer.

Vortimer's mind was racing as he tried to work out the implications of this when he heard a voice in his head. *Attack now! You must attack now!*

Vortimer looked around him and saw the old man, but no one else seemed to notice him. He nodded and glanced at the spear. The spear that would give him victory over the Jutes. 'We attack now!'

'What?' King Gwyrangon asked. 'We can't. The Trinovantes still haven't arrived.'

'He's right,' Cadoc said. 'We need the Trinovante warriors.'

Vortimer shook his head. 'They know we're here. If we don't attack now, then they'll escape.' He tightened his grip on the spear and looked at the king of the Cantiaci. 'We attack now or we lose our home to the Jutes. We still have the element of surprise. Me and my men will attack first, draw them off the island. When I give the signal, you attack with your warriors. Surround them and then we slaughter them all.'

King Gwyrangon scowled as he thought about it and, to Vortimer, it felt like too many heartbeats passed before he nodded. But Vortimer was certain that he did not need the Cantiaci. He had the spear of their god and, once the

Jutes saw him carrying it into battle, he was certain they would break. The king of the Cantiaci turned to one of his warriors. 'Sound the horn.'

The warrior nodded and put the horn to his lips before he blew into it. Warriors roared as they came to life. Men rushed to their tents and grabbed their shields and spears, while others ran for the horses. Vortimer's heart pounded in his chest as he realised this was his moment. This was the day he would make his name go down in the histories of his people. He smiled at Catigern, who was gaping at him, before he raised the spear of the one-eyed Saxon god in the air.

'We fight for our lands! We fight for our people! But most importantly, we fight for God!'

37

Berthild sensed Hengist's nervousness as he glanced at the sun. Octa should have been back from their ride a while ago and, no matter how hard she tried, Berthild couldn't help but be concerned. She looked at Hengist as he stood outside the hall, his body tense and his fingers twitching, and wondered if it had been a good idea to let his son go with Octa. Especially with the scouts going missing.

Horsa stormed around summoning warriors and ordering them to get the horses ready.

'I told you that you can't trust the Saxons!'

Berthild's anger flashed and even though she knew she should have kept quiet, she walked towards the hall and Horsa. 'Six of your Jutes went with them and yet you blame my son and Odalric!'

Everyone stopped as Horsa turned to face her, but before he could do anything, Hengist said, 'Lady Berthild is right, Horsa. Aldric and five others went with. You know this.'

Horsa's mouth twitched as he glared at Berthild. 'Men! Get ready! We ride to find my nephew.' He turned and walked towards the stables as Hengist walked towards Berthild.

'Forgive my brother. Oisc is like a son to him.'

'He doesn't have children of his own?' Berthild asked, and realised she had never seen Horsa with children. Many women, but never any children.

Hengist laughed. 'Plenty of bastards, but none he cares about. He—'

Hengist was interrupted as a warrior came racing into the town, his horse's sides white with sweat and the man covered in blood.

'Friga,' Berthild said as her hand went to her mouth when she recognised the man as one of the Jutes who had ridden out with Octa and Odalric.

'What happened?' Horsa asked as he came running out of the stables and grabbed the man's horse. Hengist rushed towards the man and Berthild felt herself doing the same.

Friga, please tell me my son is alive.

'Ambush,' the man said as he slumped over his horse. 'We found the scouts—'

'Never mind the scouts!' Hengist said. 'Where is my son?'

The warrior winced, and Berthild realised the man was losing a lot of blood. 'I... I... don't know. There were spears. They killed some of us and Oisc's horse... ran off.' The warrior looked at Berthild. 'Octa ran after him.'

Hengist, his face red with rage, grabbed the warrior and pulled him off his horse. 'Then why are you here?'

Berthild stepped forward as the warrior's face paled. 'He's here to warn us, Hengist. Look past your anger and listen to him.'

'She's right, brother,' Horsa said, and Berthild glanced at the man as they agreed on something for once.

Hengist looked at them both, his teeth bared, before he looked at the warrior again. 'Warn us of what?'

The warrior struggled to find his words for a few heartbeats as his face grimaced in pain. 'Aldric sent me to warn you. The Britons are coming. There is an army—'

The man didn't get to finish his words as Hengist dropped him and turned to Horsa. 'Get the men ready to defend the island.'

'Brother, I was—'

Hengist glared at his brother. 'My son is in danger! I'm taking the men out to find him. You get ready to defend the island. Get our men to the bridge and stop the Britons.' He softened his voice and gripped his brother's shoulder. 'And pray that I return with my son.' Hengist looked at Berthild, but said nothing of Octa. She understood why. Oisc was his only concern, as Octa was hers.

Berthild gripped the spear pendant she wore around her waist and closed her eyes. *Thunor, Friga, protect my son. Woden, he carries your spear. Bring him back to me.*

She opened her eyes and watched as Hengist led thirty men out of the town and towards the mainland, before Horsa turned to her.

'You better pray my brother returns with his son, because this is all Octa's fault.'

Berthild glared at Horsa, her heart racing in her chest. 'And you better pray my son doesn't return because, when he does, I'll make sure he kills you.'

Horsa smiled at her. 'Your son is not good enough to kill me.'

'I'm sure that's what Eadric thought as well.' Berthild stepped closer to Horsa. 'You underestimate my son and one day you will pay the price for that.'

Horsa grunted at her before he turned and walked off, while shouting orders to the warriors. Men ran into houses and the hall to get weapons and shields. The few who weren't wearing armour rushed to get them on, while women, especially the Britons, stood and gaped at them. Berthild saw the fear on their faces and wished she spoke their tongue so she could reassure them. Again, she closed her eyes and prayed. *Friga watch over these people. Do not let them suffer the same fate as my people.*

The injured warrior groaned and Berthild dropped to her knees beside him. 'Stay still.'

The warrior tried to get up, but his face paled even more and she saw how his eyes lost focus. 'I... I... need to fight.'

Berthild shook her head. 'You need to recover first.' She looked around her and got the attention of some women near her. 'Help me get him to the hall!' The women stared at her blankly and Berthild cursed the fact that she had never thought of learning even a few words in the Britons' tongue. Taking a deep breath to calm herself, she pointed to the injured man and then to the hall and, to her relief, one of the women understood. She turned to those around her and said something to them before the youngest of the group ran off and the others came to help her with the injured man. As they carried him to the hall, Berthild looked over her shoulder and saw Horsa lead some warriors out of the town while another Jute was ordering the remaining warriors to the wall.

Berthild looked at the British women who were helping her with the injured Jute and one of them said, in the Saxon tongue, 'Go. We help.'

Berthild nodded her thanks to the woman and ran after Horsa. She couldn't stay in the town and wait for news. She needed to see what was happening.

* * *

Octa heard the horn blow and his heart thudded in his chest, but he wasted no time to work out what that meant. He didn't have to as he collected his sword from where it fell and glanced at the blood of Taranis on the blade before he put it in its scabbard and limped to where Oisc lay. He groaned as he tried to pick Oisc up, but his body ached from his fight with the British god.

'Come on!' he berated himself, and with a loud scream he pulled Oisc up to his shoulders. Warda, her breathing still heavy, moved closer and Octa put the unconscious body on the horse's back, who staggered slightly before she regained her footing. Octa stroked the mare and felt her heart beating fast and was about to pray that Warda could get them both back to the island when he heard a noise behind him.

Octa turned, his spear ready, as Odalric and Aldric came out of the trees.

'Octa!' Odalric pulled his horse to a stop and then frowned at the look on Octa's face.

'Oisc!' Aldric said as he jumped off his horse and rushed to Warda. 'In the name of the gods, what happened?'

The gods happened, Octa thought, but didn't say. He doubted they would believe him. Even he still struggled to believe what had just happened and he had seen it. 'He fell off his horse. Where are the others?'

'Most are dead, but we sent one man back to the island to warn the brothers,' Odalric said. 'We chased after you, but lost you amongst the trees.'

'Looks like you fell off a mountain,' Aldric said, his eyes filled with concern as he looked at Oisc.

'Feels like it.'

The horn blew again, and all three warriors looked towards where the sound came from. 'We need to go,' Odalric said. He waited as Aldric helped Octa onto Warda and as soon as Aldric was on his own horse, they all turned towards the island.

'Get us home, Warda,' Octa said to the mare, who nodded and ran. The others followed as Octa lowered himself over the body of Oisc to protect the boy from the branches as they swiped past them.

They soon broke from the trees, all three horses going as fast as they could, but Warda struggled with the extra weight of Oisc and was falling behind the others.

'Go faster!' Odalric screamed as he noticed the same, but then his eyes widened as he saw something behind Octa. 'Go faster!'

Octa looked over his shoulder and his heart skipped when he saw the army of the Britons erupt from the trees. He didn't have time to work out how many there were, but his panic gripped him when he saw they were all on horseback. Octa saw a glint of a spear in the sunlight and he knew that Prince Vortimer was leading the army, but what worried him the most was that the Britons were gaining on them.

Octa tightened his grip on Gungnir as he turned towards the island in the distance and his heart sank when he saw they were too far away. He glanced at Oisc, whose head was bouncing up and down as he lay over the back of Warda, and prayed that they would somehow make it.

'Look!' Aldric screamed, and Octa saw a group of warriors racing towards them from the island.

There were fewer than the Britons, but Octa didn't have time to think about that. All he had to do was reach them before the Britons caught them. 'Come, Warda. I know you are tired, but we can't let them catch us.' He felt Warda speed up for a heartbeat, but then she started losing pace. The mare was exhausted from the race to catch Oisc's horse and Octa knew she didn't have enough left in her to carry both of them to safety. He glanced over his shoulder again and saw the Britons were gaining on them, and then he heard her voice again.

What will you do?

Odalric and Aldric had slowed down when they saw that he had fallen back. Octa looked at the oncoming Jutes and then the Britons and wanted to scream in frustration.

'Octa, we don't have time for you to enjoy the view,' Odalric shouted over the rush of the wind in their ears.

Octa shook his head. 'Warda is tired. She can't carry both of us.'

'Then give me the boy,' Aldric shouted, but he must have known there was no time for them to stop and put Oisc on his horse.

Octa tightened his grip on Gungnir and wished Thunor was still with him, because he could use the thunder god's strength. He glanced over his shoulder one more time as he swallowed back the fear that was creeping up his spine. The past was not important. That's what he had been told. But Octa would use the past to protect the future. A thought flashed in his mind and he dismissed it straight away. One, because he doubted he'd have the courage to face the Britons on his own; and two, because he knew it would never slow them down. They would cut him down without breaking their stride. So he shook his head and urged Warda to keep going. 'Come on, Warda. We must get the boy to safety.' Warda shook her head as she ran, and he knew she was already giving it all she had.

Thunder flashed in the skies above him, and Octa wondered if that was Thunor or Taranis. He glanced over his shoulder and saw the Britons had slowed down and couldn't understand why when Odalric shouted, 'Octa, keep going!' Octa felt a wave of relief when he realised the Jutes would now reach them before the Britons, but he knew they still needed to get to the island. He saw Hengist leading the Jutes and watched as they rode past the three of them. For a moment, Octa thought Hengist was going to attack the Britons, but when he glanced over his shoulder, he saw them wheel around and launch their throwing spears at the oncoming Britons before they raced to catch up to the three of them.

Octa didn't have time to look at the chaos the volley of spears caused amongst the Britons as men and horses died or were injured, while others tripped over them. But as he looked over his shoulder, he saw the golden spear glinting in the sunlight and knew that Prince Vortimer was still alive.

Hengist drew level with Octa, his eyes on Oisc before he looked at Octa, who shivered at the anger in the warlord's eyes. 'He lives!' Octa shouted over the hoofbeats of the horses.

Hengist nodded and, without saying a word, reached over and grabbed hold of his son before pulling him to his horse. He looked at Octa again, but Octa didn't understand the look in his eyes before he urged his horse to go faster and left Octa behind. Octa understood, though, even as his heart raced in his chest, that Hengist needed to make sure his son was safe.

Octa glanced over his shoulder and saw the Britons were catching up with them again, but they were closer to the island. Warda was spent, though, and Octa knew she would struggle to make it. Especially with his weight.

They were about fifty paces away from the bridge, but the Britons weren't far behind him. He had been left behind by the Jutes who followed Hengist. Only Odalric and Aldric still rode with him.

'Go!' Octa shouted at them, and Odalric shook his head as he kept his horse level with Octa's.

Octa found comfort in the two older warriors not leaving him behind as Hengist reached the bridge ahead of them and dismounted before giving Oisc to another warrior. For a heartbeat, Octa wondered what he was doing, and then saw the other Jutes dismount and form a shield wall on the bridge.

They were almost there and Octa was about to breathe a sigh of relief when thunder struck again and Warda stopped dead in her tracks. Octa screamed as he was sent flying over her head and did everything he could to hold on to Gungnir as he landed hard on the ground, still more than twenty paces away from the bridge. He looked at Warda, wondering what had made her stop like that, when, for a heartbeat, he saw Taranis standing in front of her, sneering at him.

I will have that spear. He heard the thunder god of the Britons in his mind, before the god disappeared.

'Octa!' Odalric shouted as he pulled his horse to a stop, but Octa wasn't paying attention to him as he stared at the Britons approaching fast. At their head, he saw Prince Vortimer, although he was still too far away for Octa to see the look on his face, but he imagined an ugly grimace.

Warda, true to her name, came to Octa and stood over him as if she was trying to protect him from the Britons, and Octa gripped her leg as he tried to get up. But then, a sharp pain shot through him and he collapsed again. Octa looked at his leg and prayed it was not broken as he realised he couldn't put any weight on it.

Odalric pulled his horse to a stop before he jumped off and ran to Octa. 'Octa, let's go, we're almost there!'

Octa shook his head. 'I can't. My leg is hurt.'

'By the gods!' Odalric looked at the Britons and then he glanced over his shoulder, his face creased as he thought of something. But then the older warrior shrugged and gripped his spear in front of him.

'Odalric, what are you doing?'

'I fear your mother's anger more than those bastard Britons. I let your father die and I have to live with that guilt every day. I'm not letting you die until I'm dead!' He glanced at Octa and smiled. 'I never thought I'd say this, Octa, but it'll be an honour to die by your side.'

Octa felt the tears sting his eyes, but then shook them away. Now was not the time to cry.

'You Saxons are witless fools,' Aldric said as he also jumped off his horse and stood on Octa's other side. He shrugged as they looked at him. 'You really think I'm going to let you make a stand while I run back to the island? The gods will never forgive me.'

Octa took a deep breath and gripped Gungnir in his hands. His leg hurt from the fall and his body ached from his fight with Taranis, while his vision blurred. Warda still stood with him, and Octa looked at her.

'Go, girl, go to the island.' The horse shook her head and Octa sighed. 'Then stand behind me.' The other two glanced at each other as the mare moved behind Octa. For a heartbeat, he closed his eyes and heard Friga's voice.

What will you do? Will you run or will you stand and fight?

Octa opened his eyes again and looked at the spear. He knew the three of them could never stop the Britons, but he would not run. Not again. *Thunor, protect us. Woden, guide your spear.* Octa gritted his teeth and glared at Prince Vortimer as the Britons charged at them. He still believed that the Saxons, Jutes and the Britons could live in peace, but for that to happen, there had to be war. There had to be fire to burn away those who did not believe the same. He glanced at the spear as he felt Woden's fury course through its shaft before he took a deep breath and launched it at the oncoming Britons.

38

Berthild stood by the bridge, her heart in her throat as she watched Hengist's force race off in the distance.

'You shouldn't be here,' Horsa said, and Berthild glanced at the warlord.

'I will not wait by the town and not know what is happening. My son is out there.'

Horsa glared at her and, just when she thought he'd say the same things he usually did, he shrugged. 'If the fighting starts, then you move to the back.'

Berthild would have smiled if it had not been for the fear she felt as she nodded at Horsa. It was a small victory over the man who was intent on fighting her and her son, and a sign that her influence over the brothers was growing. She turned her attention back to what was happening, but it was hard to see anything other than the backs of Hengist's men, and that frustrated her more than anything else. *Friga, protect my son.*

Her heart skipped when a hand gripped her shoulder and, when she looked behind her, she saw the tavern woman standing there, smiling at her.

'Your son is strong. Have faith in that.'

Berthild nodded, too concerned about Octa to wonder why no one else was reacting to the woman being there.

'Look,' one warrior said as thunder rumbled in the clear sky and Berthild turned her attention to the front in time to see Hengist lead his men around three horses. Her heart pounded as she wondered if Octa was one of them.

She watched as the Jutes threw their spears at the Britons chasing the three warriors on horseback and then gripped the spear pendant around her waist when she saw them race back towards the island, leaving the three warriors behind.

She glanced at the tavern woman behind her, and the tension she saw in the woman's face worried her. The woman's lips moved as if she was praying and Berthild was tempted to do the same as Hengist reached the bridge and jumped off his horse.

'Oisc!' Horsa shouted, and Berthild's heart skipped when she saw the boy, his face covered in blood and motionless, being helped off the horse.

'He lives,' Hengist said as he handed his son to one warrior. 'Get him to the town, now!' The warrior nodded and ran off with Oisc in his arms as Hengist turned to Berthild. 'Octa lives, but his horse is spent.'

'Then why are you here?' Berthild said before she could stop herself. Her fear for her son made her blind to what was more important to Hengist, and she regretted her words as she saw the hurt in his eyes.

'I had to get my son to safety first.' He turned before she could say anything and shouted, 'Shields! Spears!'

'They're almost here!' Horsa shouted, and Berthild saw Octa and Odalric, as well as one of the Jutes, racing to get to the bridge, but what made her cover her mouth was that the Britons were catching up to them.

'They're going to make it,' one warrior said, and Berthild's hands trembled as she saw the same.

But then behind her, she heard the tavern woman say, 'No.'

Before Berthild could turn around, another round of thunder struck and, to her shock, Octa's horse stopped and threw him off.

'Octa!' Berthild cried out as her son landed on the ground. Her mind went numb as she thought she'd see her son die in front of her and she prayed to the gods that he survived. Odalric and the Jutes jumped off their horses and stood by Octa as he struggled to his feet and Berthild realised he was injured.

'Run!' Hengist shouted, but none of the three seemed to react.

'What will you do? Will you run or will you stand and fight?' she heard the woman behind her say, and Berthild turned around and frowned at the woman.

'What is Octa doing?' Horsa asked.

Berthild turned, and they all watched as Octa threw his spear over the heads of the Britons.

'The bastard missed. I thought Gungnir never misses.'

Berthild shook her head as she understood what her son was doing. 'He didn't miss. In the sagas, Woden throws Gungnir over the heads of his enemies when he declares war on them,' Berthild said as she remembered the stories her mother had told her. 'Octa just declared war on the Britons.'

* * *

Gungnir arched over the heads of the Britons, who all pulled their horses to a stop as they stared at the spear, and as it landed in the ground a few paces behind the Britons, they all turned and laughed at Octa. He knew they believed he had skewed his throw, but Octa was sending a message to the gods. And not just his gods, but the gods of Britannia, those who had attacked him and Oisc, a young boy who had done nothing against them.

Prince Vortimer, his face an ugly grimace, raised the spear Badulf had stolen in the air as if he believed the Jutes would cower in front of it. Perhaps that was what he believed if he thought he had the real Gungnir, but he didn't.

Behind Octa, he heard Hengist's voice. 'For Woden! Kill the bastards!'

The Jutes roared as Prince Vortimer's face paled and he glanced at the spear in his hand before he recovered and shouted, 'Warriors of Britannia! Dismount! Charge!'

Odalric glanced over his shoulder and shouted, 'They're coming!'

Octa didn't have to look to sense the same as the Britons jumped off their horses and raised their weapons. He pulled the sword from his scabbard, its tip still covered in Taranis's blood, and braced himself as the Britons charged at them, trusting in the gods that Hengist and Horsa would reach them in time.

'You should have aimed for the prince,' Odalric said, and Octa wondered if he should have done, but it didn't matter. Not now.

The Britons were closing in on them and Octa felt the ground tremble under his feet as the three warriors braced themselves. None of them had shields. They had never expected to fight a battle and only had the weapons they carried, but they stood strong.

'Your father and grandfather would be proud of you, Octa,' Odalric said, his knuckles white as he gripped his spear.

'Aye, Octa the Coward!' Aldric roared. 'The bravest warrior I know.' The Jute laughed as the Britons were close enough for Octa to see the hatred in Prince Vortimer's eyes. He wanted to look over his shoulder to see how far the Jutes were as he heard their war cries, but knew he couldn't because if he did, then he might live up to that name once more.

'Kill them!' Prince Vortimer shouted, but as soon as the words left his mouth, his eyes widened as a volley of spears flew over Octa's head and struck the Britons. The prince got his shield up in time, but a handful of the other Britons weren't as lucky as they were skewered by the spears. Cries of pain filled the air as Octa braced himself to face the Britons. He struggled to stand on his injured leg and his arms felt weak, but he would not run.

Octa heard the Jutes roar and sensed how close they were as he felt his own battle lust take over. A feeling so unfamiliar to him it took him a few heartbeats to understand what it was as Hengist and Horsa ran past him, followed by their warriors.

'For Woden! For Tiw!' Horsa cried out, and the Jutes echoed his call as they charged into the Britons. The thunderous crash reminded Octa of what had happened in the forest and he flinched as if he expected Taranis to attack him again.

Hengist stabbed with his sword and killed a Briton before he could lift his oval-shaped shield to protect himself, while Horsa drove his spear into the stomach of another Briton. Prince Vortimer hung back as the ferocity of the Jutes caught the Britons by surprise and Hengist, still angry at what had happened to his son, roared as he and his brother led his men. He hacked and stabbed at the Britons, almost single-handedly driving them back as his Jutes followed. Octa took a moment and looked behind him to see his mother standing there, her face filled with concern, but what caught his attention was Friga standing behind his mother. The mother goddess smiled at Octa before he turned back to the front in time to see the Jute ahead of him killed by a Briton. As the man fell back, the Briton stormed into the gap and stabbed his spear at Octa.

Octa, forgetting about the pain in his leg, ducked under the spear and sliced the warrior's leg open with his sword. As the man dropped to his knees, Odalric drove his spear through his neck and picked up the shield of the fallen Jute before he stepped into the gap in the shield wall. Aldric had joined the Jutes as they charged past and was stabbing with his spear and killing any man within reach.

'Octa, get back to the island!' Odalric shouted as he blocked the spear of a Briton and killed the man.

Octa tested his leg and, with the battle lust coursing through him, he realised the pain had lessened and that he could stand on it. He picked up a shield of another dead Jute and took a deep breath as he fed on the battle lust in his veins.

He had faced a god and stood tall. He would not cower from another man again, and with a roar he charged into the battle. Octa raised his shield and blocked the blow from one Briton as the thought drove him on. He had found the spear of Woden. Octa turned the shield and stabbed the Briton in the chest. He was the son of a mighty warlord and the grandson of another. Octa pulled his sword free and sliced the face open of another. He was no longer afraid. Octa punched out with his shield and drove the Briton in front of him back as Odalric stabbed him in the face with his spear.

'Kill the bastards!' Hengist roared as the Jutes, despite their lower numbers, drove the Britons back.

Octa blocked another blow and glimpsed Prince Vortimer fighting with his men. He stabbed with the spear and the golden-edged spearhead pierced the neck of a Jute, before another rushed forward and the prince was forced to jump back. His men closed ranks around him and killed the Jute who had tried to slaughter their prince as he called for his warriors to keep fighting.

Hengist must have seen the same as he roared and cut down the man he was fighting before he charged through the gap and at the prince of the Britons, while Horsa killed two Britons as they tried to stop his brother. Octa followed after hacking down the Briton facing him and saw Hengist swing his sword at the prince. Prince Vortimer stepped back before he stabbed the spear at Hengist's face, but the warlord ducked under the spear and cut Vortimer's arm open. The prince stepped back and glared at Hengist.

'I fight with the spear of your god! You cannot defeat me!'

Octa heard him shout, but Hengist was oblivious to his words as he hacked at Prince Vortimer again. The prince blocked Hengist's sword with his shield and kicked at his leg. Hengist did not see the kick and, as he landed on the ground, Prince Vortimer raised the spear to kill him. Odalric, close behind

Octa, charged forward and shoulder barged the prince as Octa stabbed at him with his sword. Prince Vortimer somehow stayed on his feet and twisted out of the way of Octa's sword.

'I fight with the spear of your god!' the prince screamed again. 'Fear me! Fear the wrath of my God!'

Octa, his shield in front of him, said in the British tongue, 'That not spear of Woden.'

In the chaos of the battle, he heard Prince Vortimer's shocked breath as he gaped at Octa, before Hengist jumped to his feet and stabbed his sword at him. Prince Vortimer saw the attack and turned as he tried to get out of the way and Hengist's sword grazed off his mail vest, but the blow was hard enough to drive him back. Yet before Hengist could drive home his attack, a group of Britons rushed at him. Hengist deflected the spear from one of the Britons and tried to twist out of the way of another, but wasn't fast enough. Luckily, his chain-mail vest held, but Hengist was still sent staggering backwards.

'Brother!' Horsa screamed, but he was surrounded by British warriors and couldn't help his brother.

Odalric roared as he swung his spear like a giant sword at the Britons fighting Hengist. One of them ducked, but another was too slow and the spearhead sliced his nose open. As the man screamed and dropped to his knees, Hengist turned and hacked at his neck with his sword. Octa cut another in the leg and, as the man fell, he was forced to lift his shield and block the spear aimed at his head.

Prince Vortimer looked around him, his eyes wide before his face contorted, and he glared at Hengist. 'Sound the signal!' the prince shouted.

In the middle of the battle, Octa heard a horn, and the Britons roared with a renewed energy, but they slowly fell back as they fought the Jutes. He glanced at Hengist, who killed another Briton before he could duck behind his shield. The Britons still had the greater numbers, but the Jutes had the upper hand and the Britons struggled to cope with their ferocity as they hacked and stabbed. Spears streaked forward, piercing armour and skin, while the Britons were forced to hide behind their oval-shaped shields as they were pushed back. Despite that, Octa sensed something wasn't right as Horsa roared, 'Kill them all!'

The Jutes cheered as they forced the Britons back, step by step, away from the island and their families. Octa joined the push, with Odalric beside. He punched out with his shield and stabbed with his sword. He blocked a spear and Odalric killed the Briton before kicking another to the ground. Blood sprayed over him as the Jute beside was cut down and Octa wasted no time as he stabbed the Briton in the throat.

As they drove the Britons back, Odalric nudged Octa and pointed to a spear stuck in the ground. With his battle lust coursing through him, it took Octa a few heartbeats to realise that was Gungnir. For a moment, he stopped and glanced over his shoulder at the island and was surprised by how far they had driven the Britons back. He turned his attention back to the battle and frowned when he saw Prince Vortimer standing behind his men and constantly glancing behind him. Octa saw his lips moving as if he was shouting something to his men, but he couldn't hear what the prince was saying.

'What's he doing?' Octa asked Odalric, who was by his side, his shield and spear ready to protect Octa, as he put his sword back in its scabbard without cleaning it and limped towards Gungnir.

'Probably praying that his god saves him from the brothers.'

Odalric's words made Octa hesitate before he gripped the spear. He looked around and wondered where Taranis was, but then he forgot about the British god as he wrapped his fingers around the shaft and looked to the island. To where his mother was standing, but he wasn't surprised that Friga wasn't there any more. Although he wondered if the goddess was keeping Taranis away from the spear and why she was standing with his mother earlier on.

As the thoughts ran through his mind, he heard Odalric say, 'By the gods. It's a trap.'

39

Octa turned as he heard a new noise over the sounds of the battle and his heart skipped when he saw what Odalric had seen. Horns blew in the distance as a forest of spears and helmets glinted in the sun and, at that moment, Octa looked at Prince Vortimer and saw the smile on his face. That was why the Britons were falling back, Octa thought as he looked back at the island again.

Prince Vortimer was drawing them away from the safety of the island and, as Octa saw the new army storming at the Jutes, he knew the prince's plan had worked.

'They're not running towards us,' Odalric said, but Octa noticed the lack of fear in his voice as he saw the same thing. 'They're trying to surround us.'

Octa looked at the brothers, but they were both too focused on getting to Prince Vortimer to see the danger. None of the Jutes seemed to have noticed the new larger force racing to get around them. 'We have to warn them!' Octa said, but as he tried to pull the spear out of the ground, he felt something grip it. He turned and paled when he saw an old mottled hand holding on to the shaft of the spear and, when he looked up, he saw the rage-filled face of Taranis staring at him.

'The spear is mine!' the god roared at him, and Octa glanced at Odalric, who seemed unaware of the British thunder god's presence. 'The spear is mine!'

'Octa, what are you waiting for?' Odalric said as he frowned at Octa, who was still gaping at the British god. 'Octa?'

'Give me the spear!' Taranis leaned closer and Octa felt his fear return. All he wanted to do at that moment was to let go of the spear and run, but then images of Oisc, his face bloodied and not moving, came to him.

What will you do? Friga's voice came to him again. *Will you run or will you fight?*

Octa roared as he swung his shield at the god and caught him in the face. Taranis let go of the spear as he staggered back and thunder rumbled in the air. The thunder god of the Britons looked to the sky, his face suddenly filled with fear, before he turned his attention back to Octa.

'I will get that spear!' Thunder sounded again, softer than before, and the god vanished as if he had never been there.

'Octa, what are you doing?' Odalric frowned at him and Octa shook his head as he tried to focus on what was happening on the battleground.

The new force was closer now and some of the Jutes had noticed them as well, but the brothers and the warriors fighting in the front had not seen them yet. What concerned Octa was that the Britons had stopped moving backwards and held the Jutes where they were.

'Throw the spear, Octa,' Odalric said. 'Kill their prince and they break.'

Octa glanced at the spear in his hand and then shook his head. 'I can't.'

Odalric looked at him, his brows raised. 'Why?'

'Because he'll take the spear if I do.' Octa ran towards the battle as fast as his injured leg would let him. He could not throw the spear because he did not know if Taranis was still there, but he had to get to the brothers. He had to warn them. 'Hengist! Horsa!' he screamed as loudly as he could, but as he looked at the new force, close enough now for him to see the king of Cantiaci leading the charge, he knew it was too late.

'To the side! To the side!' Odalric screamed as he ran beside Octa. Some of the Jutes saw the new threat and warned their comrades of it.

Octa and Odalric reached the Jutes and pushed their way to the front.

'Shield wall to the right!' Octa shouted as he tried to get to Hengist and Horsa. 'Shield wall to the right!'

He got to the front, still screaming the command, when Horsa killed the Briton facing him and turned to Octa. 'How dare you order our men?' His face was red with rage and blood, but Octa ignored all of that as he pointed Gungnir towards the new force.

'It's a trap! They're going to surround us!'

Horsa's eyes widened as he saw the new danger. 'By the gods. Shield wall to the right!' Hengist looked over and saw the threat as well, before he turned his attention to Prince Vortimer, who had rejoined the fight. He stabbed with the spear he believed was Gungnir, and killed a Jute, laughing as if he thought his plan had worked. And as soon as the new force struck the side of the Jutes, Octa knew it had.

The Jutes were now fighting on two sides and they were outnumbered as Horsa led the men of the right flank and Hengist those on the front. Octa and Odalric fell in beside Hengist as they fought for their lives.

He blocked a spear before stabbing with Gungnir. He ducked as another spear came for him and felt it graze his head. Odalric punched out with his shield and stabbed with his spear. Hengist opened his shield and cut with his sword, while around them the Jutes were being cut down while they were trapped on the battleground. Octa forgot about the pain in his leg and the aches in his body. He forgot about his mother watching the battle from the island, as well as Warda, pawing the bridge as if she wanted to join the battle. All that went through his mind was to kill every Briton who faced him. Gone were ideas of living in peace with the Britons and sharing their lands with them. He roared as he punched forward and drove Gungnir through a Briton's face, before he pulled the spear back. With every stab, the spear of Woden found its mark. Every time the spearhead went forward, it ended the life of a Briton. Rage coursed through his veins as he fought for his life and Octa screamed to the gods of his people as he killed another Briton. He would bring fire to these lands. He would kill every Briton who faced him. Because he was Octa the Coward, the warrior who fought with Woden's spear.

Breathe. The words came to him. *Be calm and open your eyes.*

The words killed his battle rage and, if it wasn't for Odalric, a spear would have ended his life. But Odalric lifted his shield and blocked the spear before he hacked down the Briton with his sword. Octa glanced at the older Saxon and wondered where his spear had gone.

'Octa! Stop dreaming! Fight!'

Octa shook his head and kept his shield up as he glanced over his shoulder. The Jutes were being pushed into each other on two sides by the Britons, but they had not blocked off the way to the island. If they could make it to the island, they would survive. Hengist and Horsa could send ships to the continent and bring more warriors over. His heart racing, Octa grabbed Hengist and pulled him back from the fight.

'Octa, you bastard!' the warlord screamed as he glared at Octa, but Octa ignored his anger and repeated the words Friga had said to him.

'Hengist! Be calm and open your eyes!' He pointed towards the island and it took Hengist a few heartbeats to see what Octa was showing him. But when he did, he shook his head.

'Jutes do not run! We will fight these bastard Britons until the last of us dies!'

Octa's frustration took over, and he screamed at Hengist. 'Then you fight and die and no one will remember your name! You die here and they kill Oisc!' Octa glared at Hengist. 'Saxons don't run either, but we are outnumbered and outsmarted. Fall back and we can fight another day!'

Hengist glared at him and Octa thought the warlord was going to kill him, but then he nodded and turned to his men. 'Fall back! Return to the island!'

Horsa looked over his shoulder from where he was fighting and shook his head. 'Stay and fight! For the gods!'

'Horsa! We must fall back! We die here and our dream dies with us!'

Horsa stepped back from the fight and glared at his brother before he screamed his frustration into the sky. 'Fall back!'

'Back to the island!' Hengist roared, and the Jutes turned and ran for the island.

The Britons cheered as if they had won and perhaps they had, but Octa didn't care. He did not want to die on this day. Octa wanted to live. He wanted to find a new home for his people, and he wanted to avenge his father. Octa wanted to bring the fire the gods had promised, but he could not do that if they all died in this field. So he gritted his teeth against the pain in his leg and did his best to keep up with the Jutes as they ran towards the island.

'Octa, faster!' Odalric said as he ran next to him.

Octa shook his head. 'My leg! I can't.'

Odalric grabbed him by his mail vest and dragged him towards the island, and all Octa could do was try to stay on his feet. Another hand grabbed his from the other side and he was shocked to see Hengist was helping Odalric carry him.

The gods were with them because, instead of chasing them straight away, the Britons stood their ground and cheered, until Prince Vortimer screamed, 'Kill them all! For God! For Britannia!' The Britons roared as they chased after the fleeing Jutes.

Odalric looked over his shoulder as he pulled Octa towards the bridge. 'We're not going to make it.'

'What in the gods' names...' Hengist started, and Octa smiled when he looked up and saw Warda running towards him. Brigantia had told him she had sent the horse to him and he guessed that the goddess of the Britons wanted him to live.

As soon as the horse reached them, Odalric and Hengist threw Octa on top of her back and they lowered their heads as they sprinted for the bridge. Octa gripped the reins of Warda as she raised her front legs and cried out her own war cry, before she turned and ran towards the island.

Octa leaned forward and stroked her neck. 'Thank you, my friend.'

They reached the island, and Horsa called, 'Shield wall!' Before the Britons reached them, the Jutes locked shields across the bridge. They stood six men wide and five men deep, while other warriors ran to the edges of the island and raised their shields.

'Throwing spears!' Hengist ordered as Octa fell to the ground after dismounting Warda, but his horse stood by him as his mother rushed towards him.

Those warriors not in the shield wall or on the edge of the island rushed to collect the smaller throwing spears while Britons charged at them. Thunder rumbled in the air and Octa saw the skies darken. He prayed it was Thunor's doing and not Taranis as his mother reached him.

'Octa!'

'I'm fine, Mother,' he lied as he tried to get up. But his leg refused to let him. He looked around him and realised that Odalric was not with them and, as he scanned the Jutes, he saw the older Saxon standing in the shield wall beside Horsa. His heart raced, and he prayed to Thunor to protect his friend because Octa knew he could not rejoin the fight.

The Britons crashed against the Jutish shield wall as thunder rumbled over their heads again and, in his mind, Octa saw Thunor fighting Taranis. Thunder god against thunder god. Octa felt helpless as he struggled to his feet and watched as the Britons pushed the Jutes back on the bridge. Men died, crying out to the gods and loved ones, while the bridge seemed to bend under the weight of the warriors in their armour.

'Throw!' Hengist's voice boomed over them and the Jutes grunted as they threw spears into the packed Britons. 'Again!' Another volley went, but it was not enough as Prince Vortimer and King Gwyrangon stood behind their men and pushed them on. Prince Vortimer kept waving the stolen spear in the air, his face red as he screamed at his warriors.

'We can't let them get on to the island,' his mother said, and Octa saw the concern on her face. He looked around them, his heart racing, when he realised the tide was going out. Some of the Britons tried to wade into the water to get to the island, but their feet sunk into the wet sand because of the weight of their armour and they were skewered by spears thrown by the Jutes.

'Where is she, Mother? She can help us.' Octa looked around him, his hand tightening around the shaft of Gungnir. *Friga, I need you.*

'Where is who?' his mother asked, a confused expression on her face.

'Friga, Mother. Where is Friga?'

His mother stared at him. 'Octa, how would I know?'

Octa shook his head so that he could focus as the men on the bridge were pushed back even further. Already, the Britons were halfway across the bridge and those on the island had run out of throwing spears.

'Keep fighting!' Horsa roared as he stabbed with his sword, but the Briton he was facing blocked it on his shield. Odalric deflected the spear aimed at Horsa's head and the two large warriors shared a brief glance before they pressed their shoulders against their shields as they tried to stop the Britons.

'She was standing with you, Mother.'

Berthild frowned at him. 'Octa, what in Friga's name are you talking about? That was a woman from Jutland. She worked in a tavern there.'

Octa turned to his mother. 'Mother, that was Friga!'

'What?' Berthild's eyes widened as an idea came to Octa. He turned and limped towards Hengist as fast as he could, leaving his stunned mother behind him. The sky darkened more as the thunder rolled over them.

'The bridge! We must break the bridge!'

Hengist frowned at him, but then he looked at the bridge and saw that the Britons were almost across it as the Jutes were pushed back. 'Cut the bridge!' he roared as he grabbed an axe from one warrior and ran to the bridge. Others joined and while the last row of Jutes, led by Horsa and Odalric, still fought on the bridge, Hengist and some of the other Jutes started hacking at the joints of the bridge.

Time stopped for Octa as he stared at the battle on the bridge when a thunderous crash echoed in his ears and the bridge collapsed. Men cried out as they fell into the low water and got trapped in the muddy sand and Octa sighed with relief when he saw Odalric was not amongst them. Both he and Horsa were lying on the ground as they stared at the Britons drowning or being killed by spears thrown at them while they floundered in the outgoing tide. But as the rain fell down on them, Octa knew it would only bring them a short-lived respite, because he was certain the Britons would attempt to cross to the island as soon as the tide went out.

40

The mood in the hall was dire. It had been a few days since the battle against the Britons and the rain had not stopped. Octa didn't know if that was a good thing or a bad thing. The heavy rain kept them trapped on Ruym Island, but it also meant that the Britons couldn't attack the island. With the bridge gone, the only way the Britons could reach the island was to march over the beach, but the rain made that more dangerous than the Jutes' spears and so the Britons seemed intent to wait for the rain to stop.

On the day of the battle, after the tide had gone out, Prince Vortimer had sent his men across the beach, but they had barely made it halfway before they got stuck in the sand and were killed by well-aimed spears. Even with the rain and the tides coming and going, the water around the island was red with the blood of those who had died.

'We should have sent a ship to Jutland before they attacked us,' Horsa said, his face as dark as the clouds outside. It was not the first time he had said it, but unlike the previous times, Hengist responded.

'We should have done, but we didn't. And we didn't because we didn't think the Britons would attack us. Summer is ending and I wanted to send the ship after the winter.'

'Bastard Britons,' Horsa said, again not for the first time, as he sat in the hall, his head wrapped in bandage from a cut he got during the battle. Barely a man in the hall didn't have an injury. Odalric had a deep cut on his arm and

Aldric was stabbed in the leg. Even Octa had a cut on his scalp which he had forgotten about as the fight had gone on and only remembered when the blood ran down his face afterwards. And then there was his leg. It was still sore, but he could walk on it, with the aid of Gungnir, of course. Octa glanced at the spear and wondered what Woden would think of him using it as a walking aid.

Octa's mother had been busy these last few days, and he had barely seen her. Somehow she had formed a friendship with one of the British women, which surprised him because neither woman could speak to each other, and the two of them had organised the women on the island to treat the injured warriors. Even the men of Ruym were helping the Jutes, and it seemed to Octa that they preferred the men from the continent to their own king. Although whether they did it because they really felt that way or because they feared retribution for the battle, Octa did not know. But he was glad that neither brother held the Britons on the island responsible for the battle.

'Aye, the gods know we should have seen this coming,' Hengist said as he stood by the hearth fire.

'How do we know King Vortigern isn't behind this?' one of the senior warriors asked, and Octa knew many had wondered the same. Even he had.

Hengist shrugged. 'The gods know that we don't, but he wasn't on the battlefield so we can only guess that Prince Vortimer went against his father.'

Odalric sat next to Octa and drank his ale, his arm wrapped in a bandage and a bruise on his face. He glanced at Octa, who shrugged. His mother had warned them. She had seen the signs, but Horsa had refused to listen. Although after the battle, the younger of the brothers started treating them better, especially Odalric. The two of them had stood side by side in the shield wall. They had defended each other and killed those who tried to kill them. Octa had never understood it before, but that experience built a bond stronger than most.

'We underestimated the Britons,' Hengist continued. 'And they almost crushed us because of it.' Hengist looked at Octa, who didn't understand the look in his eyes, but he understood the glare Horsa was giving him. Octa had stood strong and even though neither brother would admit it, he had diverted a disaster for them. And Horsa did not seem to like the praise some of the warriors were giving him. 'If we are to survive here in Britannia, then we need to stand together. Jutes and Saxons. As well as the Angles, the Frisians and the Franks. If we unite, then no army the Britons muster can stop us,' Hengist said, and many of the men grunted their agreement.

Octa stared at the flames as Hengist's words washed over him. He had not wanted a war with the Britons, but just like Friga, he had failed at that. Octa thought of Taranis and was glad he had not seen the god again since the battle, although he was certain that one day the thunder god of the Britons would come for the spear again. He had not told Odalric what had happened, because he wasn't sure how the warrior would react. Just like he had not spoken to his mother again about the fact that she had been talking to Friga. Octa took a deep breath as he pushed those thoughts out of his mind. None of that was important. Not now. Now they had to find a way to survive what was to come.

'What do we do?' one warrior asked, and the brothers looked at each other. 'As soon as the rain stops, the Britons will attack again. And even if they don't, we can't just stay on Ruym. There isn't enough food to feed everyone, especially not when winter comes.'

Hengist's face hardened as he stared at the flames of the hearth fire. 'As soon as the rain stops, we send a ship to Jutland to bring the rest of our men over. And while we wait for them, we fight like the gods themselves to stop the Britons from taking this island.'

'And when the rest of your men arrive? Then what?' Octa's mother asked as she walked into the hall and stared at them all. Oisc tried to look serious as he limped behind her. Hengist's son was as bruised as the warriors and sported a new scar on his forehead, but he was determined to help Octa's mother and Octa guessed he just wanted some space from his father, who had been constantly fussing over him from the moment he woke up. 'What will you do, Hengist? Horsa?'

'We will do what we came here to do.' Horsa clenched his fists as he stared at Octa's mother.

Hengist nodded. 'We underestimated the Britons and I swear by Woden we will not do that again.' He turned and looked at them all in the hall, and Octa couldn't help but shiver at the intensity in his eyes. 'We will conquer Britannia and take these lands for ourselves. We will fight those who resist us and spill their blood in the name of the gods.' He glared at the flames of the hearth fire and Octa glanced at Gungnir, leaning against the table beside him. 'And we'll start with the lands of the Cantiaci. From this day on, we will no longer call this island by the name the Britons gave it. It is our land and it will have a name in our tongue. From today, this island will be called Thanet Island.'

* * *

Friga stared at the flames of the hearth fire in Woden's hall as his two wolves slept by her feet. Her brows creased as she tried to see beyond the flames to what was to come, but like Woden, she was blind to it. She had tried to stop a war between them and the gods of Britannia, but like Woden had said she would, she had failed. But Friga had not considered that Taranis would do what he did. She understood why though. The thunder god of Britannia was only fighting to survive, just like they were, and like Woden he had tried to use men to get his hands on the spear. Friga sighed as she wondered why Taranis and the one who encouraged him couldn't see the truth. That they needed each other to stop him.

'You can't trust them, Friga,' Woden said as he walked into the hall, his one eye fixed on her.

'Who? The men or the gods of Britannia?'

Woden stopped beside her, and she saw the exhaustion on his face. She would have felt for him, but what he was doing was unnecessary. 'Both.'

Friga smiled at her husband. 'But you trust him, the one with your spear.'

'And because you trust them, he almost lost Gungnir. They almost got my spear.'

Friga glanced at the spot above Woden's seat where he kept Gungnir. A spot that had been empty for a long time. 'But he didn't get your spear.'

'Only because Thunor intervened. And I know you told him to before you say anything.'

Friga would have smiled at her husband, but then remembered something. 'But you told Thunor when to intervene. You knew I had gone to him, but made him wait until it was almost too late.'

Woden glanced at the spot where he used to keep his spear. 'I needed to make sure I had made the right choice.'

Friga nodded. 'Octa still has Gungnir and he used it to start the war you craved so much.'

Woden grunted. 'The war between men is not important.'

'Yes, it is. Because it is the war between men that will start the war you really want. The war between us and them.' Woden stared at the flames and said nothing as one of the wolves pressed up against her leg. One of Woden's ravens flew into the hall and crowed at them. Woden smiled as he listened to the bird and Friga knew that another part of Woden's puzzle had fallen into place. 'Brigantia can help us. They all can.'

Woden shook his head. 'They couldn't help themselves. How will they help us? They are weak and with each passing moment, they grow weaker as he takes more away from them. The only way to stop him is from taking those lands before he does, and they're too blinded by their greed to see that.'

Friga turned to Woden. 'They are blinded by the same greed that you close your eye to. The greed to live and rule the lands they ruled for a long time. We fight the same war as them, Woden.'

Woden looked at her and Friga saw the fury in his eye. 'You and I might fight the same war, but we fight different battles. Now leave me, I need to think.' Friga nodded and was about to walk away when Woden said, 'You can't stop the war. Even with Brigantia's help.'

She paused and looked at her husband, whose one eye reflected the flames of the hearth fire. 'Just like you can't stop the fire.'

* * *

MORE FROM DONOVAN COOK

The next instalment in this thrilling, epic Dark Age adventure series from Donovan Cook, is available to order now here:

https://mybook.to/FirstKingdom3BackAd

HISTORICAL NOTE

Nennius in the *History of the Britons* (*Historia Brittonum*) talks about an interesting event after the arrival of Hengist and Horsa to Britannia. He doesn't tell us how long after their arrival this event happened, only that it happened some time after they arrived. What he tells us, though, is that during this time, which we can assume might have been a few years, the numbers of the *barbarians* had increased greatly and that, because of this, the Britons could no longer supply them with the provisions which they had agreed on.

There could be several reasons for their numbers to have increased. New arrivals from the continent. If you remember, this period was known as the great migration period because all across Europe tribes were on the move as they avoided wars and famine in their homelands. The Hun were rampaging across Europe while the western Roman Empire was fighting for its very survival. So it's not hard to imagine that these Germanic tribes boarded their ships and set sail for the green pastures of Britannia. Word would have spread of King Vortigern's new Saxon foederati and I imagine many men believed they could provide a better life for their families if they joined this foederati.

Another reason could be that the Jutes, Saxons and other Germanic people who originally arrived with Hengist and Horsa mixed with the local people and had children with them. Archaeological evidence suggests that there had been a large Germanic population for at least a decade before the apparent arrival of the famous brothers.

What we know from Nennius is that King Vortigern told the barbarians that they could no longer honour their part of the deal and that Hengist and Horsa had to leave. What Hengist did next, if this was all true, is quite remarkable and says a lot about his cunning and King Vortigern's lack of it. He somehow convinced the high king of Britannia that instead of leaving Britannia, he and his brother should be allowed to bring even more warriors over to protect the king and his people. In fact, according to Nennius, Hengist responded with, 'We are, indeed, few in number; but, if you will give us leave, we will send to our country for an additional number of forces, with whom we will fight for you and your subjects.'

I imagine much more was said than this, but King Vortigern agreed and the brothers sent ships back to the continent and brought sixteen ships filled with hungry warriors with them to Britannia. I'd like to think they played on King Vortigern's insecurities. All monarchs tend to be insecure and see threat everywhere. History is full of kings who killed indiscriminately if they felt someone was after their throne. Not even their own family members were safe. They must have convinced the king that his position was threatened by others, either in his own family or the other kings of Britannia, and that only they could protect him.

The Venerable Bede, in the *Ecclesiastical History of the English People*, has a different version of this event. He states that the Anglo-Saxons joined league with the Picts and demanded more supplies from the Britons. And that if their new terms weren't agreed to, then they would ravage the island. This would play into the perceived idea that this period was marred with violence and endless battles, where countless were slain and rivers ran red with blood for many seasons. But the archaeological evidence doesn't support any of this, which is why I went to Nennius's version of this event. I also felt it added a fun little twist to the story.

For this novel, I decided that his own son Vortimer was that threat and the reason for this is that Nennius tells us that Vortimer, not King Vortigern, led four battles against the Anglo-Saxons, although other sources say it was Vortigern who led these battles. Nennius tells that Vortimer and his army of Britons drove the Anglo-Saxons to the island of Thanet and trapped them there and I imagine he must have sensed a victory was coming against the men from the continent and that his name would be spoken for generations to come. But history tells us this did not happen.

Another reason I wanted to use Vortimer as the 'antagonist' was because I wanted to explore the other side of these events. Just like events today divide opinion, I'm sure that in those days there were many who did not agree to the Anglo-Saxons' arrival. The king of the Cantiaci would have been one of them because the lands of his people were given to the Anglo-Saxons to live on. Vortimer might not have liked the way his father was manipulated by the Anglo-Saxons, and if he was indeed a Christian might have seen the heathens as a threat to Christianity on the island which would not have been as strong as many believed it was.

Unfortunately, there are still many things we don't know and much of what I write is my own ideas and speculation, but I hope you enjoyed this novel as much as I did letting my imagination get the best of me while I wrote it. And I hope to see you all in the third instalment of the series.

ACKNOWLEDGEMENTS

Starting a new series always brings new challenges with it. Trying to understand the new characters and time periods. Trying to make sense of the history and the actions of those involved and trying to make it different from the series I've written before. But at the same time, all these things are what makes it such an exciting experience. I've learnt about the birth of England and the English, as well as some bizarre stories, and it's great to watch Octa grow and embrace his new role.

But as with any book or series, there is a lot happening behind the scenes. People who support and encourage and others who make sure you don't look silly by missing an obvious plot hole. And then there's our daughter and our dog who make sure I never have time to get any work done.

As always, I want to start by thanking my amazing editor at Boldwood Books, Caroline. Her wisdom and guidance always bring the best out in me as a writer and my books and I am always grateful for her support. To Ross, for his incredible insight and knowledge of the written language, and to Susan, whose keen eyes are my last line of defence against misspelled words and commas.

To my amazing wife, who has to put up with a lot more than she bargained for, but is always there when I need her, and to my daughter and our over-energetic Frenchie for stopping me from taking things too seriously.

And most importantly, to the readers. I thank you all for taking the time to read my books and leave comments.

I hope you all enjoyed the second instalment of the *First Kingdom* series and I look forward to seeing you for Book 3.

Happy reading,

Donovan

ABOUT THE AUTHOR

Donovan Cook is the author of the well-received Ormstunga Saga series which combines fast-paced narrative with meticulously researched history of the Viking world, and is inspired by his interest in Norse Mythology. He was born in South Africa and currently lives in Lancashire, UK.

Sign up to Donovan Cook's mailing list here for news, competitions and updates on future books.

Visit Donovan's website: www.donovancook.net

Follow Donovan on social media:

 facebook.com/DonovanCookAuthor
x.com/DonovanCook20
bookbub.com/authors/donovan-cook

ALSO BY DONOVAN COOK

Charlemagne's Cross Series

Odin's Betrayal

Loki's Deceit

Thor's Revenge

Valhalla's Fury

The First Kingdom Series

Woden's Spear

Woden's Storm

WARRIOR CHRONICLES

WELCOME TO THE CLAN ✕

THE HOME OF
BESTSELLING HISTORICAL
ADVENTURE FICTION!

WARNING:
MAY CONTAIN VIKINGS!

SIGN UP TO OUR
NEWSLETTER

BIT.LY/WARRIORCHRONICLES

Boldwood

Boldwood Books is an award-winning fiction publishing company seeking out the best stories from around the world.

Find out more at www.boldwoodbooks.com

Join our reader community for brilliant books, competitions and offers!

Follow us
@BoldwoodBooks
@TheBoldBookClub

Sign up to our weekly deals newsletter

https://bit.ly/BoldwoodBNewsletter